THE FALLEN CHRONICLES
BOOK 2

OBSIDIAN LIGHT

VERUSHA ROBBINS

Published by

Ink 'n Ivory

PO BOX 6321, Rouse Hill, NSW. 2155. Australia

www.inkNivory.com

ISBN: 978-1-922113-68-9 (Paperback)

ISBN: 978-1-922113-69-6 (ePub)

ISBN: 978-1-922113-70-2 (Hardback)

First Printing: 2023

Dedication

To my amazing fans on Wattpad. You inspire, motivate and fill my heart with joy. Thank you for being with me throughout this journey.

Acknowledgements

This may sound strange, but I'd like to thank the story for choosing me to write it. I never knew what I was going to write until I sat down in front of my computer, so every day was a surprise. These characters and their story have filled my days and nights and I really hope I have done it justice. It's been an emotional ride, but so worth it!

Thank you to my amazing editor Sierra and Miblart for the stunning cover. I just can't stop staring at it!

Thank you to my home team. I hope we keep cheering each other on in many lifetimes to come.

To my family... I love you and I'm so grateful for each and every one of you.

Chapter 1

Lucifer and I faced the mirror portals. They hung on the left wall of his bedroom, humming with power. The frames were ornate, gilded in gold, and set with clusters of precious stones. I dimly remembered a legend that spoke of eight powerful portals created by a dark fae king who used them to conquer worlds and spy on his followers. Some said the portals were large bodies of water that transported the might of his armies across the night sky. Others mentioned slivers of the moon that hung like sparkling tapestries from the walls.

But as I looked at the shiny surfaces in front me, rippling with variants of gold and shades of blue, I wondered if they were instead mirrors.

"These portals will take you to Kryptos and to the Fallen's domain," Lucifer said softly. Humour glinted a sharp fin in the dark waters of his eyes before submerging once more. "It's keyed only to your energy signature, so unfortunately, you will be unable to bring anyone back from the dungeons or take anyone with you to Kryptos."

Part of our negotiations involved a way for me to return home to The City of Light whenever I wanted. Though, if I did choose to leave Hell, it would mean that I wouldn't have a way of coming back.

Not directly, anyway.

I had also negotiated for a way to venture in and out of the dungeons easily in order to test my abilities and attempt to disable the dark energy cages. I was hoping once I freed the warrior angels, I could bring them back with me. But negotiating with the master manipulator of deals and contracts meant I overlooked numerous loopholes, and Lucifer had taken full advantage of that fact.

I'd have to think of another way to get the warrior angels out of Hell.

"Why are these portals in the bedroom?" I asked.

He gave me an indolent smile. "More often than not, little angel, your blood is on the ground rather than in your body where it belongs. Until you have mastered the ability to keep your life force within you, you will need to return to a place where healing can be available."

My eyes flickered up to the mandala above the bed and then back down to the bed.

"And because it makes me uncomfortable," I added dryly.

"Of course."

Arguing would change nothing and only bring Lucifer more enjoyment at being able to needle me so effectively.

I was learning. Slowly.

I was tempted to bring up the Light he used to heal me, but intuition told me it wasn't the right time. I had achieved the impossible and gained some ground with the Devil, and I was carefully avoiding anything that might set me back.

Lucifer continued talking. "By going into the dungeons, you will also have to deal with the Fallen. If you start interfering with their cells, they will demonstrate their displeasure."

I eyed him carefully. "But you stopped them last time."

There was a slight warning note to his tone. "The Fallen know not to turn you or destroy your form. Everything else would be fair play, especially if you venture into their domain. When Ezriel called the first Hell Hound, it was to test you. When he called on several more, it was to destroy you. He has been having challenges with obeying the boundaries I have set for some time, and it was an opportune moment to correct his lapse in judgement."

I blinked. Lucifer made it sound like he was correcting a misbehaving child trespassing into someone else's lands, not a deadly, dark warrior who had almost killed me out of spite.

I knew freeing the angels wasn't going to be easy, but if I had to deal with the Fallen every step of the way, it would be virtually impossible. Lucifer wouldn't let me die, but in order to develop my abilities, he also wouldn't interfere.

I walked over to the table by the corner of the room and picked up a pitcher and goblet made from dark silvery metal. I poured the contents boldly into the goblet and took a sip. The flavour hit me like a warm summer breeze in the heart of winter, making my face flush pink with pleasure. The sweetness danced across my tongue, a complex combination of honeyed fruit and dark, rich berries. My eyes fluttered closed and then opened once more.

Ambrosia.

When I turned back around, Lucifer had a small, amused smile playing across his lips. The firelight turned his skin to molten gold, making him appear like a prized statue in a lost temple of the Gods. My heart seized. It was almost painful to look at him.

"You told me you killed a God," I said.

He raised an eyebrow at the sudden change of conversation. "Yes."

"Who?"

There was a beat of silence, his dark eyes unreadable. "You already know, don't you?"

I stared back at him. I did, didn't I? There was only one God I knew of that he would hunt down and kill.

"Asclepius, the Greek god of healing," I said softly.

His lips twisted into a cruel smirk, gaze distant as if relishing the moment again in his mind.

"How did he die?"

He laughed lightly. "I didn't realise you had acquired a taste for suffering, little angel. I assure you, Asclepius suffered greatly."

"Did you burn him inside the temple?"

He tilted his head to the side curiously. "Why do you assume that?"

The memory came to me slowly. "You said that once. That if he didn't see you, you'd burn the temple down."

The corner of his lip lifted. "So I did. But no, that is not how he died." He paced a bit away until he stood in front of the bedpost. Turning, he leaned against the wooden carving of intertwining snakes to face me.

"I turned his body inside out and watched him suffer. His internal organs were exposed, pulsating outside his body. Every day for over a year, I visited him and listened to him beg."

The bottomless depths of his eyes glinted, and the darkness inside shifted like shards of steel impaling a screaming shadow. "At first, he begged for me to turn him back, promising all manner of things... riches, power, influence..." his voice sharpened, "even bringing the dead back to life. Eventually, he just begged to die."

The image he created was horrifying, and yet somehow, all I could think of was the desperation on his face when he tried to save me. When he turned, that betrayal must have seethed inside, magnifying in intensity until retribution was the only course of action. Understanding didn't make the action right, but I could see how he ventured down that path.

Guilt was a vine that tangled ruthlessly around my heart. He did it… he did it all because of me.

"So you killed him," I said bluntly.

"Apollo came to see me, and we managed to make a deal."

The God of sun and light would be a considerable foe. I turned the goblet in my hand. "He threatened you?"

The Lord of Hell looked at me derisively. "Little angel, it would be pure folly indeed for any creature, no matter their stature, to venture into my domain and threaten me. Apollo has many weaknesses, but fortunately for him, his love for his son tempered any irrational behaviour he would have otherwise expressed. I killed Asclepius so he could eventually reform, and now Apollo owes me a favour."

I cleared my throat. "Apollo now owes you a favour for killing his son?"

"Yes."

"I see."

And as strange as that was, I did see. The Devil made the gods very nervous, and as much as they wouldn't openly admit it, they feared his wrath.

I took another sip of ambrosia, feeling my head swim slightly. "How many gods owe you favours?"

"Not nearly enough, little one. The holding of a debt is sometimes more important than the payment itself." He tapped his fingers against the wooden bedpost and looked at me consideringly. "I have a present for you."

My expression must have reflected my surprise because the humour flashed once more in his eyes. "It's not usual that I bestow gifts, at least ones that are not vastly unpleasant. But this time, I'll make an exception."

"No strings attached?" I asked, using a human phrase.

"No, not this time."

He pushed himself away from the bed and moved slowly towards me, smooth muscle gleaming in the firelight, wickedness written in every hard line. As he neared, the subtle scent of apples invaded my lungs. I fought the urge to breathe deeper, to drown in the icy sweetness layered with something darker, more exotic.

Instead, my fingers curled tighter around the goblet.

I concentrated on the silken edge of his robe as long, elegant fingers curled around my other hand, intensifying our link. They travelled gently over my wrist, knuckles grazing up the outer curve of my arm, traversing a slow, sensual path until his hand curled around the skin just below my shoulder.

Under his fingers, something cold and heavy formed. It was a band of dark gold metal engraved with runes. It curved around my upper arm, fitting in place like it had always belonged there. Without looking, I knew it was a twin of his own.

His other hand curled around my other arm, and I felt the same metal coolness blossom around my skin.

My eyes met his.

"These will help protect you if you find yourself facing unfavourable odds, which I am sure would occur often. It forms a plate of armour around your upper body, which is impenetrable by most weapons. Activate it by will, but it also responds to fear."

My mouth opened and closed, wanting to say things I didn't have the words for. "Thank you," I finally said. "It's a beautiful gift. Does that mean I should still expect to be attacked randomly, even here?"

"Expect the unexpected," Lucifer said with a cryptic smile. He was still holding me close, his thumbs barely brushing the skin above the armbands.

"So there will be no sanctuary until I leave?" My tone was husky and low.

"There is one place." His voice was as smooth as warm wax sliding down a supple thigh. He leaned down and whispered in my ear. "Here. The only demon you will find in this room is me."

I closed my eyes briefly as I felt the shift of his silky hair against the curve of my face. "Hmmm," I replied, my pulse stuttering, "I'm not sure what's worse." He leaned back, and I opened my eyes. The energy between us was eerily familiar yet charged with tension that ran like fire between us. It was like a string being pulled tighter and tighter, and I knew it was on the verge of snapping.

Since our conversation in Kryptos, there was a tenuous understanding, a slight shift of power that had left me in new lands I was uncertain of how to navigate. Having him touch me, his hand wrapped around my arms, and something so perilously close to warmth in his eyes made me want to do something ridiculously stupid.

But doing that would also shift the power back.

He sensed my desire and smiled. "Tempted, little one?"

I took a deep breath. "Always," I answered.

I leaned up and kissed him lightly on the cheek. Breaking quickly away, I moved towards the door before I did something I might regret. The urge to walk back was stronger than I thought.

Before I disappeared from view, I turned, raising the goblet I had pilfered, and flashed him a smile of my own.

Amusement passed across his face, reminding me of an angel I once knew. That look stayed with me all the way back to my room.

***

The reptilian slits faded from Markos's eyes as he came back to his body. It took a couple of seconds before he reorientated back into his form. He was glad to be out of the three-headed serpent he had merged with.

The information he had gleaned whilst being in the Dragarth was shockingly delightful. It seemed that the rumours of an unturned angel in the warden's domain were true. But more than that, the warden seemed to have developed a weakness for her. His usual brand of cruelty and depravity was curiously absent. The warden watched the angel, not like a predator toying with its prey, but like she was part of his pack.

The sight of the light angel had stirred the ancient hunger within him to consume and destroy. It had been so long since he had tasted the purity of a light soul. The suffering he could cause her would quench some of the desire that had built up almost unbearably inside him. Not for the first time, he wished he could ascend into the higher levels of Hell and be chosen amongst the Fallen to fight the warrior angels. He would relish breaking them slowly and feeding from their pain. But Fallen didn't interact with seventh-level demons, as the risk of them breaking free was too high.

A pity.

Markos removed himself from the small cavity in the wall he had magically locked himself in. Merging with the Dragarth had left him vulnerable to demon attacks. If they had torn him apart whilst he was in the Dragarth, he might have been locked inside the serpent forever.

He moved slowly through the seventh level of Hell, fighting with several demons until he reached the throne of bones. He had lost the alliances he had made since his defeat at Sepheroth's hands; most of them now turned against him to curry favour with the new demon king of Hell. But he was strong enough to still hold his own.

One day he would get revenge. He just had to be patient.

Sepheroth was in the vicinity of his throne, watching a fight among the demons over a soul that was unlucky enough to have been stolen from the Underworld. Markos knew he did this to assess the strengths and weaknesses of the horde and determine who he could use for different parts of his plan. It wasn't unusual for the demon king to use another place to watch the horde. Sepheroth didn't want to openly announce who was currently in charge, as the warden liked to frequently make an example of those in power.

In that, he was different from his predecessors, who liked flaunting their power. It showed his intelligence. It proved he was dangerous.

Markos slipped into his wraith form as he got closer, enjoying his almost invisible state, moving between the throng of demons, unnoticed and unchallenged. No one seemed to notice his approach until he was a few meters away.

Sepheroth turned his head and locked his eyes on him. He smiled as if he had known he had been there all along and was just waiting to see what he would do.

As much as it pained him, Markos dropped to his knee in front of him.

"I have some information."

***

I returned to my room, eager to play with my new armbands and to plan a way to tackle the challenge of freeing the warrior angels.

Pushing through the wall became easier as I mentally adjusted the thought that the wall didn't have to be a wall, and in fact, wasn't a wall at all, but a substance that allowed me access in and out of other spaces. Once I fixed that knowing in my mind, merging through the other side became second nature.

That's not saying I could do anything else with the ability. I had nowhere near the skill level of Lucifer, who could bend reality with practised ease.

There were some people on Earth who already understood the power of manifestation. Tribes suffering from drought would band together and with their collective energy, would pray rain. Not pray *for* rain, but thank the rain that was already there, visualising the wetness on their skin, and soaking into the ground.

And the rain always came.

Our own minds gave atoms and molecules a fixed existence. If you mastered the ability to change that, you could effectively change everything around you. Easier said than done.

I merged through the other side of the wall and then jerked back suddenly, hitting the now solid surface.

"Ah, hello?"

There was a man standing in my room. A human man.

He was wearing brown pants that looked dirty and worn. Around his waist was a red and white striped cloth tied to show a triangle of material at the front. A light tunic was under a well-oiled leather breastplate. The man was a handspan taller than me and broad in the shoulders. His shoulder-length hair was speckled with grey like his beard, and brown eyes looked at me contemptuously.

"You," he spat out with a heavy accent. "There must be some mistake!"

"How did you get here?" I asked slowly.

"I will not train a woman!"

"Pardon?"

He strode towards me, booted feet clicking on the floor. I moved quickly out of the way, sliding my back against the wall. Instead of following me, he slammed his fist against the place I had emerged from repeatedly.

"Woman! How do you leave this place?" he growled at me.

I just stared at him.

This time he pursued, reaching over and grabbing me by the neck. "Tell me how to get out of this room." He shook me hard. "Don't make me hurt you. You don't want to see what I'm like when I'm mad, little girl." His breath smelt stale and foul.

I was in an interesting dilemma. This wasn't a demon that was attacking me, but a human man. As an angel, my duties involved guiding and counselling the people on Earth. We didn't interfere directly and certainly didn't harm souls on Earth as they were going through their own life cycles, unaware of the purpose of their incarnations until they left their bodies.

But we weren't on Earth. And I didn't like this man.

I felt the Light gather into my hand, intensifying until it burned beneath the skin of my palms. The white Light would probably have no effect on him as he wasn't a demon, just an arrogant, domineering individual, but I discovered I could do more with Light now.

When focused, it was a laser that could cut through objects. It could cut through flesh.

"Let go of me, or I'll hurt you," I said steadily, my voice slightly raspy from his chokehold.

I saw the doubt of my threat move through his face, but his muscles tensed slightly. I placed my hand over the wrist by my throat. There was a flicker of surprise at the heat gathered there. I didn't allow the Light to burst through my skin straight away but gradually increased the temperature until I was certain his skin was searing.

With a quick motion, he grabbed my wrist with his other hand and pinned it to the wall. I blinked, then dropped my goblet and moved my free hand to clasp around his throat. I let the threat hang there.

As the cup clattered to the ground, surprise flashed again in his eyes.

Another quick motion and my other hand joined the wall. "Now what?" he asked calmly, "Are flames going to come out of your breasts?"

I realised my foolishness straight away.

"I guess not." He echoed my thoughts with a smirk. "You had an advantage, and you lost it."

My mind raced, trying to think of a way out of my predicament. Before I tried to merge myself backwards out of the room, a feat I hadn't accomplished before, he let go of me and took a step back, crossing his arms in front of his chest.

"That was your first mistake. Your second one was making a threat and not following through with it. Your third mistake was giving away the fact that you're reluctant to hurt me. Stupid. Your fourth, that you didn't have a backup plan." The man sneered, "I've trained children still in their swaddling clothes who are better than you. Why should I waste my time with a frail-looking *lubumoto*?"

I didn't know what lubumoto was, but it didn't sound flattering.

"Because Atlas, if you fail to train her sufficiently, I will throw you in a pit of scorpions. That *is* your greatest fear, am I correct?" Lucifer emerged from the shadows in the corner of the room, voice like saccharine poison.

Atlas swivelled and flinched at the sight of the Devil, making a complicated symbol in front of his chest. "Demontorus!" he hissed in fear. Black mist extended in front of Atlas, forming the shapes of the insects he so greatly feared. "Yes, yes, I will train the woman!" he agreed quickly.

"Excellent. Do your very best, Atlas; otherwise, you won't return to your army. I'll find a nice dark hole in the centre of Hell with your name on it."

Atlas blanched.

"Lucifer," I said slowly. "Who have you brought into my room?"

His lips curved, anticipation brightening his eyes. "I'd like you to meet Atlas Huntagon, commander of the Tarigon army and the great conqueror and strategist of the north."

"You stole a human from Earth?" I asked, bewildered, looking between them.

"He is your trainer. Use him wisely." Lucifer's dark gaze shifted to Atlas. "Afterwards... we'll see."

With that dire statement, my soulmate left, leaving me with an angry commander of a human army.

Chapter 2

Lucifer faced the Fallen assembled before him, reading the subtle tension that ebbed and flowed between the ranks. Their postures were the perfect blend of strength and obedience, and, at first glance, they appeared to be the epitome of the ideal warrior.

But only at first glance.

Something feral and untamed simmered behind their eyes, lurking with teeth and claws. The darkness had unlocked an unending thirst for violence and pain, and the Fallen resisted any directions that weren't aligned with those goals. He had allowed them free reign with their destruction as long as they continued their duties in Hell. But the leash had grown an inch too long, and some were mistakenly under the impression that they weren't even wearing one.

Only a portion of them had been in the dungeons when he turned Ezriel back towards the Light, but word had spread exactly as he had intended. The touch of fear they were now forced to endure angered them. He rarely needed to demonstrate his abilities, and he hadn't for a long time. But he now took pleasure in their conflict, the battle within to rebel, and the uncertainty of facing a greater, unknown power.

His reputation was drenched with the blood of millions and engraved with the vehement curses of the dying and tormented. There were impossibilities and contradictions in every dark tale woven around him. In some stories, he was as powerful as the creator; in others just a fable to scare children at night. The truth was intangible, even to the Fallen, and he was content to leave it that way.

"The witch summonings have increased in frequency." His gaze swept over the Fallen, lingering on the leaders in the front. To their credit, they didn't flinch, but the slight stiffening of their posture gave away their growing tension. "Which means demons are still moving unhindered into the Underworld." He paused significantly. "Why is that?"

There was a moment when no one said anything, and the silence stretched, thinning out over pit holes of questionable failures. It was Selaphiel who took a step forward into the sharp scrutiny of the Lord of Hell.

"We've patrolled the higher levels and have made examples of the demons that have been breaching the walls. It seems the lure of the Underworld is still too appealing for them to resist."

Nadiel also took a step forward, his silvery hair glinting white in the dim lighting. "The positions of the Hell gates into the Underworld are constantly changing. As many as we close, there are always more opening, my Lord."

Lucifer studied them both, holding their eyes until they were forced to look away. He let the dissatisfaction creep cooly into his voice, frosting over his words. "They sound like excuses to me."

"We can send out more patrols. We could also offer a soul for information on which demons have been making deals." A new voice bled into the silence, earning sharp looks from both Selaphiel and Nadiel.

Lucifer shifted the weight of his gaze to Diager. He wasn't amongst the top ranks of the Fallen, even though he had been immersed in the darkness for a long time. It appeared that Ezriel's absence had left a power vacuum that others were eager to fill. Even those who weren't already in leadership positions. It would be interesting to see how the battle for dominance played out.

Diager shifted his weight on the balls of his feet, aware of the penetrating stares from the rest of his brethren. His dark brown hair was braided back away from his face, highlighting the almond shape of his eyes, which reflected a cool confidence bordering on arrogance.

"Finally, someone presenting a solution," Lucifer drawled, adding more fuel to the power play as triumph lit across Diager's face. "It makes me wonder how effective and frequent the patrols have been with such limited results. It seems that perhaps too much time and importance has been placed on the arena and less on your other duties."

Selaphiel opened her mouth to protest, then wisely closed it. Anything they said to defend themselves now would only increase the punishment he had already devised.

"After all," he continued, "what is the point of adding to our numbers if it still doesn't get the tasks done?" Lucifer walked down the steps of the dais until he was level with the dark warriors.

"This is what you will do." He walked through the ranks, his steps soundless on the rock floor. "As Diager has suggested, you will increase your movements through the upper levels of Hell and publicly eliminate the demons that are caught on the wrong level. But make sure you do this on the level they reside in. You will find out which demons have already made bargains with the witches and which ones are yet to be called. If you know the demons that are currently out of Hell, you inform me immediately."

"In addition," he paused by Nadiel, his shoulder in line with the Fallens, "three of you will position yourselves near the ferryman's crossing."

Nadiel spoke without turning his head. "You want us to kill any witches we see passing through," he predicted. "Hades won't like us roaming the Underworld." The feeling of agreement hovered in the air.

"No, I want you to follow them to the demons they are negotiating with. After they leave, bring the demons to me." The corner of Lucifer's mouth lifted. "I'll deal with Hades."

"You don't want us to kill the witches?" Selaphiel asked from the other side, disappointment evident in her voice.

"I would rather not send a warning that something is wrong when the witches don't return from the Underworld. There is no point in killing witches if the coven is still intact." Lucifer's voice rose, reaching every ear as if he was personally whispering into them. "Let me be crystal clear. If the demon movements have not been reduced significantly, I will close the arena, and I will end further recruitment. I will take away your toys and I will not give them back. Do you understand?"

There was a resounding, "Yes," from the Fallen. The resentment increased, their ego prickling at being handled like children, at a threat, any threat directed at them. Even by him.

"Good," he purred.

He walked further into their ranks, past the rows of dark, plated armour and sharpened weapons. He stopped at Sirus, a Fallen with long fiery hair twisted above her head, studded with black crystals like a diadem. She was one of the leaders who arranged the battles within the arena.

"How is Ezriel?" he asked, watching the slight flicker of fear his name induced. They knew the question was not asked out of concern, but to announce his current condition to everyone present.

"He..." she cleared her throat and started again. "He is struggling to... completely shed his new condition." Reports had indicated that the former Fallen leader had been screaming periodically as the memories of his darkness and violent deeds warred with his newly formed consciousness.

"Have you put him through the arena?"

"Not yet, he is still adjusting to the cells." It clearly disturbed them to watch one of their strongest revert back to being so weak.

"Well, Sirus, I have never known you to be so *kind*." Sirus stiffened at his words and the clear insult. "Put him through the arena. He is not there to get comfortable. The faster he turns back, the faster he gets back to work."

"As you will," she said coldly.

"Excellent." He raised his voice, obsidian wings brushing against the floor as he turned. "You're dismissed."

***

"… and then our cavalry will attack from the east, forcing them towards the base of the hill where our archers will pick them off from above." Atlas burped as he sat with spread knees on my chair. He drained the rest of the goblet's contents by tilting his head back and exposing the rough column of his throat. Slamming the goblet back down on the table, he reached for the pitcher of wine only to find it empty. He scowled at it.

"Woman! Bring me some more wine," he ordered, thrusting the pitcher out towards me.

I stared at him, a frown creasing my forehead. For the better part of an hour, Atlas had been boasting about his battle plans against the fearsome Kolaiths and his varied strategies for slaughtering them when he returned to Earth. I was not a human soldier, so most of the concepts and references of army formations and battle equipment had been lost to me. Also, the conversation of killing humans over something as trivial as greater lands and riches was not a topic that I found appealing.

However, my lack of response had not deterred him. Instead, his words poured forth as if I was the most avid of audiences grasping onto every syllable.

The wine he had invited himself to seemed to be of a human beverage, and not the rare ambrosia that had found its way into my room before. Ambrosia had a vastly different effect on humans than those who were classified as immortal. It was rumoured that it gave them some of the Greek God's abilities, which was why giving the sacred fruit to a mortal was the highest of sins in Olympus and punished by everlasting torment.

"I'm not your servant."

He waved the pitcher at me like it was a flag. "Well, you will have to do for now."

My frown deepened. "I think not."

The pitcher came flying at me from across the room. I was so surprised, I only had time to raise up my arm and deflect the blow aimed at my head. As the pitcher clattered loudly to the floor I glared at him.

"It is clear that you have no intention of helping me, and frankly, I have my doubts whether you can assist me at all. So, enjoy the rest of the food, and good luck with your battle if you ever return back to

Earth." I turned to merge out of the room, intending to find my soulmate and ask that he return the human back where he found him.

"Why didn't you use your powers just now?" Gone was the jovial, boasting tone. In its place was the sharp rebuke of a commander catching a foot soldier napping.

"Pardon?" I asked irritatedly, turning my head.

"I threw something at you. At your head. Why didn't you use your powers?"

I huffed out a breath and turned around. "You surprised me."

"You didn't think I would attack you?"

I paused to consider. "No."

He shook his head. "Stupid."

My eyes narrowed. "I have larger threats to worry about."

Atlas snorted, scratching the underside of his arm. I wondered when the last time he had a bath was. The smell indicated that it had been quite awhile.

"Then you will be dead quicker than a thievin' whore. Everyone is a threat. Your generals, your friends, your wife, even your damn dog. The quicker you learn that, the longer you'll survive."

"Seems like a very lonely life."

"I'm alive, others are dead. One day, I will go to the Elysian Fields and be surrounded by big breasted women," he grabbed an apple from the table and pointed it at me, "but when I'm good and ready. I already bested you before. It was foolish for you to assume I wouldn't do it again. Do you have any meat? I could do with a good stew."

A small part of me wanted to tackle everything he presumed about life, and the folly of the current path he was on. But a small part of me also wanted to throw the pitcher back at him. I opted to not say anything.

He was right about one thing. I hadn't expected him to attack me because he was human. I was not used to defending myself against humanity, as my life as an angel was designed around helping them. I shouldn't have felt safe. Hadn't being in this place already taught me that?

"So, who are you, fighting girl?"

I crossed my arms. "My name is Sandriel."

He crunched down on the apple and chewed loudly. "Fine, Sandriel. Who are you fighting?"

"The Fallen," I replied. "And whatever other demons they conjure up from Hell." So far I had only faced the Hell Hounds in their presence, and I couldn't expect that if they found me, Hell Hounds would be the only demons they had available at their beck and call.

Atlas scoffed. "The Fallen? That does not sound like a mighty name. It's like calling yourself The

Defeated, The Downtrodden, The Failures... though, the demons do sound like a bit of a problem."

"The Fallen are fallen angels who have turned to the dark, and as such, have powers that inflict great destruction and pain. Their objective is the suffering of others. They are one of the most deadly killers these realms have ever seen." When he didn't respond, I said. "The one who brought you here is one of the Fallen."

Even though he kept his composure, his face drained of colour. I wondered if he was thinking about the scorpions or the Devil himself. Then he laughed, great big guffawing sounds that made him choke on the apple pieces he was still in the process of swallowing. He hammered at his chest. "You're doomed, girl. You can't fight those things. You can't even fight me!" he snorted. "Even I'm not fool enough to wage war on those creatures, and I've fought some dubious battles."

"Do you have an army?" At my lack of response, he threw his hands up in the air. "Maybe the creature called me here to smack some sense into you, which I'd gladly do so I can go home to my wine and the buxom Jocelyn, who can crush a man's head with her sweet..."

I lifted my hand and lasered one of the chair legs he was sitting on. Atlas hit the floor with a satisfying thump. After a look of outrage, he picked up the chair leg and examined the burnt edges curiously.

"I don't want to kill them, I just want to get around them." I stepped forward. "Let me explain."

It took me a couple of hours to delve into the history between the warrior angels and the Fallen and my interactions with them both. He was intrigued by the arena, and less horrified then I'd hoped he'd be. I also caught the gleam in his eyes when I mentioned their weapons and armour. I couldn't deny the bright intelligence that flared in his eyes when I spoke. He weighed and measured everything I said and asked me careful questions if I was too light on my explanations.

"So, in essence, I need to unlock the dark cages, free the warrior angels and get them to a place where they can ascend to The City of Light."

"Well, that's the first step."

"What is?"

Atlas was now leaning against the wall, eating a slice of nut bread. "Know your terrain. You need to make a map of the areas you know, and what you need to explore. You don't have a choice of battle ground. This is it. If you don't know where your enemy can approach, where you can make a stand, and where you can retreat, then you've failed before you've started."

I nodded slowly. This made sense.

"At the same time, you need to learn everything you can about your enemy. Their weaknesses, their strengths, their movements, when they shit, and when they rut. Your problem, Sandy, is that you don't know them and you don't know yourself or what you're capable of. That in itself spells defeat."

"My name is Sandriel." I made a frustrated sound and paced the room.

"It will take me time, which I do not have, to glean what I can do. My abilities are not something that can be taught, they just manifest," my hand waved in the air, "as they will. But you are right, I need to gather more information. But even if I just observe their movements, there is a high chance they might catch me."

"Then try to blend in with them."

I blinked. "Pardon?"

"In your case, you need to beat the enemy without fighting. You need to be unseen, failing that you need to blend in." He dusted off the crumbs from his beard. "They will probably have slaves cleaning up after them. People in power rarely want to wipe their own ass, so cleaning up other people's shit would be a lesser task."

"Other people's... shit?"

"You know," Atlas pointed to his rear, "the shit that comes out of your ass? Come on, angels have to shit, right? And other stuff, like cleaning the blood and bones from the arena and cages."

My body had not lowered in vibration so much that it was functioning at a human level. I had regained some appetite, but whatever I was eating my body was using and not eliminating. Though that stage might come soon, the longer I was here. The Fallen, on the other hand, might have rediscovered those bodily functions. Atlas was right, I couldn't see them taking care of their own mess when there were others who could do the less desirable work for them.

"It could be demons," I mused. "Lesser demons who are bound to them."

"Well that's something you should find out. You can't blend with demons, but perhaps you can with other angels who haven't been turned. Either way you need to know." The human commander tilted his head at me. "You describe them as powerful without equal?"

I nodded. "They are undefeated to my knowledge, bar Lucifer himself."

Atlas smiled, his teeth surprisingly white. "Which means they're arrogant, and they won't see you coming."

Chapter 3

Lava churned thickly through the crevices of Hell. It boiled and bubbled down rocky slopes, rolling across teeming caverns, spluttering fiery acid at any who dared to approach. It hissed its way around corners, through tortured screams and unending despair, hungrily consuming flesh and bone, anything living it could latch on to.

Uncontained, it flowed through all the levels of Hell, glowing maliciously at the weak denizens it passed, curving around the stronger ones, reminding them of the untamed power of the elements. Forging new paths, it burned its way through stone, unveiling hidden crevices and grim sanctuaries, callously plundering the contents inside.

Finally, after many twists and turns, it pooled into a great opening, as wide and tall as a great mountain.

In the centre, piercing high into the air, was a tall, dark fortress, made from a smooth, seamless stream of obsidian stone. The structure had circular openings at various heights, where black-winged creatures flew in and out, sometimes circling around to perch at the top.

The lava curved itself around the fortress and squeezed, determined to bring the structure down. It boiled with red fury, steaming against the stone, watching it sizzle. The rock wouldn't give. It launched high in the air, splashing its rage about, pounding continuously at the formidable wall.

And still, the fortress would not give.

Finally, the lava lay still, seething as it slowly swirled around the base of the structure, wondering what type of creatures resided up above.

***

The Fallen left their meeting with the Devil, filing out of the large cavern, silent in their own dark thoughts. They flew through several tunnels until they reached an opening. There, the eyrie stood tall in the centre, glistening black, alight with flames as the surrounding lava reflected upon its smooth surface.

They spread out their wings and flew, the rising heat from below making their ascent easier. Soaring through the air, they carved around the fortress in spirals until they reached the summit.

Selaphiel landed on the flat surface and folded her wings back into her body. She strode directly to one of the four lavish seats towards the centre of the platform. Turning around, she draped herself on the plush cushions, pulling out a knife and flicking it across the back of her fingers as she waited for the others to arrive.

She didn't have to wait long.

Sirus and Nadiel landed at the same same time and took their seats next to her. The three of them were the leaders of the Fallen, chosen for their strength and ability to command others. They had kept their seats for a long time. Occasionally they were challenged, but it was rare for someone in command to fall.

They all avoided looking at the empty chair at the end. Ezriel's absence had been keenly felt across their ranks. He had been one of the first to fall, and the darkness had bestowed him with an enviable amount of power. Most couldn't remember a time when he wasn't a Commander, as he had single handedly brought a significant portion of them to embrace the dark. To hear him begging like a pathetic light angel was almost intolerable.

It made them feel weak. And it made them feel angry.

"Diager wants to challenge for a position," Nadiel murmured from the side.

"He's not wasting any time," Selaphiel replied, trying to spot the dark angel in the crowd.

Sirus tapped her fingers on the chair's arm in an irritated beat. "I thought we were waiting for Ezriel to regain his darkness."

"We don't know how long that will take. We have tasks to complete. You heard Lucifer." Nadiel looked at where the Fallen were assembling in groups, waiting for their assignments. They talked freely amongst themselves, their voices a low, continuous hiss of sound.

"Yes, we all heard him," Selaphiel said darkly. "I have no issue with Diager fighting for leadership... if he is the strongest. Whether now or later, it has to be done. There is no point in putting it off."

Sirus's lips flattened into a thin line. "Fine." She clapped her hands sharply, commanding attention. The Fallen fell silent. "Diager, step forward."

There was a ripple movement towards the back of the gathering and the dark angels parted to let Diager through. He walked with a hint of swagger, confident in his abilities and in the subtle claim he had made when he spoke to the Lord of Hell.

"You rang?" he said with a hint of an insolent smile.

"You seem to think a lot of yourself, speaking out of turn to Lucifer as if it was your right. Is it arrogance I wonder," Sirus gestured with her hand, "or just stupidity." There were snickers of laughter from behind him.

"Perhaps it's just the realisation that my talents lie in leading instead of following. There is a time when one recognises themselves as a hawk instead of a sparrow."

Selaphiel's smile was sharp. "Is that so? Maybe you are just a sparrow wishing it was a hawk." Diager had been making his presence known more and more recently. He had displayed an artistic flair for cruelty and pain, seeming to find the warrior angels suffering a competition. His enthusiasm almost matched hers, and had made the other Fallen take notice.

She pointed her knife at him. "Why don't you prove that claim?" Her eyes lifted to the rest of the Fallen. "Diager believes he is fit to command you. To control you. Who would like to challenge him?"

There was a slight pause as the Fallen glanced at each other. Then there was movement. Several dark angels stepped forward to join Diager. Diager glanced at them through slitted eyes, measuring the threat they posed. One of the angels was Gregori, who was only newly turned.

Selaphiel ached her eyebrow at him. Surely he didn't actually think...

Gregori stared defiantly back at her.

She suppressed a smirk. The new initiates always had trouble adjusting to the Fallen ranks. As the first flush of darkness entered them, they felt invincible, believing their knees should bend to no one. Selaphiel still carried that belief, they all did, but when you were wiser, you learnt which battles you could win and which ones you'd lose.

This one still had to learn.

There were a couple more contenders. A dark skinned female with doe eyes shifted lightly on her feet, and a male with piercings covering almost every available surface of his skin stood stoically next to her. She particularly liked Tianya, a tall, toned Fallen with an asian cast to her features. Her skill with the blade had piqued her interest, and as a result, she had taken other pleasures from her, too.

If she failed to best Diager, those pleasures would stop. She wouldn't invite incompetence to her bed.

"Well, Diager," Selaphiel continued, "it seems like you have a bit of competition. Let's see how well you hold up before we consider you." She raised her voice. "That's what we will be doing now, considering a contender for Ezriel's position. If there are any more of you who believe they are better suited, step forward now."

An edge of anticipation cut through the ranks. Several more Fallen stepped forward and joined the group.

Sirus smiled. "Looks like you have a bit of a fight on your hands, Diager."

"Nothing I can't handle," he replied, though his expression was grim. Selaphiel could almost see him mentally counting the weapons he had on his body.

Nadiel gestured for the Fallen to make a ring around the contenders. "The last one standing will be considered." He smiled grimly. "Begin."

Diager and the other Fallen pulled out their weapons and started to circle each other. Simultaneously, three of them launched, blades flashing rapidly. The winner didn't need to kill the rest of the Fallen, only maim them until they couldn't fight anymore. Killing was frowned upon amongst their ranks as it took time for them to reform again, but... it wasn't disallowed. They would regenerate, in time.

Nadiel turned to face them, distracting Selaphiel from the fight. "So what are we going to do about Lucifer?"

Sirus frowned, her eyes still looking ahead. Her elaborate braid still looked perfect despite her flight up to the eyrie. Yet another thing Sirus liked to be in control of. Though it was so tightly made, Selaphiel wondered how she still managed to get the blood circulating to her head. "What do you mean?" she asked.

"Did you suddenly lose your hearing during the last meeting? Lucifer has no intention of going to war with The City of Light. He isn't concerned about recruitment. His only concern is that Hell is kept in... *order*." Nadiel growled out the last word, as if it burned just passing through his lips.

Selaphiel could understand the intensity of his feelings. This was a revelation to her, too, and their leader, the ruler of Hell, had mentioned it so casually as if he was talking about changing the pattern of their armour.

"So," Sirus snapped. "It's not like we can do anything about it. Look what happened to Ezriel!"

Nadiel leaned forward, bracing his forearms on his knees. "Ezriel was obviously too vocal about his feelings, but that didn't mean he was wrong. He could sense this coming, a long time before we did. He just took things too far, especially with that angel pet Lucifer has."

"He protects her... from *us*. He places a light angel above *us*," Selaphiel interjected, casting a glance towards the fight. It looked like the weaker Fallen were banding against the stronger ones. Diager had three on him. So did Tianya.

Nadiel nodded at her words. "Is that the sort of leader you would follow, Sirus? I for one don't want to spend the rest of my time chasing demons in Hell. I'd rather be up there, on Earth, fighting my former brothers and sisters and increasing our strength for the larger war. Doing these… tasks, are not who we are."

Sirus glared back at him, dark eyes flat as a cold slab of metal. "Again, what choice do we have? Do you want to go up against Lucifer and have your darkness stripped away? I'd rather have power than no power at all."

"What about more power?" Selaphiel asked. "What if there was a way in which we could plan things carefully and take control?"

Lucifer was incredibly strong, but there was also just one of him, and many more of them. They couldn't just rely on strength, though; they had to be cunning, too. The opportunity to be free, to pursue their own desires, was intoxicating, but they had to be oh, so careful. This wasn't something to be rushed into, but meticulously plotted, step by excruciating step. One mistake would cost them all.

"There could be a way…" Nadiel said thoughtfully. "There could be several ways, but I would need to explore them further."

"Both your brains have been fried in this heat. I can't believe we are even discussing this," Sirus hissed, gripping the arms of her chair as if she wanted to launch away from them. "The consequences are too great to attempt rebellion. If you want to be foolish, go ahead. But don't involve me!"

Coward. Weak. Selaphiel's lips curled in disgust. Ezriel had paid for his disobedience, but at least he had the balls to stand up for the rest of the Fallen. Sirus was caught up in fear of her own punishment. She was a strong Fallen, but she would never be strong enough to really be respected. Followers never were.

She caught Nadiel's eyes behind Sirus and almost imperceptibly nodded her head. If there was a plan, then she was in.

This time, they'd do it right.

***

Atlas and I had continued our discussion for a couple of hours more before he shooed me away, throwing himself face down on my bed. Before he closed his eyes, he mentioned he needed a pot, otherwise he'd end up pissing on the floor, which was why I was now in the living room eyeing every candle holder and drinking jug, trying to determine which would be the best substitute for a chamber pot.

I held up the dark ruby coloured jug and gave it a cursory once over. This might work if he was just passing urine, but what if he needed to relieve himself even more? The opening was much too small.

I put the jug back down, worry creeping in. Picking up a candlestick on another side table, I gave it a cursory once over. Oh, no, that definitely won't do.

I paused with my hands still around the candlestick. "What are you doing, Sandriel?" My voice rang out around the room. My situation became embarrassingly clear. "By the creator, you're fretting about a chamber pot when you have more pressing things to think about!"

Atlas could worry about his bowel movements later. I could worry about his bowel movements later. Right now, I need to talk to Lucifer.

Disgusted with myself, I moved away from the table and towards the double doors leading into my soulmate's bedroom.

Tentatively, I knocked on the door and then pushed them open. "Luce?" I called out, stepping inside.

The room was empty, though his scent lingered in the air, beckoning me closer as it subtly filled my lungs. My skin prickled with awareness, my mind conjuring him in front of me like a phantom. Even now his pull on me was strong, and he wasn't even present. But then again, it had always been that way, even when he was a light angel.

Back then, it was love that bound us inexplicably together. What was it now?

My gaze flicked over to the chair in the corner of the room, where his dark robe hung from the back like a pool of shadows melting into the floor. What did Lucifer do while he was away? I couldn't imagine him in the arena, watching the angels desperately fight for their own survival. Not because the thought of him enjoying their suffering disgusted me, but because Lucifer was more practical. He liked getting things done and was rarely idle. I remembered him always being like that, even as a Light angel. His only time relaxing had been spent with me and even then it was a luxury, with demons terrorising the people on Earth.

What sort of things would Lucifer have on his priority list now?

I was about to leave when the mirror portals caught my eye. They swirled gently with white mist, like rolling clouds viewed from high above the Earth. My feet moved closer until I was standing before them. One would take me back to Kryptos, the other to the Fallen domain.

Tentatively, I touched the moving surface on the right and watched the mist fade away.

Darkness eclipsed my vision. After a couple of seconds, my eyesight adjusted and I could make out different tones and shades. Slowly these formed shapes, but they were barely distinguishable. It could be similar to the dungeon in the Fallen domain, but I wasn't sure. I was tempted to slip through, quiet as a whisper and have a peak, but Atlas had cautioned me on having a solid plan. To think that all the warrior angels were so close, suffering in their own personal hell, tore me apart.

Every moment wasted was a step closer for an angel towards the dark.

"Whatsssss are youuuuss doing?"

I jumped in the air, and almost fell through the mirror. Turning around I glared, grateful at least that I hadn't shrieked this time. The dark spectre hovered in the middle of the room, wisps of faint black smoke curling beneath him like octopus legs. I wondered if there was anything under the hood of its cloak besides the hollow emptiness that seemed to emanate outwards. The shadowy darkness of his robe shifted and I thought I glimpsed a flash of white bone.

I squared my shoulders. "I'm looking for Lucifer. Do you know where he is?"

"I alwayssss knowss where the massssster isss," it hissed.

Really? I pondered this. "Well, can you take me to him?" I asked impulsively.

The spectre demon continued to float in the air, riding invisible currents I couldn't see. Then suddenly it disappeared.

"Okay..." I trailed off. It could have just said no.

Unsure of what to do now, I headed towards the doors. Perhaps I could practise activating the armour bands around my forearms. With all the talking and debating I had been doing with Atlas, I hadn't had time to experiment with the gift Lucifer gave me.

"The masssterr sssaysss you cansss sseee him."

Shrieking, I spun around, white Light flaring in my hands. My heartbeat took a moment to slow down from the galloping beat it had raced to. I glared at the servant demon for the second time.

"Pardon me?" I spat out through clenched teeth

"I cannnss takesss you to thee massssterrr," the demon whispered, floating closer.

Instinctively, I took a step back as it approached. Even though I had asked the demon to take me to Lucifer, it was still a demon. All demons could not be trusted. There was no such thing as a friendly demon. If it acted friendly it was only because it had to or there was a hidden agenda that somehow served its own purpose. The only reason I felt a sliver of ease in its presence was because it obeyed Lucifer, and had not previously attacked me on sight. But who knew what orders Lucifer had given it?

Maybe this was another test Lucifer had conjured up.

I tossed the decision in my head from side to side, feeling the weight of each one. Deciding to take a gamble, I let the Light fade slowly from my hands. "Alright, thank you."

The demon moved in front of me, its hooded face looming from above. Its negative aura crackled painfully against mine, and I had to bite back a scream as a pale skeleton hand latched onto my wrist.

The burn of dark energy seared my skin and I struggled to keep the meagre contents of my stomach down. I felt an intense hunger radiating towards me, as if I was a juicy, roasted chicken in front of a carnivore that had been forced to eat grass for years. The armour bands reacted to my fear, the metal sliding over my skin like liquid, covering my shoulders and torso in melted gold.

Before I could react any further, we blinked away.

We appeared on a dusty street in a town. The moon hung, full and swollen in the sky, casting a silvery white light through dense shifting clouds that were eager to dampen her glow. Buildings of varied sizes pressed around me on either side, their window-like eyes glowing curiously with dim orange light. The faint noises from crowds echoed down the street, as well as the muffled slap of feet against the ground.

The burning pain on my wrist suddenly lessened. I blinked and the spectre demon disappeared. The chill in the air wrapped around my bare arms and legs like steel vises. Shivering, I looked around curiously.

What was Lucifer doing here, on Earth?

More footsteps on the street sounded around me. A group of men and women turned the corner, dressed nicely in tailored clothes and satin dresses, falling and laughing against each other.

"If you don't want to make a spectacle of yourself, I suggest you move back here," Lucifer's voice coiled smoothly through the air.

I snapped my head around towards a darkened alley between two buildings. Moving quickly before the revellers saw me, I darted towards the mouth of the alley.

I would have indeed caused a spectacle in my clothing if someone saw me. My white dress alone would be considered undergarments in this time and place on Earth. And the golden armour... it would be hard to explain that one.

He was waiting for me in the shadows, the broad outline of him barely visible as I approached. I marvelled at the people sleeping in the houses all around us, innocent in their slumber, or those casually enjoying the company of friends. They were completely, utterly unaware that the embodiment of their nightmares, the manifestation of their deepest terrors walked their streets tonight.

"Lucifer," I said softly. "What are you doing here?"

The whites of his eyes gleamed, making the darkness shifting in the centre even more disturbing. "I'm waiting."

"For me?"

"No," his eyes looked past me into the night. "For that."

I turned again, squinting in the darkness, trying to discern what he meant. At first I couldn't see anything out of the ordinary, but then I caught a flash of movement from the rooftops. Something or someone skittered across the tiles. They made an impossible leap to the next building landing on all fours. Then in a jerky, swift motion, crawled over the roof like a spider, scrambling down the wall of the building, pausing only briefly to open the latch of a window before disappearing inside.

The white drapes of the open window gently fluttered in the night cold breeze.

I turned my head back to Lucifer. "What... was that?" My voice pitched higher than normal.

"You mean *who* is that? That is Dahak. He has managed to possess a young female and as a result has decided to go on a killing spree."

Just as he said that, muffled screams of terror pierced the air, then swiftly were strangled off, leaving a deadened silence.

"You have to stop him!" I hissed.

"I will... later," he replied calmly. He shifted, bringing up his knee and placing a foot against the wall. "You wanted to see me?"

I gaped at him. "There is a demon out there killing humans! You have to stop him now!"

"I'd rather wait."

"Why are you waiting?" I yelled, not caring if anyone heard me.

"Because it pleases me for Dahak to believe he has gotten away with his brief sojourn, before I shatter that illusion. It's more satisfying that way."

"Well, you can wait. I'm not!" I couldn't just stand there and wait for a demon to continue massacring people. My blood sang with the need to take action.

Energy rushed to my hands, building with intensity and eager to burst out of my skin.

Spinning back around, I started to bolt back into the street towards the house. If I flew up to the window, I could hopefully catch the demon inside. I had no idea how I was supposed to get it back to Hell, but I figured I could work that out later. The priority was to stop it from slaughtering anyone else.

At least, that's what I intended to do.

Instead, I ran into an invisible wall of thickened air.

The air resisted the forward momentum of my body, making me feel as if I was trying to move through sludge. It slowly pushed me back inside the alleyway.

I narrowed my eyes at my soulmate who had not moved an inch. "Let me go, Lucifer," I growled.

"No, little angel, I don't think I will. I did not bring you here to interfere. This is for me to deal with, not you."

I flung out my hands wide. "Then deal with it!"

A window opened in the alleyway and a wrinkled face popped out with a blue nightcap. Eyes squinted down at us from up above. "Shhhhh! Some people are trying to sleep! Get out of here before I call the guard!" The window slammed shut with such force it spilled some loose rubble from the brickwork down into the space next to us.

Lucifer continued, "In my own time." He held up his hand and a flicker of fire appeared at the tip of his index finger. "I think you mistakenly believe I care what happens to these humans. I could light up this building behind me, listen to its inhabitants roasting in the flames, and simply walk away, forgetting the deed in the next breath because it's too insignificant to really matter." He smiled at the look on my face and continued, "Now that we have established that, why did you want to see me?"

I clenched my jaw, the hurt that shot through me making me swallow. It was pathetic really, that I was even hurt. I knew who he was, and it was a far cry from the angel he had been, despite having glimmers that achingly reminded me of the lighter version of himself. He was changing, slowly, and so was I, but at his core he was still the High Lord of Hell. It seemed a part of me was struggling to accept it.

The moonlight bathed my skin, shining softly against the white of my dress. It reached only a corner of the alley, recoiling away from the fallen angel who rested in the shadows. Again it occurred to me that I could shift straight out of the Earth plane and be back in The City of Light.

And again, I stayed.

I tried to ignore glancing behind me at the open window across the street and wondering if the demon had slipped out and was on its way to another family, another victim. Could the warrior angels in The City feel its presence on Earth? Maybe they would come down to banish it back to Hell.

By the creator, I fervently hoped they would.

"I needed to ask you a favour." My tone cooled down several degrees.

I could hear the amusement flavour his words. "I don't do favours, little one, I do deals."

"Fine," I snapped out, crossing my arms. "I need to make another deal."

His face emerged from the shadows as he leaned forward, his sculpted lips querking up at the corners, his cheekbones sharpened by blended shades of night. "Go on," he purred.

I let out a breath. "I need you to give me a tour of the Fallen domain. I need to see where they train, where they eat, sleep, spend their leisure time, torture others." Rushing to finish, I continued, "And where they... go relieve themselves. I need to see the layout of their personal quarters, including the areas that connect to the dungeons and the arena. I need you to take me safely around and bring me safely back to your domain."

Lucifer's brows raised and his smile deepened. "I see. That's quite a request. And what shall you give me for it?"

Nothing I could immediately think of. "What do you want?" I countered instead.

"Oh, so many things," he replied silkily. He slid out of the dark and I felt the combined thrill of fear and anticipation swirl almost sickly in my stomach. "But I do have one particular thing on my mind."

"And what is that?"

Lucifer came closer until I was forced to stare up into his midnight eyes. He held out his hand to me. I eyed it suspiciously for a second before I placed my own hand in his.

"Let me show you."

I tried to pretend I couldn't hear the screams echoing down the street as we blinked away.

Chapter 4

As soon as we shifted into our destination, I knew immediately where we were. My bones ached from the currents of negativity shooting through my skin. My head pounded, painful pressure building inside my skull, threatening to burst through the vessels embedded in my eyes. I gritted my teeth, struggling to blink back tears as my ears rang with a high pitch frequency.

I was back in Hell.

I squeezed Lucifer's hand in my own as the pain steadily increased. Suddenly, I felt his energy run soothingly over my skin. It blocked out the pain in a dark, comforting wave, dimming the growing pressure in my head. I shivered as his darkness enclosed around me, intimately aware of how vulnerable I was from a psychic attack.

I remembered Elindara, the female warrior angel I had bargained for in The City of Light. When she came back from Hell, her aura had been riddled with large, gaping holes, like a colour painting pierced randomly with a hot poker. Her condition was a severe case of a psychic attack from negative energy.

But Lucifer's energy didn't harm me, instead it layered over my own in a protective shield. It showed me how far we had come that I had unconsciously let him through my energetic barriers, and that once he was in, he didn't take advantage of it.

I let out a deep breath and looked around. The crepuscular lighting and the thick, heavy mist that obscured the surroundings unlocked memories in the back of my mind. I watched shapes move around us.

They were angry, and they were *hungry*.

They slithered, crept, and crawled in a range of different sizes, pressing in from all sides. Panic surged wildly, and I wrestled with the urge to flee.

It was here that my darker self was born.

"Breathe," Lucifer said, his fingers moving to lace through mine. "Take a moment to conquer your fear." He turned his head to look down at me, his voice strong and certain. "Nothing will harm you while you are with me."

I shuddered and took a moment to push the panic back down, to ease the erratic beat of my heart. Closing my eyes, I tried to centre myself, leaning on the knowledge that Lucifer would not leave me here. When I finally felt I had my fear under some semblance of control, I opened them again and nodded.

We walked through the mist, and the demons around us parted to make way. They hissed and growled at our presence, but they didn't move closer. While they inspired a deep level of fear inside me, I was a thousand percent certain that the Ruler of Hell was infinitely more terrifying to them. The tormentors had their own tormenter. The monsters in the dark feared an even greater monster.

And who was more terrifying than the Devil?

When there were no sudden attacks, I relaxed a fraction. Curiosity bubbled up to the surface. Why had Lucifer brought me to Hell?

Before I had a chance to ask, he slowed to a stop. The grey mist in front of us parted like a veil, sweeping out on either side. Hidden behind was a translucent wall, luminous and pearly in colour. It rippled like it was made from water, spanning as wide as I could see. Something about it called to me, resonating in a sweet musical note that made me want to move closer.

"What is that?" I breathed out.

"It's a barrier between the levels of Hell."

Ah, yes, of course. Lucifer had created barriers in Hell to separate the grades of demons from the most dangerous to the least.

"What level of Hell are we on now?"

"The first."

"Does it feel and look the same in all the levels of Hell?"

Lucifer shook his head. "No, each layer increases in negativity and the landscapes shift to reflect the inhabitants." He gestured in front of him. "The barriers act like a filter. The demons in the bottom level are unable to ascend to the level above as their negative energies are too dense."

I nodded. "It's like the barrier between the Underworld and the Earth plane," I murmured.

"Yes, but that's a natural barrier between realms. This one was made."

"But humans can access the Underworld. Can level one demons go down to level two?"

"Yes, but we discourage that."

And by discourage he would mean violently kill. I turned back towards the barrier, feeling its power radiating outwards. It wasn't raw magic, slammed together to create something on this scale. This was delicate and complex. This was the work of a master.

In that moment, I felt a sense of awe. "How did you learn to do this?'

There was a slight pause. "I learnt from someone a long time ago."

Interesting. I could feel Lucifer's resistance to the question, which only made me want to probe deeper. I was suddenly aware of the aeons between my incarnation as Nadia and my angelic self. In all that time since he fell, it shouldn't have been surprising that he had sought out others to assist him in honing his command and control over the dark energies. I wondered who and what they were, and why he was resistant to talk about it.

But something was off.

This barrier wasn't made completely from dark energy. I still felt the pull of something familiar, like a piece of me was hidden inside the barrier and they were trying to magnetically join together. I stared at the barrier, trying to see beneath the water surface.

The realisation hit me and my eyes snapped to his. By the look on his face, I was aware he had been waiting for me to figure it out.

"You used Light!" My gaze sharpened as my thoughts raced. "Is that why you kept yours?"

"One of the reasons," he replied vaguely and walked forward, pulling me closer to the barrier.

I tried not to enjoy the feeling of his fingers entwined with mine. That simple touch, the casual way he did it, and the utter ease in which we fit together, sent an ache to my heart. He had held my hand just like this so many times before. To have him do it again now, so casually, was beautifully painful.

Lucifer swept his hand in front of him and the barrier shimmered like a mirage. The watery light solidified into glowing lines that were woven into intricate patterns, almost like multiple starbursts overlapping each other. I could see now that the lines were a combination of light and dark.

"Dark energy wasn't enough to hold demons. When they combined their strength into one area they managed to pierce through the barrier. When I wove the barrier with Light, it held for longer, but in a place like this with demons continually testing their strength, the energy drained quickly."

"So you combined both," I concluded quietly.

"Yes, dark balanced with light to give it endurance and strength. But even then the barrier could not last forever."

A demon, hairless and small with grey sickly skin, crept closer to us from the mist to my right. When it saw me watching, it hissed, two bright red tongues flicking out between thin lips, raking over small broken teeth that were chipped and stained yellow. Without looking, Lucifer raised a hand.

The demon exploded into black flames, screeching as it was reduced to ashes.

When my heart slowed once more, the pieces started to come together. "So, knowing this you saved your Light. The darkness you had abundance in supply, but once you turned..."

"I wouldn't have access to Light energy," he finished for me.

"And you only have a limited supply," I concluded with mixed emotions. "Which is why you need me."

Besides myself, I knew there was only one other Light angel in existence and he was safely in The

City of Light. In all this time, I was the only other one since Lucifer fell. My thoughts and feelings battered against each other, causing little bursts of pain to explode inside me. I followed a train of thought I hadn't explored before.

Lucifer knew the barriers would need recharging periodically otherwise they would fail and the demons would escape. He was also very aware that he had only kept a finite amount of Light to keep them charged.

He needed a contingency plan.

He needed me.

How long had he been searching for one? Was that the reason he had brought me to Hell in the first place? My head pounded, and everything around me started to fade into the distance. Was that also the reason he had captured angels since the beginning? Maybe he had been looking for someone like me. He knew I had Light abilities from the very first moment we met. I had even used it against him.

Had I been mistaken this whole time believing that he brought me here because some part of him had been looking for me since my last incarnation passed?

I thought he had remembered me. But maybe his sole purpose was to use me all along.

The panic started to come back, but this time for a different reason. I swallowed. Don't you dare cry, I told myself fiercely. Don't you dare. Perhaps this was the real reason he hadn't hurt or turned me. Lucifer needed me in the form I was in.

I couldn't give him Light if I was dark.

I felt sick to my stomach.

I wanted to wrench our fingers apart, and move as far away from him as possible. I hated the way I was feeling. It shouldn't have mattered why. I should have felt glad he was trying to lock the demons in Hell. Through his own desire for control, he was saving the people on Earth. I should have felt grateful he wasn't trying to turn me, even if it was just because he needed me.

But I couldn't.

I didn't.

And I hated it. I *hated* it.

I curled my hands into a fist, my nails biting into my skin. I squeezed my fist harder, until I felt my blood start to pool under my nails.

Without looking at my soulmate, I said, "Am I right? That's why you need me."

"I don't need anyone. There are always other ways to obtain what I want. But you would be correct in surmising that your abilities present an opportunity I would be foolish to overlook."

My chest constricted. If there really were other ways, he would have used them by now. "I see," I said.

Something familiar yawned and unfurled within me. *Yes, finally... you do.* The words were said so softly I dismissed it in the chaos of my mind.

His jaw angled down, dark eyes unfathomable. "This would be the price for showing you the Fallen's domain. I'll require you to continuously fill crystals with Light energy during your stay here."

I steeled myself. With considerable effort, I closed off the turbulent feelings that rioted through me. There would be time to deal with them later. Now it was business. It was time to negotiate.

"That doesn't seem fair. Like you said, you are asking for something continuous. My tour of the Fallen domain should only take a few hours. Am I correct?"

A flicker of amusement sparked to life in his eyes. "Correct. But the disharmony that would result from your visit would have quite the ripple effect."

"But not worth the time and energy I would be spending filling up crystals with Light. Light and energy I could be using to dismantle the cages," I pointed out.

His lips quirked. "But I would say, my time is infinitely more valuable than yours. In fact, the fate of the world depends on it."

"And I would consider that your time invested in showing me the Fallen domain an excellent way to spend your time. I will double the amount of time it takes you to show me around, and invest that in making Light crystals. For a few hours you get more crystals to maintain your barriers. Crystals you currently don't have."

"What if I tell you that I won't show you the Fallen's domain unless you spend five hours a day making Light crystals? Negotiation is a luxury I am willing to explore, but sometimes I prefer ultimatums."

My expression hardened. "Then I would tell you that I will find another way to get what I want. You are simply the more convenient option."

He bursts out laughing and I blinked. For once, it wasn't mocking or derisive. This was full and rich and... beautiful. My chest clenched painfully.

Focus.

Lucifer smiled, teeth flashing. "Four hours a day and I'll give you another room to stay in, whilst Atlas occupies yours."

I let go of his hand. "One hour a day, and only if I'm not already drained or healing."

He raised his eyebrows. "Four hours a day, and no room. Find another way if you must."

"How much is a barrier worth to you, Lucifer? I can start on making these crystals today." I tilted my head. "How much time would that buy you? Two hours and I get my own room. Same thing applies if I'm hurt or completely drained."

"At the frequency you hurt yourself that could be some time." Lucifer's eyes glinted. "If you are hurt or drained, then the hours carry over to the next day."

That would be annoying, but I could tell the room I had to negotiate was getting thin. "I also require no attacks in my room."

"Ah… little angel. That, I can't promise. You know the one place you can find respite. Your training will continue as we specified. I will not compromise on that."

"Fine, two hours a day with everything else I mentioned." I paused. "And Atlas gets a chamber pot."

"Deal," he said softly, looking at me in a peculiar way.

"Deal," I replied, equally as soft, the lump forming once again in my throat. I needed to get away. I needed to breathe.

"When would you like to leave?"

"Give me some time to prepare," I said, knowing the time would be spent coming to terms with this new revelation and how I felt. "I'll come find you when I'm ready."

Chapter 5

My new room was mostly white.

It was located through the left wall of the bathing room and larger than my previous quarters. Soft white sheets flowed over the large four poster bed, which was covered with several downey pillows of different sizes. Ivory drapes hung invitingly from the top, flowing down until they just grazed the floor.

There was a table and two chairs made from a light wood as well as a patterned chaise in gold and cream. The only thing that remained the same was the inky floor and walls.

The new decor was obviously more appealing to me, but I couldn't help but think about how impractical white was for blood stains. A thought that would have never entered my mind in The City of Light.

I went straight to the bed, laying down amongst the cushions and closed my eyes. My mind was a mess. I tried to centre myself and reach for the calmness and clarity that was inside me, but it remained elusive, escaping just past my fingertips.

I felt used.

There was no point in hiding from it. It hurt because I had inanely started to develop feelings for the one person I should have flown as fast and far away from. As much as I told myself not to, or that it was foolish and stupid, I clearly couldn't help myself. And now I was faced with the very real possibility that Lucifer's change of temperament towards me had nothing to do with our past and the development of our bond, but because he needed me. It could all be a ploy to get what he wanted.

But he gave you the option to leave at any time, my inner voice said.

He might have gambled with the fact that the lure of saving the warrior angels was too irresistible for me to leave.

I shook my head against the cushions. No, Lucifer would have never gambled. He would have known. That's why he had shown me the dungeons.

He could have used torture to get what he wanted.

There was that. If not on me, he could have used Rushton or one of the other angels. I would have done almost anything he wanted then. But he hadn't chosen that path. He had given me choices.

So, why would he do that?

I considered this and couldn't find a definite answer. Perhaps for no other reason than my own contentment and to build a certain level of trust. I couldn't deny our soul connection, which had once more started to form, but I also couldn't ignore the coincidence of my abilities and his need to use them.

Another thing was bothering me like a splinter working its way beneath the flesh. When Lucifer talked about attempting to create the barrier with Light I had assumed this whole time he had embraced the darkness first and then descended into Hell. But from what I gleaned from our conversation, he had descended into Hell when he had still been Light.

Why had he been there in the first place? Had he known he was going to Fall? I knew Nadia's death had been a catalyst, but there were still missing pieces in the timeline. I rubbed my forehead with my hands, tired of thinking about it. This was a distraction I didn't need.

I needed to be focused on my mission.

But, I also just needed a moment.

***

I was walking through the village, steadily ignoring the looks I was getting from members of my community, and from people I had known my whole life. Everyone had started responding to me differently since Lucifer appeared in the village. Where I had usually felt invisible, now it felt like there was a cloud of faeries flying above my head.

Faeries. Apparently they also existed.

I could be an old woman before I learnt a portion of all the wonderful, mysterious things in this world, hidden just beyond the vision of an unaware human. If only I could live forever and explore the world with Lucifer. There were so many places he talked about and wanted to show me, but the demon attacks were escalating and he had to prioritise his time. After encountering one of them that fateful day near the apple tree, I wholeheartedly agreed. I couldn't imagine how many innocents had been slaughtered so horrifically by being in the wrong place at the wrong time.

An older couple who I had sold pies to every year stood on the side of the road, gapping as I walked past. Unused to the attention, I lowered my head slightly and concentrated on the ground in front of me. I was heading to the dress store, a place I had a rare cause to be. My meagre savings were usually spent on food or small comforts for the cottage. But this time was different. Not only did the frequent gifts of food and other luxuries make my small savings grow, but tonight, Lucifer was coming over for dinner.

I wanted to wear something special.

The door jingled as I opened it, alerting Mrs. Bertnam to my presence. She turned at the sound, holding the mint green edge of the dressing room curtain open, obviously talking to someone inside.

She pushed her spectacles up her long nose and raised her brown brows. "Why, if isn't Nadia Fairwood, finally gracing me with her presence. The talk of the town these days, aren't we?"

Leaning back inside the dressing room, she said to the person inside, "It looks perfect on you as always. I'll get it hemmed and have it sent over tomorrow morning."

"Nadia," a light feminine voice said to my left. I turned to see Jacinda, elegant as ever with a cream colour day gown draped over her arm. Jacinda was one of the most sought

after single ladies in town. Men flocked for a moment of her attention, and she charmingly held them off with a sure smile and a ready wit. Her hair was dark and shiny like a raven's wing, her eyes like polished amber. From her svelte figure I could observe that she did not indulge in apple pies. Or muffins.

My stomach rumbled at the thought.

We had never really talked before, not because she deliberately avoided me, but because we never had a single thing in common. While Jacinda liked to discuss the latest fashion from Eltran, the bustling town in the west, I was trying to stitch holes in my socks. Jacinda was an avid reader of poetry, I talked with the local farmers about the best fertiliser to use for growing tomatoes. But she had always been polite, and I had no cause not to like her.

"Congratulations, I heard you were engaged," she said with a smile that flashed a dimple in her cheek.

Startled, my jaw dropped. Engaged? I was engaged? "Ummmm..." I struggled to think of what to say.

"Mrs. Bedford told me?" she added helpfully.

I groaned inwardly. Of course she did. According to her, I probably already had three kids and a house by the lake.

Jacinda continued, "I've heard he is unbelievably handsome and well off. Is he a Lord?" she asked, eager to find out. "People are saying he is a prince! What is his name?"

I heard movement from behind me and a tinkle of laughter. My heart sank in my chest as I recognised the sound. I was wrong, there was only one thing I didn't like about Jacinda, and that was the company she kept.

"Thank you, Mrs. Bertnam, Derik will love it..," the voice trailed off then picked up a healthy dose of malice. "Nadia, yes indeed, you are the talk of the town."

Carmine, the miller's daughter and the shining star of my mud pie in face fantasies, glided around to stand next to Jacinda. She wasn't as naturally beautiful as her friend, but there was something striking about her flashing dark eyes and wide cheekbones… when they weren't filled with spite.

"Are you after a dress for the wedding, dear?" Mrs. Bertnam called out from the counter as she scribbled some notes on a piece of paper.

Oh spirits, she meant my wedding. "Ahhh… no, Mrs. Bertnam, just something new," I replied, my eyes still trained on Carmine and her venomous smile.

"She's not getting married, Mrs. Bertnam," Carmine called out. "She doesn't have a ring on her finger." She lowered her voice, "Everyone has been wondering how you could have possibly landed a man like that. But now it all makes sense. There is only one reason someone like that would be interested in you." She looked me up and down, taking in my worn shoes and faded summer dress. "How many men in the village have you serviced exactly?"

A chill washed through me making me nauseous. It was followed by a cold, burning anger. Something in me stirred, calling for blood. I tried not to react, reminding myself of all the conversations Lucifer and I had about karma and the unfortunate ignorance of humanity regarding their actions.

But it was hard. So, so hard.

"Carmine!" Jacinda admonished fiercely. "Don't make unfounded, disgusting rumours. We know nothing about their relationship to speculate or judge." She shot me an apologetic look. "Let's go and leave Nadia to buy her dress." She tugged on Carmine's arm, urging her towards the door.

"They're not rumours," Carmine hissed, extracting her arm from Jacinda's grasp. "Edmond and Kaleb both went to her house last week. They said she invited them over." Her eyes glittered. "And now she has money to buy a dress."

At the men's names the fury surged as I remembered their presence at my cottage. "They're lying," I snapped. I fought the urge to hit her smug face. I had a flash of her features covered in blood and a thrill of pleasure shot through me.

"Carmine, don't make a scene!" Jacinda said mortified, her face heating with embarrassment.

"Carmine Harris!" Mrs. Bertnam said loudly, walking over. "I will not tolerate such ugliness in my shop. That sort of rubbish belongs in the gutter and is completely unworthy of a lady." She planted her hands on her hips and glared at her. "I think if your father heard what you just said he would be completely ashamed. Now, kindly leave and let Nadia do her shopping in peace."

Carmine at least had the grace to look embarrassed. She shot me a look of pure disdain. "I apologise, Mrs. Bertnam for causing a scene, but you ought to know. Everyone should know." She turned on her heel and marched out, the bell ringing violently as she slammed the door shut.

"I'm so sorry, Nadia," Jacinda said. She handed the white dress she was holding back to Mrs. Bertnam "You know how Carmine is. She is having a rough time at home and she just takes it out…"

"You don't need to make excuses for her," I told Jacinda coolly. "I know exactly what kind of person she is."

She looked uncomfortable.

"Any how, Jacinda, do you mind seeing yourself out as I help Nadia?" Mrs. Bertnam intervened briskly.

"No, not at all. Good day and thanks, Mrs. Bertnam." Jacinda nodded to us and quickly left.

Mrs. Bertnam avoided asking me anything more about my personal life as she showed me a range of dresses. As she talked about the latest styles and trends I could feel myself become increasingly more furious.

I was used to Carmine's taunts and insults, but it was Edmond and Kaleb and their insinuations that made me want to tear all these beautiful clothes into pieces. They had come to my house in the middle of the night to attack me. If Lucifer hadn't been there…

I growled under my breath.

"Sorry, dear?" Mrs. Bertnam turned towards me, holding up a dress. "What did you say? This one?"

I nodded, not looking at what she was holding, my eyes glazed, my body hot. Sensing the turbulence of my energy, she quickly wrapped up the dress and handed it to me. I paid and walked out the door.

This time I didn't notice the stares and whispers. My mind was a fog with a dark, winding pathway leading me on. My stomach rolled sickly and I was dimly aware that something was wrong, but I couldn't seem to focus. My feet carried me through the streets, past houses and stalls. They were a colourless blur.

It didn't feel like I was heading into any particular direction until I saw him.

Kaleb.

I hissed between my teeth when I saw him standing on the side of the street with his younger brother, laughing and talking amongst themselves. His tall, lanky frame seemed insidious in the morning light, a thin shadow riddled with dark intentions.

My vision tinged with red and I looked down on the ground around me, searching... searching...

Something glinting in the sun caught my eye.

Leaning down, my fingers brushed over a shard of glass from a broken bottle. I curled my fingers around its sharp edges, unconcerned at the sudden bite against my flesh. It scraped along the ground as I picked it up. I casually concealed it amongst the folds of my faded peach dress and stood up slowly, eyes ahead.

I crossed the road towards them.

Distantly, I heard someone shouting as they walked past, narrowly missing crashing into me as they carried a box full of potatoes. I was a couple of metres away before Kaleb noticed me, his eyes flickering with recognition.

Kaleb's father owned a bar in town and was the frequent haunt of the younger men. My anger grew as I remembered him that night with Edmond, bottle in hand.

What sort of evil had they been planning? What thoughts had been playing out in their minds as they walked for hours on foot to reach me all alone?

Kaleb placed a hand on his brother's shoulder and turned to face me. He smiled, but it didn't reach his eyes. I never trusted people whose smile didn't warm their eyes. It made me think they were dead inside.

"Good day, Nadia," he said amicably.

His younger brother turned around too with a sunny expression on his face. "Good day."

I ignored him.

I pictured it all in my head.

The way I would step forward, the shard of clear glass, flashing almost silver in the sunlight as it breached the space between us, puncturing the white linen shirt covering Kaleb's body, again and again and again. His body would make soft sucking sounds as the sharp point cut in and out. The blood would bloom like roses over the cloth, sticking wetly to his skin. My hand would come up again, carving across the pale column of his throat, watching the flesh part and the blood bead like garnets.

Or my tentacles could come out and wrap around his limbs, pulling them apart at different angles. The bones would make a delicious pop and I could drag them closer to my mouth...

I shuddered and shook my head as the images rolled sickly through my head. Tentacles...

"Nadia," Kaleb said, his voice tense. "What are you doing?"

I blinked and realised that my hand was half way up in front of me, the shard of glass held tightly between my fingers, which were now dripping with blood.

Confused, my voice came out in a rasp, "I was..."

I was about to kill you.

Shocked and horrified at the realisation, I dropped the glass and backed away. Something was wrong. Something was very wrong with me. I turned, almost knocking into another passerby. Shoving them aside, I ran.

I ran as fast as my legs would take me, all the way home.

A dark voice intruded in my dream.

~ You could have taught them a lesson. You could have shown them you were a power to be reckoned with. Not a poor, vulnerable female all alone. But you didn't. I would have done things much differently. ~

The dream shifted.

Lucifer landed on the grass outside a small house in the middle of a forest. I was held tightly in his arms, the pain a constant burn that left me hovering on the edge of consciousness.

I gripped his arm weakly. "Where are we?" I rasped out.

He studied the house and then the surrounding forest with caution. "At a place that should give us some answers."

The door opened and a feminine figure was outlined against the fire light within. She called out to us, "Welcome, First Son of Light. I've been expecting you." She turned back and walked inside.

~ Who is she? ~ I asked in my mind.

Lucifer held me tighter against him and carried me across the dewy grass.

~ She's called a witch and sorceress by those who don't know her. But the few that do, call her the Naballa, which means seer. ~

We walked over a small wooden bridge that ran over a bubbling brook. It looked like it encircled the house, but in the dark I couldn't really tell. I felt something shift in the air as we crossed, almost like we pushed through an invisible barrier.

A fresh wave of pain rolled over me, and I closed my eyes, trying to breath through the sensation. I could feel Lucifer's stress and worry filter through the link, and I fought not to make any sounds so I wouldn't upset him further.

"You can put your Flame down over there, and come take a seat," the seer said.

I felt his immediate reluctance to part with me, but he carefully placed me down on some soft bedding. He brushed some hair away from my face before he stood up again. I heard him walk away, then a chair scraped back, followed by another.

"Do you know why I am here?" Lucifer asked.

"I would be a poor seer if I did not." There was a pause. "You have changed, Son of Light."

"You speak as if you knew me before."

"I have not, but I know how you should feel. Your energy is turbulent and chaotic. We both know you can seek your own answers by going within, but you can't connect."

This was news to me.

"Then you would also know the urgency of my mission and what is at stake."

"I am aware." There was a low groan of wood and I imagined the seer leaning forward. "Give me your hand."

I struggled to open my eyes. At first, everything was a blurry mutation of colour, then they slowly formed recognisable shapes. Lucifer had his back to me, the broad outline of him in white. Across from him sat the seer. Her face was a pale oval, her hair cascading in brown, wavy locks. She had a bowel in front of her and Lucifer hovered his hand above.

"Blood always gives the answer," she murmured.

Lucifer clenched his fist before she touched him. "Not yet," he said firmly. "First, I will know your price."

She laughed low and throaty, but there was a hint of something underneath. "Almost had you then. Ah, the things I could have asked."

"There was never an almost. I am very aware of how this works. What is your price?"

I could hear the hint of impatience in his tone. Since my time in Asclepius's temple I had noticed Lucifer had changed in a way I couldn't put my finger on. He was still compassionate and loving towards me, but it was like the light he radiated outwards had grown dimmer, blanketed by something heavy and dense. And like the seer has said, his emotions were more turbulent.

"What if I asked you to kill for me?"

"Are they demons?" There was a hard edge to his tone.

"And if they were not?"

"Then you know my answer."

"Not even for… her?"

"It's not in my nature to destroy," he said icily. "I would have to be something else entirely to be capable of such an act, but you already know that."

"Nature can change, but yes, I already knew that. How about this, Son of Light, the payment I require is the opposite of killing. It would be for you to not kill, which I believe is agreeable to you."

The word was crisp. "Explain."

"I require you to never harm me and those of my bloodline for as long as you exist."

I could feel his confusion at her request and his caution. "To ask me such a price would mean that you believe at some point in the future I would have cause to."

"A possible future, Son of Light. There are many pathways you may take. I am just protecting myself and my line from one of them."

"I see." There were a few beats of silence. "And how would I recognise your bloodline?"

"We all carry a birthmark... here." There was a movement of cloth against skin. I wondered which part of her flesh she had exposed.

"Do I get to ask three questions?"

A hesitation. "Yes."

"And you will answer my questions in full." Another pause, but this one simmering with anger. "I need you to say it, Naballa."

"Yes," she hissed. She was clearly unhappy with doing that. I'd imagine the seer would find it useful to obtain knowledge no one else knew and then use it for her own gain.

"Then we have a deal." Lucifer opened his fist.

Unable to keep my eyes open, I let them fall shut while still straining to hear the conversation.

There were a few more moments of silence before she said, "Ask your first question, Son of Light."

The question shot out fast like it was on the tip of his tongue. "What is needed to heal my Flame from the demon poisoning?"

"Hmmmmm..." she said, drawing the sound out. "You already know the answer and you have tried it. It's Light."

He had tried it. When Lucifer found me by the apple tree, with the demon blood crawling through my veins he had tried to counter it with his Light. It was excruciating. The demon energy was affected and started to disintegrate, but it was taking me with it, destroying me as it was being destroyed.

"You had the right source, but not the right conductor. Your Light was too raw and pure and needed a specific channel that could kill the demon infection without killing your Flame."

~ Is that why you asked Rapheal? ~ I asked in my mind.

~ Yes ~ his voice caressed. ~ Rapheal is our greatest healer and would have known how to get rid of the demon blood. ~

I felt the flicker of anger spark from him after his words.

Rapheal hadn't helped us and instead encouraged Lucifer to come back to The City of Light and leave me to my fate. Was I meant to die this way? I felt the sweat drip from my brow, my breathing laboured.

~ No. ~ Lucifer said sharply, hearing that thought. ~ I won't let that happen. ~

"So, the answer is Light and a specific way to channel it," the seer stated. "What is your next question?"

"Where can I find a conduct to channel my Light and heal my Flame?"

I held my breath.

"Well...well..." the seer said. "It seems there is a place you can go to that has what you need. It's a place beyond the mists, a bridge between the earthly and the celestial. There, ancient healing knowledge has been stored, where the incurable can be cured. Almost impossible to find if you are mortal, unless you have an invitation. But for you, Son of Light, I believe the mists will part. Avalon. The Island of Apples. Also known as the Island of Crystals."

A surge of hope shot through me, flaming through the darkness inside and burning through the despair. There was a way...

~ Do you know this place? ~ I asked, unable to contain myself.

~ Yes, I do. ~ I felt his eagerness to leave. ~ I'll be able to find it. It might take me a day or two, but I know where to look. ~

"Third and last question, Son of Light."

Lucifer betrayed none of the emotions he felt within. His voice was deliberate and precise. "When you did a reading of me earlier, before I came, what did you see?"

I felt the air turn cold. The door and windows of the room vibrated.

"Answer me," Lucifer said softly.

"The deal is the deal," she hissed. "Very well, I saw a great darkness in you, a great evil to blot the world. Terror, pain, and death surrounded you with every step you took. You will be the most feared creature to walk the realms, unmatched and undefeated. Your power will eclipse the Gods and you will have no mercy for those who get in your way. Compassion will be a foreign memory to you, and love a weakness to be used and manipulated."

"Evil will wear your face."

My heart seemed to stop in my chest and I struggled to breathe. That couldn't be true. No. Not Lucifer.

"You are wrong. That will not happen," Lucifer said.

"Then hurry, Son of Light. You are running out of time."

Chapter 6

I woke up in a tangle of sheets and memories. The pain of the demon infection ghosted through me, as well as the shock of the seer's predictions. I sat up in bed and took a deep breath, pushing my long hair away from my face. The Naballa had seen, even back then, the path Lucifer would take into darkness.

No, the *possible* path.

There had been a ray of hope in her reading, a shining star to follow in the desert of our despair.

Avalon.

So what happened? Why didn't we make it there? Or... did we?

I couldn't seem to locate the memory in my conscious mind, and even though the past was a tantalising lure with answers to many of my questions, I still had too many things to do than to try and linger there. Time was precious and slipping slowly through my fingers. If I wanted to save the warrior angels then I had to move fast.

I slid off the bed and through the translucent drapes. Something in the corner of the room caught my eye, making me pause. There was a smooth wooden chest with an ornate silver latch that hadn't been there when I first came in. It was disturbing that it had appeared while I had been sleeping. In my mind, I imagined the servant demon looming over me whilst I slept, its bony fingers clicking together as it resisted choking me in my sleep. Even though it appeared that the spectral demon wasn't allowed to hurt me, it still chilled me to think it could appear when I was unaware.

When I was vulnerable.

Proceeding with caution, I walked closer to the wooden chest until I could make out a thin sheet of wood resting on top. Burnt into the wood grain in an elegant, masculine script were the words:

As per our arrangement.

Picking it up, I set it on the ground, then flicked open the latch on the chest. It was heavier than I expected, but it swung open with a reluctant groan from its hinges. I felt their energy immediately. Clear quartz crystals, over a hundred of them filled to the brim.

Clear quartz crystals had many purposes and uses. One of them was the ability to absorb energy efficiently and easily.

It seemed my daily two hour quota of filling crystals with Light had begun.

I picked one up and held it in my hand, running my fingers against the rough edges and enjoying the hum of energy against my skin. I let my Light pool in my hand, illuminating my fingers all the way down to my wrist like a glove. At first, the Light only surrounded the crystal, then after a moment, it filtered through the cool surface, making it sparkle brightly.

I studied the crystal intently. This was what Lucifer had used when he had healed me. A smaller piece, but the same type of crystal. I wondered how much he had left. How close was he to the barriers falling apart?

I spent the next two hours sitting on the floor, filling the crystals with Light energy, my mind focusing on the next steps of my plan. First, I needed to see Atlas and fill him in on the events so far. I'm sure he'd have advice on how I should proceed with a few of his narky comments thrown in. Then, I had to find Lucifer and accompany him to the Fallen domain.

It made me nervous, thinking about being in their presence again with their soulless gazes focused on me. Since our last confrontation in the dungeons, I was well aware that their animosity would have grown exponentially. If hatred was a living thing, it would tear me apart the second I entered their domain, my pain the only balm to the burning rage living behind their eyes.

I had humiliated them and it had cost them one of their leaders. This game I was playing required me to balance on a razor edge. That edge was cutting into me as I traversed through Hell, and it would only be a matter of time before I slipped on my own blood and fell into the screaming void below.

I just had to get the warrior angels out before I did.

Placing the glowing crystals back in the chest, I shut the lid with a click. Surprisingly, I only felt slightly drained, not enough to lie down and recover. Feeling the urge to get moving, I placed my hands against the wall and merged through it.

My new room was adjacent to the bathing pool. The pool itself had returned back to its rectangular shape, the candles and hanging orbs of light cast a reddish glow instead of a golden one, making the water appear like it was tinged with blood. I moved along the edge quickly, not wanting to be tempted into taking a quick dip.

I didn't see it coming.

Water erupted from the pool, spraying across the floor. Something pink and rubbery snaked out, hooking wetly around my left ankle, and pulled. Slamming into the ground, my teeth smashed into my bottom lip as my head cracked against the floor. Blood spurted into my mouth as my vision blurred.

I had a second to fill my lungs with air, before I was yanked into the water.

Blind. I couldn't see.

Bubbles blocked my view as I was viciously yanked from side to side. I tried to kick my leg free but the grip on my ankle was too tight. The tentacle squirmed up my leg to wrap around my calf and my mind flashed back to the demon in my past life.

But no… this was different. This was an underwater creature.

My hands burst with Light, illuminating the water around me.

The bathing pool was impossibly larger below than above, and much deeper. Rupturing through the cracks in the tiles were three additional tentacles. It looked like the demon was trying to break through, straining to squeeze its body through the gaps in the floor to get at me. I glimpsed a gaping maw through one of the cracks, surrounded by hundreds of eyes.

My eyes widened. More bubbles escaped my lips, floating rapidly past me, escaping above my head.

I narrowed my Light into laser points. The Light shot through the water like a beam, but it was less intense. The water was affecting its strength. I waved my hands around frantically as I was thrashed back and forth, trying to cut the tentacles around me with my disorientated vision. Light careened wildly around the pool and the grip around me tightened painfully.

Then it let go.

I must have hit it! I quickly kicked towards the surface, trying to reach the glimmering light above.

I needed to breathe. I needed to *breathe*.

Suddenly, the tentacles latched onto my arms, pulling them wide apart and anchoring me in the water. My hands surged with power as I struggled desperately to move, but the demon held on tight, making my laser beams of Light ineffective and useless.

The tentacles yanked harder. I felt my shoulders pop and my mouth opened in a silent scream.

My Light disappeared.

The pain was vicious. Unless I thought quickly, I was going to lose this battle. I was going to drown. The tentacles dragged me down towards the bottom of the pool.

Do something or drowning will be the least of your problems, something softly hissed in the dim recesses of my mind.

I knew that voice. Another bout of fear injected into me like ice in my veins and I struggled to push it down. The water demon dragged me to the bottom of the pool, scraping my skin along the debris from the broken tiles. The cracks in the pool were wider and I again terrifyingly glimpsed the dark, empty mouth getting closer and closer. It opened and closed, eager to suck me inside.

The only weapon I had was my Light, but like with Atlas when he trapped my hands, I'd been rendered useless. I had nothing. My Light was gone. I was in darkness...

Except... I could still see faintly around me. My shoulders were emitting the softest of glows.

The demon pulled me down towards its jaws, its eyes glinting with hunger and glee. I channelled more power to the surface of my skin. The glow around my shoulders became stronger and veins of light rippled over my arms. My feet started to slide through the cracks, and I felt the soft, slippery edge of the demon's mouth at the soles of my feet. With desperation, I blasted the rest of my power through my body in every direction.

Light burst from my skin.

I became a living flame, glowing like a tiny, white hot sun beneath the water. The tentacles dropped from my arms as if scorched. I twisted and shot the Light from my body until it beamed out in one long stream, striking the demon in its wide gaping mouth beneath the cracks of the pool floor. The Light glowed fiercely underneath the cracks and the tentacles yanked back frantically, disappearing out of sight.

Unfortunately, I couldn't hold my breath any longer.

Water rushed into my lungs like lava, burning and weighing me down. My kicks to drive my body to the surface became more and more feeble. My eyes glazed over and I started to relax. My Light faded away.

In the back of my mind, I felt something infinitely cold grab my wrist before I was yanked out of the water, cold air biting into my skin as I was tossed unceremoniously onto the floor. I gagged, water streaming out of my lungs as I hurled the water I had swallowed onto the dark tiles. I opened my eyes just in time to see the spectral demon fade away.

I coughed, more water ejecting out of me. I took in great, big gulps of air, feeling furious and shocked at the attack. Lucifer had warned me that he would continue to test me. A warning I had forgotten in the turbulence of my mind.

He had also said that my abilities were only limited by the limits I gave it.

My hands were my limits.

Not any more.

***

Atlas looked up from where he was reclining on the bed to see me merge into the room, dripping wet with my arms flopping uselessly by my side.

"By Ares's balls, what in the bloody blazes happened to you?"

I stood there, forming a puddle on the floor. "I was attacked by a giant octopus demon."

"You look like shit."

"Thanks." I wiped away the water dripping into my eyes with a hiss of pain. "I need your help."

He frowned, one hand stroking his peppered beard. "Clearly. Your arms look a bit wrong."

I sighed, moving closer into the room. "Atlas, could you please help me set my shoulders back in place?"

He swung his legs off the bed and stood up. I noticed he still had his shoes on. "It's going to hurt," he warned.

I glared at him, my face still bruised and bleeding, my lungs feeling raw with every breath I took. "I think I can manage."

He gestured for me to lie down. I moved over to the bed, noticing the edge of a chamber pot hidden underneath. Gingerly, I laid down on the black sheets, wincing as the throbbing pain increased.

I had managed to will my armour away so that the top and sides of my shoulders were bare. Not that the armour had helped me during my last encounter. The spectral demon had finally stepped in and saved me. It seemed Lucifer had been telling the truth about me not being in danger of losing my form during these 'training sessions.'

And then there was that voice while I was fighting with the water demon. Faint, but there... my darker self had risen again. A flash of fear rolled through me as I realised the healing had not gotten rid of her. It seemed that when I went into Hell to look at the barriers, it had somehow awoken her again.

Atlas grabbed my wrist until he manoeuvred my arm out to the side and gave it a forceful jerk. I groaned as I felt my shoulder pop back into place. Immediately there was relief. He made me move around so he could do the same to the other side. I could tell that he had done this many times before.

"For all the battles you have claimed you have been in, I hardly see scars on your skin, girl."

I noticed all the scar tissue he had roped along his arms and thinner white lines that criss crossed his skin. I wondered if I did scar, how many marks I would already have on my body. "I can heal myself," I said casually.

Atlas stared at me, then threw up his hands. "Then why don't you do this your bloody self?" he shouted.

"I can heal wounds. I can't set the bones back in place," I clarified calmly.

He gripped my wrist again and pulled. I gritted my teeth as he popped the other arm back in. "That's a skill that would be very useful in battle." His brown eyes looked at me consideringly. "What would you -"

I cut him off before he could finish his sentence. "I'm not going to join your army, Atlas."

He narrowed his eyes suspiciously and stepped away from the bed, giving me the space to sit up. "How did you know I was going to ask that?"

I smiled wryly. "I could just tell." With another groan, I propped myself up amongst the cushions. "Thank you for doing that," I said, rubbing the top of my shoulder. "I don't belong on Earth, I belong in Heaven." Even as I said that the words didn't ring completely right.

"Well, you don't belong in Hell either, now look where you are!" he said cheerfully. "Let's not rule out an army altogether."

He clapped his hands together loudly and moved over to the chair in the corner of the room. I noticed the other chair had been broken. One of the legs was on the table, and the rest was in pieces on the floor.

Atlas's voice was eager and impatient at the same time. "So what has been happening, Sandy? Tell me, I've been bloody bored sitting in this room by myself. The faster we can get you freeing the angel people... the faster the demontorus will return me to my army."

"Did you have a fight with the chair?" I asked, standing up. I shivered as my damp clothes clung to me, plastering against my skin. My cheeks flushed slightly at the state I was in. The sheets were wet but I still grabbed them and wrapped it around my body sitting once again on the bed.

"I needed a sword," he said as he faced me, sitting on the unbroken chair.

I paused, confused. "And why do you need a sword?" Not that the chair leg resembled anything like a sword.

Atlas picked up the broken piece of wood and waved it at the wall on my right. "There is something moving behind these walls," he declared. He eyed the dark surface embedded with shimmering golden strands with trepidation.

"Ah yes, the Dragarth," I said knowingly.

"Ah yes, the Dragarth," Atlas mimicked me. He raised his voice. "What in Zeus's cock is a Dragarth?" he roared.

I blinked at him in surprise. It seemed I had taken for granted Atlas's capitulation in being in Hell. A human not only having to face Lucifer, but also be surrounded by threats his rational mind was barely processing was an incredible strain on the mind. I wondered if he even believed he would make it out of here alive?

The shaky ground under the layer of confidence he projected was now visible, the anger barely masking the fear. This was a man who was used to fighting battles with other men. He knew what to expect, the level of violence humans inflicted on each other and how to kill them.

Demons... Fallen... that was something different entirely.

If I hadn't met Lucifer in my past life, the trauma of being attacked by a demon would have unhinged my sanity. How could you rationalise or explain such an attack? Not only to yourself but to others around you? Atlas must have a strong mental fortitude indeed to bear the strain of the nightmarish landscape enclosed around him.

The truth was, what he probably thought was in the wall was nothing compared to what was actually there. The Dragarth was terrifying, and that chair leg wasn't going to do anything to stop it.

I took a breath. "The Dragarth is a serpent that lives inside these walls. I believe it is one of the protections Lucifer has in place in case other demons break in. It used to stop me from going out too, but now it doesn't do that." That sounded reassuring, didn't it?

He stared at me. "There is a serpent in the wall."

I nodded slowly.

Atlas turned and poured himself a drink from the pitcher. He chugged it down in great big gulps. Filling his glass, he did again, wiping his mouth with the back of his hand. "I need more wine." He banged the cup down on the table twice, looking at it with disgust. "This bloody thing only magically fills up once a day. What kind of evil sorcery is that?"

It appeared that he would be fine. I gave him a small smile.

Moving onto a safer topic I said, "I've managed to negotiate a trip to the Fallen domain like we planned."

"Good," Atlas said, his brown eyes sharpening. "Do you know what you have to do?"

"Map out terrain, observe as much as I can about their movements and numbers and also possible infiltration points." Atlas opened his mouth to speak and I hurried on. "In addition, find out where they store weapons and food and who manages these supplies."

"And steal a disguise."

"Yes, steal a disguise."

"You're not exactly going to be able to blend in like that, Sandy," he said, gesturing at me with his wooden stick. "So find something good."

"It's Sandriel," I muttered, looking down at myself. I would have to improvise once I was there. I looked back up at him, my face a mask of determination. "Okay, let's do this."

Chapter 7

Lucifer and I entered the dungeons together. His hand once again held mine, strong and sure as we stepped through the portal into the darkness beneath the arena. Uncomfortable with the emotional confusion the physical contact created, I slipped my hand away from his and looked around, avoiding eye contact with the all too perceiving Lord of Hell.

Now that I had acknowledged my feelings towards Lucifer, it wrapped around my heart like a bruise, sensitive to anything that brushed against it. A simple action, which might not have caused any emotional reaction before, now burst with a plethora of feelings ranging in a spectrum of colours. One second it was aching pain, the next, secret delight, and then a combination of everything in between. It was like I lost control of the calm, rational part of my brain. It was now overtaken by something softer, younger, and more vulnerable.

And what was left of my brain was disgusted. Especially since the cause of my burgeoning emotions was more likely based on carefully planned manipulation. The Lord of Hell was playing me like a fiddle, and part of me was smiling like an idiot and dancing jauntily to his tune.

Since I had found him waiting for me in his room, Lucifer had failed to mention the chest full of crystals or the surprise he had left for me in the bathing room. He had just raised a perfect, black eyebrow when I banged the doors open and said in a bored, velvet tone.

"Are you ready?"

Infuriating.

I had found another set of clothes in my room, laid out neatly on my bed. The loose white top and pants were comfortable, allowing me to move freely and without hindrance. They also predictably made me a visual target, but for once I didn't mind standing out. If the Fallen became accustomed to seeing me dressed in white, they would be less likely to notice if I slipped into another guise.

I conjured up a small ball of Light and took a few steps away from him so I could study the dark energy cage in front of me. I wondered which angelic soul was trapped inside. The feelings of despair and hopelessness buffeted me from all sides, making my soul ache. It was an effort of will to block them out so I could think without losing myself in the warrior angel's pain.

"Which cell is Rushton held in?" I asked.

"I've already shown you which cell he is in," he replied coolly. "It's such a pity you can't remember, as there are so many of them in this place."

I shot him an irritated look over my shoulder. "Or you could show me again."

"Information doesn't come for free, little one. Or haven't you learnt that yet?"

I turned back fuming. The last time I had been in here I had been chased by Fallen and Hell Hounds, running frantically around cages just trying to find a way out. In the dark and with all these cells randomly placed, I had no chance of recalling where Rushton was kept. I knew he was a fair distance away from the entrance to the arena, but that could be anywhere.

I let out a big breath. Rushton's cell would have to wait. Since I also hadn't figured out how to counteract the dark energy that held him inside, there was no point in trying to locate him.

Hopefully, I could. I had to.

I wasn't ready to bargain with my soulmate again. Who knew what other tasks he was eager for me to complete and had just been waiting for the right time and opportunity. The thought was bitter and it burned its way through my chest, eating away at the seeds of hope that had unconsciously been planted there and had only just begun to sprout. I pushed the feeling further down and locked it away. The lock wasn't strong and I knew sooner or later it would crumble and break. But for now, I couldn't show him any weakness.

"So," I turned around with my hands lightly on my hips, "where to now?" I asked brightly, an artificial smile beaming across my lips, stretching them wide.

There was the slightest of creases between his black brows as he regarded my exuberance. Maybe too much. I dimmed my smile a fraction.

"Since you have been here before, you are well aware that these are the dungeons where the Fallen keep warrior angels that have not yet embraced the darkness."

Interesting way to phrase it... embraced the darkness. It was more like having the darkness beaten into you and shoved down your throat until you stopped resisting.

I frowned. "But you also kept Rushton underneath the pool room. Do Fallen take their captives there as well?"

Lucifer's lips quirked becomingly. My faint Light made his hair shine like polished jet. It was tied back neatly making him appear like an elegant lord of a castle with his fine black vest, held together with small garnet buttons.

As elegant as he looked, I could still sense the weight of power that was barely leashed, giving him an aura of unpredictable violence. "That was specifically set up for you. Gregori was invited into my domain for that purpose only. Angels rarely wander my halls and neither do Fallen."

Except for me. "So, the warrior angels are taken to the arena and then back again to their cells." I looked up at him. "Is there anywhere else they go?" I only had one shot to release the angels, so I had to make sure that they were all more or less in the same location.

Lucifer clasped his hands behind his back and walked passed me. "Well, there is Hell."

My face fell. Yes, of course, how could I forget? Back in The City, the rare angels who had been released over the aeons had mentioned their experiences in Hell and the uniquely cruel ways they had been tortured.

I followed Lucifer as he moved smoothly around the cells. The temperature here was still freezing, and I rubbed at my arms in an effort to warm them up. "Do the Fallen take them there often?" I asked, increasing my pace to keep up.

"Usually when they first capture them. Hell has a way of setting the tone for the rest of their stay. In addition, it breaks their will enough for the Fallen to finish the rest of the work in the arena."

A morbid curiosity settled over me. "If they wanted to break them, why don't they just leave them in Hell?" The memory of my terrifying experience was always just beneath the surface of my mind, eager to swallow me whole and drag me under. That paralysing fear of having my body invaded, having my will stolen from me was enough to cause my hands to shake. That and the fact that my darker self was still inside me. Still whispering inside my mind.

"If angels are left in Hell for too long it can break their minds," Lucifer responded matter of factly. My small Light revealed the broad outline of his back turning around one of the cells. "Fallen angels with broken minds are hard to control. They don't seem to grasp the concept of orders."

"Oh good, so there is a practical reason," I said sarcastically, following Lucifer around the cells. I paused when I couldn't spot him. My eyes flickered around trying to determine which way he went. Meanwhile, I tested out one of the pieces of the puzzle I had gleaned from the past. "So, how come you didn't lose your mind? You were down here as a Light angel for some time."

His voice came from my right. "Hell plays on your worst fears, and brings them to life. For me, all that was here were a great many demons."

I found him waiting for me, near an open cell. The darkness inside was like a small Hell gate in itself, urging me closer with painful whispers rasping against my ears. I shivered and looked across to Lucifer, my Light illuminating his perfect profile.

"Are the Fallen aware that I have access to the dungeon?"

"No."

I tilted my head at him. "But surely they would notice the portal mirror hanging on the wall."

"I have many portal mirrors leading to different places."

"But you don't need them," I pointed out. "You can just make yourself fall into a black hole and appear somewhere else. Or disappear in a blink."

"Yes," he said patiently, crossing his arms over his chest. "But it also works in reverse, little angel. At times, I require others to enter my domain and they can't safely enter without a portal mirror."

Walking towards him, I recalled the time I met Gregori in the room underneath the pool. "Then how did Gregori leave? He just disappeared like you did."

Lucifer bared his teeth. "For guests it's easier to leave than to gain entry."

And I was a prisoner when I first arrived. The Dragarth had been tasked with stopping me from using the portal mirrors. It just occurred to me that Lucifer could have just removed the portal mirrors to prevent me from leaving. He didn't need the Dragath. Unless... he had wanted to see what I would do. Another damn test.

My eyes narrowed at him.

Lucifer stopped near one of the walls of the dungeon, and that wall had a door. It was an inconspicuous wooden door with an arched curve to the top. Old and battered, it looked like it was in danger of falling apart. At the centre towards the right, there was an old metal knob with no lock.

"Shall we carry on?" he asked smoothly, moving away.

"What is that?" I asked.

"It's a door. I'm sure you've seen one before."

A quick, impatient sigh. See, infuriating. "Yes, but where does it lead?"

He turned his head to look at me, his dark eyes gleaming. "Why, it leads to the slave quarters."

I froze. "The slave quarters?"

"As I said." Lucifer moved out of my Light and kept walking.

I stared at the door, my heart racing. Atlas was right. The Fallen did keep slaves around to fulfil the less than desirable duties. I just had to find out who or what they were. My hand twitched, eager to wrench the door open and find out myself. As much as I wanted to hasten this process, one wrong step could cost me everything. Turning, I ran in the direction my soulmate went. He had stopped here on purpose.

And if so... why?

When I finally caught up to Lucifer, he was almost at the stairs. In front of him were two of the Fallen, and to the left of them, in chains, was a warrior angel on the brink of collapse. I hesitated briefly, then moved closer.

"We were unaware of your arrival, my Lord," said the taller Fallen, with hair as rich as mahogany wood. I could see the tension in the lines of his arms, the slight quiver of his fingers. The Fallen was fighting his fear at Lucifer's sudden appearance. I could sense nothing in the smooth tones of his voice, but his body language betrayed him. "Is there someone you are looking for?" he inquired.

"Not this time," Lucifer replied. "Carry on."

The other Fallen with narrow sharp features glanced at me as I approached. His upper lip curled slightly into a snarl. He handed the end of the chain that was linked around the warrior angel's neck to the other Fallen and pivoted on his heel to stalk back up the stairs.

"Where are you going?" came the Devil's soft voice.

The Fallen froze on the steps.

"I believe you were coming down the stairs, Eldren, not venturing back up."

"I was... I was... just going to..."

"Going to what?" Lucifer asked sharply.

The Fallen straightened, lifting his chin. "I was going to inform Nadiel and Selaphiel of your arrival, my Lord."

His voice was a snake coiling its way through the dark. "Didn't I not just infer that it was unnecessary?"

Eldren's voice became uncertain. "Yes..."

With a soft curse under his breath, the other Fallen dropped the chain on the floor with a clatter and strode up to Eldren. Without missing a beat, he pulled back his arm and slogged the shorter Fallen in the face. Eldren let out a startled sound of surprise as he flew down the steps, landing hard on the back of his armour.

With a furious growl of rage, Eldren leapt to his feet. The taller Fallen jumped from the stairs with a burst of power and backhanded Eldren across his face. He grabbed the back of his armour before he could fall and threw him over his head like a sack of grain to land on the other side. Eldren moaned, blood trailing out from his mouth. He weakly opened his eyes and shot the other Fallen a look of pure rage. His hand moved on the hilt of his sword.

"You show me the length of that steel fledgling, and I'll ram it straight down your throat," the taller Fallen snapped with menace. Eldren paused, apparently coming to realise the very dangerous situation he had found himself in. With a flicker of a look at Lucifer and a slight swallow, he moved his hand.

The punishment seemed to me to be quite excessive. Maybe that was the Fallen's way of handling the slightest insubordination amongst their ranks, but something told me this was something more.

During this time, the warrior angel who was left on the side made no movement. His hair, which was the shades of a tiger's eye stone, hung limp and dirty around his head. His hands were bound together by steel, but in them he clutched a short spear, darkened with blood. Demon blood.

With the confrontation between the two Fallen, I hadn't noticed him muttering almost silently to himself. I couldn't make out the words but it was repetitive, a short phrase said over and over again.

"Apologise now to our Lord!" the other Fallen ordered his subordinate, his dark eyes flat and hard.

Eldred scrambled to his feet and then dropped to one knee, bowed over at the waist. "I apologise, my Lord."

There was a stretch of silence that thinned painfully, then Lucifer drawled out, "Like I said, carry on."

I could see the relief that flickered across both their features, more obvious on Eldreds', who stood up shakily and followed the other Fallen with the warrior angel trailing slowly behind. They headed in my direction. Both of the Fallen glanced at me as they walked past, but their faces revealed nothing. The warrior angel continued to mutter under his breath, oblivious to his surroundings and the presence of the Lord of Hell. He was so far gone in his mind, he didn't even register my Light that hung above me.

I finally heard his whisperings.

"Just kill them all. Just kill them all. Just kill them all. Just kill them all. Just kill them..."

My heart clenched.

Unable to help myself, I reached out and touched the angel on the shoulder with the barest brush of my fingertips. Nothing. He didn't react or respond; in fact, his muttering only increased slightly in volume.

Fear and concern washed through me. How close was he to turning? How much time did he have left? There was really no way of knowing, but his lack of response to anything around him and the meek, submissive way he followed his captures without any resistance spoke volumes. They disappeared into the darkness.

I walked forward until I was next to Lucifer. "They are scared of you," I said softly.

He glanced down at me, his face all bladed edges softened slightly by shadow. "Naturally."

"Yes, but more so now since you turned Ezriel back to the Light."

"Partially back," he corrected. "There is no point in undoing all that good work."

I shot him a hard look. "They are afraid you are going to turn them back as a regular form of punishment."

He cocked his head at me. "What makes you say that?"

"Just the way they reacted," I said thoughtfully. "It was almost as if he needed to hurt the Fallen in extreme disproportion to his actions in order for you not to take any action yourself."

Lucifer smiled, a dimple appearing at the corner of his mouth. "It appears that Atlas's lessons have been proceeding well."

I gave him an arched look. "Exactly how you wanted. Want to tell me why you are helping me? My success would mean that you would lose your new recruits," I said, gesturing to the dark cages around me.

"Perhaps."

"And a great number of Fallen would be very angry at that fact."

"If you manage to outwit them, and steal their prized possessions right from under their noses in their own domain, then their anger would be warranted... and entirely their own fault."

My lips twisted. "Ah, I see, another test. But for both of us this time."

He raised an eyebrow at my tone, at the slight bitterness that laced my words giving them an acidic edge.

"Shall we continue?" I asked, gesturing up the stairs.

Lucifer inclined his head. "As you wish."

Eager to leave the dungeon, the feeling of helplessness and not being able to take an action to free the warriors trapped inside, I walked past Lucifer and up the stairs. Before I could venture any further, he grabbed my arm casually and then yanked me to him. Unbalanced, I crashed into his chest, gripping his shoulders in surprise. The golden link between us hummed sweetly.

"What is it?" he asked, his dark eyes staring at me intently.

"What... what do you mean?"

"You've been angry at me since the moment we got here."

"I'm always angry at you," I snapped back. It was unnerving the way he was looking at me, like it was bothering him. Which was laughable really. And did he really have to hold me so close? The lock on my feelings trembled, weakening.

"No, you're more than that," he mused. "You're… upset." He frowned.

"I don't want to talk about it," I hissed, pushing against him lightly to release me.

He didn't. Lucifer's midnight eyes travelled slowly over my face as if he was studying every detail, every feature. "The demon in the bathing room? No… not that. The crystals…" There was a flicker of something in his eyes too quick for me to catch. "Now why would you be upset about that?"

I shoved him away, mortified, this time I was successful. Probably because he let me go. "I said I don't want to talk about it." My heart beat erratically.

I could see his mind whirling, the gears shifting in his head, trying to find pieces that fit, dismissing the ones that didn't. He couldn't possibly understand, he didn't have the capabilities, the emotions, or the empathy.

My eyes darted around the dungeon, then I turned to face the stairs, determined to head up there myself and leave this painfully embarrassing conversation. I didn't want to admit to him how I felt. I barely wanted to admit it to myself. He couldn't possibly understand that I felt used, and that him wanting me here had more to do with keeping the barriers stable in Hell than the fact that I was his flame and some horrible past we had together that tore us apart.

I started up the stairs, growing even more angry with every passing thought. The lock crumbled and my feelings overwhelmed me, making me choke. How do you dream of something so beautiful every time you close your eyes, only to feel the emptiness when you woke? How do you explain to someone who had lost their ability to relate to the subtle, complex feelings of the heart, the combination of guilt, fear and hope you felt every time you looked at them? The inexplicable sadness of losing something you only just realised you lost?

It was exquisitely painful.

My footsteps made angry slaps against the smooth surface. How do you explain that deep down you want the most reviled being in all creation to want you in Hell, just because they want you in Hell? That statement in itself was so utterly ludicrous that if I had a mud pie I'd hit myself in the face with it.

Twice.

I was almost at the top of the stairs before he spoke.

"Foolish angel," Lucifer murmured softly. I froze at the hint of exasperation in his voice and the slightest tinge of amusement.

His shoulder brushed mine as he walked past, our link, a warm caress, sparked at the touch like firelight. He smoothly took my hand once again in his own, lacing his fingers with mine. "Shall we continue?"

I blinked at him owlishly. The corners of his mouth edged up. Without waiting for a response, he led me up the rest of the way into the arena above.

Chapter 8

The floor of the arena was covered in demon blood. There were shallow pools of it in some places, streaking outwards in random smears over the fine white sand. In the centre, lying in several pieces, was the remains of a large demon. It looked like a troll, with swollen muscular limbs, a bulbous snout, and short tusks that were cracked and yellow. It wore a cloth over its lower half that seemed to be in various shades. When I spotted fine short hairs on the surface, I realised that it was several skins roughly stitched together.

The demon was brutally decapitated. Its head lay to the side with its mouth open, and murky green tongue lolling out. It wasn't a clean cut, but a slow hacking that left the edges ragged with skin and shards of bone. Its torso sported numerous puncture wounds and deep slashes, so did the legs and arms which were also strewn about.

This one had been played with.

My mind flashed to the warrior angel led by the Fallen in the dungeon below, muttering to himself. I wanted to throw up.

Fire still ringed the edges of the pit, adding an uncomfortable layer of heat, a vast difference from the freezing temperatures below in the dungeon. Metal spikes loomed up from the flames, their sharp tips glowing red as they curved inwards. They made a vicious barrier against anyone who foolishly believed the greater danger lay inside the arena instead of in the darkness beyond.

We walked across the sand, and my footsteps made an odd crunch with every step, which I hadn't noticed before. Dread rolled sickly over me as I asked, "This is not sand, is it?"

Lucifer glanced at the ground and then back at me. A diabolic glint shifting through the dark pools of his eyes. "No, it's bone."

"Whose bones?" I whispered.

"Bones of the defeated."

I sucked in a breath, then wished I hadn't as the putrid smell of demon guts washed over me. The urge to vomit became stronger, though I couldn't remember the last time I had eaten. I was standing on angel and demon bones.

I was standing on a graveyard.

If we were injured in the higher realms or on the Earth plane, the high vibration of our energy would regenerate our bodies at incredible speeds. Here in the lower realms, a minor wound would be slow and sluggish to mend. I was taught that if our physical forms were completely destroyed, we would eventually reform in the same place we had been 'killed.' And if that place was in a lower realm, then our energy and abilities would be weaker.

It gave me another understanding why the warrior angels fought so viciously in the arena. They couldn't afford to be destroyed. If they came back weaker, it would be that much easier for them to turn. But then again there was one thing to defend yourself, and another to take pleasure in the violence.

Wasn't that just another pathway into the dark?

The sound of wings in flight distracted my thoughts. I looked up to see a Fallen woman fly smoothly down. She wore leather and wore it well. The material moulded over her long legs, defining every muscle and sleek curve. Her top crossed over her breasts, leaving an enticing amount of skin in the middle lifted and exposed. Her hair was braided high on her head, and the plait fell thickly to her waist. The dark hilt of a sword peeked out over her left shoulder.

She landed in front of us, inclining her head to Lucifer, enough to show deference, whilst still maintaining a position of power. Her eyes never once looked in my direction or at our joined hands. "My Lord, do you have need of us?"

I expected him to dismiss her like he did with the Fallen in the dungeons. "No, but I did want to have a word with you."

She blinked slowly, the only indication of surprise. "Of course, how may I be of service?"

"A demon has tried to enter my domain in the fourth level of Hell. Though unsuccessful, it still managed to get past your defences." The sharp note of displeasure was like the sound of a blade sharpening against a whetstone.

The Fallen tensed. "I will reprimand those responsible for patrolling the area."

Lucifer raised an eyebrow at her. "I think the person responsible is you, Selaphiel, unless you are about to inform me that you no longer lead the Fallen?"

"Not at all," she replied smoothly. "What I forgot to say is that I will also take punishment as you see fit for this lapse."

I could tell that there were more Fallen watching us from above, but no one else flew down.

"Find out who it was, and how it got past you. The quality of information will determine what happens to you."

Selaphiel nodded. "I will do my best," she replied coolly.

He smiled. "Then, I would suggest you do the best of someone *better*."

Her jaw twitched.

Out of the corner of my eye, I caught movement. Turning my head, I noticed a group of women dressed in ragged scraps of clothing. They walked towards the piles of demon remains, shoulders hunched and eyes lowered to the ground. Most of them were older, with noticeable grey streaks weaving through their roughly tied back hair. A few wore boots, worn and fraying apart. Those who didn't had scraps of leather tied to their feet like sandals.

They started to drag the larger demon remains with their hands to form one large heap. The gooey and liquid parts were scooped up with a small bucket to be tossed on top of the growing pile. Their fear was palpable, radiating out from their bodies and they studiously avoided looking in our direction.

These were slaves. But more alarming was the fact they were *human* slaves.

"There are humans here," I breathed out.

Selaphiel finally looked at me scathingly, before replying to Lucifer, "I will return with the information you need." Spreading her dark wings she flew swiftly up into the air. I watched her disappear into one of the many circular openings against the cave walls.

My voice gritted out, rough like the bones beneath my feet. "Are these humans kidnapped from Earth?"

Lucifer tugged me forward towards the other side of the arena. His perusal into my feelings earlier had me feeling a little shaky and confused. Just as I had him sketched as one definitive outline, he then decided to change shape.

He had done that so many times, since the moment I met him, that I was beginning to run out of paper. He had never enquired about my feelings before.

Was it a deliberate manoeuvre, a chess piece moving slyly into position that I didn't have the pieces in place to counter? I couldn't tell.

What did 'foolish angel' even mean?

That you're a fool, my darker self helpfully supplied. *I agree. You continuously do things that go against your own self interest.*

I ignored her.

Lucifer's hand was warm in my own. "No, these are humans who willingly came down into the Underworld."

I stared at him in shock. "Who would do that?"

"Witches."

My head jerked back to the women in the arena. One of the younger females risked a glance at me as she held a severed arm in her hand. The side of her face had been badly burned. Scars puckered around her lips and in ridges across her cheek. One light green eye drooped, looking as it was on the verge of falling from her face. As soon as she caught me staring, she averted her gaze and quickly continued to clean the arena floor.

"They descend into the Underworld with the hope of finding demons to trade with. These are the ones who didn't make it back."

My mind ticked with this new information.

If I found the appropriate clothing, I could possibly blend in with the witches without the Fallen noticing.

If I put my head down, I could pass for a human as long as I avoided any interaction. The only issue would be if the witches discovered my presence and gave me away. These were dark witches.

They had no love for angels.

We neared the fire on the opposite side of the pit. As we got closer it parted, the metal spikes squealing loudly in protest as it bent to allow us through. As we passed, I could see a wide tunnel leading away. It was lit with hanging orbs of fire, similar to the ones in the bathing room.

"Is there another way out of the arena?" I asked, thinking about Selaphiel and how she flew into the air above.

"There is a path across the lava pit. You would have to fly across." His eyes slanted towards me. "I'll take you on the way back."

We continued to walk down the tunnel. It was wide enough to fit several horses side-by-side. Thankfully, it was rock that scraped against my feet instead of bone. "All these witches, where do they live?"

The scarlet light shot across the side of his face, making it seem like it was painted with blood. I doubted anyone had ever bloodied his face. "They have their own quarters underground, through the door you saw in the dungeons."

"And they have never tried to escape?" I asked with surprise. All those dark witches together would make a powerful force when united.

His teeth flash, also washed with red. "Of course. They are given opportunities to escape all the time. And when they do take those opportunities, because they always do, they are hunted down and made examples of." He paused. "That's only if they manage to survive Hell. No one has made it to the Underworld."

I shuddered internally. Even though the witches of the dark caused untold suffering amongst the people on Earth, I still wouldn't wish them a life in Hell, serving the Fallen. I thought about the burns on the side of the young witches face in the arena, and wondered if that might have been her punishment for trying to escape.

All of a sudden, the tunnel stopped. It appeared, at first glance, that we had come to a dead end, but then I noticed a ramp leading down.

My eyes narrowed. "Is this another dungeon?" I asked, my blood chilling in my veins.

"Why ask questions when you know you will find the answers if you just wait?" Lucifer drawled out.

"Maybe I don't like surprises."

"Knowing everything would be a very dull existence. Surprise and curiosity is the spark which fuels our passions."

"I'm not feeling very passionate. I'm feeling nervous. The creator only knows what you have down there," I grumbled out.

We headed down the ramp. I could feel the cold air billowing up from below. Lucifer's pace was quicker than mine and I had to constantly walk faster so I wasn't dragged behind. "Seers can see everything." I pointed out. "If you give them a direction to look. They did see you turning dark."

"Ah, you are referring to the Naballa. She did see the most possible path and prepared for it. But even one as talented as she is blocked from knowing certain things. She sees the shape and colour of the tiger, but not the jungle that surrounds it. There is seeing, and there is also understanding." His voice carried a soft layer of amusement. "Are you wishing for a career change?" His thumb lightly brushed the edge of my hand. "Let me ask you this, little one. If you had known your path ahead, would you have still gone to Kryptos to negotiate for the warrior angels?"

I glanced at him, a quick look under my lashes. He was watching me carefully. I thought about what I knew before and the knowledge I had gained now. It was impossible to go back, to walk away from what was in front of me. I had the power to change something for the better on a larger scale than I could ever have imagined. How could I walk away from that?

"Yes," I said simply.

He smiled at me in a way that sent a thrill up my spine. I looked away quickly.

There was no light at the bottom of the ramp, so I called a globe of my own. The soft white light illuminated the space around us. It was smaller than I imagined it would be. The room was twice the size of my own, but much higher.

On the walls were several sets of chains, long, small, thick and thin, with clamps and collars attached. They had an odd blue sheen, which made me believe they were no ordinary pieces of metal. The floor was scuffed, sporting numerous track marks, only a slight few recognisably human.

On the far wall was a portal mirror, larger than any of those I'd seen in Lucifer's domain. Spreading out my wings would only make just over half the width. It was also twice my height. Small splatterings of black ichor covered the ground and walls. Some of them looked like old stains, others were fresh. I stared at the portal and then turned to look at the ramp behind me.

"This is how the demons get in from Hell," I said softly, letting go of his hand and walking closer to the portal.

The corner of his lip lifted. "Correct."

"Which level of Hell?"

"The fifth. We don't bring in demons lower than that."

I turned back curiously. "Why not?"

"If you ever meet a demon from the sixth and seventh levels, you will understand. Controlling one or two is manageable, but entering their level of Hell and being swarmed by a horde can be difficult."

I cocked my hip to the side and tilted my head. My tone was pointed. "Weren't you swarmed by all of them at one stage? Before you set up the barriers?"

The Devil's eyes glimmered and the darkness shifted around his form as if drawn magnetically to his presence. "Let me clarify, difficult for the Fallen to manage."

The watery surface of the portal rippled, shifting from white to light shades of grey. I couldn't imagine the size and scale of the demons that would be in the lower levels of Hell. What I had seen had been terrifying enough, something beyond that was almost incomprehensible. I shivered as the cold air finally syphoned whatever warmth I had retained from the level above. I rubbed my skin absently.

"So, this is a portal to the fifth level of Hell. When I went to the Underworld, I couldn't see the portal behind me, so I am assuming this portal works both ways and is visible on the other side?"

Lucifer walked towards me, he reached out and brushed a fingertip down my arm, before walking past towards the chains on the wall. Immediately, I felt a layer of heat envelop me, blocking out the chill like a solid barrier.

I shot him a grateful look, even though he was facing away from me.

"Correct." The chains clanked together harshly as he took a set off the wall.

A sudden thought struck me. "What stops the demons from just pouring through the portal? If it's visible on the other side, wouldn't they all be fighting to break through?"

"The portals are keyed to allow certain energy signatures through. Demons are not one of them."

"Can I enter into the fifth level of Hell?" Not that I wanted to.

"Only if you said please," he replied smoothly.

I rolled my eyes behind his back.

Lucifer turned around. "I'd have to key your energy signature into the portal itself, or you'd have to wear a ring, which would then grant you access."

A ring?

"Would you like to see one?"

I frowned, distracted. "See one, what?"

"A fifth-level demon."

I shuddered, unconsciously taking a couple of steps back. "Why would I want to do that?"

Lucifer held a set of chains taunt between his two hands. Both ends had metal clamps attached. They were long and pooled on either side to the floor. Now that they were closer I could make out several runes scratched upon its surface.

"Consider it educational," he said with a mischievous look in his eyes. That look made me catch my breath. When he was a light angel that look meant he was going to bring me back a surprise, usually in the form of delightful exotic foods.

Now, he was bringing me a demon.

Turning, he disappeared into the portal, the liquid surface swallowing him up. My eyes darted around the room and I quickly hurried backwards until I was halfway up the ramp. With will, I activated my arm bands. Golden armour shot outwards, sealing my torso in a protective layer. I tensed to move quickly.

My heart thudded as the seconds ticked by. Power surged through my body, reacting to my anxiety.

The surface of the portal rippled.

A set of broad shoulders emerged, followed by long, lean legs. Lucifer looked as calm and composed as he always did, perfectly unruffled by his foray into the lower level of Hell. He shot me a wicked look and walked forward, tugging on the end of the chain he had wrapped around his wrist.

The demon was terrifying.

It hunched through the portal to crouch before us in the tiny room. Its body was roped with muscles, and covered in a hard grey-green shell. Legs bent like a cricket ready to spring and were tipped with sharp, black claws. The arms were long and powerful, also with razor tips that curved viciously at the end. I felt a flash of relief that I had decided to move up on the ramp.

One swipe and I'd be in shreds.

Its ribs were defined around the torso, tapering in towards the pelvis, reminding me of a blend of insect and man. A skeleton-like tail whipped in the air behind it, with a sharp scorpion tip that could puncture through a body, leaving a hole the size of a dinner plate.

But it was the head that caught all the attention.

The head was shaped like a horn, curving smoothly back to form a gleaming tip. There were two indents into the shell, giving a suggestion of eyes, but I couldn't visually see them. All was irrelevant to its mouth. It was as wide as a shark, protruding forward and curving high up towards the back of its head. Metallic looking teeth pierced out of its gums in several rows with knife-like edges. Sticky clear fluid stretched between the top and bottom rows as it opened its mouth and snapped its teeth viciously.

My eyes bugged out of my head.

Terrifying.

The urge to bolt up the ramp was nearly overwhelming me. The only thing that stopped me was the fact that Lucifer was between me and the demon. The chain he had wrapped around his wrist was also encircled around the demon's neck and arms, changing its size and shape to hold the demon perfectly.

That didn't stop the tail from bending around, lightning quick, to jab straight into my soulmate's face with deadly intent.

Lucifer reached up with his other hand and casually slapped the end of the tail away. It knocked into the side of the wall with a thud crumbling some of the rocky wall.

The chain glowed blue and the demon let out a piercing, high shriek. As much as it wanted to, it seemed like it couldn't move any closer with the chains holding it firmly in place.

"None of that," the Lord of Hell murmured reproachfully. "We have a guest."

The demon let out another ear piercing shriek and snapped its jaws several times in our direction with bone crunching force. It spotted my Light orb in the corner of the room and it became even more frenzied, trying to get at it.

"What is that?" I breathed out.

Lucifer turned his back to the demon and faced me. "It's a Scythin. Incredibly fast and deadly, with high adaptability to situations and environmental changes." He looked at me consideringly. "You might be able to fight one in time."

"Don't you dare bring one of those things inside your domain!" I gave a wide eyed, panicked look at the creature in front of me. "I'm not fighting that thing." As if the demon understood me, it turned its head fractionally in my direction, its none-eyes staring right at me. More fluid dripped from its mouth, between its shiny teeth and onto the floor. It became eerily silent.

"Can you take it back?" I whispered.

"You don't want to see what it can do?"

"In the arena, fighting an angel?" I spat out. "No! Why would you think I would want to see that?" I didn't want to witness one of the warrior angels being shredded by those claws, or that horribly, vicious mouth.

"I was going to propose in combat with a Fallen."

I paused. It might be a good opportunity to observe what a Fallen could do in combat, especially if I found myself in a situation where I'd have to fight. Their abilities manifested in different ways when they fell into the dark. It would be useful to have an insight on what I would be up against.

"That might be an interesting fight," I said carefully.

Lucifer's answering smile was knowing.

"For educational purposes, of course," I clarified.

"Of course."

I let Lucifer lead the way with the Scythin in tow. He shot me an amused glance as I followed behind, out of reach of that dangerous seeking tail. It swayed back and forth, high in the air, the tip always pointing in my direction. I knew I could have stood next to Lucifer and been perfectly safe, but I couldn't be at ease having my back to that demon.

"Are the demons in the sixth and seventh levels of Hell larger?" I asked, imagining a creature as tall as a double story house with teeth as long as pillars.

"Not necessarily. Those in the lower levels are more powerful and even more intelligent." He glanced at me over his shoulder. "Some are half your size, but they can tear down a creature like this," he gave another tug on the chain and the Scythin hissed, "in a matter of seconds."

Imagining Lucifer surrounded by all those demons when he first entered Hell, and not just surviving but thriving, gave me a whole new perspective on the Lord of Hell and fueled me with a lot more questions. As much as the Scythin towered over Lucifer, looking as formidable as anything I had ever seen, there was an inherent dangerous quality to Lucifer that eclipsed the terrifying countenance of the demon.

Even though his beauty was the first weapon that struck you, the intuitive part of your brain screamed there was something else under the surface. Something that triggered the flight part of your brain. Hard.

The Scythin tail jabbed at me, missing me by half a metre. I glared at its back.

"Why don't you have a chain around its tail?" I growled out.

"It's not bothering me," came the bland reply.

It doesn't respect you, came the sinuous whisper in my mind. *Your obvious fear of it says you're prey. Says you're weak. I wouldn't have such fear.*

I said I don't need you, I returned, but my darker self's comment stung. She was right. And it bothered me.

I could see the silver spikes and feel the heat of the arena fire up ahead. How frightening it must be for the warrior angels to wait inside, not knowing what type of demon would emerge through the flame eager to kill them. Though, in the last battle I saw, it had appeared that the demon was trying to escape and it was the angel driven with a blinding killing rage. There was obviously a certain method in how they broke the angels, and I was certain which demons they selected to fight was part of that process.

The steel claws parted before us, as did the flames. Lucifer led the Scythin through and I followed behind.

A Fallen was already waiting for us in the arena.

His silver hair was startling, tied back at the nape of his neck. It contrasted nicely against his buttermilk skin. I absently wondered what colour his eyes would be when they weren't infused by darkness. His lips were set in a serious line and he bowed low in front of Lucifer. If he was startled by the sight of the demon, he didn't show it. Like Selaphiel before him, he ignored my presence.

"My Lord, you summoned me?"

Had he? I hadn't noticed Lucifer calling for the Fallen.

"I need a recommendation for a fighter. Someone who can demonstrate their skills."

The Fallen stared a beat too long at Lord of Hell. "You mean one of us," he said slowly.

"Yes, Nadial, that's exactly what I mean." The demon screeched behind him, trying again to move. The chains seemed to hold it immobile, much like when Lucifer had used his air bindings to hold me still once.

Nadial raised his eyes and stared at the creature. His jaw twitched slightly. "I believe I have a contender. We have recently promoted one of our members in our ranks to assume Ezriel's position. It would be a worthy inauguration for them."

Lucifer slowly smiled. "Excellent. Arrange it at once."

He deftly tossed the end of the chain to Nadial. At once the Scythin came alive, its head whipping towards its new captor. Sensing an opportunity, it launched at the Fallen swifter than a shark in the water.

Nadial cursed and barely dove out of the way. The sharp edge of the tail came down, a mere finger span away from his head. Nadial gripped the chain and it glowed a muted blue.

The demon instantly stopped moving forward, its head thrashing in frustration.

It had all happened in a split second.

Nadial bowed gracefully to Lucifer. "As you will."

The Devil turned towards me, the same mischievous glint in his eye. "Let's take a seat, little one. Some fights are best viewed closely, and I wouldn't want you to miss a thing."

Chapter 9

Dark eyes stared at us from every direction.

Word of a battle between a Fallen and a demon had spread like a fire storm and a sizable audience had gathered in the alcoves. Lucifer and I were standing on a platform, dead centre in front of the arena, closest to the floor. I could feel the heat from the flames below, almost singeing the fine hairs on my arms.

I twisted my hair into a loose knot at the nape of my neck. Hot, cold, then back to hot again. The temperature in Hell was a torture in itself, though no one else seemed to be bothered by it.

Two dark wooden chairs appeared behind us and Lucifer gestured for me to sit down. I sat down gingerly on the padded seat and leaned carefully against the high back. My hands gripped the edges of the chair arms.

Yes, I had been the one to bargain for a tour of the Fallen's domain, but sitting with Lucifer on a mock 'throne-like' chair in front of my darker brethren and watching them fight seemed a little too orchestrated to me. The hostility emanating in my directing was beginning to make me twitchy. I wasn't their queen, and I would never be their queen. And yet, their ruler was treating me as his equal.

And I was sitting on a god loving throne.

Lucifer reclined on his chair, confidence and power written in every line of his body, clearly created to rule. I fought not to hunch in my seat.

The Scythin, now free from its chains, prowled around the arena floor, its deadly tail flicking around continuously like a large, agitated cat. I was fairly sure that the fire enclosing the arena wouldn't cause too much damage to that hard exoskeleton if it wanted to jump through, but it was those spikes behind the inferno that would be the problem. They were too close together to squeeze past, and there was risk of being impaled.

As the Scythin stalked the circumference of the arena, letting out a series of angry screeches that displayed its impressive set of teeth, it seemed like it knew it, too.

Then, the energy in the cave shifted.

I could feel a thick current of anticipation permeating the air. Glancing up, I spotted a spread of dark wings gliding swiftly down towards the arena. The Scythin sensed the incoming Fallen and paused, turning to watch the approach with its creepy shell-covered eyes.

"Interesting," Lucifer murmured softly as he saw the Fallen about to battle the Scythin.

The Fallen contender was a gorgeous female with long dark hair, left loose and open like a satin sheath. Her face had a slight asian influence, visible in the slanted eyes and pale milk skin.

Ezriel's replacement was lean and slim like a long reed, and in her hands were two, slender blades made from dark metal. She landed gracefully on the soft arena floor and faced the Scythin with a calm, cool expression on her delicate face, swords pointing down on either side of her.

Her composure was enviable. If she felt nervous at all in front of the fifth-level demon, she didn't show it.

Nadial's voice echoed throughout the cave. "Our Lord has commanded that one of us perform in the arena." He looked up at us, but I could feel his eyes on me. "Today must be a special day," he said slowly.

I raised my brows. I doubted the Fallen ever fought in the arena. I suspected they would consider it demeaning, as this was where they had been broken. Or saved... depending on who you asked. Even still, the arena was a training ground used to humiliate, debase, and cause suffering to their lighter family.

They might have considered it an insult to be asked to fight here, like they had yet to prove themselves to the darkness or to Lucifer himself. And Nadial had just lightly suggested this unusual, degrading request was all because of me.

Great. What made it worse was that it was true. At least partly. I was pretty certain I was just one of several motivations Lucifer had for this to take place. But it wasn't like I needed another reason for the Fallen to want to destroy me.

I shot a look at Lucifer out of the corner of my eye, but the Lord of Hell remained impassive, as if Nadial hadn't said anything out of the ordinary.

Nadial continued, "As you are aware, Tianya has fought successfully for the leadership position and she will now solidify her victory by battling a Scythin. I am confident she will represent us well. Begin."

While Nadial had been speaking, Tianya and the demon were slowly circling one another. I felt momentarily surprised that the Scythin hadn't launched itself at the Fallen and attacked in a rabid frenzy. Most demons I had encountered appeared as though they couldn't control their hunger or their rage. Their emotions bypassed every rational or controlled thought. This demon was different. It watched the dark angel's every move.

It showed intelligence.

It showed how dangerous it was.

Tianya approached slowly, tucking her wings back inside her body. The Scythin leaned forward and screeched at her, teeth snapping in warning. As soon as she was in range, the demon flung out its deadly tail. My breath caught in my lungs as the tail whipped through the air, almost too fast to see.

The Fallen leaned back in a graceful arch, her dark hair flowing like a stream behind her. The bladed tip whizzed passed, just missing her porcelain face. As soon as it cleared past her, she stepped forward and spun low to the ground, blades cutting into the air.

The Scythin reacted instinctively, bunching its powerful legs and leaping up and over the dark angel, just narrowly missing her swords. It landed on the other side. They both turned and faced each other again.

Round one and no one had scored a hit.

The demon bared its impressive spread of serrated teeth at her. Her own mouth stretched wide, even white teeth flashing in a challenge.

They sped towards each other again.

The demon dipped its tail in the arena bone-sand and sprayed the fine white grains in the Fallen's face. Her hand jerked up to protect her eyes as the Scythin's jaws went for her throat. For a second, she looked vulnerable, but Tianya allowed herself to drop back into the ground away from the perilous teeth, using her momentum to skid, feet first, past the Scythin. Her other arm curved out languidly as she went by, and the edge of her blade, clipping the back of the demon's leg.

Even though the demon's exoskeleton seemed to be made of armour like shell, the edge of her dark sword slid through like it was made of soft dough. The Scythin screeched in pain and whipped around. Dark blood slowly seeped through the wound.

Tianya rolled up in one smooth movement and faced the Scythin again, tossing her hair out of face.

Point one for the Fallen.

There was a whistle of approval from up in the cave and a few clanks of steel against steel. I unfurled my fingers from the wood of the chair arms where I had been gripping with a considerable amount of tension.

The demon turned its head up to look at where the noise was coming from and snarled. I wondered if it knew it was surrounded, and death would be its only escape. It glanced back again at Tianya and then launched with speed.

This time, its tactics changed.

Claws extended, it battered at her deadly swords, trying to disarm her while its teeth finished the job. The Scythin's tail also aimed at her from behind, counting on her distraction to deliver another deadly blow. The movements were fast, precise, and delivered with incredible speed. It was almost impossible to avoid such ferocity.

Propelling herself backwards, Tianya's body twisted back effortlessly in the air, both swords cutting up and downwards to sheer the deadly claws off at the tips. Her body just curved over the point of the tail as it jabbed forward, and her booted feet kicked up, snapping the head of the demon back before it could bite down.

The demon stumbled backwards as she landed on her feet. She smiled mockingly, and did the strangest thing... she turned her back on it and walked away.

I leaned forward, confused. What was she doing?

The Scythin raised its clipped nails and roared. I resisted the urge to cover my ears as the sound reverberated through the cave.

She kept walking nonchalantly away as if the beast didn't bother her, pausing only to fling her swords point first on the ground, the dark hilts quivering slightly from the force of her throw. The Scythin raked the bone-sand with its feet as if sensing a trap but appearing unable to determine where it was.

Its enemy had thrown its weapons away.

Now would be the perfect opportunity to attack.

With the Fallen's back still turned, the demon bounded forward, favouring its right leg. It ate up the distance towards the dark angel with massive strides that launched it partially in the air. It gave a great final leap, mouth terrifyingly wide open and tail flicking behind like a whip.

Metres before it could reach her, the bone sand stirred.

The fine particles shot up into the air, melding together to form a gleaming white spike. It jammed through the underside of the demon's mouth, piercing through to jut out the top of its skull.

My mouth dropped open.

The Scythin trembled in the air, violently twitching for a couple of seconds before it stilled. Tianya finally turned, a small smile playing across her lips. The sand dissolved and the demon slammed into the ground, unmoving. The sound of steel against steel in a unified rhythm became louder and louder in the cave. My fear increased as I glanced down at the dark angel who faced Lucifer and gave a short, perfunctory bow.

She could have ended that fifth-level demon in the first five seconds.

But she didn't.

It was clear that she had wanted to demonstrate her incredible skill, before she displayed her power. The Scythin had never had a chance. The lesson was delivered. The Fallen were an incredible force to be reckoned with. They seemed faster and stronger than they had been as warrior angels of the light. Once upon a time, Tianya had been an Earth angel.

Here in the dark, her powers had grown.

Lucifer inclined his head slightly back at her in acknowledgment.

Yours could grow, too. You have no idea how much power you could have, my darker self whispered. *These Fallen would be nothing compared to you.*

I took a deep breath and mentally pushed the voice out of my head. I spotted Nadial flying into the arena. He landed on the other side of the demon and waved for the noise to stop. Instantly, the banging ceased.

"Are you satisfied, my Lord?" he called out.

"The demonstration was sufficient," Lucifer replied casually, his voice carrying around the cave. He addressed Tiyana directly. "You have shown your skills in a battle, but being a leader means that you take responsibility for everyone beneath you. If they fail, you fail. And then, you will answer to me. Time will tell how well you do."

He stood up from his chair, putting his back to Nadial and faced me. Holding out a hand, he said, "Shall we?"

I was aware that all eyes had swivelled once again in our direction. I tentatively placed my hand in his and allowed him to pull me up. "Where are we going?"

"I'm going to show you the other exit."

"Oh, okay," I said, nervously running my palm down the fabric of my clothes and trying not to glance above me. The thought of flying through the cave full of Fallen was intimidating to say the least.

"Would you like me to carry you?" A teasing glint in his eye.

"No," I said, mortified. Pride had me squaring my shoulders back and looking at him with confidence I didn't feel. "Lead on," I said, gesturing ahead with a couple of swishes of my hand.

His lips quirked at the corners and then he turned back to face the arena. Obsidian black wings swept out gloriously behind him, blocking my view. Even though they were the mark of a Fallen, they drank in the light, absorbed it into each feather until it glistened like polished jewels.

Stunning. But just in a different way.

Maybe I was becoming accustomed to my soulmate's new appearance. His midnight eyes, which had disturbed me before, had become familiar and almost comforting. It wasn't as if I didn't miss his former countenance, because I did. Fiercely. It was connected to a time and an angel that I had loved and lost. But I also seemed to have found some beauty in what he had become.

Because the darkness was meant to be beautiful and seductive.

Why else would you fall?

Power, that voice purred. *You forgot power.*

That, too.

Lucifer turned his head to look at me. "Make sure you follow close behind." He took off into the air, soaring up and away.

I quickly spread out my own wings, the gleaming white colour a taunt to everyone around me. I might as well have turned around and stuck my tongue out. I flew up, my back prickling and muscles tensing, almost like I could expect a spear to be hurled in my direction at any second. I was only grateful I still had my armour on.

I followed Lucifer as closely as I could. A glance down showed Nadial talking quietly with Tiyana who had just retrieved her swords. That was the frightening thing. The Fallen wouldn't even have to touch me to kill me. The only thing that prevented them from tearing me apart was Lucifer. And with the tension rife in the air between master and his warriors, I wondered how long that loyalty would last.

Lucifer landed on one of the many alcoves in the cave. You wouldn't notice anything different about it from the rest, but once I landed beside him, I could see that instead of a hollow groove carved out, it was a tunnel leading into the dark. Hanging orbs of light flickered on as we passed as if sensing our movement.

"The Fallen don't seem very happy with you," I said.

"Don't they?"

"You know they don't. And I'm not helping the situation."

"I told you what would happen if you went into their domain." He glanced down at me. "It didn't bother you before."

"I'm not saying it is bothering me." It was really bothering me. "But shouldn't it be bothering you?"

He smiled. "Do I look bothered?"

"No." But that could also be because you're not quite right in the head. "If they all try to gang up and kill you, it's not my fault."

He shot me an amused look. "I'll be sure to remember that."

There was an opening to our left, and I followed him down another ramp. At the bottom, it widened out into another massive room carved out of rough rock. It appeared almost empty except for a raised dais at the back.

"What is this place?" I asked.

"It's where we hold meetings." Lucifer didn't walk further into the room, so I assumed there was nothing else interesting to see. I could picture them gathered here, their numbers swelling slowly to fill out the space. Two growing to ten, ten to one hundred. An army of dark warriors, all bent on destroying the light. What plans they would have conjured in this room, hunting our kind.

Movement behind us had me veering to the side. Fallen filed into the room from the arena. They glanced at us as they walked past, all bowing their heads to Lucifer and ignoring me like I was a piece of fungus on the wall.

They moved steadily across the chamber floor towards the outer edges and it was then I realised there were more portals lining the walls. One by one they disappeared into different mirrors as if they had been preassigned.

Perhaps they had.

Five portal mirrors. "The first five levels of Hell?"

Lucifer nodded without looking at me, his dark eyes on the Fallen. When the flow of Fallen stopped, he turned around and walked back up the ramp. I followed, hurrying to catch up to him. We didn't have to walk long before the tunnel abruptly stopped. It was cut off by a sheer cliff that dropped kilometres below into a raging pool of lava.

The heat blasted violently upwards, sending a burning, searing pain across my skin. The lava spread out before me in a thrashing, spluttering blanket of waves, as far as my eyes could see. It seemed alive to me, sizzling with hatred, boiling with malice and eager to devour anything that got too close. The negativity was almost overwhelming. It felt like the lava knew I was there standing above, and it hated that I was out of its reach.

This was the Hell that humans talked about in their stories. This was the burning fire pit of destruction that could torture souls for eternity. Where had that recollation been born in human minds and in their stories? Perhaps some had been trapped here in Hell, the playthings of demons and the Fallen, and when they finally escaped and reincarnated, the memories still lingered deep in their subconscious. A trauma that had lasted through lifetimes.

Further out, close to the horizon, I could make out a tall, dark fortress looming up through the lava. The tiny figures of the Fallen flew around the structure, before disappearing within.

"Over there is where the Fallen live. There is no accessible way into their eyrie except over the lava, going through a portal, or if you have the ability to teleport."

I shivered, despite the overwhelming heat. "The lava, it feels alive."

"That's because it is," Lucifer replied frankly. "It's a demon."

My mouth dropped open. "That's a demon?"

He turned to face me, enjoying the mingled look of horror and surprise on my face. He spread his wings wide. "Demons come in all shapes and sizes; you should know that by now." He looked down at the lava and then back up again. "I wouldn't fly too close."

Lucifer stepped off the ledge and flew backwards a couple of metres, before twisting in the air and speeding away with a couple of beats from his powerful wings. Hesitating for a second, I leapt off the ground and followed him.

The flight over the lava was a harrowing experience. I kept imagining large fists of fire reaching out to snatch me from the air, or a wide blazing mouth to open and swallow me whole. Those sorts of thoughts made flying difficult. The heat helped me maintain a reasonable height, and even though it was a distance to the fortress, the journey was quite easy.

As we flew closer to the Fallen's home I could tell that the dark stones that it was made from were inlaid with threads of gold, much like my walls in Lucifer's domain. Little arch openings were visible from all around the upper half of the tower. Lucifer disappeared in one of the arches closest to the bottom. I landed a few seconds behind him and went inside.

Opulent would have hardly described it.

I was immediately bombarded with a range of textures and rich, dark colours. A wide, plush carpet of crimson, gold, and black spread out along a dark opal floor, which shimmered with an array of colours. On the walls were large Greek and Christian inspired paintings of battles and wars, of Fallen angels fighting demons and angels of God. The paintings were exquisitely done in great detail and were set in ornate gold frames.

Chairs and lounges of dark wood and plush red velvet were scattered about in front of tables of wine in crystal chalices and fruit piled high in crystal bowls. Pillows of all different jewelled colours were scattered over the furniture, contrasting against black fur throws draped over the arms. Burnt amber orbs were set in concentric rings just below the ceiling, casting it in a rich golden hue.

There were two arches to my left leading to other rooms and a spiralling staircase to my right, leading to the floor above.

Lucifer's domain had an understated elegance to it, a reflection of the dark angel himself. This was over the top. It was as if every square inch was a blatant showcase of wealth and status. Even the drapes that framed the arches were made from a rich copper brocade that fell thickly to the floor.

It was a statement that said, 'I have all this just because I can.' Or more likely, 'I have taken all this, just because I can.' I had no doubt this was all stolen from the world above. I wondered about the paintings though, who had created them?

Soft footsteps came from my left. Through the arches came three nubile young women. They walked into the room with a rolling sensuality that takes years of practice. Their bodies were lean and toned and scantily clad in sheer silks of emerald green, scarlet, and white. The tips of their firm breasts pressed against the fabric and the exposed length of soft flesh from their thighs was enough to bring heat to my face as it flashed through the silks. The scraps of clothing only served to emphasise what was underneath, and in the dim lighting you could see the outline of every curve, dip and hollow.

These were human women. Young, lovely, and clearly captive.

Dainty gold collars encircled their slim necks with runes inscribed on the metal. It reminded me of the chains that were used on the Scythin, but much prettier. A bruise marred one of the women's faces, a short brunette with flashing hazel eyes. The pretty, dark-skinned woman next to her had a busted lip.

They looked shocked when they saw me, but as soon as they registered Lucifer's presence, they knelt prostrate on the ground, exposing more of their chests. The woman with the short blonde hair and sweet face started to tremble.

"My Lord Lucifer," the brunette said softly, in a voice that conveyed respect and obedience. "How may we serve your pleasure?"

A voice from the stairs spoke in a rich timbre before Lucifer could give a reply. "My Lord, are these slaves bothering you?"

A Fallen, shirtless and wet, as if he had just stepped out of a bath, made his way down to our level. His skin gleamed with droplets of water that trailed down his smooth skin and his smile held a sharp, abrasive charm. His dark hair was shaved away from a strikingly handsome face.

It was the beauty not of high princes and aristocratic nobles, but the bold alluring features of warlords and conquerors. But after being around Lucifer, I could only catalogue his attractiveness in a vague, distant way.

"To be bothered, I'd have to care," the Lord of Hell replied.

My body coiled with tension. "Who are these women?" I asked softly.

The Fallen's smile widened at my question, and he looked at me with a glimmer of interest I found uncomfortable. He strode over to the women on the floor and raised the dark-skinned beauty by cupping a hand under her chin and lifting her up.

"These lovely creatures," he murmured, studying her features and rubbing a thumb over her swollen lip. She flinched. "Are witches." He turned to look at me, his hand stroking the collar around her neck. "We keep the pretty ones here to pleasure us and serve all our... needs. And you love it, don't you, pet?"

The witch nodded enthusiastically, though her eyes flickered to mine with a different message. My jaw clenched. It didn't matter one whit that she was a dark witch. I could feel the disgust curl through my belly and rage unfurling in a slow, hot simmer. My brain conjured up images of what the Fallen might be doing to these women. It made me want to throw up.

"Fascinating," Lucifer drawlled. "These are the slave quarters and where they entertain their masters. The next level is the Fallen quarters." He turned dismissively and carried on upstairs.

I shot a cool look at the male Fallen who watched me with a smirk playing on his lips. As I walked towards the steps, his eyes travelled down my body as if he was picturing what I looked like without my clothes. Perhaps even with a chain around my neck. This was a Fallen that was used to getting what he wanted from women, willing or unwilling. He enjoyed their fear, their shame and their suffering. He didn't just enjoy his women being broken, he enjoyed the process of breaking them. Slowly.

And I could tell he wanted to do that with me.

The power I was holding back rolled through me and I let my hand crackle with white flames. It burned harshly around my fingers, a promise of pain to the darkness embedded within him.

Come and get me, I said with my eyes.

I gave him a smile of my own and I caught a flicker of surprise at my response.

I followed Lucifer up the stairs.

Chapter 10

I was already angry by the time I reached the next level of the Fallen's domain, but once I caught sight of all the walls on the next level, that anger hardened like welded steel.

The Fallen quarters had a small landing area with multiple corridors leading outwards. The floor was the same dark opal as the level below, but instead of paintings on the walls there were swords. Light swords, hanging in rows like trophies. The silvery light they once held, was now dull and empty.

My mind whirled and the implications hit me like sharp, little darts to the chest. But I wanted him to say it.

I met Lucifer's midnight eyes as I came to a stop before him. "How do the Fallen get their dark blades?"

He looked at the walls, his gaze travelling over the numerous weapons. "Our blades are transformed when we embrace the dark."

That glorious Light sword of his, which shone like a blazing star through the darkest night, was now something twisted and deformed. What a beacon it would have been for hope on the Earth plane, giving courage and strength to those fighting Hell's creatures. Now, there was no champion of light in the upper realms.

Even though Lucifer argued that the demons weren't walking the Earth like they were before, he had instead created and unleashed the Fallen... who, in my opinion, were infinitely worse.

"So all these blades here..."

"They are from the angels who have yet to be transformed," he finished.

I had suspected that from the moment I walked in, but I still sucked in a breath as I looked at the multiple rows of weapons. I couldn't get a gauge before of how many angels were trapped in the dungeons below. I had believed that some of the cells had been empty. But now... this... there must be almost a hundred. A hundred yet to give into the dark, still fighting with every breath they had to hold on.

A hundred.

I felt the overwhelming enormity of the task before me, like climbing a mountain and realising the path before you was endless and the destination way beyond your sight.

How in Heaven was I supposed to save them all?

My anger turned like a large ship, veering back on course. It turned towards my soulmate. This had been *all* him. That he had chosen for himself to Fall was one thing, but to force the other angels of light to do the same by means of torture was the epidemy of evil.

In a way, every Fallen I saw was a victim. A victim of Lucifer. The look of terror on Ezriel's face when he had partially turned back was barely enough to understand the trauma he had undergone for far too long. Those seconds of realisation of what he had done to his fellow angels must have been beyond horrifying.

How long would one take to heal from that? And would he ever be given the chance? Right now, he was in the nightmarish process of turning again.

Lucifer was responsible for all that. And yet... he had also given me the opportunity to save them. The question was, why? It bothered me like a splinter travelling under my skin, journeying to my heart. It was a question that Lucifer had declined to answer.

I had this overwhelming, crippling fear that if I managed to free the angels from their cages, I would find Lucifer blocking the way out, laughing mockingly at the fact that I had believed him... the Father of Lies. For wasn't that one of his names?

Part of me felt something very much akin to hate when I thought about all he had done. The other part of me... well, the other part of me was stupid.

My feelings for Lucifer continuously jumped from one extreme to the next.

It was exhausting.

As if sensing the fire of my gaze upon him, Lucifer turned to look at me. He raised an eyebrow at my expression as if he could read the thoughts flickering across my face.

"Is there a problem?" he asked coolly.

My nostrils flared slightly. "Where do I begin?" I responded in the same tone.

He tilted his head. "You do realise you are in Hell and if you didn't have a problem I'd have to redesign."

I glared at him. "This isn't funny."

"Do you see me laughing?"

"You're laughing on the inside."

His lips curved at that and he casually said, "Perhaps if our link was stronger you'd find out."

My eyes widened into round orbs of shock.

He... he could feel our link. He *knew*.

Lucifer hadn't said *anything* regarding its reappearance before. I had assumed that he had yet to feel it, as his sense of that fragile cord might have been diluted by the darkness that rode inside of him. How long had he known? Surely he couldn't be *happy* with its existence.

Because he would know that would mean... that he had... that I had caused...

He left me spluttering and continued to walk up the stairs. "This level and the next four above are the Fallen's rooms. They are organised according to rank. The lowest being at the bottom and the highest at the top."

"I... you..."

Lucifer looked down at me, midway up the stairs, his voice just a touch impatient. "I do have other things to do, so I would appreciate it if we didn't waste any more time dawdling."

He disappeared up the second flight of stairs. After a couple of moments, when I finally pulled myself together, I followed, heart racing. Just another thing to shelve and dissect later. If I started to think about it now, I'd drive myself crazy trying to understand Lucifer's rationale for what he did, when he did it and why.

And what the retaliation would be.

The next four levels were more or less the same, but with an increasing amount of space as the occupants per level decreased. A couple of Fallen emerged from their rooms, but after giving a respectful greeting to Lucifer, they quickly disappeared. I was again ignored.

The highest ranking Fallen quarters had its own private pool, training area and meeting space. The decor was even more elaborate, if that was even possible.

But it was the next level that interested me the most.

We couldn't reach it by the stairs. Instead, we flew outside the eyrie and re-entered through a single opening. It was clear this level was meant to be separated from the rest, with limited access from the non-wing occupants. It was dark. The lighting was dim and eerie, with only a few flickering candles on the ground and in little recesses along the walls. There were thick, rectangular solid slabs of marble spaced out evenly on the floor, about waist high.

On these slabs were Fallen. And they all looked dead.

Some were visibly injured with large and small wounds on their faces. A few were horribly burned and deformed, their features unrecognisable. There were lumps of flesh on one marble table, which I didn't want to look too closely at. Another just had a leg.

Other tables had perfect corpses, features soft and relaxed, their hands arranged neatly clasped on their chest. They all wore long, black robes with their feet bare. It was strange to see them without their armour, as besides the colour of their clothes there were no other visible markers that differentiated them from the lighter angels. I felt like I was in a tomb, where people buried their dead, but it also strangely reminded me of the healing chambers in The City of Light. Except without all the crystals, high vibrations, and peaceful atmosphere.

I opened my mouth.

"Before you ask," Lucifer said, leaning his large frame against the wall. The candle light unfairly accentuated the perfect symmetry of his face and the sensual curve of his mouth. "This is where the Fallen are kept until their soul energy and physical bodies reform."

I nodded my head slowly, fascinated. I started to walk around the room, looking at the dark warriors spread out before me.

"Wouldn't it take longer without healing crystals?"

"You would think so, but the darkness increases our natural ability to heal."

"Where do the light angels reform?" I asked.

"Back in their cells."

I looked at him sharply. Back in their cells, surrounded by negative energy. I could only imagine how painful that process would be and how weak they would feel after they reformed.

A body a couple rows down caught my eye. Moving closer, I recognised Gregori, the Fallen angel I had met in the room underneath the pool. He had been the reason Rushton had been captured for the second time. His face was pale like the bark of a Birch tree, and the cruel smirk that had twisted his lips was gone, leaving his face in peaceful repose. Besides an ugly bruise that had flowered up on the left side of his face, there weren't any other visible injuries.

"What happened to him?" I asked.

"I believe he tried to fight for Tianya's position... and failed."

Something glinted off his finger. It looked like a ruby ring, but the stone was much brighter like fresh blood trapped under glass. It was a rectangular stone cut into several facets and held together with a twist of dark metal. My eyes travelled over to the Fallen, lying on the slab next to him. She, too, had an identical ring on her right hand.

My mind joined more dots together and I felt a flicker of excitement.

"Have you ever reformed here in Hell?" I asked, still looking at the ring. I moved around to another slab where a Fallen lay peacefully on top. On his hand, another ring.

"Someone or something would have to kill me, little one. And no creature has had the pleasure of doing that yet."

I glanced towards the dark corner he was leaning against. "Yet?"

"Like I told you before, every warrior accepts that they could fall. Not likely in my case, but possible."

"So, you are not as infallible as everyone believes you to be."

Lucifer blinked at me slowly like a satisfied lion after its meal, watching the baby deer play in the grass. I felt a twitch of nerves.

"Only the Gods are arrogant enough to believe they can't be defeated."

Archangel Michael had been the only being that had come close. I couldn't imagine a creature stronger, more powerful than Lucifer. Especially if they were dark.

I shuddered at the thought. The spirits help us all.

We left the tomb of the Fallen and flew up to the level above, just under the top of the eerie. This level had one wide entrance that could fit twenty angels side by side. The room was large and barren except for seven glimmering portal mirrors hanging from the air several metres apart. I imagined the Fallen filing though, an army of darkness intent on destruction.

I frowned, spinning around to face him. "I thought you said the Fallen were not allowed access to the sixth and seventh levels of hell."

His midnight wings were still out, and the heavy weight dragged the tips of the feathers across the ground. "They aren't. There are five to the first five levels of Hell, one to the Underworld, and the other…"

I breathed out, staring at him. "Earth…"

He nodded.

I turned back, facing the mirrors, my eyes flickering rapidly from one to the other. "Which one?" I asked softly, urgently. If I was correct, this could change everything. Hope burned like a tiny, fierce flame inside me, giving me that extra bit of strength to face the mammoth task I had placed around my own shoulders.

"The last one on the right."

I walked towards the portal mirror at the end, until I stood in front of its glimmering surface. The only difference I could make out between the portal to Earth and the others was a slight variance in the runes carved into the frame. I didn't know what the runes meant, but I guessed the particular order in which they were placed must act like a map to the intended destination.

"Plotting, little one?" His voice was amused.

I turned back to face Lucifer, a picture of innocence. Or at least I hoped I was. "That's why I'm here, isn't it?"

He prowled towards me, all innate grace and rippling power. I fought not to take a step back. "You know," he said smoothly as he neared, "the Fallen are not adversaries to be taken lightly. They will attempt to destroy anyone and anything that gets in their way. And so they should. I have trained them to be very effective killing machines."

He gripped my chin lightly, tilting my face up to his. "Though, if I had to place bets on who would ultimately win," he murmured softly, the golden hum of our link thrumming through us both, "I think I'd place them on you."

My heart fluttered in my chest. "Flatterer," I accused lightly. "I know the odds are very much *not* in my favour."

"And that, little angel, is when we fight the most." The corner of his mouth lifted. "When we have something worth fighting for."

By the spirits. It was so easy to hate him, but then he went and said something like that.

He let go of my chin and took my hand in his. I felt his energy stir, just a sliver of power, and we blinked away from the portals and appeared once more right on top of the eerie. Not for the first time I felt how vast this realm was.

Lava spilled out in every direction, a single demon so large and powerful, an embodiment of rage that extended further than the eye could see. I knew I should be feeling the searing heat upon my skin, but the temperature was akin to a tropical climate, balmy and humid. I cast a quick glance at Lucifer. That sliver of power still ran lightly along my skin.

We had appeared near the centre of the platform, and I noticed four, elaborately carved chairs in a row, facing opposite me.

Lucifer spoke again before I could ask. "The Fallen gather here privately to conduct meetings."

I noticed patches of the black stone in front of the chairs looked stained. "Do they fight here like they do in the arena?"

"Sometimes for practice, other times to determine hierarchy."

"Has any Fallen challenged you?"

He smiled and tilted his head, as if remembering a fond but distant memory. "A few."

I raised an eyebrow. "What happened to them?"

"I sent them to the seventh level of Hell. If they survived the week, I would face them in single combat for the position in the hierarchy."

It would take a lot of confidence for a Fallen to believe they could take on Lucifer. "Did you end up fighting them?" I asked.

"No. No one lasted the week."

I opened my mouth, then closed it. I was about to ask if the Fallen were still down there, but then realised Lucifer preferred to set an example, and what better way then letting the rest of the Fallen see the slow regeneration of the remains of the one who challenged him.

"When was the last time that happened?"

The glow from the lava covered his wings in flames. "A few hundred years ago."

"Maybe you've made your point."

"Unfortunately, people always forget."

We blinked away again and I found myself once more in the dungeons, in front of the portal to Lucifer's room. The temperature dropped dramatically and the overwhelming feeling of hopelessness made my mood plummet. Nothing killed a vibe faster than being in the same place your family was trapped and tortured in cells.

"And this concludes the end of your tour," Lucifer said dryly, folding his wings back into his body.

As soon as he spoke, I heard the soft rush of footsteps. In the distance, a door creaked open and then slammed shut. Slaves. They must have heard us and scattered out of sight. They were the elderly, the scarred and broken. The slaves in the eerie flashed through my mind, chained and practically naked. The pretty ones used for the pleasure of the Fallen… whatever that pleasure may be. My stomach churned sickly.

I let go of Lucifer's hand, and my eyes lifted up to his dark ones. "Have you used them? Hurt them? The witches? The pleasure slaves?"

If he was surprised by the vehemence in my tone, he didn't show it. He absorbed the heat of my anger like the stones surrounding us and reflected a barren, coolness back at me. "Hurt them? Of course," he said dismissively. "Used, in the matter in which you are implying…" Lucifer looked at me archly. "Would it matter if I did?"

I felt my chest tighten. I let the disgust drip from my voice. "That you would force yourself on women? Absolutely." Any act of torture was abhorent but somehow the thought of my soulmate violating these woman brought back my memory of when I was Nadia, watching as the two young men of the village knocked on my door late at night. It seemed more personal, somehow.

Lucifer laughed, and the sound was surprisingly free. His eyes shone with dark amusement. "I've never forced or coerced a female to lie with me." His voice became a touch smokey, though the humour remained. "All my lovers have been very, *very* willing."

I blinked.

I looked at the startling perfection of his form and face. His sheer beauty stuttered the brain, and the rich sensuality that poured off him was a potent drug to even the staunchest of women, rigidly determined to cling onto their virtue.

Even on Earth, the lust filled gazes followed him wherever he went like a hovering cloud. And he wasn't even trying. I couldn't imagine his effect on others when he actually was trying… when he actually wanted to…

And he was a Fallen now. I was sure those physical desires were even more heightened in his dark state and he had sated himself often. The thought was uncomfortable. It felt like jealousy.

Angels weren't naturally possessive, even with their soulmates. We understood that love wasn't about control or limitations, but about expression and freedom. Angels had a few soulmates, which extended from our human incarnations. In one life we might be with one, in another a different person. It was all dependent on what lesson we had to learn by being with that being.

Flames might be with each other for several incarnations, and then choose to test themselves in other relationships. When you realise life is about growth and evolution, jealousy was a foreign concept.

In saying that, some Flames had chosen to be with each other monogamously in the spirit realm, and if through the aeons that decision changed for a short period of time, they always ended back together.

My circumstances were a little bit different. Lucifer had never had a human incarnation. He was created as an angel. We had never had lifetimes together bar one, as brief as it was. I never got to fully experience the feeling of fulfilment of being with your other half for lifetime after lifetime, feeling the joy and pain and contentment of finding a home in another soul. The depressing thought was that now he had turned, we would never experience that again.

That uncomfortable feeling of jealousy was not directed towards Lucifer and his very willing past lovers, but towards Nadia who had experienced something, which I in my current incarnation, never would.

As depressing as it was, I was jealous of myself.

It left a bitter taste in my mouth.

I realised I had been staring at his face for quite some time as my brain spun around with all the thoughts in my head. Flushing, the words poured out in a verbal jumble as I tried to cover my awkwardness. "Well good, then. Good. I'm glad. That with the slaves you haven't had to… that they were…" I gestured erratically with my hand. "Because that's the main thing. Willingness. Good to be willing."

Shut up, shut up, shut up, shut up...

I almost felt my darker self roll her eyes.

I flushed brightly again, certain my cheeks were scorched crimson. "Shall we go?" I breathed out, my voice high.

The amusement had mortifyingly deepened. He gestured courteously with his hand towards the portal. I all but bolted through.

I merged through to his room, and then turned around to face him as he stepped through. Opening my mouth I rushed a goodbye. "So, thank you for–"

"The pleasure slaves in the Fallen domain," Lucifer said smoothly, cutting me off. His hands slipped casually into his pockets. "I didn't touch them."

"Oh. Really? Not that it... I mean–"

Lucifer entered my personal space like he was entitled to it. His hand shot out to grip my throat lightly. My eyes widened. I could feel his breath fanning against my skin and that golden hum prickling just underneath.

Lucifer drew me closer to him by the throat. Both my hands came up to grip his wrists. "I was with many people after I fell. I went from one to the next and the next and so on. I wanted to lose myself in the flesh, in the pleasure. And I did." His eyes were fathomless dark pools. His voice had turned silky and dangerous, and I felt an answering thrill shooting up my spine. "Do you know why?"

"Why?" I whispered carefully.

He brushed his lips along the soft curve of my cheek and whispered delicately in my ear. "How else was I supposed to get the taste of you out of my system?"

I drew in a sharp, hard breath and pulled back to look at him. His lashes lowered, and the heat of his gaze made my pulse tremble. "And now that I remember once again…" Leaning down, he brushed his lips sensually over mine. Tiny sparks erupted under his touch, fizzling sweetly through my blood. My hands tightened over his wrists.

I just want more, he said in my mind.

He kissed me, and my control slipped.

Desire that had been building over days washed over me in a tidal wave, drowning my thoughts until they became white noise in the dim recesses of my mind. My lips parted under his, and I was lost. This wasn't seduction. This was raw, primal *feeling*. He kissed me with anger, with a touch of pain, but mainly, overwhelmingly, he kissed me with a violent hunger.

I responded in kind, surrendering to the powerful emotions all but detonating between us. My hands slipped up his wrists to the back of his neck, pulling us closer until my chest pressed tightly against his. The muscles in my body clenched hard, then shuddered apart.

He tasted like apples. He tasted like cinnamon and spice. He tasted like everything I wanted but had forgotten. I felt him let go of my neck and grip my hips hard. He kneaded the flesh there, until sliding up my skin under the back of my top. His hands curved around the sides of my chest, thumbs just brushing the curves of my breasts on either side. The feel of his hands on my bare skin took me to another, insatiable level of pleasure.

I, too, wanted more.

I made a low, breathy moan against his mouth.

My feet left the floor. Lucifer swung me around and my back hit the bed. His body covered mine in a feast of smooth muscles and feline strength. He blocked out my world until all I could feel and see was him. Mouth never leaving mine, he tore my top to shreds.

Our link felt stronger.

Liquid gold filled my mind, binding his darkness to my light. My back arched as his hands ran up my chest in a languid caress. He pulled my hands high up above my head and trapped them there. His lips finally left mine, travelling with burning heat down the side of my neck.

I could feel the barest brush of his emotions. Desire. Need. Control. Even now he was holding himself back.

I could feel what he wanted.

He wanted to devour me, until I was mindless beneath him, burning with pleasure until I could barely breathe. Until I wanted nothing more than to stay in his bed, in a tangle of limbs, moaning his name. He wanted me like that for days, weeks, months, until the desire clawing inside him finally sated.

He also wanted to kill me.

Fear shot through me, banking the desire like a shower of ice. The bands on my arms responded, and metal slid over my skin, covering my chest in a protective layer.

My eyes flew open, heart pounding, and I stared at my Flame who was hovering slightly over me with midnight eyes as dark as I had ever seen it. He removed his hand from my wrist and slid a finger tip slowly down the centre of my chest plate. Somehow, I knew he could break it with ease.

His voice was husky and low. "Do you fear me, little angel, or yourself?"

I struggled to tear my eyes away from that poet's mouth, wanting more than anything to feel it again, against my lips. Scared that if I did, I wouldn't be aware of what could happen next. He was a weapon of desire and erotic dreams. A lust induced fantasy made real. He was also a weapon that could kill me. That wanted to kill me. Part of me didn't care.

And that's what scared me the most.

"Both," I whispered back.

He growled low in his throat, like a predator forced to let go of his meal. He was angry.

He bent his head to the side of neck and breathed me in. He shuddered and I felt his control slip a fraction more.

Then, he disappeared, leaving me alone on the bed.

Without knowing why, tears filled my eyes and spilled down my cheeks. I stayed on his bed, under the mandala, silently crying until I had no more tears left inside me.

Then, I quietly left.

Chapter 11

Socrates placed a finger on a white Ludus stone and pushed it slowly forward one square. He leaned back in his seat and stroked his semi-transparent beard with his right hand, then glanced up at the Lord of the Underworld, who was hunched forward, scowling at the board.

"You've been playing in my absence," Hades growled, glaring at his old friend. "Frequently."

The philosopher raised his white brows. "What makes you say that?"

"You appear to move your pieces like a general in Ares' army, reckless and bold, yet your deviousness is revealed as I find myself in several traps I am unable to manoeuvre out of. Tyche must be favouring you." He glanced darkly at his captured black stones on the side of the board. "Or maybe it's Hermes, whispering in your ear."

"It is more likely that Tyche is disfavouring you, rather than favouring me," Socrates pointed out. Before Hades could glare at him again, he continued, "You know better than I that Ludus is primarily about reading the opponent rather than reading the board."

"Are you saying I've become predictable?" There was a warning note in the God's voice.

Socrates ignored it. "Everyone is predictable to a certain degree. You predict that at some point during our conversations I will engage you in an ethical or theological debate you will deem pointless and annoying, and I've predicted your usual delightful mood souring and your concentration vanishing as soon as Persephone leaves." He let a smile flicker across his lips to ease the sting the Goddess's name brought and then looked down at the board, which was covered with mostly white stones. "Thus, providing me with many advantageous opportunities during this game."

Hades involuntarily glanced to his left at the beautiful blue saffron flower that bloomed on the stone pedestal. Persephone had left that there in her absence. She had said to him that when the flower died in six months, she would return. He drummed his fingers against the top of the table. He was tempted to walk over and crush it to dust in his fist. But that would not bring her back any sooner.

He hated flowers.

"I should have given her twelve pomegranate seeds," he muttered under his breath.

"Curbing your Flame's freedom is not what I would call a grand demonstration of love," Socrates said dryly.

"It's her mother that's the controlling one."

The philosopher let out a huff of laughter. "I don't believe it was her mother who manipulated her into eating sacred fruit, which forced Persephone to live with her." He watched as Hades stood up, evidently done with the game, and paced in front of the wide opening of the tower they were in, overlooking the Underworld.

"She doesn't need fruit. Unfortunately, she has a weapon infinitely more powerful," Hades said darkly. "Emotional manipulation."

"Ah," Socrates nodded in agreement. "A mighty weapon indeed. If only you had such power," he said with a twinkle in his eye. "What fear the Lord of the Underworld would inspire in the hearts of his subjects."

"You mock me, old man, at your peril." Even without his armour, his dark grey himation embroidered with gold couldn't disguise the formidable strength of his form.

Hades looked out of his tower, which rose high above the marsh lands. The five rivers of the Underworld converged around the structure, swirling around thunderously at the base before dropping off a cliff in an enormous cascading waterfall.

"I think I shall drop you in the river Phlegethon and watch you burn slowly, while it takes you to the depths of Tartarus."

Tartarus was a dungeon for the wicked, a realm of profound suffering, and a prison for the Titans. It was an old and frequent threat, one that held no power behind it.

"If mocking you gets you out of this tower, I'd consider that a success."

"You make me sound like a recluse."

"You haven't moved from this place for weeks. If you are not a recluse, you are certainly becoming one."

Hades turned to glance pointedly at Socrates. "I have people around me. Some you would say I've even honoured enough to play Ludus."

"Ah, but my Lord, we have to be here. We have no choice, being dead and all." He paused as if straining his mind in thought. "Do you have any voluntary guests?"

The dark God crossed his arms, unimpressed. "I seem to recall you voluntarily leaving the Elysian Fields to voluntarily float your ghostly form all the way to my tower. Uninvited."

"Someone had to do it. Unfortunately for me, I drew the short stick." The humour in the philosopher's eyes dimmed a little. "Your presence, my Lord, has been missed in the Underworld. Things have been slightly... crowded."

"I am aware of the activities in my realm, old man." Hades moved towards a large, stone pedestal basin in the centre of the room. Water filled the basin to the brim, and it only took a sliver of will to transform the smooth surface into flickering images of the Underworld.

"You haven't been patrolling as frequently as before, and there have been a few guests from the land of the living."

"Witches," Hades face darkened, his eyes roaming the images before him. "Cerberus and I have caught a few, and dissuaded them from making the journey again." His voice held a fond note as he thought of his three-headed Hell Hound.

Socrates raised his white brows. "Are they alive?"

"I'm surprised you have to ask. You should know me better than that." At Socrates' stare, which was surprisingly piercing for a spirit, the Lord of the Underworld finally added, "Mostly... just with fewer limbs."

The philosopher shifted uncomfortably in his chair. "I thought you might have threatened to make them a permanent resident, but then again that would only be determined by their belief system. Awfully anti-climatic if they weren't Greek."

Half distracted by the movement of his patrols around the western edges of the Underworld he asked, "What do you mean?"

"You have noticed that all the spirits in this realm are Greek? It goes to reason that when you leave your body you go to the realm of belief, not just to the Underworld. Imagine if they were Nordic, they might believe that dying in battle would send them to Valhalla, or if non-religious or Christian then The City of Light."

Hades looked up at that. "They entered the Underworld, which is only accessible through Greece. They're Greek."

Socrates lifted a finger. "Perhaps not. Would you say it's possible they travelled to Greece from a different land?"

There was a pause. "Possible," Hades said reluctantly. "But unlikely."

"Would you say it's possible they might not believe in the Greek religion?"

Hades just growled a response, then smiled, his expression almost wolfish. "I assure you, by the time I had finished with them, they had ample belief."

"Ah," the philosopher said, his eyes bright. "They might believe you exist, and do exist, but they might not necessarily believe *in you*. You might just be a creature of the Underworld, not necessarily a God to be worshipped. People are aware of other religions and deities around them, but that doesn't mean they follow them."

"Humans can believe in more than one God."

"True, but there is only one that they call out for before they die to save them. Maybe the afterlife is determined on the strength of such beliefs."

Hades turned his head back to look at the pool of water. "You're right," he said with irritation.

Socrates blinked in surprise. "I am?" He didn't expect the dark god to capitulate in a discussion so soon. Some of their conversations had lasted months, and even some of those they had agreed to disagree.

"Your theological debates are annoying."

The old spirit smiled. "And pointless, apparently. I do remember what I meant to say before I got distracted. Ah yes, the constant level of witches has also brought about an increase of Hell's citizens, which is always an unpleasant experience for the spirits getting caught in between their negotiations. The demons take their pleasure wherever they can get it."

Hades felt a cold anger flow swiftly through him. "Lucifer," he hissed, hating to even mention the vile creature, "was supposed to curb the demons infiltrating on his side." His knuckles tightened on the edge of the seeing bowel. The demon king was obviously not doing his duty. "If I see a demon I'm going to squash it."

Socrates cleared his throat. "Well, in saying that, there has also been sightings of Fallen in the area, which has also made it uncomfortable for the dead. Fallen don't seem to care about collateral damage in the midst of their destruction. I'm assuming they're there to curb the demons, as you said."

The Lord of the Underworld's first instinct was to rampage around his domain and kick the Fallen back to where they belonged, out of his domain. He hated the thought of Lucifer's minions skulking around, causing trouble.

But at the same time, he could acknowledge that this was likely the way Lucifer planned to recall the demons in the Underworld. And if he wasn't also there to limit the witches infiltrating from Earth, then the Fallen and the demons would be in the Underworld longer than necessary, hurting the dead.

He couldn't let that happen. The dead were his to manage and protect.

With a growl, he summoned his armour. Black metal appeared out of thin air around him, then slammed onto his body simultaneously, covering him from the neck down. It moulded neatly to his large form, and gleamed gold in the low light before turning back to black. A dark grey cloak materialised behind him and settled delicately about his shoulders as if the wind had placed it gently there.

Fingers flexing in his spiked gauntlet, his double pronged staff appeared in his hand. It was his favourite weapon, versatile and deadly. He also called his double bladed great axe and secured it on his back, its wickedly sharp edges gleamed high above him.

Hades skill with weapons was almost comparable with Ares himself, even though he was rarely found in battle in the upper realms. He had sharpened his blades on those who dared to trespass the Underworld and they had paid dearly for it. It spoke volumes as to why the other Gods took an immediate dislike to him.

Powerful and unbending Hades did not bargain with the Gods or any other being over the dead.

They were his to command and his only. He was their guardian and he was also their protector.

He could not forgo his duty and Socrates had been counting on that. He had just needed a push.

Turning to his old friend, Hades spoke, his voice like a crackle of ice on a winter's day. "I'm going hunting," he said with finality.

His helmet appeared, covering his nose and the sides of his face. If Socrates thought he was formidable before, now he was absolutely frightening. The armour he wore only enhanced the cold, brutal strength that was caged within his form. His power was palpable, almost uncontainable, as if he had allowed the edges to ripple out around him.

With a loud snap in the air, the Lord of the Underworld disappeared.

The philosopher waited a couple of minutes before he let the smile curve his lips. "Good hunting, my Lord," he said quietly.

***

The witch appeared in the Devil's domain and tried not to tremble.

Her eyes remained on the inky black floor, refusing to look up at the creature before her. The Fallen who had taken her through the portal still had a vise like grip on her arm. He bowed low, and then squeezed her flesh painfully to indicate that she should drop to her knees. It was easier for her to let her knees give out, than to stop them shaking.

Bowing her head low, she let her long, dirty hair cover most of her face.

"My Lord," the Fallen said, "the witch as you requested."

"You may leave," came the rich, velvet voice. It sent an involuntary ripple of pleasure down her spine. Her fear escalated.

The Fallen let go of her arm, and she could feel the blood flowing through her veins once more in a wave of sharp prickles. As soon as the dark angel who brought her left, the room instantly felt colder as if the seasons had instantly changed from autumn to the dead of winter. She clasped her hands tightly together on her lap and wondered if this was going to be her last day with the breath of life still in her body.

"Helena," that voice said her name as if it was a ribbon and he was sliding it slowly through his fingers. She was surprised he even knew her name."You're here because you are the last witch that has infiltrated the Underworld and who has had the unfortunate luck of being caught."

Frustration spiked through her at his words.

She had made the deal, and obtained the demon names. Her and her sisters had paid the ferryman and avoided Hades and his guardians. No easy feat. She only needed to get back out to the Earth plane, where the members of her coven were waiting for her. But then another demon had found them, and dragged her and her sister towards Hell. They had fought, but the demon was too strong.

They hadn't been prepared to face such a creature and had suffered severe injuries. The tendons in one of her legs had been severed. Even now she couldn't straighten it properly. One couldn't know how to counter every demon in the Underworld. Her sister, Mariana, had managed to kill herself with her small stiletto knife. The demon, distracted by her blood, gave Helena an opportunity to escape. She had dragged herself away, lost in the maze of the Underworld...

...and stumbled into the Fallen.

Her hope of escaping died, as well as the opportunity for a swift death.

She had been living with the witches in Hell for the past couple of weeks, and they had helped her heal, giving her a brew that had taken away most of the pain. The gruelling day to day chores in the arena, the constant pain and abuse all but drained her spirit and her will to fight back. As witches on Earth, they had been powerful and respected. People either avoided them or wanted to be them.

Here they were nothing.

There was only an endless fear, which had them scuttling like mice in the dark. They all but reeked with the scent.

And now she had been brought into the presence of the Devil himself for some unknown, terrifying reason. If she didn't know better, she'd believe she was cursed. As it was, she was dangerously close to letting go of her bowels and pissing herself.

She kept her mouth shut, saying nothing and waiting to die.

"There has been a power struggle amongst the demons in the Underworld. A few dead bodies are unremarkable, but when that number increases significantly in a short space of time, it makes me take notice." Her skin rose in warning bumps as she felt him move closer. She kept her eyes down. His hypnotically beautiful voice continued and she had to try to concentrate on the words, rather than the sound. "As these demons are the witch's main point of contact in the Underworld, you would most likely know why."

The Devil's voice deepened to a purr. "And you, Helena, are going to tell me."

She bit the inside of her lip, heart pounding like a rabbit caught in a trap. The air shifted and she felt him move. He didn't make a sound, but the part of her brain that was sensitive to danger suddenly started jumping up and down and pointing fingers in his general direction. Helena saw the curved front of his black boots enter her vision.

Then something sharp pricked the underside of her chin. A searing pain well beyond the small injury made her gasp. Her face was forced up and she found herself looking down the length of a long, dark blade, covered in runes. She couldn't help herself any longer.

She looked at him.

Her stomach immediately clenched with desire. That face. That body. That perfect colouring and texture of skin and hair blended together to create a thing of such beauty. He was dreams made flesh. It wasn't that each individual feature was exquisite, which it was, it was the sum total of all the parts that left an impact like a lightning bolt through the chest.

She made a small, dry whine in the back of her throat.

"Tell me what you know," the dark, carnal apparition in front of her said silkily.

It was a colossal effort, and she panted with the strain to tear eyes away from him and the haze of lust that fogged her mind. She wasn't high in the ranks of her coven for nothing. She closed her eyes and built a solid wall in her mind, mentally blocking out any magic that was trying to manipulate her.

Demons could project lust or tweak the part of your brain that centered around pleasure, making your body react without your control. She had seen a witch or two fall under the spell of such magic, writhing on the ground beneath their feet.

That's why defences were taught, to shield your mind from outside influences and control. She was talented at it, in fact, she taught other witches how to protect themselves.

Her mind now carefully shielded, Helena looked back at the Devil.

Lust hit her is a slow rolling burn, rocking her back on her knees.

There was no magic here. He was... just as he was.

But she couldn't give him the secrets of the coven. She couldn't. Her loyalty to her dark family had been embedded deeply in her since she was a little child. When she had been taken from her blood parents they had been all she had known. The dark witches had become her mothers and her sisters.

The coven was on one side of the battlefield, and on the other was everyone and everything else. But even though those loyalties ran deep down all the way to the bone, she knew that if he touched her... she might give him anything he wanted.

She clenched her teeth, and shook her head minutely. She waited for his touch, dreaded it and yearned for it all at the same time.

The blade fell away from her throat, and the Devil walked back towards the end of the room. It was then she noticed a fire pit built in the corner. Wood piled neatly on top of each other in a wide circle.

There were two, tall wooden stands on either side that were secured to a horizontal beam over the pit. Hanging from the beam was a round metal cage. A cage, say big enough to fit a human. Perhaps a dark witch who wasn't willing to speak.

"Still feeling resistant?" the Devil said.

Sweat beaded along her forehead, starting to slide down the sides of her face. It was a horrible way to die, being burned alive. It was a death not unfamiliar in their collective psyche.

There was an ancient fear attached to fire, of that burning, acidic smoke searing your lungs. The cumulative screams of the witches over the centuries who had roasted on pyres, could shatter every window in a city of thousands.

Her voice was hoarse, a raspy croak. "Yes, I'm ready to die." She would do it. She would do it for her family. For her coven.

Who knew where her soul would end up. Helena had traded an afterlife of singing angels for a lifetime of power and glory. There was only darkness ahead on her path, a darkness she knew and pursued. She had made her choice a long time ago.

"Who said *you* were going to die?" The Lord of Hell gave her a small, cruel smile.

Confusion spread across her face, making her sit up straight in caution. At her focused attention, he walked slowly to the other side of the fire pit. A large section of the air shimmered and then dropped as if it was a piece of fabric. In its place was another cage, a cube on the floor approximately two metres in height and length.

In the cage were children.

There was a little boy about five years old, and a girl not much older than him. They clutched each other terrified, huddled close to the ground. Now that the veil was gone, she could hear the sniffles and whimpers of distress. She recognised them instantly. It was Kasim and Analise.

They were two children of the dark witches in Hell. Some of the witches who had been captured over the years had been unknowingly pregnant. Their offspring had grown up in Hell, living in a land full of the most deadly predators, learning the single most important skill... how to hide.

Apparently they didn't hide well enough.

She took in a sharp, pained breath, understanding the deviousness of the beautiful creature in front of her. He knew straight away what her weakness would be. Family. And now he was planning to prod that weakness with a burning stick.

A section of the cage fell away in front of the children, and they shrieked, cowering at the back trying to get as far away from the dark angel that had put them there. Analise looked over at her, eyes green like a lagoon and Helena saw her lips move.

"Help us. Please."

Helena paled. The Lord of Hell waved his hand and the pile of wood under the cage burst into flames. He fixed his dark eyes on the children and they started to be dragged out of the cage by invisible bands of air.

Analise gripped the cage bar tightly with one hand, trying to resist the force moving them from the cage.

Her other hand held tight to Kasim's little fingers, who wailed loudly, face red and splotchy. Their feet suddenly lifted off the floor as the pull became stronger. Analise started shrieking, too.

Helena struggled awkwardly to her feet, breathing hard. Their screams raked through her like vicious claws.

Separate covens didn't exist in Hell. You either banded together or you died. The witches from all over the land were her family now, and they helped each other to survive. It was them against the rest of Hell.

The information she had could compromise her coven's power on Earth, yet if she didn't give the Lord of Hell the information her family here would die.

"Stop," she whispered desperately.

The Devil turned towards her, as he had been waiting for her to speak. "Yes?" he purred.

She told him everything she knew.

Chapter 12

Atlas had gone crazy.

The room looked like it had been torn apart by a pack of Hell Hounds. The table had been broken into several pieces, its remains scattered across the floor amongst shattered pieces of glass and pulverised fruit. Wine dripped down the walls, leaving small puddles on the floor. Strips of black silk, which used to be the bedsheet, were thrown like pieces of confetti across every available surface.

Then there were the feathers. The pillows were ripped apart and feathers layered the whole mess as if a flock of chickens had gone to battle.

Atlas stood in the centre of the room, eyes wild and hair sticking up in every direction. His tunic was torn in several places and covered in food and wine. With a yell he brandished a chair leg in my direction.

"Sandy!" he roared, waving the piece of wood at my face.

"Uh, yes?" I said, eyes wide, almost too scared to move.

"Get me out of here or I swear by Ares' balls I will smear shit all over this place!" He bared his teeth at me like a fighter facing his last battle, willing to go down hard.

I glanced in trepidation at the chamber pot, which was leaning precariously against the wall. Atlas also eyed the chamber pot, then looked back to me. Throwing down his chair leg, he made a move towards it.

"No!" I yelled, holding out my hands in front of me placatingly. "Okay, okay, okay! Let me think. Let me think!"

Thankfully, he stopped before he reached the wall, and instead crossed his arms over his chest and stared at me impatiently.

Taking a deep breath and letting it out slowly, I quickly thought about my options. There was no way I was going to find Lucifer and ask him if I could let Atlas out. Just thinking about my soulmate made my eyes blur. I wasn't ready to deal with everything that had transpired between us yet. There were too many layers, too many emotions burning within me that if I stopped for a minute and thought about it all, I might implode.

I looked back at the wall I had merged from and then back at him. There was that. The problem was I only knew how to merge myself out of the room. I didn't know if it was even possible to take someone else with me.

What if I hurt him? Worse, what if I killed him?

I bit my lip and stared at him worriedly. It was clear that Atlas had not been coping well on his own. I hadn't stopped to consider how a warrior such as he, a general of his own army, would feel after being locked up in a room for days on end. Not just any room, a room in Hell where there were unknown threats he couldn't see and had no comprehension of how to deal with.

To be honest, I hadn't had *time* to consider his feelings. There had been too much going on, too much at stake. There still was. But now, I could see the impact isolation had been having on him.

Atlas Huntington was not a man who liked to feel helpless, or bored for that matter. He was a leader, who kept his mind and body sharp by fighting and facing the fires around him.

And I needed him.

He tapped his foot impatiently, his face looking like a growing storm and I knew if I didn't do something he was going to make good on his threat. The whole room already smelt awful, I couldn't imagine him doing... I shuddered. As a threat, it was a really good one.

Taking another deep breath, and immediately regretting it, I looked at him squarely. "There is only one way out of this room." I jerked my thumb over my shoulder towards the wall. "And I'm not sure if you can get through."

Atlas glared at me. "Well then you better be sure, because I ain't staying in this room."

I sighed. "Atlas, I had to mentally blend my energy into the wall, believing that there wasn't a difference between me and a solid object. It takes a fair amount of control. It might mean that for you to go through the wall you would need to apply the same belief. And while you are a formidable man, who is clearly intelligent," it didn't hurt to flatter him a bit, and it was true, "I don't think that you have or can acquire the ability to manipulate energy."

"What's energy?"

Point proven. "Look," I said, turning my body sideways so I was in line with the wall. With a couple of seconds of concentration, I stuck my hand inside the surface all the way to my elbow. I pulled my arm back out again and then pushed it back in. "Do you think you can do that?"

"No. But I can do that with a knife. In someone's guts."

"Not the same thing. This is going to take a little bit of time to work out," I tried to explain.

Atlas growled low in his throat. "No more time! I could be with my army right now, hunting the Kolaith scum and being embraced by many questionable women. I'm done waiting around, doing absolutely nothing. Find a way to get me out now, or the next time you come back..." he trailed off meaningfully, not even having to look at the chamber pot. "And," he said with a note of absolute finality, "you'll get no more help from me. Good fortune trying to battle the Defeated Ones."

It took me a second, but I realised he was talking about the Fallen. I graciously didn't correct him, and also graciously didn't point out that he was helping me because the Devil told him to. And if he didn't train me, then Lucifer had promised to feed him to a nest of scorpions. One didn't point out to their friends that they didn't have choices.

And that's how I had begun to see Atlas. As a friend.

And this friend needed to have some control over his life.

My shoulders sagged as if the air had been sucked out of them. The sigh I let out was a mixture of bemusement and exasperation. I placed my hands on my hips. "Calm down, I didn't say I wouldn't help, only that I needed to think of another way."

At my words, the rigidity of his posture eased, though the scowl was still in place. I looked around the room. It was possible that I could take Atlas with me, but I didn't want to jump ahead and try merging with him without at least some practice to determine if it was even a possibility. My gaze snagged on the only unbroken chair in the room, which had toppled sideways, half under the bed.

"Okay," I said with determination ringing in my voice. "Let me try to merge with the chair."

Half an hour later

"You broke it!" Atlas shouted, sitting on the bed facing me. He had taken off his shoes and now sat in a cross legged position watching me practise.

I merged the rest of my body out of the wall and spotted a part of the chair arm on the floor. I had tried for the seventh time to take the chair with me through the wall, but it was clearly resisting. It was easier to blame the chair.

"Oops," I said. I placed the rest of the chair carefully down and gingerly kicked the broken piece of wood out of the way.

"That could have been my arm," he accused. "Are you trying to get me killed, Sandy?"

I tossed my hair out of my face. "It's Sandriel. And aren't you glad we're practising?"

Another hour later

"I'm tired," I groaned, slumping against the wall. My fingertips pressed against my temple, massaging the skin in slow circles. I closed my eyes briefly and wished I was back in my room, surrounded by pillows. It had been a long day.

"You're not trying hard enough. You need to *believe* you can get the chair through the wall." Atlas leaned comfortably against the opposite wall. Now that we had been practising for a while he was in a much better mood. I suspected it was mainly because he had company.

I let my arms flop on either side of me. "How would you know?" I grumbled. "You didn't even know what energy was until a couple of hours ago."

An apple struck me on the chest, bouncing off my armour.

Opening an eye, I shot him an annoyed look. "Hey!"

"You need to concentrate," he said disapprovingly. "Be disciplined."

"I am concentrating! That's why I have a headache."

"You whine like a little girl," he sneered. "See yourself winning here," he pointed to his head, "Before it can happen out there." He pointed to the wall.

Atlas chewed on a piece of bread that he found on the floor. His brown eyes looked intently at me, holding the power of a priest in the middle of a sermon. "Believe, Sandy. Believe," he said, his voice gaining strength.

Bits of breadcrumbs shot out of his mouth as he spoke, sticking like adornments to his beard.

"Believe."

Yet another hour later

We both stood together, looking at the wall. The silence stretched thinly between us, making me want to cringe. Atlas was not a silent man, but right now, even he couldn't find anything to say.

The chair was stuck solidly inside the dark stone. Its legs stuck out facing us, the rest of it was on the other side.

The silence ticked on.

Shifting uncomfortably, I flicked a look at Atlas. He was frowning. "Uh," I said, trying to break the tension. "So... what do you think?"

He turned his head and glared at me. "This..." he gestured towards the chair, "is the same as me stuck in the wall. How is it any better?" he growled.

"At least it's *in* the wall."

"Would that be my head on the other side or my arse?"

"Preferably your head so I don't have to listen to you any longer," I muttered. Tilting my face to the side, I studied the chair for a couple of seconds. "You know, if you look at it optimistically, it's a nice piece of art. We can call it... *halfway there*."

He looked at me excitedly. "Or how about, *moranga*."

"What does that mean?"

"It means you're a bloody idiot." His face went flat. "Again!" he commanded, spinning around, pointing one finger up in the air.

This was going to be a long night.

Chapter 13

We had made it.

I lay on the bathing room tiles, eyes half closed with the fingers of my right hand trailing gently in the water. After hours of practice, I finally managed to get the chair through the wall.

After a few more successful tries, I decided to attempt the processes with Atlas. Thankfully, it was a success, otherwise – if his loud, booming threats and curses had come true – I would currently be boobless with a face of a donkey's arse.

Very telling if that's what Atlas considers the ultimate threat for a woman.

Unattractiveness.

As soon as I showed him the bathing room, he had taken a running leap and dived into the pool with all his clothes on, spraying water everywhere. He reminded me of a great, big shaggy dog that had been roaming in the forest for far too long, covered in weeks worth of debris.

I deliberately didn't mention that this was the place where the octo-demon almost ate me. The poor man needed a bath so badly, I refused to scare him away. Though, I did have a quick look in the water to make sure there wasn't anything there.

The splashing grew louder as I heard him come closer. Wet bits of cloth suddenly sailed through the air and landed on the other side of me. Great. Atlas was naked. I closed my eyes completely.

"So Sandy," he said, his voice muffled by food. In the short time I'd known him, he seemed to be always shoving something in his mouth. "What happened on your tour?"

My mind flashed to the Scythin fighting the angel in the arena, to the witches bound and held captive in the Fallen's domain, to Lucifer's lips and hands on my body... my breathing increased, and I squeezed my eyes tight, willing the images away before I fell into them.

"Huh," he said.

Face slightly hot, I told him everything that had happened but avoiding the heated interlude with Lucifer at the end.

"Did you get a disguise?"

My eyes flew open and then my face crumpled. "No," I said, utterly disgusted with myself. After everything, I had forgotten one of the most important elements of the mission. I needed a disguise in order to enter the dungeons without being immediately recognised. I couldn't stroll in with my white pants and golden armour and start tinkering with the dark cages like I was dismantling a wheel from a carriage on a busy street. I needed to blend in.

"I'm so stupid," I whispered. "I forgot." *Stupid. Stupid. Stupid.*

"Eh," said Atlas. "Well, you can use mine. They're dirty enough anyway and you can rip them to fit your size."

I blinked. That was… an excellent idea. Somewhat disturbing and a mite disgusting imagining wearing Atlas's soiled clothes, but a surprisingly excellent idea. Any clothes that I would have managed to obtain in the dungeon were bound to be filthy and torn anyway. That was the point.

I avoided turning my head to look at him, staring instead at the ceiling where the gold veins of light puslated through the dark stone.

"Thank you," I said softly, gratefully. A frown creased my forehead. After a beat, I said, "What are you going to wear?"

There was a soft sound of water moving, then a relaxed sigh. In my mind I could almost picture his head leaning back against the tiles. "Why do I have to wear anything?" he asked, genuinely confused.

I stilled. "Atlas," I said patiently. "Please don't take this the wrong way, but I'd rather converse with you with your clothes on than without."

"I don't have clothes on now," he replied pleasantly.

"Yes, and I'm trying not to look at you."

"Are all angels prudes?" he scoffed.

My mouth dropped open. He was right, angels weren't exactly prudes. Angels didn't notice the physical form the way humans did. We did not view nakedness as something to elicit any extreme emotion. The body was just a vessel of something much more important. And yet, from the very first moment I had met Lucifer, I was keenly aware of the physical form, and I had only become even more sensitive to its state of dress and undress.

That I was so uncomfortable with the notion of Atlas's nakedness revealed yet another symptom of being in a lower realm.

In acknowledging this... I still didn't want to see Atlas naked.

"Could you perhaps wear a towel?" I suggested carefully.

He ignored me. "Let's concentrate on the important things, Sandy," Atlas said amiably. "Now that you have gotten more information you need to work out a few things."

I sighed, sifting the water through my fingers. "A great many things," I said deflated.

"Firstly, you still need to find a way to free your warrior friends. The whole plan depends on getting them out of the cages, so if you can't do that you might as well pick something else to do. You have a disguise, so best use it and work on the cage closest to the portal in case you alert the Fallen people. What are you going to do if the Fallen become aware of you?"

"Run? There is no way I'm going to be able to beat them in a direct conflict."

"You best hope that doesn't happen," he warned, "Otherwise, it will be virtually impossible for you to free the angels from the cages with them looking out for you." He paused, thinking. "What you need… is a distraction. Something to draw the Fallen away from the dungeons and the arena."

I nodded in agreement. That would be ideal. The less Fallen around, the less likely I would be at risk of being discovered. "Like what?" I asked.

"I don't know yet… we will have to work that one out. You still have other problems to deal with. How are you going to access the portals? From the way you put it to me, it sounds like there is a hierarchy amongst the angels and not all would be able to access every portal. How do you know you can get them through to the Earth plane?"

Pointing my finger in the air in triumph, I smiled and announced excitedly. "I think I figured that one out!"

I risked a quick glance in his direction, letting my hand drop. Atlas was leaning back against the edge of the pool a little further up from me, with his arms stretched out on top and his eyes closed. His hair was wet and slicked back, making it look almost black.

Now that his face was scrubbed clean from all the dirt from whatever he had been doing before he arrived in Hell, I could see white scars marring his skin. There was a particular nasty looking one, which was long and thick. It travelled down his muscular arm, looking like the corpse of a worm with its raised, stringy surface.

A thin line also bisected the side of his forehead, but I couldn't determine how far down it went with the thick growth of his beard covering most of his face.

He looked less… animalistic now, and more like the veteran leader of an army who had earned his scars. I considered offering to heal them for him, but I sensed he would want to keep them. It was apart of him now.

"How?" Atlas asked, breaking my thoughts. The water was deliciously warm. A perfect temperature to relax and fall off to sleep. Just thinking about sleeping made me want to drift off, so I kept them open and turned back to look at the ceiling.

"It's the rings they wear. Lucifer said the portals are keyed to allow certain energy signatures access. He either configures it himself, like he has done with the ones leading to the dungeon and to Kryptos. Only I can access those," I clarified. "Or he grants access through the use of rings. And since individual Fallen might change their position in the hierarchy frequently, due to their successes or failures, it makes more sense that the portals are configured by the rings they wear rather than the mirrors itself."

"Ha. And are you sure all the Fallen wear these rings?"

"I noticed them in their healing chambers. Every Fallen I saw had one on their finger. And now looking back, I'm pretty certain the other Fallen I've encountered were wearing rings, too."

"Well done," he said. I felt the corner of my mouth lift at the praise. "But that still means you have to get the right rings at the right time without being seen and without them noticing you've taken them."

"Yes, that," I said dryly. "And I'd need at least two rings." Two angels to go through the portal, and one to return with both rings to take another one through.

"At least," he agreed. "Be faster if you can get more. You also need to think about how you are going to get the angels to the portals. A bit hard to disguise a hundred angels flying across the lava to the Fallen domain. Assuming some of them are even in a state to fly."

"Ah! This is so complicated!" I complained dejectedly, my voice echoing through the room. Bending my knees, I sat up raking my hands through my hair, then rested my forehead against my arms.

There were so many variables, so many impossible challenges, and so very many things that could go wrong. It all seemed insurmountable.

Hopeless. My eyes filled with tears of frustration.

"It's a great risk, Sandy, with almost too many holes to succeed."

Even Atlas thought this plan was doomed to fail. I felt even more dejected.

"Almost," he continued. "There is one thing you could consider that might just give you the chance to pull this crazy plan off."

My head shot up. Atlas was looking at me steadily, his head turned, brown eyes bright. "What?" I whispered.

"The witches. You need to speak to them and come to some sort of deal."

I raised my eyebrows. Working with the dark witches. That was something I thought I'd never do. Their hatred for angels was probably amplified to instant violence since being tortured in Hell. There was a strong possibility they might try to attack me the moment I made contact. I wanted to instantly reject the idea, yet what if I had something to bargain with? Something they wanted?

It was worth thinking about.

At my silence, Atlas encouraged me further. "It'll make one damn interesting alliance if you can pull it off."

I nodded at him, consideringly. "I'll think about it." Yawning, I got up from the floor. "I need to sleep, and I don't want to leave you here."

Walking over to where a platter of food was laid out on a tray, I picked up the large, black towel that was folded next to it. "Here," I said, turning away but dangling the towel towards him by my fingertips.

"Why can't I stay here? I don't want to go back to the room," he said stubbornly, refusing to take the towel from my hand.

"Atlas, you're not safe here. Demons attack at any time. And where I might have some ability to protect myself, you don't. What will happen if I leave you here and a demon appears? You don't have a weapon nor the ability to deal with them." My voice softened and I shook my head. "If I could send you back home I would. I know you'd do anything to get back to your army. I promise I'll take you out of your room every chance I can, but the best way we can get you back to Earth is for me to complete this mission. And for me to do that I need you to be safe."

I thought about everything I had yet to do and what was at stake. My throat constricted. "I really need your help."

"Ahhhh!" he growled in frustration and grabbed the towel in a vicious swipe. I heard the water splash as he got out. "I hate that bloody room! Of course you need my help," he muttered as he dried himself off. "You wouldn't be able to do any bloody thing without me. Useless, utterly useless."

I smiled in relief. Once I was reasonably certain I had given him enough time to drape a towel over himself, I turned around.

And shrieked.

Atlas stood with the towel held out to the side, grinning at me. Naked.

Trying not to look directly at him, I said through clenched teeth. "Put some clothes on. I'm not taking you through the wall like that!" I focused my eyes just above his right shoulder, trying desperately to blur out everything else.

He laughed, loud and booming. "You're such a prude, Sandy, you deserved that. Might loosen you up a bit. Haven't you seen a naked man before?" He spun the towel around and around like a whip. "Do angels not have crotches? Is it just blank down there?"

"Atlas," I hissed. "*Now.*"

"Awww... you're no fun." He wrapped the towel around his waist and tucked it in at the top. "There. Happy now? Most women would have loved the eyeful you just got. You wouldn't believe the camp bedfellows that throw themselves at me."

"I'm sure," I said blandly.

He started telling me about a story involving a lady called Beatrice. She apparently went into a jealous rage because he had lain with her sister. We successfully merged through the wall after which I listened to Beatrice's antics to catch him in the 'act,' in which she failed. After that, she made several attempts to end his life because if she couldn't have him no one else would. I was dubious as to whether this person actually existed.

I walked down the hallway towards Atlas's room. His steps slowed behind me.

"I'm just going to grab a tray of food from the room here. If you call that food. Where is the bloody meat?"

I turned and watched his back disappear around the corner, muttering to himself. I crossed my arms and waited for him, my mind whirling.

I was lucky to have Atlas around to help me. Lucifer had apparently really done me a favour in bringing him here, as his advice had so far been invaluable. Then again, if Lucifer was really helping me, I still found it strange that he was throwing me in front of the Fallen with target rings painted all over me.

The fight between the Scythin and the Fallen woman was portrayed for my amusement. And the way Lucifer was treating me had not gone unnoticed. If the Fallen caught me alone now, they might not hold back, even with Lucifer's demonstration of what happens when he is not obeyed.

He had made the price of me being caught even higher? Why? What was he trying to achieve?

"Sandy! Are these the portal mirrors you were talking about?"

My eyes widened in horror. "Atlas, no!" I screamed.

I bolted down the passageway, fearing I was too late. A ripple against the wall to my left alerted me, moving rapidly like a bolt flashing through the water. Tearing around the corner, the sound of my heartbeat was the only thing I could hear. I saw Atlas by the portal mirror, his hand pulling back from the misty surface he had just touched.

I lifted my arm. Light shot out in a stream, hitting the wall just in front of the ripple.

It was the only thing that saved him.

The light spread across the surface in a rolling mass of white flames. The ripple paused. I raced in front of Atlas. He looked at me, his brown eyes full of surprise. At my expression, I saw his hand twitch down to the side of his waist, as if he wanted to pull out his sword.

Then the Dragarth bursts out from the wall. At first, all you could see was a mass black scales sliding out in a continuous stream, smashing through several tables and chairs.

Then it raised itself up.

"What in Athena's tits is that!" Atlas screamed behind me. I lashed out with my hand behind me and grabbed his arm holding him in pace.

"Don't move," I spat out between clenched teeth.

Three sets of glowing red eyes swivelled around to face us. The serpent reached the ceiling and looked down with undisguised fury. Their tongues flicked out of their mouths as if anticipating the flavour of our flesh, and one opened its enormous mouth to reveal its dripping white fangs. To the left, its tail slithered on the ground, covered in spikes.

I lifted my finger and pointed at it. "No!" I yelled sternly.

Three sets of eyes blinked. Hissing at me in anger, its black heads bobbed up and down. Then one darted down and snapped its jaws just a few millimetres from the tip of my finger.

"Stop that!" I said, glaring at the reptilian head. "You know you are not allowed to touch me. I'm under Lucifer's protection. And this…" I jerked my head towards Atlas, "human is under mine."

The Dragarth raised its tail and smashed it down into a table, splintering it into several pieces. The heads darted this way and that, as if trying to get around me to snap at Atlas.

The Dragarth was driven to protect the entry ways into Lucifer's domain and Atlas had trespassed, just as I had done when I first entered Hell. Even though Atlas wouldn't have been able to go through, the simple act of touching them had triggered the Dragarth.

I had to get Atlas away.

Calling up a shield, I moulded the Light to curve around the front of our bodies. The heads reared back from the glow, but stayed within decapitation distance. I could hear Atlas breathing hard behind me.

I cautiously moved, pulling him along. The Dragarth turned to face us, knocking over more furniture as we inched around the room. We passed Lucifer's double doors and Atlas backed up to swing them open.

"No! Not that room!" I gritted out harshly. Hearing the warning note in my tone he freezed without opening the door. It was one thing if I went barging in, another completely if I did it with Atlas. Also, I didn't exactly leave in the best of circumstances. The last expression on Lucifer's face was definitely anger. I doubted I'd find him in an indulging mood.

"Why? What's behind the door," he whispered roughly. I could tell that Atlas thought there must be something infinitely more terrible in the room behind us if I refused to go through them and escape the Dragarth.

He was right.

I wasn't exactly scared of the Dragarth, and it wasn't because I didn't find it terrifying in all its black scaled glory, because I certainly did. The three-headed serpent would be enough to make even the warrior angels pause and consider calling for reinforcements. But ever since I tried to empty out the pool with the portal mirror in an effort to try and get to Rushton, the Dragarth had been ordered to leave me alone and I had been unable to move the mirrors again.

The Dragarth wasn't allowed to attack me. I was safe from its wrath. Atlas was a different story.

"You don't want to go in there," I whisper back, my eyes on the serpent. "We have to get back to the room. I don't think it will attack if you go back to where you are meant to be." I hoped, at least.

"Yes, yes," Atlas agreed quickly. "Happy to go back to my room now Sandy."

We managed to inch our way slowly to the passageway leading to the room with the shield hovering over us. "We're leaving now," I announced, unsure whether the demon would even understand me. "You can go back into your wall now."

"Stop talking to it like it's a pet," Atlas growled. "Let's just move. For the love of Zeus, *move!*"

The Dragarth slithered a little closer watching us creep away like a snake watching a darting mouse. When we started to move backwards down the hallway, its three heads curved around the corner, bobbing up and down. It stopped and watched us with its crimson eyes, still hissing but less aggressive. Hope surged in my chest at the possibility the demon might not pursue once we were away from the portals.

Once I got to the wall, I let down the shield. It faded and flickered away, leaving us vulnerable. I felt a moment of panic and I readied myself to put it back up again the moment the Dragarth made a move towards us. But it stayed watching us intently, not moving any closer.

"Good, good Dragarth," I whispered.

"Are you *insane*?" Atlas hissed back.

"Tell me if it moves," I said and turned my back on the demon.

"What? Ah! It's staring at me!"

I concentrated on merging through the wall. It was difficult, with a demon behind me, salivating at the thought of eating us. Atlas' grip on my arm became increasingly tighter and tighter. Painfully so. But after a couple of tense minutes, I felt my hand pass through the solid surface.

Grabbing Atlas, I pulled us through.

***

The Warden of Hell was not a tall creature. He did not tower over demons like a mountain over the sea. Nor did he sport curving horns, elongated claws, or any other appendages that could rip or tear into his enemies with vicious glee. He was tiny, with only a modest amount of muscles attached to his slender frame. His teeth were white and even, with no protruding fangs, and his jaw was disproportionately small to his face.

His appearance was that of a lesser creature, an omnivore who ran at the sound of swift, sure feet. He looked weak, like prey modelled after the soft things that roamed the upper world.

Appearances were deceiving.

Sepheroth was aware as soon as he appeared in the seventh level of Hell. The warden could have veiled himself, hidden his presence from the demons until he was ready, but it seemed he wanted to make an entrance. His dark bladed swords were out, held ready by his side, and his eyes glowed molten red as if the fires of Hell had suddenly taken residence inside.

It had been some time since he had made a visit, so most demons were not prepared. As soon as they felt his energy mingling amongst them they all froze. Not the type of stillness that ceases motion, but a stillness of breath and heartbeat. Then motion resumed once more, away from the Warden of Hell.

He moved past them, swords smoking with power. No one touched him.

They had witnessed many times what happened when one fought with the First Son of Darkness. The temptation was there – it was instinctive, the need to throw off the chains that bound them – but yet no one made a move. The price was high to be defeated.

Sepheroth dismantled his form until they broke into seven aspects, sliding away. The different forms of himself moved separately around the crowd, getting lost amongst the demons. He didn't want the warden to feel his combined strength and recognise him for who and what he was.

Lucifer walked up to the throne of bones. On it sat Ezoridath.

The demon was larger than a bear with muscles upon muscles that bunched high up over his shoulders. His arms were the same width as his legs, his chest like slabs of clay. Raw, angry red flesh covered his body, making him look as if when he was created, someone had forgotten to add a layer of skin. Needle sharp spikes covered every inch of him and several silver piercings lined his thick, black lips. He was a formidable strength, a worthy ruler of Hell's most damned.

Sharp black nails tapped the edge of the bone throne he sat upon. He hissed out a greeting, "My Lord Warden, how good of you to join us. What can we–"

The bones on the chair melded and moved.

Before Ezoridath could react, the sharp edges of bone pierced *through* him. They moved sinuously like numerous pale snakes, flowing in and out of his chest, arms, and legs. They went in white, then emerged, streaked with black demon blood.

After a few moments, the throne completely changed colour. Ezoridath screamed, a sound of agony ripping through his lungs and hurtling through the air. All the other demons leaned closer, the sight and sound of torture too exquisite to ignore.

But he wasn't defeated yet.

His muscles strained and the bones began to crack. Then, the warden whispered a word. The power of it shuddered through the air, rippling like a storm. The throne froze, crystalising within a block of solid ice. Ezoridath was inside, a frozen face of agony.

Creating ice in the middle of Hell took a considerable amount of power. The coolness usually had to manifest from somewhere, had to be drawn from an external source like the deep soil of the ground, from the atmosphere or the depths of water. It took an extraordinary amount of skill to draw the elements together and channelled so elegantly in one direction. In Hell, all the levels were surrounded by lava. There was no external source of cold, which meant... the power was coming from him.

The warden flicked his fingers dismissively.

The throne exploded.

Bits of ice, bone, and demon flew in every direction like little sharp knives. Some of the demons on the side had the foresight to block, shift away, or shield. Others that weren't as quick, got impaled.

Hisses, growls, and other sounds of anger amplified from every direction.

Ezoridath was not truly gone. He would reform and come back eventually, but when he did, he would be weaker, his power diminished. Ezoridath would slide down the scale to be more prey than predator. Fighting and losing in Hell had its consequences.

Sepheroth had been planning for this night, when the warden would come. This is why he had put Ezoridath on the throne in the first place. The demon thought Sepheroth had been elevating him to a position of power, but he had only been setting him up to take the fall.

Oh yes, the warden was not only making an entrance, but a statement. Whether or not he knew that the demon on the throne was the true leader of Hell, it didn't make a difference. He was saying that he was not to be contested, to cease fire, to desist. Any opposition would be effectively destroyed.

He was also saying that he *knew*. He knew there was a power shift, a change in hierarchy, and it would only be a matter of time before he found out who it was.

But Sepheroth had not been planning to oppose him directly.

The First Son of Darkness turned and stared at the demon horde of the seventh level. They surrounded him, straining to pounce on his slender form. He cocked his head in invitation. No one moved.

Having made his point, he turned with his back to them and casually tested the barriers of their cage, searching for weaknesses, filling those he found with a complex weaving of power. The demons watched, their hatred mounting to violent levels.

No one was stupid enough to attack.

Then, he disappeared.

Sepheroth called his forms back together, once he was sure the warden's presence was gone They converged in a mass of darkness and flesh, and he grew rapidly in strength and power. He stretched, feeling his seven aspects settle once more in his body, their needs and desires finally becoming one.

The demons gave him room as he moved towards one of the walls. Rock shattered as he struck the hard stone, crumbling like sand from the impact of his fist. It made a flat indent large enough for him to sit on. Once seated, he turned and glared at the horde surrounding him.

"The warden's presence has escalated our plans. We had planned for this, so we will now move forward." He waited a beat for the objection or a comment to challenge his command, but none came.

They had learnt.

"The light angel needs help freeing the warrior angels, so help we shall give her." He pointed his finger to the demons he needed. "You, you, and you, create the necessary distractions." The demons gave their acknowledgment and blended back into the crowd.

"And after that?" a demon hanging from the side of the wall asked. It was just a shadow, moulded to the rocks, but it spoke in a painful rasp from unseen lips.

Sepheroth's lips curled. "Then we take her."

Chapter 14

I left Atlas in his room.

His quarters had returned to its former state, the bed and furniture restored as if the destruction had never occurred. I wondered if the rooms were spelled that way, or if the spectre demon was responsible for keeping Lucifer's domain in order.

It disturbed Atlas more than I thought it would, and he immediately wanted to trash the place all over again. He said it made him feel like his anger had never happened...

...and that bothered him immensely.

I couldn't understand why it mattered so much. Perhaps it came down to his belief that he had only this one life to live. If he truly believed that, it made sense that he would feel a deep subconscious pull to leave a mark for the world to see. Otherwise he'd feel lost, tumbling aimlessly through the endless pages of existence. Like a man slowly scratching his name into the wall of his cell, he wanted others to remember his suffering.

Those humans that understood the circle of birth and death and the continual illusion of life, still felt the need to leave an impact on the world, but that need became more about the change they saw in others as a result of the life they lived, rather than basking in the ego of all their accomplishments.

Then there were those in their own ignorance, who viciously sought power and prestige like the ultimate final goal, sacrificing everything and content to leave the world in ashes and dust to live a life of luxury and fame. They did not realise that the future generations they so easily ignored could house their very next incarnation.

We are all born with a passion and a purpose, but we have a choice with how we pursue it.

But Atlas was a warrior, a man who mentally and emotionally saw purpose in physical acts. He was not used to seeing things holistically and perceiving that the reason he was in Hell was perhaps a part of a larger purpose. There was no point in pursuing this philosophy with him, even though it could potentially ease his suffering.

Everyone was on their own spiritual path, and one needed to be ready and open to embrace any new paths of thinking.

I stayed with Atlas for another hour, just to make sure the Dragarth wasn't going to attack him in his room. His pride wouldn't let him ask me to stay, so I chattered about my life in The City of Light until his body slowly relaxed. Then, I left for my own quarters.

I passed the sitting room, which had also been restored, the tables and chairs the Dragarth destroyed, now perfectly whole. The serpent was thankfully gone, presumably back into the wall, or reporting back to Lucifer. Imagining the three-headed demon complaining to Lucifer was so disturbingly humorous that I snorted quietly with laughter. It was the first time I found anything amusing in Hell.

I finally made it back to my room. On the bed was another set of clothes, pants and top all in white. Calling my armour back into the arm bands, I quickly changed and collapsed back into the plush cushions.

It felt so good, I fell immediately into a deep sleep.

I ran through the dungeons, my breath loud and frantic in my ears. I veered sharply around one of the dark cages, feet slapping against the floor, the Hell Hound fast at my heels. The taunts of the Fallen echoed around me, promising pain, promising retribution. The click and scrape of sharp, elongated nails picked up speed.

My wings furled out and I leapt into the air. The snap of teeth was too loud, too close.

Flying erratically through the maze of dark cages I tried to desperately find my way to the stairs. The stairs were my only chance of escape.

Chancing a quick look behind me, I screamed as the Hell Hound vaulted through the air with sharp claws and even sharper teeth. I crashed into one of the dark cages, limbs spasming. Blinded by the pain, I fell onto the floor in a crumpled heap.

The scene suddenly froze.

I was immediately standing outside myself, watching my body on the floor. Darkness pressed around me, cool and foreboding. Illuminated on the dungeon floor was the other version of myself, frozen in place. This had already happened before. I had run exactly like this through the dark cages away from the Fallen and the Hell Hound. I knew I was dreaming, and yet the dream was too orchestrated.

"That's because it is."

The shadows converged, moving and shifting like swaths of fabric, moulding into a distinctive feminine shape. Once the shape solidified, the shadows parted like smoke, revealing my darker self. Her long, golden hair was pulled back away from her face in a tight, complicated braid, making my features look sharper and more distinct. She was sheathed in supple leather, all in one piece, covering her arms down to her wrist and over her chest up to her throat.

As always, she appeared to wear my form with a grace and control of someone assured of their strength and capabilities. It was the subtle cues you could read in a person's body language. The straightening of the spine, shoulders slightly back, neck long and slender, chin tilted up. It was the way a person looked directly into your eyes and not at your mouth.

"I want to show you something," she said softly.

I crossed my arms and looked back at her coldly. "Why are you still here? I thought I got rid of you." I knew she hadn't really gone. I hadn't forgotten the whispers in my mind, soft at first, then becoming increasingly louder. Even though I knew I hadn't banished her forever, it was still frightening looking at my face with those dark, cunning eyes.

She smiled at me, a mix of pity and disappointment. "You still don't understand, do you? The pieces are right in front of you and you haven't put it together." Turning towards the version of me on the dungeon floor, she shook her head sadly. "Pathetic, really. I offered you power moments before and you didn't take it. Do you remember?"

I did. "I didn't need it in the end," I said stiffly. "I managed to survive."

She raised an eyebrow, the expression strangely reminding me of Lucifer. "Barely. And I'm not talking about surviving. I'm talking about thriving." My darker self gestured towards my crumpled form. "Since you seem to lack comprehension, I'll show you what I mean."

The scene reversed, the sequence of events going backwards. I watched myself lift off the floor and into the air, wings spread out. I bounced back off the dark cage, flying back through the twist and turns of the cages, wide eyed and panicked. The Hell Hound once again narrowly missed my leg. It arched back down to the ground, muscles bunching in preparation to leap.

Movement came to a stop once more.

"Now," my darker self said to me, her eyes gleaming in anticipation. "Let's see what could have happened."

The scene resumed its normal pace. Unable to look away, I watched as the Hell Hound vaulted into the air. Instead of screaming with terror, my eyes flashed with dark, terrible power. I moved my hands and black energy extended out from the cells on either side of the Hell Hound. It wrapped around the demon dog like crackling ropes of power, squeezing tight. The Hell Hound whined, high and piercing, shaking as if it was being fried. Then the dark roped loosened, melding back into the cages.

The Hell Hound dropped to the floor, still and silent, steam rising up from its fur. The smell of roasted meat permeated the air.

"See," my dark self said happily, lifting a hand and shoulder up lightly. "Was that really so hard?"

My lips flattened in a tense line, even though a small part of me was thrilled at watching the power I had possessed. That part wondered how it would feel to be unafraid. The fact that I even felt that made me even more angry. "Like I said before, I took care of it myself."

"Oh," my darker self said in mock surprise. "You mean like this?"

The scene in front of me blurred like a chalk painting splashed with water. The muted colours melded and swirled before forming distinct shapes. I saw myself, my back towards one of the open dark cages, arms shredded with blood running down in thick rivulets. Desperation and fear burned in my eyes as I faced the Hell Hound in front of me. I barely remembered the moment I had come up with this plan. Everything had happened so fast, I was just reacting on instinct.

I watched the Hell Hound barrel towards me, leaping for my throat.

"This is where you throw yourself out of the way and lock the Hell Hound inside with your tiny, fluffy ball of Light." The scene played out just as she said. She tilted her head and smiled at me patronisingly. "How cute."

I glared at her. "It worked, didn't it?"

"Oh yes, that is until your Light ball faded and the Hell Hound was released. What was your plan then? Scare it away with your screams?" The scene moved forward rapidly. "Oh, and let's not forget when Ezriel called in for more and Lucifer had to intervene and save you. Again." She looked at me questioningly and slightly confused. "Don't you ever get tired of that? A couple more minutes and you would have been smeared all over the dungeon floor."

I gave her my best bored tone, but the comment stung. "Is this where you show me how you defeat all the Hell Hounds? Because I really don't care. Just tell me what you want and get out of my head. I assume you aren't going to leave until you do."

"No, no, no," she said softly. "That would be a waste of time. The Hell Hounds aren't your problem. The Fallen are. You are now aware of what they are capable of. What they can do. They will grind you into dust before your cute, fluffy Light ball can annoy them."

My darker self took a couple of intimidating steps closer to me, staring me down. I could feel the pressure of her gaze like a weight pushing me back against my heels. "You don't have the power to defeat them, but I do. I can help you, I can save everyone here, all the light angels trapped in their cages. Whereas all you can do is fail."

I met her eyes with steel in my own. "Really? Why would you want to defeat them? You are one of them. Don't think for one moment that I believe you are on my side."

"Of course I'm on your side, you fool. I'm you. I'm what you become if you actually survive this place," she snarled, looking surprisingly savage. "I want to defeat them because they think we're weak. Pathetic, and needing a big, strong angel to save us. You are weak," she spat, "but I'm not." The disdain in her voice was as clear as a chime of crystal in a filthy tavern.

A bolt of fear rippled through me at her words, at her absolute certainty. I raised my voice to a shout. "I won't become you. Get out of my head!" I spun around looking for some way out of this place, even though it was inside my mind. I called up a hanging orb of Light, then randomly picked a direction, heading out into the inky darkness.

My dark self laughed, her anger dissipating in the face of my denial. "You think this is how angels fall? That they have Fallen versions of themselves appear in their minds?" I gritted my teeth and kept going. I had thought about that, but I couldn't come up with a single answer.

From what I had gleaned, angels were tortured in the arena, choosing to kill for pleasure and anger rather than defence or the protection of others. No one in The City had ever mentioned a mocking apparition in the mind, taunting their every decision.

At first, I was terrified that she was a parasite I had unknowingly picked up in Hell. Perhaps a creature that had latched on, worming its way into my head before I could detect her. But after I was tortured in Hell, Lucifer said there wasn't any darkness within me. Surely he would have sensed it?

Unless... he had lied.

But then the healing mandala in his chambers should have destroyed any demon still inside me. So my darker self must be a product of something else.

"Why do you think he wants to kill you?" she called out behind me.

I froze in the darkness.

I shook my head and told myself to keep going, that she was baiting me. But my body slowly turned back to face her, compelled by those words like it was a string tied to the hidden nooks in my heart.

I had been so close to surrendering to the desire that burned between Lucifer and I, moments from letting down a wall between us, which could never be constructed again. Then his darker desires had chilled me down to my core, shattering the fantasy I had woven between past and present.

There was nothing like having your Flame wanting to murder you to make you pull back from the edge of a cliff you were about to jump off.

And by the spirits, I desperately wanted to know why.

My darker self was still standing where I had left her. At my attention she gave me a knowing, pleased smile.

"Why?" It came out harsh, like a strip of gravel road.

She drew it out, building the tension like she was an actress in a theatre, delivering the final line of a play. "It's the soul link. You're making him lighter, just as he is making you darker. Where did you think that energy would go when it flows between you? The stronger the link becomes the stronger the energy and the faster the transformation."

"Wh...wh..." the words stuck in my throat. Stunned, I stared back at her.

Was she right? Was I becoming darker because of him? It was his energy flowing through me, his darkness slowly corrupting my soul. It didn't feel that way, but then again, slow transformations never did. I had attributed my change in emotions as a result of me being in the lower realms, but what if it was something more?

Fear spiked as I looked into her face, seeing what kind of creature I could become. I couldn't do that. I couldn't be that. To change so much that hurting those around me became a joy to be pursued repulsed me on the deepest level.

She couldn't be right. Could she? And if she was right, that also meant...

"Are you saying he is becoming a light angel again? What he once was?" I asked thickly, hope flaring wildly like a sudden fire lit in a land of drought.

If his darkness was infecting me, then my Light would be affecting him.

Her smile grew. She tilted her head slightly. "You would like that, wouldn't you? To have him back again the way he once was, loving you the way he once did." She breathed in as if she was smelling something sweet. "How badly it must hurt looking into his dark eyes and wishing with every fibre of your being that they were blue."

"You didn't answer my question."

My darker self shrugged. "You are in Hell, so I don't believe that's possible. You can't retain a high vibration in Hell, but you are changing him." She looked at my face. "Oh darling... does that make you sad? Why would he even want to be Light? You make him weak in a place he needs to be strong. Not just strong," she corrected, "stronger than everything and everyone else. That's why he wants to kill you."

My eyes widened. As much as I didn't want to believe it, it made sense. A sadistic, awful kind of sense.

She took a step closer. "That's why you need my help. You're running out of time. The longer you stay here, Lucifer will kill you. He may not want to, but he will need to in order to survive. I also have a vested interest in surviving. You want to free the warrior angels?" Her eyes glittered like the ocean under the moon at night. "I can lend you my power to dismantle the cages." She let the promise flow sweetly from her lips. "All you have to do is ask."

I was reeling, processing too much for my mind to respond quickly. "I... I..."

"Think on it. I can help you achieve your goals faster. Help you save all those innocent angels before they get turned. Every second you waste is an angel getting closer and closer to giving into the dark. You are their only chance

to return back to The City before it's too late." She smiled wickedly. "Sure, you will have to resist the temptation to draw deeper upon the power I offer. I'm not going to lie. But you seem so certain that you won't become me, so it's a risk worth taking, isn't it?"

I didn't answer her.

My mind flickered to the portal to Kryptos, my way out of this realm, back to the safety of The City of Light. But even as the temptation rose swiftly in me, I knew I couldn't do it. I couldn't really die here. My Fallen self was using human terms to be dramatic, but I could keep reforming weaker and weaker until maybe my Light would be too insignificant to be a threat.

If that happened I would be of no use to anybody.

"Like I said," she said softly, "think on it."

The scene to my right was still frozen. Lucifer had emerged from the shadows, facing Ezriel with the Hell Hounds sitting down like puppies waiting for a treat. I was crumpled on the ground, covered in blood. I wasn't a fighter, but I had still managed to survive.

Would that be enough in the coming nights?

I didn't know, and too much was at stake to leave it like that.

The dream faded and I slept.

Restless.

Chapter 15

Diager moved cautiously through the Underworld tunnels. Spirits passed him, moving aimlessly along the rocky floor. Those who ventured too close to his aura flinched away as if sensing the darkness living within him. Usually their fear of him would be warranted, but fortunately for them, he had other things focusing his attention.

Eventually, these souls would be called to judgement and processing. He understood it to be a long and arduous process designed specifically for the Gods to feel like they had some grandiose importance over the realm of men. Some souls would be granted entrance into the higher realms, uniting with friends and family until they chose once more to reincarnate. Others would be assigned to the lost realms, or purgatory until a guide helped them move forward.

Then there were a few that the demons took down to the below.

Diager didn't know what happened to those souls. And... he didn't care. The only souls the Fallen really took an interest in were the ones that were yet to embrace the dark.

He waited before turning a corner, avoiding an upper demon that had escaped from Hell. Once the whiff of sulphur passed, he continued on, his feet gliding over the rocky terrain with casual ease.

It wasn't the demons he was avoiding, though he made sure he was out of their awareness just to be cautious. He didn't want some of the Fallen to mark his presence. There were factions within factions within their numbers, loyalties built from promises of glory and power. A translucent bond that could shift and dissolve without much effort.

It was better to keep his thoughts and plans close for now. There was only one he would share it with and she had as much to lose as he, and just as much to gain.

Diager slipped silently into a narrow opening in the wall, almost invisible by the way the large uneven rocks formed around the hole. Being one of the older Fallen, he had spent a significant amount of time in the Underworld, mapping out pathways in his head. He was aware that his knowledge was greatly inadequate to the true extent of the vastness of the Underworld, but he knew enough to feel confident within its dank confines.

The narrow tunnel branched outward for a while before splitting into two directions. He turned left and almost immediately found himself in a small confined space.

It was a perfect spot for an attack.

He watched a shadow detach itself from the back wall. Selaphiel's cat shaped eyes blinked impatiently back at him.

"You're late," she said.

It was also a perfect spot for a meeting no one should know about.

"I had to avoid a couple of our patrols," he said. "Sirus had a few marks on me, too, which I had to shake."

Selaphiel frowned. "You should have just stabbed them and claimed it was an accident." Her hand waved up dismissively. "That's what I did."

Diager's brows shot up. Selaphiel was always an inch away from violence at any given moment. He initially had his reservations about working with her, but despite her instinct to solve problems with physical solutions, she had a sharp mind and something even greater. Power.

"Don't look at me like that," she continued. "Sirus is already suspicious that we are plotting something or other without her. If we don't hit back, it will make her even more paranoid. At least now she just *thinks* we are plotting. If I did nothing about the eyes following me, then she would *know* we were plotting."

"I sometimes wonder at your logic."

She bared her teeth. "Subtle is your thing, not mine. We better not dawdle. Tell me your plan. We need to do something or things are going to escalate."

Diager moved to the side of the wall and leaned against it. He was equidistant between the exist and

Selaphiel. He wasn't paranoid, but some habits were ingrained too deep. "They are already escalating. Lucifer now treats an angel as an equal in front of us all. He goes too far and I can't understand why." The Lord of Hell was not known to be reckless, in fact he was everything *but* reckless. "Surely he knows how perilously close he is to sparking a rebellion."

"Perhaps he believes we wouldn't dare." Selaphiel frowned darkly. "Sirus is a perfect example. She is too much of a coward to make any decisions on her own. It makes me wonder though, and questioning this is an act of insanity in itself but... Lucifer's actions aren't those of the dark." She held his gaze firmly, as if the strength of her eye contact would outweigh the innate wrongness her words invoked. "We always knew he was different than us, and most of us have assumed that meant a deeper relationship with the darkness. But is it really?"

Dangerous thoughts, dangerous questions. "Look at his power," he replied. "He commands the darkness like no other. He is stronger than any one of us. It doesn't seem plausible that the darkness would favour one not in alignment. But... you are also right." He admitted. "His actions are contradictory."

"It's that angel," Selaphiel hissed, anger elongating the muscles in her face. "It all started with that angel. What is it about her?"

Diager hesitated. "It seems like he *cares* for her." The sentiment left an unfamiliar, foul taste in his mouth.

Immediately, she scoffed. "Impossible."

"Don't dismiss the idea because the thought of it is obscene. You see the way he acts," he pointed out. "You tell me. She is a Light angel. An enemy. One that needs to be eliminated before she becomes too much of a threat and yet he does nothing. But you are wrong about one thing, it started before the angel's appearance. We have lost our focus, our purpose for being."

Selaphiel threw her hand up dismissively, then stalked to the wall opposite him, leaning her toned form against the rock. "We waste time debating things we don't have an answer for. I agree, the issue is not just her, it's a lack of leadership. We aren't doing anything proactive. We are all wasted weapons, collecting dust in the back of a closet. Ezriel was right. He was always right, just impulsive. The most exciting part of our day shouldn't be babysitting demons. So, Diager, tell me your plan. I hope I won't be disappointed."

"This goes no further than you and I for now," he cautioned.

"I find it insulting that you would even ask," she drawled out.

"That means Tiyana." He knew about her relationship with the other Fallen and didn't want Selaphiel to utilise the other Fallen in any subsequent plans before it was time.

Selaphiel raised her brows. There was a slight beat of silence. "Fine."

Diager nodded. He had been waiting to say this next part for a long time. He took a breath, "Were you aware that there is a ninth level of Hell?"

The silence stretched like thin wires beneath quivering flesh. Selphiel's eyes burned. "What?" she snapped. The top of her body leaned forward towards him. "What did you say?"

"You heard what I said."

"What do you mean there is a ninth level? I wasn't aware there was an eighth level, Diager," she hissed.

Diager absorbed her disbelief and anger. He didn't allow the small smile of satisfaction to creep onto his face. He knew she was wondering how he knew something this significant and she didn't. It would shake the foundation of superiority she had built all these years.

He nodded. "Ezriel told me once, while we were on Earth. Being one of the First, he was here when Hell was still… settling in its new form. I'll get to the eight level later, that's not as important. The ninth level is the one we need to focus on. We haven't been told about it for a reason. Most of us have assumed that the demons in the seventh level were the darkest of all the levels and that there was nothing below." He shook his head. He was still coming to terms with the information himself and the implications. "But there is."

Her eyes glowed, anger warring with fascination. "Why has it been kept a secret? What's down there?"

The leather on his arms creaked as he crossed them. "Ezriel wasn't a hundred percent certain, but he strongly suspects it's where Lucifer keeps the strongest of them."

Her lips pursed in a thin line. "More demons?"

"Not just any demons. The seven."

Selaphiel froze, and for a moment there was only the low moan of the Underworld winds in the background.

"The seven," she said slowly. "As in the seven deadly sins?" At his expression of affirmation she whistled slowly. "I wasn't sure they existed."

"They do," he said quietly. "And Lucifer has been keeping them locked up in the ninth level all this time, in small isolation cells."

Her lips parted. "So what? I sincerely hope your plan is not to release them and hope they kill Lucifer."

Diager snorted. "No. I'm not an idiot. Assuming Ezriel was correct, there would be no way we could control them. They'd turn on us just after they turned on him. No, it's the cells themselves I'm interested in. If they are strong enough to contain each and every one of the seven then they would be strong enough to contain *him*."

Her eyes widened fractionally in the dark.

"They are the strongest barriers. Practically impossible to open. Which is why the seven haven't been seen or heard from. They are almost a myth. And there are rumours there had been more than seven cells built. Several just open and waiting for occupants." He let the implications rest heavily between them.

She frowned. "You are basing too much of this plan on rumours, Diager. What proof do we have that this all exists? It's too risky and," she paused, "very unlike you."

He smiled charmingly at her. "That's because I haven't yet told you the way to validate Ezriel's claim."

"Go on," she said impatiently. "We are on a time limit here."

His smile sharpened at the edges. "The demon, Selaphiel. The demon that follows Lucifer everywhere. He has access to the below, and he is our key to getting in there."

***

I woke up with a headache.

The pounding in my skull was a sign of the building stress my body was just barely containing. I rubbed my forehead wearily and hauled myself out of the bed, feeling as if I hadn't rested at all. My darker self was still lingering in my consciousness, like a stain on a valuable piece of cloth you just couldn't wash off. She was lying dormant for now, but I knew that at any time she could unfurl, rest a finger lightly on my shoulder, lean in and whisper in my ear.

It put me on edge.

The dream I had and the information that spilled from her lips like droplets of the sweetest poison made me want to run straight through the portal mirror to the safety of the realm above.

Here were the facts I was dealing with.

Lucifer wanted to kill me. But it was because I was changing him away from his dark self. Yet that meant he was also changing *me*, corrupting me towards the dark. If he succeeded in destroying my form I would become weaker and weaker and my mission to save the warrior angels would fail anyway.

Not ideal.

I could leave... but then the warrior angels would be lost. Also not ideal.

I could help them escape by leaning on my darker self, but that could also mean I could lead myself further into darkness. Terrifying.

If I didn't use my darker self, then I could potentially run out of time and Lucifer would kill me. Again, terrifying.

I was surrounded by enemies inside and out, and I couldn't see a clear path to win this battle. I walked over to the chest at the end of the room. With a click I opened the wooden lid and reached down to hold a crystal in my hand.

After a few moments it glowed brightly, radiating outwards. I placed it down next to me, and picked up another. I still had a debt to pay, and more than that, if this was what it took for the barriers to still stand then I would gladly pay it.

How close was Lucifer to running out of Light? The City of Light really didn't know how close to destruction the Earth really was. And that was the issue, the warrior angels would love the opportunity to battle Lucifer, but ironically they didn't realise he was the only barrier holding back the infinite tide of darkness.

It meant that I couldn't leave. Where would he get Light from if I went back? I would be essentially condemning the world to a plague of demons. It also meant that it was in his best interest to keep me Light.

I hesitated, one hand holding an empty crystal. I needed to tell him about my darker self.

We needed to talk.

After a couple of hours I felt calmer, the monotonous task giving me some time to think through my next steps.

I left my room and ducked quickly into the pool room, grateful to see Atlas's discarded clothes still carelessly thrown on the edge. I contemplated washing it, but decided its current state was adequate for the task ahead. I pulled off my pants and let my armour stream back into the bands around my arms.

It had been really uncomfortable to sleep with metal encasing my chest, but apparently my body hadn't cared that much. Quickly, albeit reluctantly, I slid into Atlas's tunic. The sharp scent of sweat and musky male enveloped me as the hem fell just below my knees.

The neckline threatened to fall off my shoulders, so I ripped the edge of the tunic around the hem and tied the long length around my waist like a belt. I pulled the neckline up and down tight at the back, securing it in place. I ripped a smaller piece of cloth and loosely plaited my hair, securing it at the bottom.

Peering over into the water's edge I studied myself critically, turning my face from side to side. I still looked too clean, too fresh. Maybe I needed to find some dirt and rub it on my face? I looked around at the pristine bathing room.

This would have to do for now.

I left the bathing room and decided to visit Atlas. It would be nice if I checked in on him after the Dragarth encounter. He seemed calmer after I left him earlier, but then again I would imagine it would be hard to sleep knowing a three-headed serpent might be eyeing you through the walls deciding when to eat you.

I merged through and the sound of his deep, reverberating snores under the bed sheets had me grinning. Clearly sleep had not eluded him. I admired people like that. The whole world could be collapsing around them and they still managed to shut off and rest like a baby. Perhaps I should wake him? I should really discuss my next steps with him, after all. What I was going to do would be reckless without a thorough plan.

And yet. I didn't. I knew what he would ask me. What was I going to say to the dark witches? What could I offer? What was my alternative plan if everything went to pieces and I was attacked, or worse, given to the Fallen?

And the truth was… I had no idea.

I had never even seen a dark witch before the Fallen domain. They were the mistresses of chaos, seeking the destruction of others in their pursuit of power and pleasure. All I knew was that they willingly contaminated the energy of their own souls for the gift of a longer life.

In a way, they feared the indiscriminate embrace of death, which hovered always at the edge of their shadows. They would have no control or command in the afterlife, and would finally face the consequences of their actions. So they bargained with demons and other dark entities, not only for power but for the hope of eternal life.

So no, I had no idea what I could offer the witches. As for the fact that things could go horribly wrong, well, I was already half drowning in that murky swamp anyway.

I left Atlas's room and headed to another that I really didn't want to be in.

I pressed my palms against the wooden surface of Lucifer's bedroom doors. My heartbeat accelerated and after a couple of seconds I managed to find the courage to push them open. His scent wafted beguilingly over me and my lungs breathed in deep, like an addict getting a hit of what they craved after so long. He wasn't in the room, but I intuited he had recently been here.

Had I wanted him to be standing here when I opened those doors?

Yes. No.

We needed to talk, but that conversation could be held later.

I glanced at the portal mirrors on the left side of the room. One to the dungeons and the other to Kryptos. Then my gaze was drawn magnetically to the bed. The black silken sheets were smooth and untouched, the pillows without a crease. My feet wandered over before I made the conscious thought. My mind flashed back to that kiss we shared, unfettered with desire. I had felt my resistance crumble into ashes against the fire of feelings between us.

He was another angel now. No longer was he soft and gentle, loving and warm. Oh yes, the longing had still been the same, but it was a slow burn that pleasantly consumed me until I was boneless.

My fingertips brushed the cool sheets and I closed my eyes briefly, letting myself indulge in the memory of feeling his skin under my fingertip, his lips sliding down my neck as I lay beneath him.

Now he was like a living flame covered by a thin layer of skin, all consuming and careless with the devastation he wrought with his touch. He didn't care to be gentle, no, I knew once that control finally snapped he would...

I shivered.

My fingertips left the bed just as I felt an awareness through the link. As if sensing the unbidden desire I felt, dark eyes snapped their attention on me.

I jerked back, stumbling away from the bed. Somehow, he knew what I was feeling.

The awareness increased, like a great beast raising its head from slumber, sensing movement in its domain. It stretched languidly and came lazily to its feet.

And just like that, I knew he knew exactly where I was.

Was desire like waving a raw cut of meat in front of a lion's face? I didn't know. My eyes darted around the room and fell on the mirror behind me.

The sorry truth was I didn't think I had it in me anymore to resist. Giving in to the extent that I did before had changed something for me. It was like I knew too much now. Felt too much, and I couldn't unfeel it again no matter how much I tried to push it into the deep recess of my mind. And it didn't matter if he wanted to kill me. There was only so much I could resist. If he kissed me one more time I wasn't convinced that I had the will to pull away.

I stood frozen and then, after a second, shook my head. "What are you doing, Sandriel?" I whispered to myself. "Move."

With haste, I turned and almost ran through the mirror.

It was time to meet the dark witches. Come what may.

Chapter 16

My eyes adjusted to the darkness slowly until I could see the outlines of the cages before me. My breathing was abnormally loud in my ears, blocking out my capacity to hear anything else.

A sliver of fear shot through me as I came to terms that I was truly alone. I wasn't accompanied by Lucifer or even Atlas. If the Fallen found me now, I would pay dearly for being placed above them in the hierarchy of Hell.

The dark energy of the cages surrounded me. It was like a seething animal waiting to inflict pain. It strained on an invisible leash, eager to destroy. Mingled at its feet, shivering and raw, was despair. I knew where that came from. About a hundred angels were spread out before me, locked in their own private cells, hope slowly draining from their bodies as the night rolled into one continuous, endless wave.

There was a prison a few metres in front of me, and I couldn't help but wonder who was inside.

I looked around, straining my senses, trying to perceive if there was anyone nearby. Minutes ticked by, and the silence around me was unchanged. I focused my attention back on the cage and walked cautiously towards it, feeling the energy thicken at my approach, almost as if the darkness was gathering itself.

I stopped a short distance away, then put my hands in a prayer position.

I slowly spread my hands apart. The Light gathered between my palms, condensing into a solid, pure beam. I held it, about shoulder-width wide, and let it intensify in brightness. My hands trembled as the pressure built between them, trying to burst free. With nerves battering its wings in the hollow of my stomach, I turned my hands sharply outwards.

Light blasted at the centre of the cage. It streamed out in a blazing flash and hit the darkness.

The darkness caved inwards like a vortex, swirling inwards, its tendrils flying around in a frenzy. Then a hole stripped painfully away in the centre, widening slowly. I kept the stream steady, widening the light outwards to force the darkness back. As I pierced through the cage wall, all I could see was inky black. It was only as the hole got wider that I noticed a figure lying prone on the ground.

"Hello!" I hissed. "Can you hear me?" I whispered desperately. The darkness struggled against my Light, fighting against my hold. My stream of energy started to waver. "Hello? Please, can you hear me? I'm here to help you!"

The shape on the floor stirred. I moved closer, sweat beading on my brow, my breath coming out in pants.

Good try, my darker self whispered patronisingly. *But you aren't going to be able to hold that open for much longer.*

"Please," I said, ignoring her. My voice was strained. "You need to come out quickly! I can't keep your cage open!" The brightness of my Light radiated out around me. I grew increasingly worried that I was attracting attention, all but screaming my location. It didn't matter that I was somewhere towards the back of the dungeon. The Fallen could be anywhere, pulling warriors in and out of cells.

I looked at the cell opening and muttered to myself. "I'm going to do something stupid now, aren't I?" I shook my head. "Sorry, Atlas." Without giving myself too much time to think about the consequences, I leapt through the opening I had created.

My stream of Light winked out, and the jaws of the cage snapped shut behind me. I stumbled over the angel still stirring on the ground, barely missed stepping on them, and fell awkwardly to my knees.

I was in a god-forsaken cell.

Immediately, the darkness pressed against me, its negativity feeding gleefully off my energy, its presence weighing me down. But there was something else. I could also feel an external energy flow linking to the cage. It was like an open channel, seeking a connection. I knew if I extended my senses to it, I could possibly...

"Who are you?" a voice rasped out.

I glanced over my shoulder at the huddled shape on the ground. Turning carefully around so I could face the warrior angel, I called a small globe of Light into the palm of my hand. Two things happened at once. The angel, a dark-haired male, widened his dull, dove-grey eyes in shock, and the cage whipped a long, angry tendril at me.

I slammed up a shield just in time.

It hit my Light shield and flinched back. More tendrils whipped out, reeling back to strike me. I let the shield glow brighter, and it writhed away. The cage hummed angrily but didn't make another move to strike.

While I was holding Light, I couldn't feel it syphoning off my energy, but I knew once my Light ran out that would be a different story. It would wait until I was weak, then feed off me, making me weaker and weaker so I'd be unable to summon a drop of brightness to defend myself.

"You're a Light angel..." the warrior angel breathed, a spark of life flickering behind his eyes. He pushed himself up onto a bony arm. My lips turned down at the sight of his frail body, covered in dirty scraps of clothing. His muscles were wasted away, unable to reform. The Light of my shield illuminated his face, revealing numerous scars and welts that layered over his skin. Most of them were old. He hadn't been in the arena recently.

Despite his beaten appearance, he was still an angel of The City, and his inherent beauty shone through the grime like a pearl tossed in the corner of a city's dirty streets.

"Are you a dream?" he croaked. He looked terrified, as if I was some sort of new torture sent to him from the Fallen.

Shaking my head, I said, "No. See…" I let the front part of my shield dissolve and reached out my hand towards him. "I'm real."

His hand lifted off the ground. It was unsteady, the fingers trembling as if he was half convinced something bad would happen as soon as he made contact with my skin. When I felt the soft brush of his fingertips against mine, his whole body sagged. He grasped my hand, twining my fingers with his own, and trembled.

"They do that sometimes. They send illusions to make us believe that we are finally being saved. Did The City finally send a team down? Have we defeated Lucifer?" The hope in his reedy voice was painful to behold.

I swallowed. "I… no, The City didn't send a team. Just me." Pulling my gaze away from his, I looked down. "I'm trying to find a way to get you all out of here, but it may take me a little more time."

There was laughter in the back of my mind, full of dark, feminine amusement.

I heard him move, and I glanced back up to see him sitting up, leaning towards the glow of my shield as if it was a campfire in a barren, lifeless land. He squeezed my hand. "Can you get me out? Both of us? Now? Can we go home? Please…" his grey eyes hollowed. "I can't stay here anymore. I can't… I don't think I can… much longer."

Oh, Heavens. I didn't think this through. "I could," the words were hard to get out, "I could get you out of the cage, but I can't get us out of the dungeons. Not yet."

He looked shattered. My heart clenched. Tears gathered behind my eyes. How do you walk out of an angel's prison, knowing you are leaving them there to suffer alone?

"What's your name?" I whispered.

"Isolain..." He brought his knees up to his chest.

"Isolain, do you have any idea how long you've been down here?"

He shook his head. "It feels like forever, but it could be several years... a bit more?"

I knew time moved differently in Hell while the rest of the realms resumed a different pace. Years could fly past in darkness while only days flittered by in the worlds above. I couldn't remember him from The City, but then again, I didn't interact with the warrior angels often.

"I think I'm turning," he confessed brokenly. "I'm failing," the tears slipped down his face as he regarded me with a pain so deep it was almost bottomless. "I'm failing The City, who I am, what I am. I don't *care* anymore. I just want it to end."

The warrior angel, who was once a pillar of strength, a representation of compassion, resilience, love, and righteousness, put his head down on his knees and cried.

"Hey… shhhh… hey…" I went up on my knees and put my other hand on his arm. His dark hair brushed my arm, the silky threads matted. I didn't know what to say, so I did the only thing I thought would ease his suffering. Closing my eyes, I let my senses merge with his energy.

I felt his wounds and bruises, which were barely healed, but more deeply than that, I could feel his intense emotional pain. I wove white energy threads in my mind with healing green. It was a clumsy attempt, lacking the sophistication of a true healer. But it would do.

I channelled the cords of energy into his body, directing the flow with my intention to the places that needed it the most. Isolain gasped softly.

After a few minutes, the tension in his body relaxed. I closed most of his physical wounds, healing old scars that hindered movement and speed, but the worst wounds were beyond my meagre skill. Isolain's aura was darkened.

Streaks of grey and black tones marred the usually soft, bright colours of a healthy energy body. Parts of his aura had also been removed as if an animal had taken big bites out of it, tasting the different colourful flavours.

It appeared Isolain had been under a constant, psychic attack.

Something clicked in the back of my mind.

Raising my eyes to the cage ceiling, I cautiously felt for the energy conduct I knew was there. Steeling myself, I energetically connected with the channel.

I wasn't prepared.

The weight of pain fell on top of me, sizzling over my nerve endings and skin, pulsating in my mind making it impossible to think. I let out a strangled sob and shut it off.

My wide eyes met grey ones.

"The worse thing is that it's a choice, you see," his voice was flat and drained of emotion. "They let you choose to take the pain for as long as you can bear it."

"Why would they do that?" I whispered.

"Because if you don't, another angel would have to take your share. It spreads the suffering around, allowing those who have been recently tortured to have some respite." He laughed humorlessly. "But you can't sleep; you can't ever recover. You just have to keep enduring, knowing if you stop, you are failing someone else."

I noted that the channel wasn't in use when I entered the cage. "What if everyone stops all at once?"

Isolain laughed humorlessly. "I've thought about that, but there is no way of coordinating such a thing to find out. If everyone doesn't stop at the same time, there will be those that will be impacted, carrying the weight alone. You don't want to know the level of pain it would be for them." He closed his eyes.

"When you first arrive, you can take it for a while, the sharing of it. It fluctuates with intensity as angels drop off and pick it up again. You have to put yourself in a meditative state and just bear it as best you can," he whispered.

"Then after they send you to the arena, time and time again, or to Hell… it gets harder. The time between getting back into your cell and picking up the pain becomes longer. You just want to sleep. You think, one more minute. One more minute, and then I'll do it. And then you lose yourself… you lose…" His voice was riddled with shame.

"I'm sorry." The words were inadequate, but I said them anyway. "I'm so sorry." I had no idea. I thought the arena itself was the worst of it. But this. What chance did they have? We both didn't say anything for a while. The silence was thick with guilt and fear and a weariness of a warrior who foresaw his end.

"Isolain," I said. "Look at me." He opened his eyes once more. "You need to hold on for a bit longer. I *promise* you I'm going to do everything I can to get you out of here. I'm going to try and free you all. I know it sounds impossible. I know. But I have been sent here for a reason. Archangel Michael sent me." At the sound of Mikail's name, his face became more alert, like a shadow of his former self. "It's not over yet, not while I'm here. I need you to be strong for a little while longer. Please. I'll find a way. I promise."

I could free them all now, came the sly whisper. *Look at how much pain he is in. Look at how he suffers. Just say the word, and you could have an army of a hundred angels by your side.*

I gritted my teeth. It was getting harder to ignore her. Seeing Isolain's torture was enough to make me tempted, but I wasn't at the point yet to give in to my darker self's wishes. There were still pieces I needed to put in place. Avenues I hadn't explored. She wasn't my only option... yet.

"I have to go," I said.

He reflexively gripped my hand tighter.

"I *will* come back for you," I reassured him.

Reluctantly he let go of my hand. "What is your name?" he asked quickly as I moved away from him to face the way I had entered.

"Sandriel." Turning my head back, I gave him a soft smile.

"Sandriel," he repeated to himself like it was the thinnest of hopes. It probably was. "I will wait for you."

I nodded back. The pressure to succeed was even higher now.

I couldn't fail them. I just couldn't.

Channelling my Light into my hand once more, I blasted a hole into the cage. The darkness fought me, straining to reclaim its prize, but I managed to hold it back once more, giving myself enough time to jump out to the other side.

Tumbling onto the floor, I turned to see the cage shut behind me, cutting Isolain from the outside. I trembled from the drain of energy. I couldn't imagine opening ninety nine other cages just like that. There had to be another way.

There is.

"Without you," I muttered.

And if there is not? Even you need to prepare for that very likely event,

My lips formed a grim line. *We will see,* I thought.

I stood up, fixed Atlas's tunic, which had scrunched up slightly above my belt, and looked up to lock eyes with two women who stood across from me.

One was older, weathered with grey hair and hard, cold eyes. The other was younger but hunched slightly like she had hurt her back. They had both watched me leave the cage, blazing with Light.

Ah, perfect. Witches.

Chapter 17

The witches stared at me. I stared back.

Even though they were slaves, their powers suppressed by punishment, their resources limited, and their spirits stripped to the bone, they were still dangerous, and I would treat them as such. The older witch held herself with natural authority. I knew in the coven hierarchy, seniority wasn't attributed to age but power. A younger witch with more potential would rise through the ranks much quicker than someone twice her age.

"Should I go tell them?" the younger witch murmured. She was attractive, tones of brown set in olive skin, which made me wonder if the hunch was a permanent thing that kept her here instead of the Fallen's domain across the sea of lava.

The Fallen didn't seem to like their pleasure slaves flawed.

The older woman held up her hand. Her companion hissed, "It's not worth getting in trouble for."

"I've been looking for you," I ventured hastily, not wanting to give the other woman time to change her mind and potentially alert the dark angels. "I saw some of you last time I was here, and I've been waiting for an opportunity to meet with you... in private."

They continued to stare at me, though the younger witch couldn't hold back her contemptuous expression. I tried not to reveal how nervous I was. My ears strained, trying to listen to the sound of anyone approaching. Though if the Fallen had any awareness of something going on, I wouldn't see them coming until they were right in front of me. The thought didn't make me feel any better.

"Can you take me to someone in charge?" I asked.

"Why?" the older witch asked flatly. "What do you want?"

Biting my lip, I thought quickly. "I need your help, and I think I can help you in return."

"If you can break out of an angel prison, why would you need our help?" The steel in the elder witch's voice had me tensing. She was thin and boney and looked like a strict governess that would whip you if you showed any disrespect.

"Why would we trust you?" the younger witch's lip curled. I saw her hand slip inside one of the pockets of her ragged, brown robe.

My hand lit up with a soft, white glow. "You know I'm not one of them." I let the Light wind like a coil over my wrist. "I have different gifts than the others. You have knowledge I need, and as you can see," I gestured to the cell I had come out from, "I can break out of prisons." I looked the older witch in the eye to make sure my meaning was clear.

"You're working with the Fallen," the younger witch accused. Even though she was clearly not in charge, the elder witch let her speak. Her head turned. "Dominique saw her the other night with… the *Forsaken*."

My brow creased. By the tone of abject fear, she must mean Lucifer. Oh yes, I could see how that would look bad. I sighed inwardly. Clearly, wearing Atlas's clothes hadn't camouflaged me as well as I had hoped.

"I can explain," I said, hands out in a placating gesture. I thought quickly, my mind racing through information that wouldn't get me killed. "Lucifer abducted me from Kryptos and brought me to Hell. I'm not a warrior angel, but I have an ability he needs. Light. That's why he hasn't turned me."

The younger witch scowled. "Don't lie. If he needs you so badly, why are you here? I see what the Fallen do with their prisoners. The Forsaken wouldn't let you come here unless he wants you to."

I took a step towards them and stopped as they tensed. "You're right," I agreed. They both exchanged glances. "He has allowed me to come here, but as a test. I've never used my abilities before in The City, it's not the type of gift that's whetted with light, but with things of the dark. He has given me access to the dungeons to see if I can use my gifts and break the warrior angels out without getting caught by the Fallen."

"I don't believe you," the younger witch snarled softly. "There is no way the Forsaken would let these angels be freed. They are recruits for their goddamn army! You are a fool or a liar." She looked me up and down with contempt. Her eyes narrowed. "You seemed awfully friendly above ground. Doesn't seem like someone who doesn't want to be here."

"I do want to be here!" I snapped back, feeling like this opportunity was eroding fast, "I have a chance to free my family no matter how slim. I would do anything I could to help them escape, no matter the cost! I can't bear their suffering. If I have even a sliver of a chance of freeing them, then I have to take it. Surely you can understand that. Wouldn't you do that for your people?"

The older witch was unreadable, but the younger just clenched her jaw.

"And as for the rest of it," I flushed. "Would you say no to the Forsaken if he touched you? Would you say no to anything he asked if you were his prisoner?"

My darker self laughed liltingly. *Oh, what lies.*

The younger witch paused and looked quickly over her shoulder. We all froze.

There was a tense moment of silence before she turned back and whispered. "Even if you are who you say you are, what's stopping me from turning you in to the Fallen? We have no love for you, angel," she said, her voice dripping with venom and hate. "The dark and light versions of yourself. Both have caused my people pain. If I could blight you all from existence, I would."

I took a deep, steadying breath. Her outrage was ironic. The number of innocent lives the witches had extinguished for their pursuit of power reached horrifying numbers. Plagues, demons, wars... so much pain was attributed to their action, but when karma, the law of cause and effect, brought that pain back to them... they acted the victim.

"You might hate me and despise my kind, but I'm the only hope you have to escape this place. I have access to areas you don't. I have abilities you don't. I have leverage, you don't." I stared at the two women. "I could be your one shot in a thousand years. Do you really want to throw that away?"

They glanced at each other again.

"Do it," the older witch said softly but sharply, her eyes never leaving my face.

The younger witch took her hand from her pocket. White stones flung in my direction. Instinctively I put up a light shield in front of my body and braced myself for the impact. As the stones neared closer, they exploded into powder, which glittered against my Light.

It went through my shield and hit me in the face.

I coughed and shook my head sharply as the fine powder settled over my hair, face, and clothing. It shimmered and then disappeared from my skin. I cursed inwardly, quickly monitored my body, ready to heal any afflictions that could suddenly surface. My only adversaries this far had been creatures born or infected with darkness. My Light was an effective weapon against its powerful opposite, but magic of a neutral nature or ordinary objects like a knife could pass through my defences as if they were mist.

A stupid thing to only realise now. Atlas would be furious.

My heart tripled in speed as I frantically waited for the spell to take effect. I looked back at the portal mirror. It was only a few metres away. I could head back and heal myself. Angels had a natural immunity to certain magics, their energy being too high a vibration to be negatively impacted. But we were in Hell. Holding a high vibration here was like walking with a cup of water across a desert and still expecting it to be full on the other side.

When nothing initially happened, I put down my shield and glared at them. "What... was... that?"

The elder witch frowned at me, making no more moves to approach. "Show me your wings."

Anger at myself and the witches burned bright, but I also understood this was a test of some sort. I undid my belt and turned my back. Looking at the witches over my shoulder, I pulled up the hem of Atlas's tunic. My wings unfolded out, white as snow settling on a mountain. Pulling them back in, I released the hem of the tunic and turned back around, and waited.

The older woman pursed her lips almost as if she was displeased with what she had discovered. "Humph. Follow me," she said briskly. To the younger witch, she ordered, "Get someone to replace me. We've already lost time."

"You're taking her in?" her face went slack with surprise, and her eyes darted back to me.

"Marella will sort her out," came the crisp reply. "Now go."

The younger witch scurried off, picking some buckets up ahead before disappearing into the darkness. Even though the older witch looked gaunt and weathered, she moved fast. Weaving through the cages with confidence, her spindly legs moved so rapidly that I had to hurry to keep up.

Witches, my darker self sneered. *They are like children playing dress-ups, pretending to be adults. That creature would have spent her whole life seeking one-tenth of the power we have. And when they finally obtain it, they have no idea how to use it properly.*

Not willing to engage in any further conversation, I powered ahead, tying my belt back around my waist and looking anxiously around. My darker self probably had the same opinion of me. Here I was with one of the most powerful abilities against the dark, and I was clumsily trying to figure out how to use it effectively. My darker self's ego was larger than mine, and I knew it frustrated her to watch me stumble up the learning curve.

We headed towards the door I had discovered last time.

I wondered if there were other, less obvious pathways into their living space. All this time that they had been confined here, they might have been able to slip a few things under the Fallen's watchful gaze. The elder witch opened the door with a firm tug on the worn brass knob. Despite its dilapidated appearance, it opened smoothly without a creak.

Turning towards me, she gestured for me to go inside with a short wave of her bony fingers.

I stared at the dark opening for a second, contemplating how many dark witches I would find inside. There was no choice about it. If I was to have any chance against the Fallen, I needed this alliance. I needed this alliance badly.

My inner thoughts were absent from my face, but the older witch watched me carefully. I suddenly intuited that behind her severe countenance and oak-coloured eyes, she viewed me with trepidation. She was just as unsure of me as I was of her. I suspected though that any fear she had was me being a Fallen in disguise, not an angel from The City of Light.

The smooth, solid floor of the dungeons gave way to small rocks compacted down. The air smelt damp and faintly of hearty cooking you would find in a common tavern. But unlike a tavern, I couldn't hear much. It was still cold, but not bitterly cold like it was beyond the door. Sounds were dull and faint, which made me think that this place where the witches lived was larger than I imagined.

I was in a small hollowed out passageway that opened up into a larger space ahead, lit with an orange glow. As I took a few steps in, a faint tingle of magic brushed my skin. The door clicked closed and I turned my head. The dark witch moved her chin up indicating for me to keep going.

I walked down the passageway and into the opening ahead. It was a small circular space, the passageway intersecting it in the middle. Deep, horizontal grooves were hollowed out all along the wall, three in a row. There were clothing set in them on one side, worn cloth, a mixture of different faded colours and shoes of various materials and styles. On the other side it looked like an assortment of cleaning equipment like brooms, buckets and mops.

A woman was bent over rummaging through the brooms, muttering to herself. Her faded blue dress was too short, as it stopped a couple of inches above her ankles, and engulfed her slender frame in large folds of fabric. Her dark blonde hair was knotted at the nape of her neck in a careless, hurried fashion, strands escaping and falling against a long, slim neck.

"Marella," the witch behind me said.

The woman stiffened, then glanced up. Her pale blue eyes looked in our direction but landed somewhere on my right shoulder. Straightening slowly, she reached next to her and grabbed her wooden cane.

"Agatha," her voice was sweet and gentle, "you're not supposed to be here." Turning her head, her eyes moved across to my other shoulder. "Who be that with you?"

I opened my mouth to speak, but the elder witch jumped in. "She claims she is an angel untouched and wishes to speak to us. She said she wants our assistance and will offer hers in return. Tia tested her. She wears no illusion, but believes she was the one with the Forsaken the other night in the battle circle. We saw her leaving a prison out of her own accord." Agatha paused. "She also came through the mirror."

My mouth closed and I blinked at the stream of information. The witches had used an illusion disruption spell, which was why I felt no ill effects. Isolain had also mentioned that the Fallen were fond of trickery as another form of torture. It appeared this was a common theme. I was concerned about the witches being aware of the portal.

If things didn't go well here, I was well aware I might not be returning to Lucifer's domain anytime soon.

The blonde witch raised her brows. "Hmm… that be interesting indeed."

Tired of being talked about, I asked, "Who is in charge here?"

Even though the witch was blind, her eyes seemed to lock straight on my face as soon as I spoke. "Myself and a few others, but you will gain no introduction to them until I can verify you for who you are."

"I thought that already happened, otherwise why would you bring me here?" I could hear the clanging of pots in the distance and the distant hum of voices.

Marella shuffled closer, the dark wood of her cane leading the way. "We only know you hide behind no spell, but as for what you say we can't be sure of the truth of it. If you want our help we need to confirm what you say is true."

I narrowed my eyes. "And... how exactly do I do that?"

"You could give me some blood–"

"No," I said, immediately on the defence. "I have some understanding of the value of blood to witches."

Blood was a key that could work the most deadliest spells against the person it belonged to. Everybody's blood was unique, carrying a special energy signature beholden only to them. You could tell much about a creature by analysing their blood, delving into their past and even piercing their future.

When Lucifer saw the Naballa in my past life and gave her his blood, she predicted the events ahead with devastating accuracy. If she had kept some of his blood she could have potentially used it against him.

Marella placed a finger against her lips. "Trust must be given both ways."

I spread my hands wide. "I'm here in your living quarters, by myself with the knowledge that you could alert the Fallen of my presence at any moment. I would say that qualifies as a significant amount of trust, don't you? My blood is not negotiable."

Her pale pink lips quirked up on one side, her soft tone honed to an edge. "You are correct, you are in our quarters now angel and you are vastly outnumbered. Asking is merely a formality. We could take it from you and there would be nothing you could do to stop us."

I was aware of how close Agatha was behind me. A silent threat not to be taken lightly.

I smiled and said conversationally, "You are welcome to try. I am not entirely without defences of my own." My smile fell from my lips and my tone carried an edge of its own. "And if the Fallen do take me and manage to turn me to the dark, I'll make a promise to you." I pointed at her even though she couldn't see me. "The first thing I will do is find you. And then I will spend a considerable amount of time making sure that your every kindness you have shown me tonight is repaid in *full*."

My darker self laughed.

Agatha took a sharp breath behind me. Marella stared at me in silence, then tilted her head, like a fencer acknowledging a point. "Hmm..." she said again. "Perhaps there be another way we could come to an agreement. Come," she said sharply. She turned around and walked out of the circular room, down the passageway.

I glanced at Agatha and she motioned with her hand for me to follow like I was an errant child. I followed the younger witch and the soft thud of her cane. The passageway extended further than I thought, down in a straight line with rooms on either side. Rusted lamps hung from the ceiling, casting a warm yellow glow against the dark rock walls.

Marella passed through another opening on either side of the passageway. This one was larger than the room where the clothes and cleaning equipment were stored. A quick glance showed a similar setup but with bedding in the grooves of the wall. Some were occupied by witches, only a small expanse of skin and hair visible from blankets pulled up high above their chin.

The blonde witch turned right up ahead, her steps confident as if her vision was restored. I turned to discover another sleeping area. At the sound of our approach, dishevelled heads rose and startled eyes blinked sleepily at me.

I noticed a couple were young. Children.

"Over here," came Marella's soft voice. She was in another room attached at the back.

"Go back to sleep now," Agatha scolded a child with a mop of curly brown hair. Even though her tone was stern it had a thread of fondness and exasperation that was universal.

"Whose dat?" came the childish whisper as I walked passed.

"Shh! Nothing for you to be concerned about," Agatha replied in a no nonsense voice. There was some more murmuring and a rustle of blankets.

Marella was standing on a faded red carpet in a room with similar groves and bedding in the wall, though not as many. This room was furnished. A chest of draws with several missing handles was against one side, used wax candles strewn on top. There were several cloaks hanging from hooks and two stools facing each other with a small wooden crate between them.

The blind witch moved off the fraying carpet, then bent down and flipped it over, revealing a trap door underneath. Agatha brushed past me and hauled the door open by curling her fingers into several grooves hollowed out in the wood.

She gestured for me to go down.

I eyed the dark hole below then smiled and said, "You first."

She scowled and opened her mouth to speak but Marella's voice intruded. "It's alright, Agatha. You go first. Our guest and myself will follow."

Agatha's lips flattened, but she obeyed the younger witch's command. She crouched to the ground and turned, extending her leg down into the darkness until it hit something solid. Climbing further down, she disappeared from view.

I followed into the darkness below, climbing down what appeared to be an old, uneven ladder.

As soon as my feet hit the floor I heard Agatha mutter something under her breath. The hairs on my arm stood up. An instant later the room lit up in a golden blaze. Lanterns hung from various sections of the rocky ceilings illuminating a surprisingly bare room. The air was musty and very dank as if we were near a body of water. There was a long table on one end with various sorts of copper bowls, candles and blades. Symbols were painted onto the wall, in what appeared to be old dried blood.

The sight made me instantly weary.

My eyes caught on a large white symbol painted on the floor. A five pointed star was drawn in the middle with the five points extending outside the circle touching the edges of a larger surrounding circle. and my trepidation rose.

I turned to face Agatha who was helping Marella down the stairs.

"I hope you are not going to ask me to get inside that thing," I said, pointing to the symbol on the ground.

"Don't be concerned," Marella said once both her feet touched the floor. "But yes, that's exactly what I intend for you to do."

"Why?"

Marella made a face as she dusted her hands from the grim they collected as she climbed down. Agatha walked briskly around me towards the table at the back.

"Because it's the only way we can verify your intentions without taking your blood. I give you my word that will be our only intention. To gain the truth."

Rustling behind me made me turn my head. Agatha gathered several white candles in her arms and was heading towards the symbol on the floor. She bent down and placed a candle at each point of the star.

I pulled my eyes away from her activities. "Why would I take your word? Dark witches are not known for their sense of honour."

"Oh, that's where you are wrong, angel. We very much take our word seriously. In fact, we stake our lives on our word." She smiled at me challengingly, her teeth even but slightly stained. "We summon demons, powerful ones that could singularly destroy cities in a night. If we don't keep our word, our end of our bargain, we die. Our loved ones die. Our coven dies. We know the power of your word once given. In addition, it's bad business. If we broke our word no one would trade with us."

This made sense to me, but at the same time I felt like this was the same as making a deal with Lucifer, but with someone who perhaps didn't have the best twisted intentions for me in mind. "If I enter that circle would I be able to leave when I please?"

Marella, steepled her hands together. "Of course."

"Say it," I said, narrowing my eyes.

She sighed as if I was wasting her time. "You will be able to leave the circle at any time."

"And what are you going to do when I enter the circle?" I asked.

"As I said before, to ascertain the truth. May I remind you that you came here seeking our help. We aren't the ones on trial." Her cane lifted to gesture back up the stairs. "If you don't wish to proceed, please leave. We aren't holding you here against your will."

"Yes," I agreed, glancing at Agatha who had finished ringing the circle with white candles and was now in the process of adding black ones at specific intersections. "But it's only a fool who would get into a circle constructed by dark witches without knowing the specifics." And I had been foolish enough for several lifetimes. "How are you planning to determine the truth from me?"

Marella's lips pursed in a thin line. I could see her anger building. "The candle flames will be gold if you speak the truth. If you tell a lie, they will turn blue."

"It is ready," Agatha said, her oak coloured eyes giving nothing away.

Filled with uncertainty I turned and walked towards the edge of the circle. Before I stepped over the white painted line I hesitated. "Will there be pain?" I asked. I saw Agatha still out of the corner of my eye and glance towards the blind witch.

"No," she said.

For some reason that felt like a lie. This could be a perfect trap. This could be a stupid, catastrophic mistake. This could send me in a world of trouble and pain.

But what other options did I have?

Atlas would call me a fool.

I stepped into the circle anyway.

Chapter 18

I stood in the centre of the circle with candles ringed around me on a five pointed star.

No angel in their right mind would put themselves under the control of darker beings. And yet, I was not only willingly allowing myself to be spelled by dark witches, but had also chosen to stay in Hell when I had a perfectly good opportunity to leave. I would think I was mentally unstable if it wasn't for the look in Isolain's eyes as I closed the jaws of his cage once more. I would be convinced I was under Lucifer's influence if I hadn't heard Rushton's desperate plea to save them all.

Agatha was chanting, soft ancient sounds spilling from her thin lips. Her eyes were distant, as if she was listening to a song just out of my hearing. Her hands were spread at her sides, palms down and fingers separated. The flames on the white candles flared brighter. Marella stood in front of me, hands clasped over her cane. Her eyes rested on the hollow of my neck where my pulse beat erratically. A strange smile curled over her lips.

A cold sweat formed on the back of my neck.

"Feeling comfortable?" Marella asked, the candlelight flickering like long lizard tongues against the contours of her face.

I gritted my teeth and pushed the swarming buzz of nerves down. I smiled with great difficulty. "Perfectly."

Her smile widened. "Let's start with something easy. What is your name?"

I waited a few seconds to see if I could feel a magic compulsion to speak, but there was nothing I could sense. "Sandriel," I replied cautiously.

The candles flared gold.

"Good," Marella said.

Agatha stopped chanting and walked over to stand beside her. She rested her hands on her hips and focused an eagle-like stare on me, as if she was perched on the branch of a tree preparing to swoop. They were both facing me now only metres away.

"Now, I'm going to ask you to lie, just to make sure the spell is working," Marella said soothingly as if she could sense my nerves. "What's your favourite fruit?"

Urgh. "Apples..." I said cautiously.

The white candles flared gold.

Marella frowned. "I said to lie."

I winced internally and wisely didn't mention that I thought I had. It also didn't escape my attention that she shouldn't be able to see the colour of the flames, yet she had known it hadn't turned blue.

"Pears."

The white candles turned an indigo blue. I glared at the change of colour as if it was somehow responsible for my dubious food choices.

Marella's smile returned. "Excellent. Let's move on, shall we? Who are you?"

I took a breath. "My name is Sandriel and I'm an angel from The City of Light."

The white candles shone gold.

"Have you turned Dark?"

"No."

The candles remained gold. Agatha's shoulders relaxed a fraction. I wondered if she had any fear of me now, knowing for certain that I wasn't a Fallen in disguise.

"How did you end up in Hell?"

"Lucifer abducted me."

Gold.

Marella's golden eyebrows shot up towards her hairline. "Do you mean personally? He came himself and not one of the other Fallen?"

"Yes." I felt like fidgeting so I crossed my arms over my chest instead.

"Why?" she fired back.

I had to be careful here. "He has never directly shared his reasons with me, but I suspect one of them is because I'm a Light angel."

Gold.

There was a squeak of the trapdoor above as someone walked over it. Marellla waited until the sound faded before she continued.

"Why would he need a Light angel?"

Because he needs my Light to reinforce the boundaries between the levels of Hell so the demons don't escape. It was an answer I was hesitant to give. Why? Maybe the witches would want the demons to be released. Maybe they wanted the Fallen to be so engaged with battling the horde that they could escape. Whatever their priorities were, it wasn't about protecting the humans on Earth. Somehow being aware that the barriers might fall if Lucifer didn't have my Light to stabilize them wasn't information I was very willing to share.

But I had to say something.

"My abilities counteract the Dark and I can assist Lucifer with certain activities in Hell."

Marellas tilted her head curiously. "Activities like what?"

I expected that question, so I had a ready response. "Lucifer doesn't tell me all his plans."

Gold.

"Have you assisted him yet with your Light in any... activities?"

I took a breath. "Yes."

"And they are?" she asked patiently.

"I've stored Light in crystals."

"Why?"

"Lucifer doesn't tell me all his plans," I repeated.

She looked suspicious. I tensed, praying I had got away with the answer. "Do you know why he needs your Light?"

Now was an appropriate time to use one of Atlas's curse words, but I refrained. "I know what he told me, I'm not certain if that's the true or only reason."

She honed in like a falcon after its prey. "And what reason did he give you, Sandriel?"

I took a breath. Here it was. "I prefer not to divulge that information."

"That would be a mistake," Agatha interjected cooly, her face disapproving. "How do you expect us to trust you if you don't tell us the truth?"

My voice was firmer than I felt. "I am telling you the truth, but I'm not going to reveal everything because you ask it."

"This information could sway our decision to aid you," Marella warned me, her hands slowly rotating the cane on the floor. "The Forsaken's plans for you could impede our safety and wellbeing."

"I can tell you now, the reason he gave me for using my Light will not endanger you," I countered.

The candle remained gold.

Marella's lips thinned. Agatha opened her mouth to speak, but the coven elder held up her hand to forestall her. "That should be for us to decide."

"Well it isn't."

Gold.

Her pale pink lips smiled at me grimly. "Let's table that question for later. Why did you come here to the Fallen's domain?"

"To determine if I could make an alliance with the witches." I wasn't sure, though, how this attempt was going.

"To what end?"

"To free the warrior angels and lead them out of Hell."

Marella abruptly laughed. Despite her lovely appearance her laugh was raspy and low as if it belonged to a much older woman. "How did you think we could assist you?"

I was not amused at her laughter and the edge of mockery that accompanied it, but I kept my feelings off my face. "I was hoping you could tell me. You know this domain better than I do. If the Fallen have any blind spots or weaknesses, I assume you would have catalogued them by now."

The expression on the elder witch's face was calculating. Instead of confirming my theory she asked, "How did you get into the Fallen domain?"

"Through a portal mirror."

She didn't appear surprised by my answer. It made me think that the witches had discovered its appearance earlier. "Where does it lead?" she asked mildly.

"Lucifer's domain. You can't access it, but I suspect you already knew that."

"Does the Forsaken know you are here?" For some reason the witches refused to call Lucifer by name. Forsaken was a term I hadn't heard before, but it did make sense. Most angel's believed Lucifer was forsaken from the Light. Was it a sign of respect or a mild way to diffuse his authority amongst them?

"Yes."

"This is what confuses me. Why would the Forsaken want you to come here and try to free your angels?" She paused, and then her voice came out as a whiplash. "Is he testing us?"

I blinked at her. "No, not that I'm aware of."

Her voice rose slightly. "So he could be, but you just don't know?"

I shrugged. "He could be," I acknowledged. "But I don't believe he is concerned about you disobeying. I would imagine he would view your people as insignificant and a problem for the Fallen, not for himself."

Agatha's jaw stiffened and her brown eyes darkened. I was aware my comment stung. It wasn't wise to point out to a former powerful clan how weak and unimportant they had become. But I had to convince them that my presence here was not to test their loyalty, otherwise they would never agree to help me.

"How nice to know we don't warrant any concern," Marella said with saccharine sweetness. "So why has the Forsaken allowed you access to the Fallen domain?"

My finger tapped lightly against my bicep. "He wants to challenge me. Lucifer knows my desire to free the warrior angels. To achieve this will be a test of my skill and abilities. I believe he wants my powers to grow and this challenge is a way to do that."

Despite the golden flame, Marella's face was a picture of utter disbelief. She turned her head towards Agatha, who was frowning at the candles almost as if she was wondering if they were broken.

"He is obviously deceiving her and she is too stupid to realise," Agatha concluded decisively.

"I'd have to agree," Marella said, turning back to me.

"I'm only telling you what has been imparted to me. So far, Lucifer's actions have not suggested otherwise."

Her cane lifted and pointed at me. "You speak about him with an air of familiarity." Even though she was supposedly blind, her gaze was shrewd. "Do you despise the Forsaken, like most other angels?" This was a more direct question, one with only a yes or no option.

My heart beat faster and my skin all of a sudden felt clammy.

"I... I don't know," I said.

The candles turned blue.

"That... be a lie," Marella said.

I bit my lip. "No, I don't despise him."

Agatha stared at me. "You seemed very close with the Forsaken when you were here previously. You claimed before that it was under duress. Is that true?"

"Why is this important? How I feel about Lucifer doesn't alter my mission or my intentions. I still

need your help and I can also assist you in return."
I didn't like this line of questioning. There was no
way I could reveal my past or my connection with
Lucifer. That was a weapon that could be catastrophic
in the wrong hands. "As hard as it might seem to
you, I want to be here. I have a chance that no other
angel has had to save our kind." I let a sliver of
insinuation deliberately flavour my words. "And I
will do *whatever* it takes to free them."

Let them believe I was a willing concubine for the
Lord of Hell and nothing more.

There was silence for a couple of heartbeats then
Marella smiled. "My... my, you almost had me
there." Her gaze landed on the pulse of my neck
almost like she could see the flutter of movement
under my skin. "Unfortunately, I'm a *much* better
liar than you."

She whispered a few words under her breath and
the hairs on my arms pricked up.

The black candles, which had been lying dormant,
suddenly lit up with pale, yellow flames.

My sense of unease grew exponentially. Nothing
good would come from those candles being lit.

Marella's voice deepened, the tones hollowing out
as if they rolled along a cavern floor. I felt the sounds
reverberating in my ears.

"Why does the Forsaken want you in Hell?"

Pressure immediately built in my skull. My hands
fell to my sides and tightened into fists. I glared at

them both. "So much for our truce," I gritted out. I took a couple of steps to stride out of the circle and slammed into an invisible wall.

I immediately called my Light into my hands, but when I reached for it, I was blocked.

I had plunged head first into trouble and was beginning to drown.

"We only want the truth," Marella said calmly. I felt the press against my will, a comb of power shifting over my mind trying to push through. Angrily, I pushed back.

Let me take care of these insignificant humans, my darker self whispered. *They think to use dark magic to keep us here. Let us show them the folly of their ways.*

Pain edged through the pressure like needles pressing against the surface of my skin. I fought for the calm centre within myself and built a wall of light against my mind. If they wanted to break me they would have to work much harder than that.

"Answer the question," Marella said sharply.

I looked at her and bared my teeth. "What question?"

Her grip on me tightened and I felt my head swim. "Why does Lucifer want you in Hell?"

The sound of his name ringed with power forcefully unearthed the memory from where it was buried.

I woke up in darkness, a scream tearing from my lips. My hands were clammy as I tangled furiously with the silken sheet above me. The demons from my dreams ripped into me, stripping my flesh off my body with slow, ragged slices.

The bed dipped and a large, dark shape hovered over me. My hand came up defensively to block the oncoming attack, knowing they would seek the vulnerable curve of my neck. Warm, masculine fingers curled around my wrist holding it above my head. My other hand swung up and that too was pinned to the bed. I opened my mouth to scream in terror when his voice curled like a smokey ribbon around me.

"If you hate the bedsheets that much, I can remove them."

I gasped in recognition, my eyes widened, searching. "Luce?"

He stiffened above me.

"Luce," I whispered in relief. I tugged my hands under his and he reluctantly released me. Without another thought, I threw my arms around him and sobbed into his neck.

"I'm not who you think I am," his familiar voice was soft but laced with an unfamiliar disinterest. He wasn't hugging me back.

I pulled back, confused. Images swirled in my head of a woman in a black dress, screams… angel screams... The reddish-gold light from the fire revealed his beautiful profile.

"Lucifer…" I whispered.

"No."

I jerked away, fear making the words almost too thick to form. "Are you a demon?" I choked out.

His voice took a sinister edge. "Oh, much worse."

My vision blurred and the world around me seemed to bleed black. I could feel the thick, dark liquid crawl up my legs in tendrils. "This is a dream... this is a dream... thisisadream." I wrapped my arms around my head, nails digging into my shoulders. The blood would get inside me now, infiltrating my limbs, then it would consume my mind...

I snapped out of the vision gasping, still feeling the pressure burning in my head. I was on my knees in the circle, my hands braced on the floor in front of me. Agatha and Marella were holding hands. Their chanting was louder, each unholy syllable piercing into my defences. My mind was still closed to them.

The memory I had recovered was when Lucifer had saved me from Hell. I had lost time, days after that incident and I hadn't consciously remembered any of it.

It didn't appear that the witches had captured that memory, but the flashback had distracted me enough, letting my mental guards slip.

They were breaking me down.

The pain was bad, but then again... so was going through a Hell Gate.

"I'm warning you," I gritted out. "Stop trying to get into my head."

"There is no escaping this circle. You don't have access to your magic. This is our domain and you entered at your own risk." Marella's lips twisted. "I'm going to find out what the Forsaken wants with you, his domain, his weakness, all the conversations you've had..." she leaned closer. "Everything. So settle in, get comfortable, you are going to be here for awhile."

I braced my hands on my knees and tilted my head to look at both the dark witches standing over me. "You best get a chair then," I replied, my voice thankfully not as shaky as I felt.

Kill them, my darker self hissed.

Marella laughed, husky and low. She crouched down on the ground so we were at face level. "If you weren't an angel, I think I might actually like you. A pity I'm going to have to break you." She stood up again with the help of her cane.

The candle lights flickered. Agatha started a low, hypnotic chant, different from the one before. Each word blazed into my head like a brand. Marella joined in and their voices melded together in a hair raising harmony, intensifying the pressure in my head. Liquid trickled down my lips. It was blood dripping from my nose.

My hand slid slowly up my knee right at the edge of my tunic. My words came out rough but clear. "One last chance–"

My vision dropped into another memory.

I was standing in a room in the dark. My fingers raked continuously down my arms, tearing brutally into the soft skin. I had to get the demon blood out. I could feel it churning through my veins, slowly absorbing all the humanity in my body like an insatiable leech. Soon I'd just be a creature of violence and savagery, hungry for pain.

I had to get it out.. I had to get it out… I had to tear it out of me before it was too late…

The pain felt cleansing. My blood dripped steadily to the floor.

Hands gripped my arms from behind me, yanking my nails from skin. "Stop that," the smooth masculine voice was like dark honey with a hint of underlying heat.

Panic overwhelmed me and I struggled frantically. "No, no, no, no! Please, no!" I screamed. The demons, the demons had come back to drag me to Hell. The hands turned me around and through the curtain of my hair that tangled wildly around my face I glimpsed a terrifyingly, beautiful face.

I froze. "You…" I took in his midnight eyes and his flawless golden skin. "No… it can't be…"

The fallen angel studied my face intently. "Who are you tonight?" he mused. "Nadia or Sandriel?"

I snapped out of my shock. "Let go of me," I said, tears blurring my vision.

Surprisingly, he obeyed. His hands dropped from my arms but he was still tantalisingly close.

I shoved him with my hands as hard as I could. He didn't move. My fist hit his chest. As it connected, he gripped it hard against his skin.

"As enjoyable as this is—" he started to say.

"You promised me," I hissed at him. "Luce, you promised me! You gave me your word. Why?" I looked at him beseechingly, feeling a different kind of fear grip my heart. Fear, terror for him. "Why?"

Something cold passed over his face, eclipsing the small amount of warmth that previously softened his gaze. "Your delusions have overcome you. Your babble makes less sense now than the previous nights."

He reached out to touch my forehead but I jerked my head back quickly. There was a flash of annoyance in his dark eyes and something else I could decipher. Somehow I knew if he touched me there I would succumb to sleep.

"Don't lie to me," I said, my voice thick with barely restrained emotion. "Not you. Never you. I'm in Hell. I know I'm in Hell. You promised you wouldn't come here. You promised me you wouldn't wait here for me."

I reached out a shaking hand to touch the curve of his lips. "What happened to you?" I whispered.

He let me touch him for a few moments, me overflowing with emotions that warred with each other on a treacherous battlefield of fear and elation and him, as distant as a comet passing through the inky skies. I could feel the demon blood moving sinuously in me. I was dying again. Could I die twice?

Would he always be the last face I saw?

Lucifer's fingers curled around my wrist, slick with my blood. He pulled my fingers away from his lips. The smile he gave me was chilling. "I lied."

I sucked in a breath and took a step back to move away from the sinister note in his voice. His hand tightened, pulling me forward once more. It hurt.

"As for what happened to me. Are you sure you want to know, little angel?"

"I'm not an angel." As soon as I said those words, images of a crystal temple flashed in my mind filled with beautiful beings with wings. I flinched, confused. My head pounded.

His smile widened like a predator sensing weakness. "How ironic that at the very end you became an angel and I became... something else."

"What did you become?" I asked hesitantly.

"A nightmare."

"Did the demons get in you?"

"No, I became the demon. The worst kind."

I shook my head. "I don't believe that. No, it's still you. It is. You've just forgotten." I stared up at him. "And if you've forgotten I can remind you again of who you once were."

"You can't fix me, Nadia." The way he said my name was different. The lilting gentleness was gone. In its place

was a hard, controlled edge. He pulled me closer until our foreheads were almost touching. We were but a kiss away. "It's been centuries and I have done things your pretty head couldn't fathom. I have become the thing in the dark you run from."

He titled his jaw until his teeth brushed the outer edge of my ear. I shivered involuntarily. "The old Lucifer loved you. You meant more to him than the air he breathed. You meant more than his own divinity," he whispered slowly, his words tearing me apart. "He died a long time ago. I killed him. The new one loves nothing except your pain."

My heart was breaking. It was a physical pain that wounded me more deeply, more fully than any torture in Hell. Tears slipped down my skin, a pitiful expression of the depth of my sorrow. My love was a terrible curse and it had consumed his soul. I saw its mark in the empty darkness of his eyes.

"I'm so sorry. I.. I never meant to do this to you. I asked you not to wait for me in Hell. I asked you! Why didn't you listen to me?" I cried, bowing my head down, unable to meet his dark gaze."

He let go of my hands and scooped me up in his arms. I resisted the urge to burrow my face in the crook of his neck. He placed me down carefully on the bed. Our link was gone. That warm, golden feeling that connected our souls together had completely disappeared.

I closed my eyes. My voice shook as I used his own words back at him. "Tell me a truth. Do you hate me now?"

I could hear him moving around. When he didn't respond, more tears slipped away from the corners of my eyes. My face crumpled and I covered my face.

Light filtered through the fragile skin of my eyelids. I opened my eyes to see an intricate crystal design above me ablaze with light. My lips parted as the beautiful colours washed over my skin. It felt peaceful. It felt healing.

I sensed him near and I turned my head. He was watching me, his face expressionless. He was still so achingly beautiful it hurt. He wore the face of the angel I loved, but his feelings for me had been destroyed.

He was wrong. I had killed him.

A wave of exhaustion forced me to close my eyes.

I came out of the vision, gasping for breath. Tears rolled down my face as I desperately tried to regain my sense of self.

The pain in my skull was almost unbearable.

Sandriel. I was Sandriel, an angel from The City of Light.

And I had reached my limit.

My hand slipped under the hem of my tunic. Deftly, I pulled out the crystal I had strapped to my thigh. It blazed with pure, white light, dwarfing the glow of the candle flames.

The chanting faltered around me.

With a shout of pain, I raised my hand up and smashed the crystal on the ground. Light exploded around me, snuffing the black candle flames out. The pressure in my head immediately dissipated.

I smiled grimly and my darker self stretched in anticipation. I reached for my power and it flowed strongly through my body. Agatha quickly began another spell and Marella hastily joined in.

I only had moments.

I focused my Light into the centre of my palm until it became a laser point.

Then I cut off Agatha's leg.

Her chanting stopped abruptly and she screamed high and hoarse, collapsing to the ground holding the stump of her thigh. There wasn't any blood. The heat of the laser had cauterised the wound, but the smell of cooked flesh permeated the room.

I watched her groan in pain on the ground and disgust gripped me. What had I done? I pushed the thought back down. Power was the only thing dark witches understood. If you didn't have any power, you were nothing.

Shock stole over Marella's face. She fumbled amongst her clothes and I held up my hand.

She froze.

"I wouldn't do that if you prefer your hands where they are." I walked out of the circle. Nothing stopped me.

I stopped a couple of steps away from her. "I came here in good faith to gain a mutually beneficial alliance. I could have helped your people, but your actions have shown that you are not to be trusted. I'm done with you. I'll do this on my own. Try and stop me or betray me to the Fallen and I'll turn into your enemy."

I moved past her towards the ladder, then hesitated, my conscious screaming at me. My head turned towards Agatha who was shaking in shock.

Oh don't ruin it now, my darker self hissed.

Disgust curdled in me once more and I turned back, walking towards the witch who was pale faced, shaking on the floor. As I moved towards her she tried to scramble backwards with her arms as if I was a monster. I knelt down in front of her and said calmly, "I can heal you, if you let me."

I waited for her panic to ease and for her mind to register my words. Agatha glanced to my right at Marella then nodded briefly. I carefully picked up the leg I had lasered off and moved it so the cut edge was against the wound of her thigh. She bit back a scream at the contact.

"Don't worry, the pain will be gone soon."

I gathered my strength and wove a pattern of healing light in my mind. Luckily, it was a clean cut. I doubted my skill to do anything more complicated. There were angels in The City of Light who could regrow limbs in a matter of minutes even without the assistance of crystals. But I had not specialised in Raphael's Temple, so that was completely beyond anything I could do.

I channelled the light into Agatha's leg through my hands, concentrating on holding the healing pattern firmly in my mind. My hands became hot like embers trapped beneath my skin. Agatha's gasps became slower and slower until I couldn't hear them at all. Time slowed as I focused on the blood flowing through her body, the hard ridge of bone and the delicate layers of skin. After a while, I snapped out of the semi trance I was in, aware that Marella had crouched down next to me.

"Will she be okay?" There was genuine concern in her voice. Her hair had come out of its messy bun and spilled across her shoulders. Her dress was drenched in sweat.

"Yes," I was about to point to her leg which was whole, the skin perfectly healed when I realised she might not be able to see. "Her leg is whole again. Healing takes energy so she will just need to rest for a couple of days before she is at her full strength."

Marella nodded, brushing her hand gently over Agatha's arm.

I got up once more, dusting off my tunic. Without another word I turned and walked towards the ladder.

"Wait," Marella said.

I turned back to look at her. She slowly got up, facing me, eyes landing on the space between my nose and lips. She looked as tired as I felt. Clearly, trying to keep me in the circle had taken a toll on her.

"We can help you." Marella sighed and clenched her jaw as if the words were difficult to get out. "We don't trust outsiders, especially angels. Obviously your kind have imprisoned and tortured us. There is no love between us. We would kill you all if we had the means." She gestured to the level above us. "But we have children to protect and perhaps you can help us with that. We can provide you with the means to escape Hell."

I frowned, crossing my arms. "How?"

"The Fallen wear rings that give them access to the portals."

I nodded, "Yes, I know."

"You will need them in order to get your people out. We can help you get those rings and assist you in getting into their tower to access their own portals."

I raised an eyebrow. "And what would be the price for that? You mentioned protecting your children?"

She pursed her lips. "Let me talk to the other elders. Can you meet us here again tomorrow?"

I nodded. If I could get a step closer to freeing the angels then tomorrow couldn't come soon enough. "Am I in for another few surprises or are we going to have a proper negotiation?"

Her gaze was cold. "You could have left her," she gestured to Agatha who was asleep on the ground.

"After what we did I wouldn't have even blamed you. But you didn't. For that reason alone I am inclined to trust you. I can promise we will not work against you or your mission in freeing your kin. I'm willing to create an alliance with you for now as we both have things we want."

I looked at her consideringly. Her word was debatable after what had just transpired but I had a feeling that we were on more of a level playing field now.

"Tomorrow then," I said.

Her eyes flickered directly into mine. "Tomorrow it is."

Chapter 19

Selaphiel wiped the trickle of blood dripping from her elbow and determinedly ignored the other claw marks, bruises, severe burns, and tooth gouges she had collected during her trek through the fifth level of Hell. Her only consolation was that Nadiel had suffered a similar fate.

His silvery hair was matted on one side with blood; his lips split when a particularly nasty demon threw several jagged boulders in his direction. Their dark armour had protected them from the most grievous wounds, but their journey wasn't over yet. They still had to trek back to the portal, back to the eyrie.

"He better be here," she hissed to Nadiel.

Nadiel stood at the opening of the cave peering inside into the darkness beyond. "He is here."

She wondered at his confidence and the source of his information. How he knew that Lucifer's personal demon was here was beyond her. More than that, the potential revelation of the ninth level of Hell and the isolation cages had made her ground her teeth almost to dust. Knowledge was power and in this, Nadiel had more than an edge; he had the whole goddamn sword.

She made a mental note to have some of her allies keep a closer watch on his movements. If he caught one of them, she could always claim that it was Sirus's minions trying to ferret out their plans.

She should also pay Ezriel a visit. What his broken mind could tell her, she didn't know, but perhaps in his vulnerable state, hovering painfully between darkness and light, she could torture some information out of him. Who knew what else was hidden in the ancient recesses of his mind? It would be a long time before Ezriel could ever join the higher ranks again. His humiliation at being partially turned back would be a stain on his otherwise fearsome reputation.

Nadiel moved deeper into the cave, and she followed.

The air smelt more rotten than usual. The sulphur that excreted off demons like a hideous perfume seemed exceptionally pungent. It was usually the case in the lower levels. Demons were much stronger, and the scent of sulphur became more intense when they gathered in groups.

They were in the fifth level of Hell, the lowest they were permitted to go. The sixth and seventh were deemed too high risk by the Lord of Hell. Not that some of them didn't venture down to the sixth anyway. Killing a demon from the sixth level of Hell could fast-track your way up the ranks of the Fallen.

If you made it back.

The risk of being trapped down there with a horde of demons eager to carve out their displeasure in numerous creative ways was enough of a deterrent to all but those who were the most ambitious or the most insane.

She was a bit of both.

It took her weeks to recover, knitting flesh and bone, but it had given her an unpredictable edge she relished. It wasn't long after that she became one of the leaders of the Fallen. She had toppled Hestien, who was still currently holding a grudge. She smiled inwardly, thinking fondly about all times he had tried to kill her and failed.

The cave narrowed significantly, then abruptly opened out again.

Four demons hung from the ceiling in chains, hissing and permeating the air with low, furious growls. Two of them were as large as boulders, a mixture of human and animal. The other two looked more reptilian, with scales and slitted yellow eyes. The chains glowed a lightning blue, engraved with runes, effectively holding the struggling demons like rabbits caught in a trap.

Lucifer's pet demon hovered underneath, face covered by the hood of its robe, skeletal white hands steepled together. It turned to face them as they entered, wisps of smoke forming and disappearing beneath it.

"Ruin-aith," Nadial said, addressing the demon.

Selaphiel once again fought the urge to stare at him. How in the *below* did he find out the demon's cursed name?

"Fallenn," the demon hissed back.

Nadial casually strolled forward and circled underneath the demons hanging from the ceiling. Ruin-aith remained facing forward, the empty space under its hood boring into her like iron screws. It was disturbing that this demon managed to make her feel a twinge of unease.

Not for the first time, she wondered at the origins of this demon and what level it had originally resided in. Either way, its bond with Lucifer allowed it to travel between the levels like no other lower-level demon could.

"Why are these demons hanging from the ceiling?" Nadiel asked conversationally.

"Masssterss orderss," it replied.

Selaphiel frowned. These must be the demons the witches already had the names of. Lucifer was probably waiting for the summoning to then be able to track the coven. They had better act fast. If the summoning occurred while they were here, the Lord of Hell would turn up, and their presence would be questioned.

She glanced at Nadiel and, from the expression on his face, determined he had come to the same conclusion.

"Ruin-aith," Nadiel said from behind the demon. The demon finally withdrew its attention from her and turned slowly to face the other Fallen. "Do you like serving our Master?"

"Do youu, Fallenn?" the demon instantly replied.

Nadiel's mouth twisted. "I'd like it better if I pulled my own strings, demon. Wouldn't you?"

"Evensss the lowliessst creature desiress to be free," it hissed.

Nadiel flicked a blade up from his wrist and jabbed one of the demons strung up. It growled and snapped at him, but the chains held it fast. "It must be difficult for you to be at the beck and call of the Warden. That's what you call him, isn't it? Your prison guard?"

Ruin-aith didn't reply.

Nadiel continued. "I wonder what your brethren think of you, always running errands when they despise him so much. They must see you as nothing more than an obedient hound."

Selaphiel didn't see so much of a reaction but could feel an intense, cold hatred filtering through the cavern like a vaporous gas. She tensed, her body ready to explode in motion and unleash her powers if the demon suddenly became more of a threat. She sincerely hoped Nadiel knew what he was doing.

The demon said nothing.

She wondered if it could actually attack them or if its actions were controlled or limited by the bond between Lucifer and itself. They had taken a significant risk by coming here. If things went bad or if Nadiel had read the situation incorrectly, the demon would expose them immediately to Lucifer. They might as well join Ezriel and lock themselves in the dungeon cages.

But there was one thing they could rely on that the demon wanted more than anything else.

Nadiel cast his lure with the sweetest of baits. "What if we could weaken your bond with your Master? Give you some... flexibility to move?"

Ruin-aith appeared unmoved. Wisps of smoke curled under the demon in sharp coils. "And howss would youss do that Fallen?"

Nadiel carefully wiped the black demon blood from his knife on the supple material of his pants. "By bonding you to the two of us."

"How doess two more chainss sserve me?"

Tired of being left out of the conversation, Selaphiel cut in, bringing the demon's attention to her once again. "It will weaken your bond with Lucifer without cutting it off and alerting him. That way, you can take his instructions to you more as... suggestions. In return for your increased freedom, we only ask for a few small favours."

Nadiel shot her a slanted look. He wasn't pleased she had intervened in his momentum. Screw him.

"We want access to the ninth level of Hell," Nadiel said bluntly.

"Whyss?"

Selaphiel felt a jolt of excitement at the fact that the demon didn't deny its existence.

"We have an interest in the isolation cells."

"You playss a dangerouss game Fallen. Ifss the Masters findss out you will be no more."

"Well then, he better not find out," Nadiel said in a hard voice.

And there it was. They had planned for the outcome that the demon would not take up their offer. If that became the case, then they had both been prepared to kill it. They couldn't risk the demon going back to Lucifer and revealing their plans. Selaphiel braced herself, her dark magic seething under her skin. She would have to move fast. The demon could blink between levels, and they couldn't risk it getting away.

"You will needss three people if you want the bond to be ssufficiently weakened," Ruin-aith finally said.

"Three? Why?" Nadiel had moved closer to the demon as if he, too, were preparing to attack.

"The bondss with the Master is old and sstrong, sstronger than just one or twoss of you."

"We don't want him to be aware of the bond weakening," Selaphiel snapped.

The demon's head swiveled towards her. "Thatss why we do it in sstagess. One persson bondss now. The otherss later."

Nadiel took another step forward. "We do the first one now. With me."

Selaphiel gritted her teeth. Of course, it would be him.

The demon spread its bone-white hands wide. "That won't be possible. I don't have the neccesssaary ingredientss."

Nadiel flashed a wolfish grin. "We'll then, it's lucky I brought them with me." He pulled out a small dark silk bag from beneath his armour filled with little items of considerable power. It had taken time and careful planning to obtain all the ingredients they needed. Now that they had to do the ritual two more times, they would have to be even more careful to not draw unwanted attention.

With his knife, he made a quick slash across his palm. Blood instantly began to pool and drip.

"Shall we begin?"

***

"Thank you for meeting with me." I sat in a sturdy wooden chair, surrounded by witches in a half circle. I was back in the underground chamber in the witches' domain with five women facing me in their own high-backed chairs with a mix of expressions on their faces.

Marella, I already knew. The other women of varying ages were introduced to me as Hasbeth, Delta, Joan, and Edith. It wasn't completely clear if

314

there was anyone who held the majority of power or if they all shared in the decision-making of the coven. But Hasbeth was in the centre of the five, and from the limited experience that I had, positioning was deemed important.

This time there weren't any black candle circles or pentagrams on the floor. There weren't any blood-painted symbols or the thick current of magic building in a bottle waiting to be released. The room was cleaned out, bar the basic furniture and the additional chairs, which the current coven leaders sat in.

Despite all this, I was still surrounded by a group of powerful witches with only one way out. I might have had the advantage of raw power that could be destructive, as I proved the previous night, but they had the luxury of combined abilities and foreplanning.

There was a lot a witch could do with the time and tools to prepare.

Was I nervous? Of course, but I didn't let that show on my face.

I was not in the power seat during this conversation, but I was relying on a mutually beneficial arrangement to get me through this negotiation. That and a few more crystals stashed up my tunic.

Atlas had drilled me when I arrived back the night before, none too happy with being left out of our strategy session.

"You were lucky," he growled at me, red-faced. His dark brows twitched like they wanted to leap off his forehead and strangle me.

"Yes," I acknowledged, "but I did have a backup plan." I had thought about the Light crystals at the last minute, and fortunately, I did, as they were the only thing that saved me.

"Blind, dumb luck!" he roared. "You're like a lamb wandering up to a starvin' man's campfire, batting her eyelashes and bleetin, 'hello'!"

I placed my fists on my hips and glared at him. "You make it sound as if I'm completely powerless! Which we both know I'm not."

His face turned purple, and he jumped up from the bed, using his considerable bulk to tower over me. "Power and strategy are two different things, you nitwit! How do you think larger armies fall to smaller ones!"

The conversation had gone downhill from there.

"So," I said, turning my gaze to Marella, who I was still deciding if was blind. "Let's discuss how we can help each other. I was led to believe that you might be able to provide me with access to the Fallen portals."

Hasbeth, the witch in the centre of the group, couldn't quite disguise the flash of contempt. She had strong-boned features under a smooth, even tone of chocolate skin. Smooth, except for several deep slashes that ran up the length of her face, damaging one corner of her lip. She would have been attractive if it wasn't for the scars.

Now she looked dangerous, someone you would pause before provoking. She was on the heavy side, built solid and thick, but without flab. Her dark fringe was even, and her clothes were spotless. This woman cared about appearances, and she clearly didn't care for mine.

I fought the urge to discreetly sniff at Atlas's tunic.

"We have ways of obtaining the rings," Hasbeth said. "But there are limits."

I frowned. "What do you mean?"

"Quantity and access level." Her eyes were flat, shrewd marbles of cedar brown. "If we take more than a couple of rings at one time, the Fallen will catch on to the theft. That's unacceptable. In addition, higher access rings to the Earth realm will be all but impossible to obtain."

My heart sank. This was what I had been hoping to obtain. "Why?"

"Because," she said with exaggerated patience, "The Fallen who have higher access rings don't die often."

Right. This escape plan was looking more and more unlikely. "So, what access can you get me?"

Hasbeth glanced at Delta, the witch to the right of her. She was older, with a short crop of faded red hair and lines around her eyes that indicated she used to laugh, but that was a long time ago.

Delta responded. "Almost any level in Hell and perhaps, if we are lucky, to the Underworld."

I wanted to rub my temples at the building tension there. The Underworld. How in the heavens was I supposed to lead a group of bone-weary, half-turned, desperate angels through the Underworld? I was hoping for direct access straight to Earth. Once we arrived on Earth, we could shift back to Heaven or call for help.

Marella cleared her throat. "You have heard how we can assist you. We can get you access to the portal by giving you what keys we can. But just to be clear, we won't intercede on your behalf. If you find yourself in a confrontation with the Fallen, do not expect us to reveal our alliance."

I basically interpreted that as, if you are dying on the floor, we will just step over you and carry on our way. Message loud and clear.

"And we will need something from you," Marella continued.

Here it was. I was waiting to find out what the witches wanted. I had some suspicion, but I wasn't certain.

"We want you to take some of our children back to Earth."

I blinked. "And how exactly would I be able to do that?"

"Through the portal mirrors."

I frowned. "I thought you said you couldn't get access to the Earth portal mirrors?"

Hasbeth cut in. "We don't mean through the Earth portal, we mean through the Underworld."

I leaned forward in my seat, and it squeaked in protest. "You are aware the portals are only keyed to angels. That's why you can't go through them. I can't take your children through."

Hasbeth smiled, but it was grim. "That's why they won't be alive when they go through."

My mouth opened again. "Please explain," I managed to get out.

"We are aware that the portals are keyed only to angelic energy signatures. But we have also observed that angels have managed to take through inanimate objects and sometimes..." Hasbeth's face twisted, and I caught a brief flash of inner rage, "dead body parts with them. We have deduced that if you were to carry a small, lifeless body with you, you should be able to make it through the portal."

I continued to stare at her. When she just looked back at me expectantly, I responded impatiently, "Clearly, you have more to tell me. I don't see how carrying a dead child's body to Earth is going to serve you."

She raised an eyebrow. "I was waiting for you to protest what I mentioned so far. But since you seem agreeable I will continue"

"Oh, I haven't even started with my objections," I retorted. "I'm just waiting for you to finish."

"Fine," her lips turned up in a shallow smile. "We will stop the children's breath just before you take them through the mirror. When you go through, you will immediately give them an elixir that will then resuscitate them."

"Risky," I said. My gaze flicked to Marella. "I don't know what will be waiting for me on the other side of the portal mirror to the Underworld. If I'm attacked, then that could be a problem."

"As you demonstrated your abilities last time we met, I have full confidence in your ability to handle yourself," Marella said dryly.

I shake my head. "I'm not foolish enough to believe I can overcome every demon in the Underworld. Besides, you seem to indicate that time is critical in administering the elixir. If I'm distracted, I won't be able to resuscitate them. What happens to our deal if the children don't make it?"

Edith, an older witch with a shock of white hair and glacial blue eyes, answered fiercely. "Then the deal is off," she rasped.

My lips thinned. "I see." I leaned back in my chair, and the wooden groan had me silently praying it wouldn't fall apart. "It seems like I'm taking most of the risk in this arrangement." How was I supposed to keep children alive in the Underworld when the last time I was there, I barely made it out myself?

"On the contrary." Marella's golden blonde hair shone in the low candlelight. Her eyes fixed on the tip of my nose, making it seem like she was staring right through me. "If the Fallen find out we have given you access to their portal mirrors, they will punish each and every one of us. Severely. We, too, take a high risk in aiding you."

"The last time I was in the Underworld, I was dragged into Hell," I said bluntly. "You are taking a high risk with your children too." I shift in my seat. "How am I supposed to find a way to Earth? I assume the coven has methods?"

There was no way the witches were wandering through the Underworld blind. Not after so many centuries.

"We can give you a spelled orb that will guide you to Charon, the ferryman, and from there to the portal to Earth. We will also give you the location of our coven once we reach an official agreement," Hasbeth responded briskly.

"And to find my way back?"

I swear Hasbeth looked disappointed that I asked. Perhaps she hoped after I fulfilled my side of the bargain, I would disappear down some demonic dark hole and never bother them again.

She glanced at Joan, a young-looking witch with loose long, brown hair and a dark hood covering half her face. The effect was slightly chilling, but I assumed the covering was to hide a physical imperfection rather than an act of intimidation.

From what I had observed, it was unlikely a young, attractive witch would remain here instead of inside the Fallen domain.

"We can spell an orb to find your way back to the portal." Joan's voice was so soft that I had to strain to hear it.

Marella lifted her hand in my direction, drawing my attention back to her. "So, what is your answer?"

I stared at her hard. "I need time to think about it."

The scars on Hasbeth's face shivered as she shot me an impatient look. "The sooner, the better, angel. The more you delay, the higher the chances that our meetings come to the Fallen's attention. And neither of us would like that particular outcome."

***

"For the love of Ares, tell me you didn't agree!" Atlas paced his room like a caged animal, his hair ruffled like an outraged bird.

"Of course, I didn't." I sat on the edge of the unmade bed, swinging one foot above the marble floor. "I just wanted to gather more information, and what I did gather didn't seem to be very promising."

"You mean they basically gave you a big piece of shit, tied it with a bow with a little note saying it could blow up in your face."

I frowned and shook my head sharply, trying to clear the mental image from my mind. "Well, I wouldn't exactly put it that way."

He spun around and stared at the wall to the left of me, eyes flickering over the gold veins running through the surface as if it was a map and was reading the terrain. "It's going to be bloody difficult for you to get the angels to Earth from the Underworld."

"I could ask them to create another orb for me to lead us to the Ferryman."

Atlas snorted. "And have you transported a handful at a time?" He paused and looked at me. "Can his boat carry a hundred of you?"

I shot him a bewildered look back. "I have no idea."

He flicked his hand dismissively and looked back to the wall. "Anyway, you still have to pay him. That whole access point is a time clog. You don't know who is watching the area, and you could be on the run from the Fallen."

I stared at the wall like I could, too, see something. "Who would be watching the area?"

"Hades, demons, Fallen... I don't bloody know, but none of it would be good when you are trying to make a quick retreat."

A sudden thought struck me, and I jumped to my feet. "The Elysian Fields!"

Atlas swung his raptors gaze my way. "Do you know where it is?"

"No, but the witches might. If I can get to the Elysian Fields, the angels can go through and shift straight to The City of Light. *And…*" I put emphasis on the last word. "The Fallen won't be able to follow. Or any demons."

The nod of approval gave me a swift burst of pride. "Good, go ask them. And tell them you will only take two of their children back to Earth. Any more is suicide. One before the mission as an act of good faith and one as you lead the angels out of the Underworld." He pointed a finger at me. "That way, they will be hesitant to stab you in the back on your way out."

I nodded. "So, say I can access the Elysian Fields. How would I get a hundred angels to a portal in the Fallen domain?"

"You can't."

I stared at him.

He shrugged. "I think you need to ask for a favour."

I stared at him again until it finally clicked. My eyes widened. "Oh, by the spirits, no, that is the last thing I want to do. Especially now."

"There is a point in time where every army has to look towards its allies."

"He is not an ally!"

Atlas continued. "If you can get your own portal to the Underworld that the other angels can use, this whole mission would be easier." Atlas made a gesture outside the room. "Can't you use one of those other ones outside? Surely you can make a deal of some sort. If you could move a portal to the Underworld into the dungeon, then you wouldn't have to go to the Fallen domain at all. You might still have to buy the witches' silence, but your chances of success automatically increase to probable survival instead of probable suicide."

"He's not in a favourable mood," I hissed.

I hadn't seen or heard from Lucifer since I left his room the last time. I was still filling up my quota of crystals and at some point, the ones I filled disappeared. The thought of seeing Lucifer again made me feel like walking into a thunderstorm. There was a very real danger of being swept away, fundamentally changed by the lightning cord that ran between us, that I might never recognise myself again.

Even coming back from the dungeons made me hold my breath in suppressed panic. Fortunately, when I went through the portal, his room was empty.

"Well, unless we can think of a way to move a hundred angels undetected through the Fallen domain without it being a bloody massacre, you're pretty much screwed." His face scrunched up in thought, and he absently scratched his belly through a brown cotton robe he had somehow acquired. I didn't want to ask where he got it from. I just counted myself lucky he was wearing clothes at all.

"Or… if you can find a way to move the Underworld portal to the angels."

My eyebrows shot up. "How?"

The Commander of the Taragon army glared at me like I was an imbecile. "If I knew, I'd bloody say so, wouldn't I? Do I look like a flamin' oracle?" He pointed his finger at me. "Your best bet is to get another portal. Go ask the demon king," he ordered.

I stood up, my jaw set in determination. "No. There has to be another way."

"Well, you tell me when you think of something Sandy because we are running out of bloody options and time." Then Atlas delivered a blow that had my guilt bubble up like acid, searing my throat. "If you fail, do you think I get to go back home?" His face turned into a thundercloud. "No! I'm going to be stuck down here with a demon king who will probably rip my bloody balls off on a daily basis because you were too bloody stupid to ask for help!" he roared.

My mouth opened and closed. I didn't *want* to bargain anymore. I had nothing left to bargain with. If I could avoid thinking about Lucifer at all, I would consider it a blessing. Every time I saw him, it tore out a little piece of me and left a desolate emptiness that blew through the gaps in my soul.

But Atlas was right. I hated that he was right. I would regret it forever if I didn't try everything in my power to get those angels out.

That's why, a few hours later, I ended up in front of the apple tree.

I was finally doing the inevitable. Finally putting the last piece of the puzzle together. I was ready to face the memory that I dreaded and yearned to know at the same time. If I was to face my soulmate again, I had to know the truth of what happened in my past life. As much of it that was buried deep inside my subconscious.

I reached up, and the apple fell easily into my hand like it was waiting for me.

Chapter 20

This wasn't just any apple, this was an apple from *my* tree. A tree that impossibly had been preserved, suspended in the fullest bloom of its life, in a place surrounded by death, darkness and lost souls. The ghosts of the past were thick and heavy, whispering to me snippets of conversation that triggered feelings and flashes of memory.

But there was only one memory I was interested in now. The very first, and I suspected, the very last.

He was in pain. Oh, he was in so much pain. I would have done anything, anything for him, but I could not fix this. I could feel his silent screams, his turbulent rage and knew others would be able to feel it soon. They would come for him. He was not safe. I would have gone to him, but this body would not obey my will. The darkness that seeped through my veins was both alien and terrifying. It was a battle for my soul. A battle I was losing.

I pulled back, gasping from the phantom pain that suddenly invaded my body. Then the memory slammed back into me.

The apple fell from my fingers.

~ Luce ~ I whispered in my mind through the fraying threads of our link. ~ Come back inside. ~

I shifted in the bed I was lying in, propped partially up by a pile of colourful, feathery cushions. The agony that small movement caused was exquisite. The demon blood had taken over my body, showing up under the translucent cover of my skin as black, inky veins.

I could feel the dark entities hate overwhelming me, feeding from my pain and syphoning off my patience, my tolerance and my love. It was draining me slowly until there would be nothing left but an empty husk. I was losing who I was, falling backwards into darkness and there was nothing anybody could do about it.

Not even Lucifer.

We had finally found Avalon, a much needed beacon of hope that with the aid of crystals could dilute the evil riding within me. Lucifer had flown for days, following obscure leads about the hidden city with utter relentnesses. The city was in a separate dimension, only intersecting with Earth periodically or through invitation. Since Lucifer couldn't be with me during his search, he had asked a favour from a healer he had saved from a demon attack to tend to me in his absence.

Draga was the most unusual woman I had ever seen.

Black hair in tangled coils framed a slight boned face, which was always covered in some kind of white paint of strange connecting lines. She had an ageless quality to her features but old eyes that had seen many things and not all of them pleasant. She spoke a different language, a rapid fire of short, clicking syllables and even though

I couldn't understand a word she managed to make her intentions quite clear.

She prodded me, poured strange concoctions down my throat until I gagged and chanted for hours. It helped cool the burning edge off some of the pain. Even though she wore almost a permanent scowl on her face, her hands were gentle and warm as they massaged my skin with fragrant oils.

The demon whispers were fainter then, as if they were muffled by a moving fog. But they always came back, and they continued to get stronger.

When Lucifer returned with hope blazing bright in his cerulean blue eyes I was elated. We all knew I was almost at the point of no return. Avalon was the last bit of ledge to cling to before the fall. Draga had stemmed the demon infection as best she could, and bought us a little more time.

But it had all crumbled to dust.

For a while, it appeared we would make it. Lucifer would take me to the Island of Crystals and channel his Light, healing me from my torment and the risk of losing my soul to the dark realms.

Then, Archangel Michael stopped us.

Lucifer's brother was almost as beautiful as he was, golden hair to Luce's ebony colouring. The brightness of the sun to the pure light of the moon. There was a natural glow that emanated from his skin. I dimly recalled Luce having that same aura about him when we first met, but his time on Earth had caused that ethereal light to fade.

I only managed a small glimpse of Michael through the window before they moved out of my view. But I could hear them.

"I'm sorry, brother, but you cannot go to Avalon." Michael's soft, rich voice floated through the window. It was a voice you could listen to for hours and never be bored. Though, it also carried a weight to it, a resigned reluctance of someone facing a confrontation they had been dreading for days.

"And why is that?" There was a distinct undercurrent of suppressed anger arching through our link.

"Because," a short sigh, "you will succeed in your endeavour and that is a path and a future you must not take. The Earth will suffer and your Light, as bright as it is brother, will not be enough to stop it."

"Another prophecy, Michael? I'm tired of people telling me what I must or must not do. Even you. We are all in charge of our own destinies. I will make my own choices, as I have always done, and shall live with the consequences."

"The consequences of this, Lucifer, is not just a slight ripple in the waters, it's an implosion of change that will have a devastating impact on billions of souls. If you heal your soulmate now, in this life, billions of souls over time will suffer in the lower realms. If you don't, you will save many of them. One soul, as important as that soul is to you, cannot be placed above the rest to the detriment of all humanity."

My eyes widened.

"So my soulmate is to be a sacrifice?" His voice was incredulous. "How can you ask that of me?"

"Because I must."

"There is always another way."

"There isn't. Not this time."

"I can't make that choice. I could lose her forever. She is mine to protect," he said fiercely. My heart squeezed in anguish. "I will not sacrifice her to the darkness on a prophecy. Futures can be altered."

"Not this one," Michael said quietly. "Please brother, I know this choice is one beyond any of us to make... but you are the best of us. The strongest. The closest to the Light. You must, for the highest good of all, as much as it will cost you." There was a soft hesitancy. "If I could take this burden from you, this choice, and make it my own, I would. But this weight was not given to me. It was given to you."

"Then you are the better angel."

The silence stretched. Then, movement in the grass, soft thuds, and the flutter of wings.

"Don't." Michael's voice was resigned.

"Ezriel, Selpahiel. Do you all intend to stop me, brother?"

"If we have to," came the resigned reply. "Please don't make me."

The fury in Luce's voice made my fingers clench on the windowsill. "Move Michael, or I will make you move."

"We must all do as we must. Know I take no joy in this."

They fought. I couldn't see it, but I could hear the ringing clash of swords that were musical but teeth grindingly discordant, as if those angelic blades weren't ever meant to touch each other. The sounds of combat moved further and further away from me.

Fearing for Lucifer, I struggled to make my way outside, cursing the weakness in my limbs.

~ Stay where you are, Nadia. I will come back for you. ~

~ I'm scared, ~ I replied, tears forming in my eyes.

I could just sense something terrible was going to happen. Lucifer's emotions were already scraped into a fine edge. I knew this confrontation with his brother Michael and the other two angels could push him to do something he might never come back from.

My emotions triggered the darkness inside me. A flash of intense pain forced me to stumble back to the bed. I collapsed on the edge, breathing heavily. A blur of soft light fluttered agitatedly in front of me. A wind elemental. I reached out my hand and it landed on the tips of my fingers.

~ Don't be. ~ His voice was a soothing caress, despite the touch of strain that coloured the edges. ~ I'll be back soon. You need to rest and gather your strength for the journey ahead. Hold on a little bit longer. Please, for me. ~

Their battle took to the skies and the elements let loose their fury. Winds raged, sweeping through the land with howling screams. Rain thickened the sky, until it was just a grey blur outside. Flashes of light streaked above, accompanied by a booming echo that was deeper and more encompassing than any thunder I'd ever heard. I was sure the sound reached across the oceans and even up to the heavens themselves.

It seemed like the end of the world.

Despite the canopy of violence around me, my little cottage remained untouched. Protected from the elements by some invisible barrier, I could only watch and pray from the safety of Lucifer's power. Day turned into night and then into another day.

I weakened further, struggling to manage the searing bite of pain that forever nipped at my flesh. Without the balm of my soulmate's Light, or the healing potions of Draga, the demon's hold on me increased, pushing me further into dreams of blood and flesh and washing my faith away in a haze of red agony.

I wanted to call out to Lucifer, to tell him to hurry and that I was afraid I wasn't going to make it. But I didn't want to distract him from the battle above.

Time blurred. Finally, Lucifer burst through the door in a cloud of desperation. But it was too late. He was too late. We would never make it to Avalon in time. I had only a few hours left. Our tiny flame of hope had been extinguished.

Archangel Michael didn't need to beat Lucifer, he only had to delay him... and he had succeeded.

During those hours apart, I had time to replay Michael's conversation with Lucifer. I couldn't really blame Lucifer's brother. No, I didn't want to die. I definitely didn't want my soul to be lost in a realm ravaged by darkness, unable to find any peace. The thought terrified me to my very core. But at the same time, I didn't want billions of lives to suffer because of me.

How could I place my life above so many others? It seemed so selfish. I just didn't know how saving me contributed to the suffering of so many lives. Surely Lucifer wouldn't forget his duties as a Light angel if I survived?

These final months he had been distracted, trying to find a cure. He told me other angels had come down to assist in the battles with the demons escaping Hell. But once I was well Lucifer would have no need of the other angels' assistance. Surely things would go back to the way things once were?

Michael hadn't believed so. Neither did Rapheal when Lucifer had asked him to heal me. I didn't know much about prophecies and how true they were, but so far we had heard two and they were both grim. Naballa's words to Lucifer still gave me chills.

"Evil will wear your face."

How was all this possible? My heart refused to believe it.

The door opened and Lucifer came back inside, shoulders hunched, his stunning face ravaged by the pain bleeding through from the inside. When he had realised the path to my recovery had been obliterated, I saw an expression on his face I had never seen before. It was pain wrapped around a deep, bottomless hate.

It scared me.

Sensing my reaction, he left my cottage and vented his emotions out into the open sky. The lightning storm would have shaken the world. His rage would have broken it.

"Are the... Angels... coming back?" I rasped. Would they force him to return to Heaven now and restore him to his former self?

He dropped to his knees by my bed and took my hand in his. It felt burning hot compared to the icey cold that had seeped under my skin.

~ Save your voice, little one. ~

He lifted my hand to the side of his face as if it was made of glass then turned his head to place a kiss into the centre of my palm.

His head dropped, dark hair falling across his eyes. Defeated. I had never seen him look defeated.

"I don't know what to do," he whispered. "Tell me what to do." There was a pause long enough that I thought he wouldn't speak again. Then finally the words came out soft and low. "What I am has always been in service of You and our higher cause and I have served gladly. I ask nothing for myself, only for you, to help this soul to not be lost to the darkness. Please... show me another way."

He waited with his head bent.

I held my breath in anticipation. A slight kernel of hope unfurled. When the minutes stretched on and the tension in his body remained, my heart broke and that hope turned to ash. Would God not respond? Were we being punished? Angels weren't meant to fall in love with mere mortals and I had kept him too long away from his duties.

~ Forgive me, ~ his voice was anguished.

~ Oh, Luce. ~ I curled my hand around his. ~ There is nothing to forgive. ~

The darkness crept into the corners of my eyes. My head spun like a whirlpool. Lucifer's hand tightened around mine.

"Stay with me, Nadia," his voice was panicked. I tried to focus on his face.

~ Luce... what's going to happen to me? ~ The ball of terror within me grew at what I would have to face when I passed from this world.

I knew he didn't want to answer. The mattress dipped as he climbed into the bed and sat against the headboard, moving me until my head rested against his chest. His arms were tight as they wrapped around me. After a couple of moments, he forced the words out.

~ Because you have been infected by a demon, you will be pulled into a lower realm once you pass from the Earth plane. There are more than a few lower realms and your soul could enter any one of them. Some of these realms have pathways to the upper realms. The light of your soul will recognise those paths if you come across them. There are guardians there who look to guide lost souls, like you, back to where they belong. If you end up in one of those places, the guardians will find you and help you transition out. ~

I felt his fear for me. He tried to suppress it, but it was like a thin layer of acid under the sweet.

~ What aren't you telling me? ~

Lucifer pressed his lips against the side of my forehead. His arms tightened further. ~ There is a chance... you could enter a realm with no path to the higher levels. There might be beings there that could pull you lower to places where no guardian can reach. ~

He was talking about Hell.

Unable to hold them back any longer, I felt my tears flow. Terror gripped me once again and the demon inside me latched greedily onto that feeling, drawing it out like a leech. My mind conjured up visions of demons tearing me apart, over and over again. I struggled to breathe.

Strong fingers gripped my chin and turned my face towards his. "No, I won't let that happen. Listen to me. I swear it," he said almost viciously. "If you end up in one of those realms I will be there. I will find you. Until I know you are safe in one of the higher levels, I will be there in case you are pulled through. I won't let them have you. I promise you on everything I am," he swore, eyes burning like blue flames. "I won't let them have you."

He pressed his lips against mine desperately, as if his will alone could anchor my soul to him. I kissed him back just as desperately. I didn't want to die. By the spirits, I didn't want to die and leave him. The demonic energy inside of me pulsated, dragging me deeper like a heavy chain tied around my ankle pulling me towards the depths of the ocean.

I pulled back with a gasp. ~ No you can't. Luce... I don't want you to go to Hell. ~

I felt his body stiffen.

~ I saw what it did to you last time you went down to get the demon blood to heal me. I… I don't want that for you. Angels don't belong in Hell. ~

He took a breath and kissed me on the side of the temple. ~ You don't belong in Hell. I can't make that promise. ~

~ You have to. For me. It's the last thing I ask of you… please. I couldn't bear it if I knew you were down there. ~

I let my tears fall as I felt our link start to fade.

"Please," I croaked out. "Please." My voice became frantic as I gripped the edges of his vest. Tears flowed down my face in earnest. "Please, I couldn't bear it. Don't go there. I might not even be there. I could go somewhere else. Don't wait for me there. You can't. I couldn't bear it. Please, Luce, please–"

"Nadia, you don't know what you ask of me."

"I do know, Luce. I do." *I gripped his vest tighter with the last of my strength.* "Don't let our last moments be like this. Please!"

"Nadia…"

"Please! For me, please!"

His voice was strained. ~ If that's what you want ~

~ Promise me.~

He didn't respond.

"Promise me, Luce," *I sobbed.*

He sighed. ~ I promise.~

The energy drained out of me and I sank boneless into him. My vision greyed. I laid my ear against his chest and closed my eyes. His heartbeat was steady and strong..

Thud... thud... thud...

It was a sound I had grown familiar with and somehow... it calmed me.

~ Luce... tell me a truth... a beautiful one. ~

Our link disappeared. The emptiness felt like a hole in my chest.

His fingers ran through my hair soothingly. The strands were tangled, but he patiently unravelled them, smoothing them down with infinite care. When he finally spoke, his words were soft and sweet against my ear.

"In the beginning of time, the Creator, being all that was, yearned to experience itself, its own Light, in all its facets. So from parts of its essence it created billions and billions of little lights that you call souls. These souls were content and happy, but over time they yearned to experience themselves too. They knew they were light, but they wanted to feel what it was to be light. Being the light didn't mean just being bright, it meant being loving, kind, considerate, grateful and all those things that are of a high vibration. But they ran into a problem. How would they know what being the light was if they were surrounded by all the other lights? So the Creator created what we call darkness, for without the dark the light could not truly shine."

"The darkness was everything the light was not. It was fear, envy, greed, anger and all those negative emotions that pull your energy down. But through the darkness, those souls could finally experience what it was to be the Light. The Creator said that many would forget who they really are. When surrounded by darkness, they would forget their ability to shine."

"So the Creator decided to create a fail-safe. Flames."

"These were souls that matched perfectly with each other. They weren't alike, but opposites, a perfect counterpoint to create harmony. If souls ever became lost or forgot who they really were, these Flames, if reunited, would eventually bring each other back into balance."

Lucifer twined my fingers with his. His voice thickened and turned husky. *"One touch would forge a link of light that would over time, lead a soul out of the darkness. It was a way that if a soul forgot who they really were, they would start to remember. It was a way that a lost soul could finally find its way back home."*

"So, little one... our story is not over yet. Souls linked like ours will always find a way back to each other. It may take time, it may take many lifetimes and the path may be faint and perilous, but we will find each other again," *he whispered.*

Thud... thud... thud...

~ I love you, ~ I thought, even though I knew he couldn't hear me anymore. ~ You were the most beautiful dream I didn't believe I could ever have. ~

I faded away to the sound of my name on his lips.

Chapter 21

The memory left me like wisps of smoke from a fire banked long ago. My breath came out in short, sharp gasps as past and present merged completely. Emotions surged inside, hot and chaotic, burning away old preconceptions to reveal a barren truth. All the reasons why he did what he did finally made tragic sense.

"No, no, no-no-no. What did you do?" I whispered in horror, clasping my hands in front of my face.

After my soul left my body, Lucifer went to the only place that, if I got pulled into, I'd never find my way out. There were no barriers in Hell at that time. The demons would have descended on him in droves the moment he entered. To have an angel in their midst would have made them ravenous. He would have had to fight continuously in a never-ending battle, just to make sure he would be there if I arrived.

The Creator only knew how he had survived.

My hands dropped in front of me, fingers curling into my palms. I felt my power hum just underneath my skin. That's why he made the barriers. He had to separate the demons in order to stay in Hell. But as he had mentioned to me before, his Light only kept them at bay for so long. Light couldn't maintain its vibration in a realm of dense negativity.

"So you fell." My throat felt raw as I said those words out loud.

The devastation of my death and the time spent in Hell would have eroded his angelic light. He gave into the darkness to build another layer into the barriers, keeping the demons under control.

And the most tragic part was that he never knew I had left the lower realms. At least, I assumed he didn't. I was aware a soul could roam for an endless amount of time in the lost realms, never finding a pathway out unless they were helped by a Guardian. I couldn't recall it without delving deeper into my memories, but I must have been pulled out.

Did no one tell him? Why hadn't Archangel Michael let him know?

Nadia hadn't been my only incarnation. I had reincarnated several times afterwards before I evolved into my higher self. I had never recalled my past life as Nadia until I met Lucifer. The trauma of that life must have buried itself deep into my subconscious, and only seeing my Flame had resurrected it.

Did Lucifer know about my reincarnations? Or had our time together faded away as he eventually lost himself to the darkness?

My fists clenched. He *promised* me he wouldn't wait in Hell. He promised.

Tears pricked my eyes like tiny needles tipped in flame.

He lied.

Spinning around, I screamed. It was raw, deep, and full, rising up from the belly to shatter the silence around me. Light burst from me in a wild, uncontrolled torrent, illuminating the room in a blinding flash. Channelling more light into my hands, I threw orb after orb into the darkness. They shattered against the walls in a violent spray.

I felt uncontainable. Uncontrolled.

A frenzied mess of feelings; guilt, anger, and sorrow, pulsating through me in huge waves.

I wanted a demon to turn up just so I could destroy it. I wanted to tear it apart, make it explode, shatter it to the smallest possible particles and scatter them so far it would be impossible to put it back together. I *ached* to vent all the pain built up inside me.

He had loved me. By the *creator*, he had *loved* me.

It hurt.

I wrapped my arms around my middle and hunched slightly over as if I could contain the agony radiating out of my skin.

A low sound escaped my throat. Wounded.

I can help you, my darker self whispered. *You want to take the edge off that pain and anger? Let's destroy those cages. Free all those angels. Kill anyone who gets in our way. Imagine how good that would feel.*

I sucked in a sharp breath. Destroy. Kill.

The word 'yes' almost escaped. I struggled to suppress the syllable. Rolled with it on a landscape of whispered encouragement and deceptive arguments until I finally, with the last scraps of my will, pinned it down.

There was weakness in me. I could sense it. My darker self could sense it, too.

"No," I hissed through clenched teeth.

All those angels in pain. Their pain never ends. You could help them. They are suffering, and you can do something about it. Now.

More tears slipped down my face. Weak.

I reached out for our link, grasping onto the thin golden cord that bound me to Lucifer, needing to see him with an intensity that blinded me. I tried to sense him but got nothing.

~ Where are you? ~

***

Selaphiel watched with satisfaction as Tianya finished the ritual with the demon Ruin-aith. They had managed to obtain the necessary ingredients to form the third bond to the demon and thereby weaken the Lord of Hell's hold. She suspected Sirus was suspicious that they were planning something after their last talk, but so far, her attempts to investigate their movements had been carefully thwarted.

She knew their misdirection would only last for so long. If Sirus persisted in her perusal, they would have to come up with a more permanent solution.

It wasn't as difficult as she thought it would be to convince Nadiel to bring Tianya on board. She was expecting more resistance, but surprisingly, he gave in to her suggestion. She frowned slightly. A little too easily. Shaking her head, she dismissed her paranoia. If she started to see daggers in shadows where they weren't any, they wouldn't get anything done.

It suited her nicely that Tianya was the third bond. Even though her lover had ascended to become one of the leaders of the Fallen, she would still defer to her leadership. Selaphiel had carefully moulded her over time to become her ally with the allure of power and position. Tianya had potential, but not too much to become overly ambitious. The threat of her disinterest constantly swayed over Tianya's head like an axe. Tianya knew that if she wanted to remove her from her newly won leadership position, she could.

Selaphiel tugged energetically on the bond with the demon. She could feel the cord that bound them, oily and thick. Ruin-aith had told them that all they needed to do to call him was to send a thought, and he would respond. She also knew that the bond acted as a way to physically control the demon, but with the addition of the three of them, their ability to command him was weakened.

Which was the point.

Yes, the plan was to use the demon to neutralise Lucifer, but now Ruin-aith had a measure of free will. But it was also to be expected the demon would try and neutralise them in the process. They had banked on the demon's cooperation to get out from under Lucifer's heel, but she knew Ruin-aith wouldn't willingly trade one master for three more.

He would probably wait for them to act against the Lord of Hell before he made his move. And likewise, they would wait for him to give them access to the ninth level of Hell before they did the same. It was going to all boil down to timing and cunning.

Tianya strode up to her, cool as a shard of ice. "It's done," she said.

Nadiel pushed off the wall he was leaning on and came over to join them. His silver hair glinted in the low light, a stark contrast to the black leather that contoured his muscular frame. In certain lights, it almost looked like armour.

Selaphiel locked eyes with the demon. "When can you take us to the ninth level?"

Ruin-aith faced the three of them, his tattered wisps of shadow trailing beneath him as if moved by an unseen breeze. "Patience..." he hissed. "The bondsss will need a few hourss to ssettle and for me to tesst itss limitss. We musst proceed with caution in casse the Masster is alerted to what we have done thiss night."

"You have 24 hours," Nadiel said. "We will not be delayed. How will you contact us?"

If the demon was angry at the directive, he did not show it. That was one thing about Ruin-aith that made Selaphiel uneasy. You couldn't easily read him. Most demons were reactive, prone to lose control as easily as a child. Ruin-aith kept his emotions hidden as skillfully as his face in the shadows of his hood.

"Through the bondss," the demon said. "You will feel my call, and I will feel yourss."

"We will meet here," Nadiel confirmed. "At least two of us will go with you."

"Until then, Fallenss." The demon disappeared in a cloud of black smoke.

"How do we trust that he will come back," Tianya asked once he was gone, her dark gaze flickering around the cavern walls as if expecting an attack. They were in the fourth level of Hell. An attack was not out of the ordinary. They all had to fight their way to reach this meeting point and would have to do so again on the way back.

"Because he values his freedom," Selaphiel said.

Nadiel nodded. "The demon is aware we can break these bonds, which will leave him tied once more to Lucifer like a bound puppet. He won't act against us now."

Selaphiel crossed her arms over her chest. "Which leaves us to our next problem."

Nadiel raised an eyebrow.

"Sirus."

"Yes, she is becoming overly inquisitive. We can't afford for her to go to Lucifer," he mused.

Selaphiel sneered. "That bitch would do anything to promote herself. Her lips are so glued to his arse there is a permanent print on there."

"We could get rid of her," Tianya said quietly.

Nadiel gave her an indulgent look. "And how would you propose we do that?"

Tianya touched the hilt of her blades that crossed over her back. She stared at Nadiel without blinking.

Selaphiel admired her enthusiasm and had no doubt that the Fallen was completely capable, but if they got rid of Sirus, it would cause even more scrutiny. "She has too many followers for us to make her disappear. They'd know it was us, and then we'd have an uprising to quell."

Nadiel's fingers rhythmically tapped the outside of his leg. His eyes flickered left to right, and she knew he was sifting through his thoughts at lightning speed. Nadiel was smart. A little boring and uninspiring at the best of times, but he had a few more wheels turning than the average Fallen.

Tianya opened her mouth to speak, but Selaphiel raised her hand slightly, stalling the words before they left her lips.

She stared at Nadiel and waited.

A full minute passed.

Nadiel cleared his throat. "I have an idea."

"Really?" Selaphiel said in mock surprise. "Do tell."

"We have another problem. While we are taking trips down to the ninth level of Hell and planning how to bind Lucifer to the cells, we need to figure out a way to distract him while we work this all out."

"That's not an idea; that's another problem," Selaphiel said flatly. "And isn't that angel distracting him?"

"I'm getting there." Nadiel pushed off the wall and turned to face them. "And no, he is still out of his domain more than he is inside. He has been checking on the demon summonings and the witches and monitoring our progress with closing the Hell Gates. If we are not there to constantly lead our brethren, he will notice."

"So, how do we distract him?" Tiyana inquired.

"Hades."

Selaphiel's eyebrows shot up. "You want to bring a God into this? That could be catastrophic."

"That's the point," Nadiel said dryly. "We need a problem large enough to consume Lucifer's time. If we do it carefully, we can take out Sirus, too, without looking like we were involved."

Selaphiel leaned forward and finally smiled. "Tell me more."

***

I pushed open the heavy double doors to Lucifer's room.

He wasn't there.

I felt sick with the feelings churning in my stomach. It took an effort to not throw up. Nadia was no longer a ghost that had lived a long time ago. She wasn't even my yesterday. She was in every breath I took, a second set of lungs that moved against my own.

Go to the dungeons, my dark self insisted.

I needed Lucifer. I couldn't… it hurt…

I still loved him.

My breath came out hard, and I stumbled across the midnight floor as the truth of those words hit me.

How could I resist when little cracks of his former self had started to appear through the layers of darkness embedded into his being? They were rare moments, as precious as jewels in a starving man's hands. A look that hinted towards warmth, a smile that reached his midnight eyes, and the amused tone of voice all reminded me of the angel I had once loved.

Oh, and that laugh. Unrestrained, full, and... beautiful.

It tore at my heart with its deadly sweetness but it also gave me hope.

He was changing. I was changing him. I wanted to believe so badly I was changing him. Maybe my darker self was right. Perhaps that's why he wanted to kill me. But he didn't. Instead, he was training me to survive. He was pushing me to become stronger.

That had to mean something.

He still wants to kill you. The more you push him towards the Light, the stronger that urge will become. Here in Hell, what do you think he will do? The darkness is strongest here. Your best chance is to free the angels and leave. You are an idiot to tempt the dragon by fluttering your virgin eyelashes in front of its jaws. Soon, it's going to take a bite.

I shook my head, in denial of my darker self or the real possibility of her words... I didn't know.

The fire that ringed the room was pleasantly warm against my chilled skin. But this cold I felt ran deeper than bone. I didn't even realise I was shaking. My eyes caught on a cloak hung neatly over the back of a chair near the table. Even when he was Light, Lucifer had always been meticulous. He felt a deep sense of order and took care of things around him.

Likewise, the room was neat and minimalistic. It was a stark contrast to the Fallen domain, which was ostentatious at best. The furniture and belongings he did have were clearly of good quality, simple but luxurious.

Walking over, I touched the cloth. It felt thick and heavy, the fabric some unknown weave that managed to also be incredibly soft at the same time. I was still wearing Atlas's dirty tunic. The smell I had managed to block, but now I wanted to strip it off and burn it.

Pulling Lucifer's cloak off the chair, I spread it out in front of me and twisted it to drape over my shoulders. Instantly, his scent hit me. Smoky, exotic, and masculine with just a hint of apple. My eyes drifted shut and some of that turbulence inside eased.

Why him? Why us?

If he ever became Light again, would he cope with all he had done? Would I ever get him back?

My eyes opened slowly.

My feet drifted towards the bed, and I sat at the edge. Running my fingers through my hair, I clutched the back of my head. I could wait for Lucifer, though I didn't know how long he would be. He could be gone for hours, or he could be gone for days. After our last encounter, I wouldn't have been surprised if his absence was significant.

We needed to talk.

There was so much to say, and the time for half-truths and double entendres was over. Though getting anything out of my soulmate was like trying to carve a mountain out of ice with a blunt knife. But I was determined this time.

I laid back against the soft covers of the bed and looked up at the exquisite mandala above me, inlaid with precious stones and gems. I could feel its healing energies even though it wasn't activated. It was the only thing that reminded me of The City of Light, and I still didn't know why he had it here.

I reached for our link again.

~ Where are you? ~

***

"You can't kill me," she croaked. Her hands pressed into the ground, the small stones and sticks cutting into her palms as she tried to push herself further backwards. The thing was, she was already as far back as she could possibly go, flush against the rough bark of the tree.

It wasn't far enough. It would never be far enough. If she could fly across the earth into a different part of the world, it still wouldn't be far enough. Her mind chatted in fear, an insane ramble of thought that made it almost impossible to speak.

Brianna said the words again with difficulty, her faith in them fracturing in a hundred excruciating deaths as she looked into his dark, dark eyes. Eyes set in a face that Adonis, the Greek god of beauty and desire, would kill for. But her grandmother had told her he couldn't. And her mother before that, and so on and so on.

Please, Goddess, let it be true.

Was it all a lie? Some deluded tale an old woman made up to feel significant and as her skin turned to parchment.

"You can't kill me." She hoped, though the bodies of her coven sisters lay strewn like broken dolls all over the ground. Their necks and limbs were painful, unnatural angles. Blood, there was so much blood.

She was cold. Maybe she was already dying. The ice in his eyes made the warmth flee from her skin.

"You can't–"

"So you said," came the silky voice. He stepped over Amrita, a once vibrant young witch who spoke several languages. Amrita had been teaching her Gaelic.

Brianna gasped as her body slid up the tree as if held up by ropes made from air. The bark scraped against her skin through the rough fabric of her dress. Her feet dangled uselessly a few feet from the ground, and then suddenly, she was at eye level. She stared into those soulless eyes and trembled. On instinct, she held up her left palm where the red crescent-shaped birthmark marred the pale skin of her wrist.

She scrunched her eyes shut.

"Fortunately for you, that mark from your ancestor protects your bloodline. Otherwise, you would have joined your sisters tonight," the Devil said conversationally. He smiled.

Her eyes flew open, "So it's true..." she whispered in fear and awe. "My ancestor was a seer, and you made a deal with her."

"A long time ago. She had the foresight to protect her bloodline from harm." His long, elegant fingers wiped a speck of blood from his arm. "But then... I don't really need to kill you."

"You don't?" Brianna cleared her throat. "I mean, you can't hurt me either."

"That's the thing about pain. People always assume the worst kind is physical. Wounds heal eventually. Even death is a kind of peace. Emotional trauma, that's far more interesting." His eyes glinted in the moonlight. "How is Andrew?"

She took in a sharp breath that went nowhere. He knew about Andrew.

"And then there is Kayla, and let's not forget Richard, your father. He isn't blood-related to you, is he?"

She felt sick.

His teeth flashed like a wolf in the dark. "I've spent a considerable amount of time with a witch infinitely more powerful than you and your coven."

He lifted his hands, and darkness flowed between his fingers in several complex, geometrical shapes. They layered over each other until the patterns were too hard for her eyes to trace. Old power symbols were drawn in the air, the majority of which she had never seen in her lifetime. His power was ancient and potent, born from a time when cities were just mounds of sand unstirred by human potential. She felt his power charging the air like a storm. It called to her in recognition, making her blood sing.

What she would give to possess even a cup of it. She could rule the world.

"What are you doing?" she whispered, struggling against the air bonds to no avail. The Goddess only knew what he was conjuring.

"There is a certain spell that, when applied correctly, attaches itself to every person you connect with, any animal you bond with, your neighbour's cat, the dog that follows you home, anyone who smiles at you, shows kindness, or attempts to befriend you. The next day they die," he said easily, despite the complex spell he was weaving. "It can be an isolating existence. In fact, the last time I cast this spell the person took their life within the week."

The Devil stared at her. "I give you three days," he said softly.

Brianna's eyes widened as her mind flashed to the face of every person she cared about. Every person that could possibly care about her. "No!" she said loudly, her voice high and panicky.

"Unfortunately, 'no' is not enough of a deterrent."

"Please!"

The Devil looked bored. "When you die, please pass my regards to your ancestor."

"Wait!" She let out a shaky breath. "Please... what... what do you want?"

A smile grazed his lips though the ebony pools of his eyes remained unstirred. "Your obedience. Anything less, and the spell will go into effect."

She swallowed. "Forever?"

"A given. Until you choose otherwise. Then you know what happens."

Clouds shifted across the moon, briefly veiling the ruler of Hell in darkness. When the soft light bathed over the killing ground once more, she felt that he kept some of that darkness with him.

"What do you want me to do?"

The spell in front of her disappeared. Her invisible bonds released her, and she fell to the ground in a heap. She peered up and him through her curtain of dark, wavy hair. "You are going to be my mole. I want you to find where the other dark covens are located, infiltrate them, and find out how they are obtaining summoning names."

Her mind reeled at the scope of the request. Not request... command. She dusted herself off and stood up slowly. "Covens are a very protective and close-knit family." She avoided looking at her own on the forest floor. She would mourn them later. "Why would they even let me in?"

"Because Brianna, you are special. You have the mark. The Devil can't harm you," he said with an amused edge to his tone. "Other covens have already been eliminated, and being a sole survivor will be all the proof you need. Your bloodline will be coveted."

"If they know I'm spying on them, they will kill me."

"Then I would suggest you don't let them find out. I would hate for you to die when I've gone to such an effort to recruit you."

Brianna opened her mouth to speak and then flinched as the Ruler of Hell straightened suddenly. His expression became distant, and that focused attention pulled in a different direction. The urge to crouch down and crawl away was embarrassingly strong, but she managed to hold still.

His smooth voice became a touch more velvet. "I believe it's time I took my leave."

She nodded enthusiastically. "Yes, of course." Her throat locked tight when his dark gaze once again found hers.

"Do carry on with your task. Lack of progress would be… disappointing." The implications were as clear as if he put a sword against her throat. She'd be lucky if it was that quick. His midnight eyes became piercing. "And I would dismiss all thoughts of escape. There is nowhere on this Earth that you can hide from me."

She shook her head frantically, unwilling to admit the thought had crossed her mind. "I won't," Brianna whispered.

"There is no God or Goddess that would bar me entry, no place of worship that I cannot enter. No faith that will protect you. Do you understand?"

She cleared her throat. "I understand."

"Excellent." The Devil smiled, and she could not help but stare. "Please, enjoy the rest of your night."

She nodded helplessly and tried not to look at her dead sisters scattered around her. Part of her wished she could join them.

When she opened her mouth to ask when he would come back to check in on her... he was gone.

Chapter 22

The sound of movement woke me up.

Disoriented from sleep, I tried to process the soft bedding under my body and the warmth enveloping my skin. I wanted to sink back into oblivion but subtle noises pulled me reluctantly back to awareness. I stretched, back arching, fingers brushing satin.

My rest had been blessedly dreamless, the nightmares that chased me gratefully absent. Eyes flicking slowly open, I stared at the mandala hanging above. I blinked, confused, and it took me a couple of seconds.

I sat up so fast my head spun.

Lucifer was untying his vest, midnight eyes locked on mine.

Everything came back to me in a heady rush and all I could do was stare. I took in this angel who had descended into Hell, fought, bled and, in a way, died for me. I drank him in as if he was the last cup of clean water on Earth when all I had been consuming tasted of ash. I savoured every detail, bewildered how I could have possibly forgotten a connection that had lit my soul like a forest fire; blindingly bright and equally destructive.

Longing had my fingers itching to trace that hard jaw and soft, sculptured lips that used to map the shape of mine with reverence. Those stunning cerulean blue eyes he once had was a relic of the past, of a connection so beautiful it hurt to remember. But the darkness that had now replaced them was not as empty and cold as they had once been. Now they shimmered like a shadowed pool, concealing layers of emotion hidden within.

I ached to mend the lacerations Fate had inflicted upon our souls. We had both been bleeding for far too long. But some wounds were too deep and complex, and I was at a loss on how to even start the healing process.

Maybe in our own way, we already had.

I looked at him with eyes softened with memory. My throat felt thick, words swollen and stuck as all the things I wanted to say blurred and fought with each other. I opened my mouth to finally speak but then his vest dropped away and there was a wide expanse of muscled golden skin. Dragging my gaze up from where it had unwittingly dropped, I opened my mouth again.

His hands went to his pants.

My mouth snapped shut with an audible click.

More clothing disappeared. Midnight eyes locked onto mine, pinning me in place. The tension between us tightened and my pulse picked up speed, racing like thunderous hooves beneath my skin. Every cell in my body prickled alive, heightened with awareness. The firelight seemed brighter, the heat a lick of flame against my skin, my clothes rough and abrasive.

Anticipation had my muscles tightening, away or forward... my body was teetering on the edge. The connection between us filled the air, a lure that wanted to drag me closer until I could feel the heat of his skin pressed against my own. Part of me wanted some space to breathe and gather my thoughts. I had wanted to control this next confrontation, but of course, without even saying a word Lucifer had taken the upper hand. When he wanted to use his beauty as a weapon, it was devastating.

Then his body dipped down.

The floor transformed into a small circular bath. A flicker of awe bloomed at the ridiculous ease with which he manipulated matter. He lowered himself in the water, steam rising up, making the exposed part of his torso glisten in the firelight. Raising his arms, he rested them on the edges of the bath, leaned back and watched me through half-lidded eyes.

Waiting.

Taking a deep breath, I scooted towards the edge of the bed and stood up, holding the cloak tight around me. It was harder than I thought to take those few steps forward to the opposite side of the small pool of water. Lucifer was the one naked, yet it was I who felt stripped to my skin. Exposed. I sat down on the edge, pulling the cloak up to my knees and slide my legs in the water. It was hot but not uncomfortably so.

We stared at each other, the silence filled with a charged energy that could erupt at the slightest spark. His eyes travelled over me, taking in his cloak I had pilfered earlier, pausing at the hem of Atlas's tunic that peaked through before sliding to the bare skin of my knee and the length of my legs below. My skin tingled as if his gaze had been a caress.

"Luce..." I whispered. Would we dance around each other once more, using words like swords to deflect, parry and hurt? I refused to play that game anymore. "I remember everything."

His expression remained unchanged at my confession as if I had merely told him I had tripped over a rug. I waited, watching a bead of water slide down over his collar bone. The silence thickened and stretched between us. When there was no response, I soldiered on.

"Is our link turning you back?"

His chest rose and fell with his breath, dark hair brushing the edges of his shoulders. Anxiety flared at his continual silence. Was he going to say anything at all? My palms pressed against the edges of the bath. His dark eyes were veiled, but there was a certain tension in the line of his jaw. That slight shift in expression made me open my mouth again, forcing more words out.

"Is that why you want to kill me?"

More silence.

Frustration had the next breath hissing through my lips. I stared at him as if I could will a response, reach down and pull out the words his body so adamantly resisted.

Answer me, I pushed through our link.

His midnight eye bore through mine and his lips flattened. "Take off the tunic."

I blinked. What?

There was a flicker of emotion I couldn't quite catch. "You want answers. Get rid of the tunic."

Bewildered, I glanced down at my chest. Lucifer's cloak had parted around Atlas's tunic, which was covered with dirt, blood and other fluids my noise refused to identify. "I need it for my cover in the dungeons."

His voice curled around me like spiced honey laced with threat. "Get rid of it." The energy between us prickled with thorns.

My eyebrows raised. He was annoyed. I stared at him through the shifting steam, trying to decipher this change of mood, any hidden intent behind his words. This didn't feel like a ploy or a pathway to seduction. Lucifer was just simply irritated that I was wearing Atlas's clothes.

Interesting.

I debated what to do, fingers tapping against the edge of the pool. Hesitating only briefly, I shrugged his cloak off my shoulders, letting it spill to the floor around me. I could have stood up and turned my back or left the room to change. In fact, that is what I would have done not that many nights ago, but I remained where I was.

My fingers skimmed the edges of the tunic that rested on my lower thighs. I slid the rough material up, leaning my body weight forward slightly to shift it over my hips then pulled it off entirely in one quick motion over my head. I tossed the material to the side. I didn't look at him until I picked up his cloak and slid it back over my shoulders, wrapping it loosely around me.

I might have appeared calm and nonchalant about the whole thing, but on the inside, my lungs felt like they were weighted with stone and I couldn't cram enough air inside.

I looked up… and shivered.

Sheer lust flashed across his face before he slammed it away. In its place was a controlled, cool mask. But I saw it. Underneath that controlled civility was something raw and animalistic skimming just under the surface.

Voice unsteady, I pushed again. "Tell me."

I felt the lightest brush of phantom fingers graze the edge of my collarbone. The side of his lip tipped up. "Perhaps you'd like to have this conversation a little closer?"

"I feel that would be counterproductive."

"I assure you it would be very productive." His eyes gleamed, the shadows created by the firelight giving his face a wicked edge.

"You owe me some answers," I softened my voice, refusing to be distracted. "Let us finally lay the truth between us."

Lucifer raised an eyebrow. "Truth. You say that as if our conversations have thus far been riddled with lies."

"Perhaps not lies," I acknowledged with a tilt of my head, "but slivers of truth that can be open to too many interpretations. I don't want to dig for answers or the meanings behind your words. Humour me by speaking plainly for once."

"The meaning of my conversations have been quite clear. Your lack of comprehension is your burden to bear, not mine."

I let out an exasperated breath. "Perhaps try to be even more clear." I gave him a flat look. "As if you are talking to a child."

Lucifer's brows lifted. After a moment he finally said, "Three questions. No doubt, little angel, you have a long list and I can think of much better ways to occupy myself for the rest of the night," he purred, the double meaning behind his words clear.

Despite my best intentions, my face flushed. Clearing my throat, I nodded. "Three questions, then. Fully answered. Deal?"

His lips tilted up again. "Deal."

Pondering my questions, I was reminded of the same deal that was struck with the Nabala. I had to choose my questions carefully as I didn't know when I would be presented with an opportunity like this again. A completely honest answer from Lucifer? That was like glimpsing a sunbeam in Hell.

After a couple more moments of careful deliberation, I asked my first question. "How do you feel about our link changing the darkness within you?" I had to assume he was already aware the link was making him light. I didn't want to waste asking a question with a yes or no answer. I wanted to know if he was angry at our soulmate link and as a result still wanted to harm me.

"How do I *feel*?" He drew out the word like it was foreign and found it distasteful. "I find it of little consequence."

I looked at him incredulously. "I find that hard to believe," I shot out.

"Are you implying that I'm lying?" he asked casually, but it felt like I was standing on cracking ice. "I wouldn't want you to *feel* like I was breaking our deal."

Unperturbed, I narrowed my eyes. "You wanted to kill me not that long ago. Surely you could understand why your answer is confusing."

"Then is not now, little angel."

"What has changed?"

"Is that another question?"

"No," I corrected. "It's an expansion of the first question. Fully answered," I reminded him.

He smiled and I felt another brush of phantom fingers circle lazily around my ankle. My leg twitched. "It's of little consequence because I've realised it is something I can reverse when I choose to."

My mouth dropped open. "Reverse? How in everything holy can you reverse our soulmate link?" Surely that couldn't be possible.

"Is that your second question?"

"Yes," I said, leaning forward intently. "What do you mean, reverse our soulmate link?"

"The link is not completely formed. It will take time. Before it does, I will re-embrace the darkness and severe it."

Horrified, I whispered, "Why would you do that?" I shook my head quickly and held out my palm to stall him from answering. "Wait, I need to clarify. What do you mean by re-embrace the darkness? What are the implications with that?"

"Re-embrace. To let the darkness consume me once more and eradicate what is not in alignment."

My lips parted. "And then your soul would be gone again," I murmured.

What did that mean for us? Lucifer had changed since the first time I had met him in Kryptos. Gone was the cold, aloof and cuttingly cruel Ruler of Hell. His abrasive nature had weathered away by the ghosts of the past and in its place I had witnessed an amused, charismatic host whose harsh almost brutal allure had warmed and softened like golden honey. Would it all go back to the way it was? I didn't think my heart could handle it.

"Why?" I asked softly. "Why would you want to go back? Is being this way really so intolerable?"

"Hell would not bend to an angel of the Light," he said simply.

Disappointment surged. "And you still wish to rule."

"There is no one else strong enough."

I raised my brows, disappointment blending into anger at the inevitable end of us. "You make it sound altruistic, but perhaps you also just love to rule. If there was a way for you to leave, I wonder if you would even take it."

His eyes glittered. "Tell me, if I left, what do you think would happen if one of the Forsaken replaced me, or perhaps a demon strong enough?"

I swallowed thickly. "Chaos for Earth and the higher realms. I'm not a fool. I know you are keeping the demons at bay and the Forsaken, as well... to an extent." I paused. "Why is that, by the way?"

His fingers tapped on the glossy black tiles. "I do believe, little angel, that you have already asked your three questions."

I smiled at him and lifted a shoulder. "How about you throw a free one… for old times sake." My tone was light and teasing to mask how much I really wanted to know the answer. He appeared to hate the warrior angels and The City of Light. Why hadn't he let demons roam the Earth and force The City to concentrate a larger force of warrior angels on Earth? By doing that, he could have enslaved and turned more of them. His one hundred Fallen could easily be triple that number.

So why hadn't he? Wouldn't that be the action of someone truly dark?

"I'm not known for giving exemptions. But…" he looked at me thoughtfully, "perhaps we can renegotiate? How about a question for a question?"

I blinked. What could he possibly ask me that he didn't already know?

"I… can agree to that," I said cautiously.

Phantom fingers grazed the curve of my hip and then ever so lightly dragged across my lower stomach an inch below my belly button. My lips parted. What was he doing? Was that the drag of teeth against the base of my spine? I shivered, my eyes glazing as desire swirled within.

His voice was silk. "If I had you underneath me on that bed like I did not so long ago, would you run?"

Immediately, the memory I had so desperately tried to put out of my head slammed back in front of me. The way it felt to be underneath him, having that gloriously muscled skin slide sensuously beneath my hands. The addictive taste of his lips and the overwhelming thrill of his caress.

I hadn't wanted to think about it. Not because I didn't want to, but because I *wanted* to, too much.

~ *He wants you, too, even now. Just take a step and what you desire could be yours* ~ My darker self purred inside me. ~ *That's really why you came here, isn't it? Or did you really believe you sought him out to have a conversation?* ~ She laughed huskily.

Get out of my head! I hissed back. I mentally shoved her deeper inside. My darker self withdrew, but as if she had decided to graciously leave herself, trailing laughter as she disappeared.

I realised Lucifer was waiting for an answer. I blushed furiously. Nervously, I tucked some of my hair behind my ear, pulling the strands around my face to play with the ends. His phantom touch had disappeared but now he had me anticipating when and where I would feel it again.

"That's..." I cleared my throat, "that's what you wanted to ask me? What kind of question is that?"

I was panicking.

"The type of question you answer or don't."

I was going to ramble. I could feel the words jumble up on my tongue, waiting to spill out like a verbal barrage of nonsensical statements that were designed to embarrass me further and confuse the person on the receiving end. With great effort, I swallowed what I was going to say. It felt like a lump of rocks going down my throat.

My eyes burned with the effort.

"No," I forced out, in a falsetto whisper. I refused to look at his face. "No, I wouldn't run."

I looked at the surface of the bath as if I found the steam rolling across the surface fascinating. "Your turn," I croaked out.

There was a long silence and I wondered if he expected my response. "Leverage," he finally said softly. "The threat of releasing every cultural religious nightmare in force has bought me leverage amongst the Gods, fae, your City of Light and other beings of power or influence. A small example here or there has been enough incentive to pull strings when and where I wish to. If I let the demons roam free I lose that power and I run the risk of uniting a diverse group of higher beings against me by giving them a common enemy," he paused. "That's the first reason. The second is the Law of Balance. Each force has an equal, opposite force to balance it out. If I create too much chaos I will also manifest the means to reorder than chaos. Since I can't predict how exactly that will manifest and the impact it will have I would rather control my sphere of influence and take measured responses."

"Right," I muttered and finally looked up. The darkness in his eyes was softer but there was an intensity there that sent my pulse thrumming. "Why did you bring Atlas to me when you could have trained me yourself?" I asked, exasperated.

Lucifer's laugh was light and husky. "That's another question, little one." The smile lingered on his lips and my own curved up in response.

My foot flicked out, spraying water at him. "I'm not paying for another question; the Creator only knows what else you are going to ask."

"Is Atlas not worth the price? I think he would be insulted."

"I don't think you could dent Atlas's self worth even if you threw a boulder at it," I mused.

His brow raised. "I could always try."

"Don't you dare!" I laughed, my foot flicking out again.

His hand wrapped around my ankle, stopping me from spraying him. I froze. The heat of his hand was starkly different from the cool phantom touch. Our eyes locked. The room felt small and then also not small enough.

His body tensed and his grip on me tightened. Then slowly he let go of my leg, one finger at a time. The humour that had lit his face left and he leaned back until he was once more against the edge of the bath.

"I have things I need to attend to," he said coolly.

"Oh," I said, bewildered at the change of tone and unwilling to look too closely at the disappointment curling inside. "Of course."

He moved to stand up and I quickly averted my eyes. I heard the water slosh in the bath and then lighter drips hitting the floor. Sliding my legs out of the water I stood up slowly, and wrapped Lucifer's cloak even tighter around me, holding it together with one hand.

I glanced up and my breath hitched.

When Lucifer was light his beauty was magnetic, pure and utterly bewitching, like watching a star being born. Now that he was dark, he was still beautiful, but it had transformed into a seductive sharpness, his every movement radiating a carnal heat that was impossible to ignore. It was distracting at the best of times. More so now with just a towel draped low around his hips and his armbands glinting in the light. It transportant me back to when I had seen him in the lake near my house in my past life. Then too he didn't seem real.

I finally realised he was waiting for me to leave.

Flushing again I took a couple of steps backward. "Thank you for your time. I'm glad we had the chance to talk about things and clear some points up." Did we clear things up? I had no idea. I'm sure I was supposed to talk about something else. "I shall leave you now to... er... do what you do." I gestured around him randomly and noticed the rumpled bed.

"Ah, sorry about disturbing your bed. I could…" I took a hesitant step forward towards the bed, " make it…" I said uncertainly looking at the blank expression on his face. "Or… I'll just leave you."

You're rambling. Get out, get out, get out!

I spun around and started to walk out the room. As I passed by the table with the fruit platter and pitcher of wine my body slowed. My hand reached out and grazed the glossy red apple balancing on the top. The colour was a deep, rich crimson, smooth and perfectly shaped.

I picked it up and felt its weight in my hand. The firelight reflected on its surface, giving it an almost golden glow. The subtle scent wafted up to me making my mouth water. And then like in a trance, my lips touched the skin and I took a bite.

Crunch.

Divine… Delicious...

Closing my eyes, I savoured the flavour unfurling along my tongue and saturating my mouth. It was even better than I remembered. The balance between sweet and tart was perfect. Its crispy flesh held the juice within, releasing in bursts with every movement of my mouth. How had I avoided eating one for so long?

Movement behind jolted me back to awareness.

I turned quickly.

Lucifer was close enough to touch, midnight eyes staring at me intently. He watched me finish eating the piece of apple in my mouth and swallow it down as if he couldn't look away. Without thinking, my hand lifted up and I offered the red fruit up to his lips.

"Do you want some?" I whispered.

The look on his face made my mouth go dry.

The apple dropped from my fingers. My hands tangled in his thick, dark hair. A different flavour seared against my lips, snatching the oxygen straight from my lungs. My knees buckled. Lucifer's hands fisted in the back of his cloak drawing me back up against his chest until I was off the floor and pressed against his skin. He kissed me as if he had been waiting for this moment for a thousand years. More. It was desperate, consuming, and I couldn't get enough.

Our link burned bright gold like a lance of sunlight piercing through us both. It hummed through my body igniting every nerve and I could feel... *feel... so much.*

I moaned as desire tore through me and the sound was a spark on a mountain of tinder. We clawed at each other's clothes until they fell, shredded on the floor. White noise blurred through my brain. Lucifer's hands shifted to my thighs, lifting me up so my legs could wrap around him. He walked us towards the bed then stopped. His hand wrapped around in my hair, tugging my head back sharply, breaking the seal of our lips.

I gasped and struggled to understand the sudden distance. The beast shifted behind his eyes.

"No more running," his voice held an edge as if he was daring me to oppose him. "Do you understand?"

I stared at him, then nodded.

A flash of triumph flashed across his face, but through our link I could sense different emotions; anticipation, hunger and … longing. It was the last that brought my lips back to his in a silent demand.

We kissed again and fell onto the bed in a tangle of limbs. I yielded beneath him, glorying in the feeling of his hard body against my own, letting my hands explore, sweeping across his broad shoulders and down the muscles that shifted and moved along his back. I wasn't running now. There was nothing but this fallen angel in my arms and the burning need to finally make us one.

My thighs tightened around him and when he brushed against me I gasped into his mouth. Cords of air lifted my hands from his skin and held them down on either side of me. My eyes fluttered open. His control was hanging by threads, yet something made him refrain from taking what he so clearly wanted.

"Not yet," he murmured huskily, almost to himself.

More bonds of air untangled my legs from around his waist and held them to the bed. I yanked against the restraints. "Why are you–" The words dried up in my throat as his lips skimmed delicately over my breast.

I shivered with pleasure but the contact was far, far too light than what I wanted. My back arched to press closer but Lucifer leaned away. His lips travelled gently over my other breast, circling around its peak, making me move restlessly. The slightest brush over my nipple had me jerking off the bed.

"Luce," I whispered, a plea and a question.

Then he set about showing me with deliberate, excruciating patience the difference between a light angel and a fallen one. Lucifer brought me to the edge of madness with his lips and hands alone, stroking the flames of desire higher and higher. Every time I got close to releasing the well of pleasure growing uncontrollably inside me, he pulled back and began his beautiful torture somewhere else.

When his phantom touch added to his caresses I was almost to the point of begging. When he turned his attention between my legs I *did* beg, in every language I knew.

His connection to my feelings had me completely at his mercy. He knew when to give and when to take away. He knew how hard or soft to tease and stroke, watching me tremble from the onslaught. His own hunger was a beast inside him and only the fine sheen of sweat glistening on his skin gave away how much his control was costing him. He had wanted this too much. Me, beneath him, pleading and desperate.

Only when I was balanced on the fine edge of pleasure and tipping towards the pain, did he finally join our bodies together and release my bonds. My body bowed back on the verge of snapping and I shattered in a million pieces. Bliss overwhelmed me, exploding through every atom and I gripped him hard, trying to hold onto sanity.

It was like nothing I had ever imagined.

He moved within me. So oversensitised from his earlier ministrations that I came apart again. And again. His teeth grazed against the curve of my neck and shoulder, biting down hard. The growl that emanated from him was pure animalistic. His smooth, sensuous strokes turned deep, passionate, almost savage.

Fingers bruised my skin and his grip tightened like steel. I took the force of his desire and matched it with my own. Our bodies pressed into the bed, our hands linked together and we kissed like we were each other's worlds.

I cried out as an endless wave of ecstasy broke over me and felt his body release, muscles going taunt. Dear Creator, I could feel his soul... a beacon of light that was so achingly familiar, trapped beneath the dark. Tears leaked from my eyes at the sheer beauty and moment of utter completion as our souls merged into one.

Nothing could ever match this. This was what it was like to be with your Flame.

I floated back down, completely limp. My face turned to brush against his, eyes closing from the weight of exhaustion. Instinctively, I reached out through the link and tapped into a mixture of emotions churning through him. At the forefront was still a deep, thrumming hunger for more, a clawing desire that had me shifting restlessly despite feeling depleted. Underneath, I caught hints of confusion and even anger, but I was too tired to delve any further.

Lifting my head slightly, I pressed a kiss to his shoulder then started to drift. A minute later the bed moved as his body gently untangled from mine.

And then I knew no more.

Chapter 23

Hunger... is weakness.

It controls your senses, focusing your mind exclusively on the need that *must* be fulfilled. It pecks at you incessantly like a scavenger. You can only ignore hunger temporarily, pushing it down briefly before it claws its way back up.

Not a mild irritation to be swatted away, but a toothy predator shifting through the foliage. You cannot turn your back on a predator. Sooner or later, it will pounce and consume you.

The hollow pain was manageable, but when the very thing he yearned for paraded itself right in front of him... that was a special kind of torture.

And he knew all about torture.

He had been starved for centuries. But no more. A sharp thrill jolted through his soulless form. He tempered the need to move faster, to hurry the pleasure that awaited him at long last. But such things should not be rushed but savoured.

Ruin-aith moved through the Underworld, obscure like any other shadow. He had learnt how to be unseen when he wished. He liked to amuse himself by testing how near he could get behind his target before they sensed him. Most of them couldn't. Being so close to their vulnerable backs and unable to do anything about it made him itch fiercely inside.

His instincts raged at him to take what he wanted, but his bond prevented him. He hated that bond.

A flicker of white moved just on the edges of his vision.

His mouth salivated.

Yes, yes… that one. He wanted that one.

Ruin-aith followed the white glow silently through twists and turns in the Underworld. The soul floated gently, drifted almost aimlessly down the rocky corridors. All souls that arrived in the Underworld by the ferryman wandered at their own pace before they were judged and processed to the appropriate realm. Their bright energies were irresistible to demons, a juicy morsel just waiting to be plucked, but Hades' guards, especially Cerbeus, were quick to deliver punishment to those interfering with souls.

A soul's screams tremored along the walls of the Underworld. Like a vibration along the silken strands of a web, one needed to get away before it alerted the spider.

His elongated fingers flexed in anticipation as he neared closer to the soul. It was alone, a middle-aged female in a long skirt and tattered blouse. The pearly luminance of her form hid the colour of her skin and hair that life would have given her. But the pure light of her soul was all the brightness she needed. Nothing else mattered.

Nothing else would sate his hunger.

Ruin-aith waited until the soul turned into a shadowy bend of a tunnel. She would momentarily be invisible to any other being that happened to be nearby. He had to be careful, and he had to act now. He disappeared only to appear again directly in front of her.

The hood of his shadowy cloak fell back.

He swallowed her screams before they pierced the air. He swallowed and swallowed, sucking in her essence, drawing it inside him like marrow from a juicy bone. Her pain was ecstasy. Her screams continued to echo deep inside him, warming the cold places inside. He shuddered in pleasure and swallowed more and more. He could have kept on swallowing, feeling like he had only just begun, but then suddenly... there wasn't anything left.

The light that she was had disappeared.

Too quick. The pleasure was gone in a flash. Oh, he could still feel her screaming inside him. Long, endless wails of despair. She was his now, forever. But there was nothing quite like the consuming. They were so much better as they were going down than when they settled inside him.

The hunger inside wanted more. Demanded more.

Patience. Patience, he told it.

Immediately, he could feel the effects. Power trickled inside of him, feeding his form. It was like taking a sip of cool, fresh air after being locked in a cage. It wasn't enough, but soon it would be.

Soon, he would be what he once was. He had gone by many names over the ages, most forgotten when he had been chained in servitude. But one still echoed down the passages of time. A name that still made others tremble.

Even the Gods.

Soul Eater.

***

He was gone.

I could feel the absence of his presence without opening my eyes. It was like a blanket of warmth that had been removed from my skin, leaving me chilled and exposed. Through our link, I could sense him somewhere in the distance.

My hand moved across the rumpled sheets to the spot he had occupied. I wasn't quite sure how long I had slept, but it felt like some time. Sleep still clogged my mind, and I struggled to will it away. Lucifer had left just before I had fallen asleep amid a swirl of conflicting emotions. Now that I was awake, I instinctively wanted to go to him and ease some of that turbulence, but I knew that was not what he needed.

What my Flame needed was space and time to manage the opposing forces going to war inside of him. His mind was a battleground, and both armies were determined to win.

He had made his intentions very clear. Lucifer planned to re-embrace the Darkness. Just thinking about it was almost enough to crush the euphoria of being with him. But until he did, his soul and his conscience would fight him every step of the way. And that meant he would fight what was growing between us every step of the way.

Did that worry me? Yes. Could I do anything about it? No. I knew I had to tread carefully in this emotional minefield and take each step with the utmost care. Despite him leaving, we had progressed, and the last thing I wanted to do was push him too far and end up further backwards.

I sat up and immediately regretted the movement. My body felt like a mass of aches and bruises. I winced as I raised my hand to run my fingers through my tangled hair. My fingers snagged halfway through my wild mane, and I pulled, trying to force my fingers through.

"Ow." My eyes watered as my roots threatened to leave my scalp.

I sighed and gave up. At least I'd blend in while in the dungeons.

A short snort of laughter escaped my lips, and I slapped a hand over my mouth. Giddy. I was feeling giddy. The smile remained on my face, then softened to a rueful curl of lips. I would give my Flame time, and in the meantime, I would hope.

Swinging my legs over the side of the bed, I stood up slowly. My body protested vigorously, and I immediately sat back down. No... this would not do at all.

A short time later, after I had healed myself, I took a quick dip in the bath, grateful that it was still warm. It also gave me a chance to detangle the snarls in my hair and curl it in a loose bun at the nape of my neck. That slightly nervous, anxious feeling I usually had when being in Lucifer's room had all but disappeared. The fear of my emotional and physical safety from the Lord of Hell had been replaced by firmer ground. At least for the moment.

Lucifer's room was probably now the safest place in Hell, but at the same time, I didn't want to overstay my welcome.

I scooped up Atlas's rags from the floor and clenched them to my chest as the portal mirror caught my eye.

"Oh, for the love of..." I smacked my hand against my head. I knew what I had forgotten to ask Lucifer. "Stupid, stupid, stupid," I muttered to myself as I hurriedly put on Atlas's clothes, the feeling of tranquillity all but dashed.

My brain had clearly stopped functioning in my soulmates' presence, and I had completely forgotten to mention my problem with the portal mirrors. It was one of the biggest challenges I had in getting the warrior angels out of Hell. There was no feasible way I could lead a hundred angels into the Fallen domain to access the portal to the Underworld without starting a war we couldn't win.

I had planned to ask Lucifer if I could 'borrow' one of the portal mirrors he had here. If I could fix one to the Underworld or, even better, to Earth, I would have no need to go to the Fallen domain at all. In fact, my bargain with the witches would also be unnecessary.

But I didn't ask. It didn't even enter my mind. Granted, I was a little stuck on clearing the air about Lucifer's intentions to kill me and our soulmate link dissolving, but I also had the lives of other angels in my hands, and I couldn't afford to miss any opportunity to help them.

I didn't even know if Lucifer would even agree to help me. Just because our relationship had evolved didn't mean he would also make things easier on me. If he thought this situation was somehow helpful to my training, he wouldn't just throw me in the fire; he would marinate me first.

I had to regroup and work on another way forward.

It was time to see Atlas.

***

I merged into Atlas's room and blinked. The room had expanded, more than doubled its size. Beyond the bed was a mostly empty space with rows of different types of weapons hanging from racks against the wall. Atlas was moving precisely around the room with a long sword held in both hands. He had also been gifted with new clothes. A plain brown tunic hung loosely on his form to mid thigh and dark brown leggings encased his legs, leaving his feet bare.

His hair, which had previously hung wildly about his face, unlike mine not too long ago, was braided back roughly, revealing a strength to the bones of his cheeks and jaw. He looked more like a commander of an army than he ever did before.

His dark eyes lit up as he caught sight of me. "Sandy! Where have you been?" And then, with jubilance, "Look what I've got!" He spread his arms and turned slowly around the room so I could take it all in.

"I can see," I said, amused and impressed. Walking towards him, I marvelled at the vast array of weapons. There were bows of all different sizes, wooden staves, swords, which were long, short, or curved, axes, daggers, and other weapons that I couldn't find a name for.

"Do you know how to use all these things?" I asked in wonder as I faced a board of throwing implements of all different shapes, ranging from teardrops to stars.

He laughed with a touch of manic glee. "It would take me many lifetimes to be proficient in all of these, but he promised me a trainer for as long as I help you. Imagine the new skills I could show my men and surprise those ball-sniffing Kolaiths! I can take any weapons I want with me." He twisted his sword in his hand admiringly.

I paused at what he said. "What do you mean 'he' promised you a trainer?"

Atlas looked at me and wrinkled his nose. "Sandy, you should really get some new clothes. You reek like a boar pen."

I stared at him. Had he forgotten these were his clothes? I shook my head and waved my hand dismissively, "Atlas, who were you talking to?"

He looked at me as if I was a bit slow. "The demon king, Sandy. Remember him?"

"When did he come here?" I demanded.

Atlas shrugged his shoulders. "A little while ago. What have you been doing?"

Lucifer had visited Atlas after I had fallen asleep? Why?

"Atlas, you are not explaining yourself properly," I said in exasperation. "Why would Lucifer, who has threatened you with death by scorpions, all of a sudden gift all these weapons and someone to train you in them?" That didn't sound like my soulmate at all.

He scratched his beard with his free hand. "Ah yes, I may have had a moment." He waved his arm casually. "A man is not meant to be locked up in a cell with nothing to do. You're off doing things that will probably eventually get you killed, and I'm left to wonder when the Draga serpent thing in the wall will eventually eat me. I threatened to off myself and other things. We had a chat and renegotiated our terms."

My eyebrows climbed up my forehead. "You threatened to kill yourself?"

"Well, I can't exactly help you if I'm dead," he snapped.

My face fell. If Atlas truly threatened to kill himself he must have been miserable indeed. "I'm sorry he brought you here," I said softly, wringing my hands together. "If I could make him send you back, I would."

He studied me sceptically. "Would you? If I could help you free your angels, would you really want to send me back?"

I looked away, aware of the conflict inside, the balancing of the scales. I wasn't surprised that he thought I would or could use him without any consideration for his own needs. If I was honest with myself, if the choice was there, so was the temptation. But I had been taught better than that. I believe that we were all created with a purpose, and that purpose didn't manifest when we took from others to get there.

When I finally looked back into his brown eyes, I said quietly, "If it was in my power to set you free, I would never make you stay here against your will. I have to believe that I have been given everything I need to accomplish the task set before me. I'd have to have faith that this is one of the reasons I've been sent here."

He stared at me for a long moment, then cleared his throat. "You'll never make it out of here without me. I can't have you flap your lips and tell people I've trained you and then do something stupid and fail." He scowled. "What would that do to my reputation?"

My lips twitched. "Why didn't you negotiate to go back to your army every few days?"

A shoulder rose up and down. "I might have pushed and asked for a few more other things, and the demon king's made it… ah, clear, I was not indispensable."

Ah. That sounded more like Lucifer. It was still unusual that he would have negotiated with Atlas where torturing or threatening him would have obtained his continued corporation. Was this another glimmer of his soul influencing his actions? I was aware there seemed to be more details to the conversation, but Atlas didn't seem like he wanted to elaborate.

"Now I can teach you how to fight." He beamed at me.

My head reared back in alarm. "No, thank you. I think I'll be fine."

"Sandy," Atlas said patiently, advancing on me with his sword raised. "You need to learn how to defend yourself."

"I can defend myself," I said hastily, backing away from the sharp, moving point.

Lifting his sword, he countered, "But what are you going to do if—"

The top half of his sword fell to the floor with a clang. He looked down at where the short length of steel had fallen to the ground and then back up at me.

I dropped my hand, which had shot out a focused beam of heat.

He gritted his teeth and growled, "I *liked* that sword."

"I was just trying to show you that I don't necessarily need to learn how to use your weapons," I explained.

"I know you can use your other abilities, you little nit," his voice started to rise, "but what are you going to do if you find yourself surrounded by a ring of witches and unable to light a candle?"

Oh. I pointed at the stump of metal in his hand. "Well, do you think if I had a sword, I would be any more effective? They would incapacitate me with magic before I could take a step."

"Who said anything about a sword?" he roared, waving the broken edge of his blade around.

"Well, what…. I don't…" I sputtered.

He threw the hilt at me. It bounced off my chest. Ow. "You could have used a small throwing knife and taken out one of the witches or a bloody candle; I don't know! It doesn't have to be big and dramatic, " he said, waving his arms violently, "it can be small and effective."

"But I don't think that's the best use of my time," I countered stubbornly. "Right now, the witches are currently on my side. The problem I face is with the Fallen, who would be infinitely more superior than me with weaponry no matter how long you take to train me. There is no point in spending all this effort on learning a new skill when I should be honing the ones I have and figuring a way to free the warrior angels and escape."

"The Fallen ones don't expect you to know anything about weaponry, which is why learning a few things might give you an element of surprise that could save your stupid, stupid life."

"Atlas," I beseeched, "What's going to save my life is to find a way to open the cell doors holding the warrior angels as quickly as I can. Please, the weapons can wait. I can't afford to waste any more time battling with one cage at a time and exhausting my strength. By the time I open ten cages, the Fallen will have a fair idea of what I'm up to."

He scrunched his lips at me, then suddenly twisted his head to the side with the help of one hand. A loud crack sounded near the vicinity of his neck.

Fascinated, I asked, "Did that hurt?"

"No," he replied distractedly, rolling his neck loosely around. His brown eyes sharpened. "Okay, Sandy, we will work on this problem first. But…" he poked his finger at me, "after that, you will learn to at least throw a dagger. Daggers can be easily hidden and can be used at long and short ranges. Just don't stab yourself with it."

I huffed out a breath. "Okay, deal."

"Now," he said, pacing towards the wall full of long and short swords. "Tell me how you opened the last cell."

I explained to him how I generated a bar of white light and bore a hole through the dark cage, allowing me to jump inside. He grabbed another sword and practised a series of surprisingly graceful moves as he listened. "The angel inside was almost delirious. I had to convince him that I was real. Even if I open the cages, how do I get them out?"

Atlas stabbed at an imaginary foe. "There are three things a successful general does if they want to win a war. Firstly they need to be able to move their army quickly. Speed is everything and gives you the ability to position your troops exactly where you need them to defend or attack. Or, in your case, retreat."

He blocked a series of unseen blows. "Secondly, you need to be innovative and flexible with your plans. Even the best-laid plans can be shat on. If you can't think quickly on your feet and work with what you've got, then you've lost. That will come down to your attitude."

Atlas slowed down and faced me. "Lastly, you need to give your men morale. They need to believe they can win. A man without the belief he can win is a man looking to die. And soldiers need to find that from their general or the commander of the army. Do they have a general?"

My lips twisted as I thought. "I wouldn't know. The only high person of rank that I am aware of is Rushton. There could be others that are higher."

"Good enough. He would know how to get soldiers moving. Warriors instinctively obey commands and tone of voice. Bark orders at them, and they will obey even if their bodies tell them not to. If he is good enough, he will also give them the belief. But that will also depend on how you impart your plan to him and if he will listen to you."

"He'll listen to me," I said quietly. "I'll need to find him, though. That might be a bit difficult." I only had a vague idea of where Rushton was located, and since the last time I had seen him, he could have been moved. Did the Fallen keep the warrior angels in one cell, or did they move them around?

"Can't you ask the witches to help find him?"

I tapped my chin thoughtfully. "I could ask them, but it would be hard to describe him." To a human, if they looked at Rushton, they would see a beautiful angel with brown hair and lighter brown eyes. I doubted they would be able to get close enough to notice that his eyes were actually dark, burnished gold and his hair, not one solid colour, but the varied hues of cedar trees in the spring. So a description of that detail would be useless. "I'll need to show them a picture," I muttered. It would be easier if they could see his face, then they could recognise him even from a distance."

"Can you draw?" Atlas asked curiously. "My nephew was an artist. A terrible one." Smiling at the memory, he continued, "He drew naked pictures of his wife, but they looked nothing like her. She found them in his desk one morning and thought he was sleeping with the maid. So she stabbed him with a steak knife." He shuddered. "Vicious woman."

"Oh…" I was unsure how to respond. "Did she find out the truth in the end?"

"You know," he said thoughtfully, crossing his arms. "I think so. He had written a love letter to her on the back of one of the paintings."

"I'm sorry, that's awful."

Atlas didn't look that upset. "As I said, terrible artist." He snorted loudly. "What a useless profession anyway."

I opened my mouth to educate him soundly on the connection between the spark of creation, with the oneness of spirit and art, and then snapped my teeth shut, remembering who I was talking to. Instead, I cleared my throat. "Well, I haven't ever tried my hand at drawing… but," my mind ticked over, "I could use crystals."

He frowned at me and, with considerable doubt, scoffed, "Are you going to build a statue of Rushton out of crystals?"

"No." I laughed, pausing at how ridiculous that would look, "but I can store a memory in one. Quartz crystals can store not only power but information. It would be better than a drawing."

He stared at me blankly. "Sure."

I still had to finish my quota of storing Light into the crystals Lucifer gave me. I hadn't forgotten. Those crystals had come in handy more than once. Earlier, I had been able to use the stored Light to dissolve the dark energy of the witch circle. Too bad I couldn't use the same tactic with the dark cages. I'd need to have a steady stream of Light to have any effect on the cages in order to hold them down.

"I still have the problem of dismantling the prisons." I bent down and picked up the bottom half of the broken sword I had previously sheared in two. "This won't work unless I can figure out a way to open the cages all at the same time." A touch of fear slithered into my voice. "I'm running out of time, Atlas."

It wasn't just the situation with Lucifer that was like walking on cracking ice, unstable and perilous. It was also the fact that the longer I waited, the more warrior angels I would lose to the dark.

He raised his brows in question. "Didn't you ask the demon king for help?"

And there it was. "I didn't get time," I said, desperately willing my face not to flush. "Also, it was the portal mirrors I was meant to ask about, not opening the cages."

His frown told me he wasn't buying it. I signed inwardly. My face must be as transparent as glass.

Voice rising suspiciously, he asked, "What is Ares's asshole were you doin' then?"

I opened my mouth and then closed it again, unsure of what to say.

His annoyed face slowly became a look of dawning understanding and then swiftly into complete, utter disgust. Atlas shook his head at me, his lips curling as if he had eaten something sour. "Didn't you think that after you screwed the demon, it would have been, I don't know, a *good* time to ask for a favour?"

This time I could feel the blush flushing across my skin. "I forgot, and... he was gone by the time I woke up."

"Well, I hope it was a damn good lay, Sandy, because this is how far we have progressed." He held up his fingers and curled them into a zero.

I can do it, my darker self whispered, interjected in the recess of my mind. At the sound of her voice, my grip convulsed on the hilt of Atlas's sword. *I can open all the cages at the same time.* My green eyes reflected back at me on the surface of the blade.

And what would that cost me? I asked grimly.

What would be worth the price?

My jaw tensed. *Your price would be too high.*

Would it?

I didn't answer and didn't want to think too much about the answer. Instead, I lifted my gaze to Atlas. Frustration burned from within me, and I let the emotion light up my skin with power. I raised my hand, wreathed in white flames, and shouted, "What's the point in having this power if I can't make it do the things I need it to do!"

Atlas squinted at me through the blazing white glow. "I can't see."

"Maybe I'll just blind the Fallen," I muttered snarkily, then tilted my head, wondering if I could do that. How quickly would they be able to heal?

"Can't see."

It would be too risky. Focused Light that was too intense might bore a hole instead of blinding them. But then they would regenerate eventually. It wasn't like I would be killing them permanently, just knocking them out of the game for a while.

"Put the damn Light out, Sandy!" Atlas snapped at me.

I started from my thoughts. "Oh, sorry." I let the Light disappear.

He suddenly frowned and looked around. "Do that again." At my confused look, he gestured impatiently. "The blazing Light, Sandy. Put it back on!"

I acquiesced and let my hand glow brightly once more.

"Make it brighter," he ordered, his brown eyes unusually intense.

I did as he asked. My Light brightened the space around us, spilling across the floor and walls like liquid starlight.

"Brighter!" he yelled, pointing a finger at me.

Not sure what he was up to but willing to try, I channelled more Light until it flowed down my arm over my shoulder. The Light in the room stretched further.

"Brighter, Sandy!" he howled, raising his arms skyward. "Brighter!"

Unnerved by his howling shriek, my Light trembled, threatening to wink out, but I quickly steadied it. Brighter? Fine. I visualised the Light expanding from the centre of my body, growing, stretching until it filled my skin, almost bursting through. Then I let it explode out of my pores. It flooded the room in a fast blazing wave, chasing the shadows to the furthest corners.

My vision went bright, and Atlas lifted his forearm to shield his eyes. After a moment, I realised he was laughing.

Confused, I let the Light fade away. "Atlas," I asked patiently, "what's so amusing?'

His laughter died down to a rumbling chuckle. Once he could see, he placed a hand on my shoulder and lightly shoved me backwards. "That's what you do!"

"Pardon?"

"Sandy, I know you're a bit slow but can't you see? This is how you take down the cages." His smile widened, stretching the corners of his face. "You glow, you nit. You glow your little, itty-bitty heart out."

Chapter 24

The Ferryman glided slowly across the river Acheron. The soft mist billowed gently across the water's surface, flowing across the sides of his boat in a thick, lush stream. His long pole dipped almost rhythmically into the river, sliding fluidly past the screaming souls trapped within.

The silence was broken occasionally by a distant moan or a low snarl. Otherwise, the sound of water was the only type of music that reached his ears. Charon didn't expect many visitors to bother his shores, except those he ferried across the river.

He gazed serenely ahead, eyes fixed on the burgeoning shoreline, wondering what manner of death his passenger had experienced. The varying degrees of trauma altered the level of confusion a soul experienced when they passed. Some passengers were silent as they came on board, others full of questions he often had no inclination to answer. And then there were some who screamed in terror, still believing they were alive, convinced that somehow the Gods had made a mistake. Bargaining, threatening, or pleading, he enjoyed it all.

He could feel the pull of the soul waiting for him getting stronger as his boat neared. The mist thinned, revealing a cloaked figure standing patiently at the edge of the river, hands together in front of their body, hidden by their long sleeves.

This figure didn't glow, which meant they were still alive.

The fact didn't phase or deter him. He would still ferry across any passenger as long as they had a soul and they paid the price.

The boat bumped gently against the shore. He moved towards the front and slowly extended his hand. His passenger approached, graceful and confident, without a trace of fear or trepidation. His intrigue increased a notch. Perhaps this person had travelled with him before.

Slim, pale fingers reached out and placed a coin in his hand. He instantly knew from the weight and feel that it was a silver obol. He learnt something else. His passenger was a traditionalist.

To cross the river Acheron into the Underworld, one only needed a silver coin. Through the ages, souls had crossed his palm with multiple coins, sometimes a sack. Gold, copper, and precious stones, all had been offered to ensure a safe crossing or special treatment in the afterlife as if he, the ferryman, could be bribed by material wealth. What use would he have of that in the Underworld? Some had even offered paper with faces on them. Those he left in the waters to think about their foolishness. A single silver was all that was needed to cross the river and an obol was one of the most ancient and traditional methods of payment.

Charon moved backwards, indicating the passenger was allowed to board. They climbed in carefully and stood at the back. He vaguely wondered if his guest was male or female. Their hands appeared towards the feminine side but the stance and posture exuded more masculine energy. He had many mysterious travellers enter the Underworld to conduct dealings of all different natures.

Many never returned.

He moved once again to the front of the boat and dipped his pole through the waters, starting the journey once again back to the other side.

It wasn't until he was halfway that he sensed movement. Charon turned around and found his passenger directly in front of him.

They had moved fast. Surprise flickered across his mind. A sudden sharp pain had him looking down.

A dagger protruded from his chest.

He almost laughed at the sight. Did this mortal truly think a simple blade would kill him? Charon started to smile, anticipating the moment he drowned his passenger in the unforgiving waters of Acheron. But then the blade burned inside him, starting a fire that swiftly spread agonisingly through his body. He shuddered. Runes lit up on the hilt of the dagger, ancient runes of power.

Demon runes.

This was no ordinary blade. This was a blade made to kill someone like him. A weapon bargained for.

His pole dropped into the river with a splash. Hissing in pain, he felt his body disintegrating alarmingly fast. No, this could not happen! Not to him. Who would even dare?

Anger howled through him and he vowed to make this traveller suffer for eternity. He may have looked like a disarming old man, spindly and frail, but Charon was an ancient demon, chosen by Hades from the beginning of time to transport souls to and from the Underworld. His strength was formidable.

His hands shot out. The hooded figure moved to the side as swiftly as a viper. The blade slid out, then went in again and again and again. Charon stumbled to his knees, hands to his belly. Black blood seeped out from between his fingers.

"You don't know what you've done," he hissed, looking up at his dark hooded passenger.

The voice that floated down to him was feminine and cold. "Oh, but I do."

A booted foot slammed against his shoulder and the ferryman tumbled over the edge of his boat and into the icy river, joining the screaming souls still trapped within.

**

The ferryman's boat bumped against the shores on the opposite side of the river Archeron. One figure disembarked, stepping onto the short strip of sand and then moving swiftly away to blend into the Underworld shadows, away from watching eyes.

After a few minutes of navigating through the twists and turns of the Underworld's labyrinth, Selaphiel pulled back the hood of her cloak. She stripped the rest of the garment off, discarding it in a darkened corner. She had thrown her dagger in the river, where it hopefully wouldn't be found until much later.

Tugging on the chain around her neck, she pulled out a glowing blue sphere from her shirt. The soul inside pulsed softly. Pressing her fingers against a shallow indent in the middle, the orb gave a soft click. Selaphiel twisted either side in opposite directions and the orb came apart. The soul immediately brightened and expanded in size. It floated gently to the ground, taking the shape of a young boy in tattered clothing. He looked dazed and confused, looking at his surroundings but not focusing on one point, or even her. He wandered off in the opposite direction, none the wiser of his short travelling adventure across the river Archeron.

Nadiel's plan had been admittedly brilliant.

To create the distraction they needed to keep Lucifer and the rest of the Fallen from discovering what they were doing in the ninth level of Hell, they had to kill Charon, the Ferryman. He wouldn't be dead permanently, of course, but by the time he reformed, the Underworld would be in chaos. There would be no one to ferry the souls across the river to be processed, which meant Hades power would start to diminish.

It was effectively an act of war. And who would Hades immediately suspect?

Lucifer.

Hades wouldn't have the luxury of not acting on his suspicions because finally the balance of power would tilt in the Ruler of Hell's favour. Lucifer would finally have an opportunity to make a move for the Underworld and expand his territory in the lower realms.

Hades couldn't afford to let that happen.

He would have to act, even if he wasn't entirely sure it was Lucifer's hand that took out the guardian of the gate.

Selaphiel smirked. Lucifer was going to be so busy trying to fend off Hades and the rest of the Gods, he wouldn't have time to uncover their plans. And by the time Charon reformed and informed Hades that it was in all probability a witch that had destroyed his form, the damage would have already been done.

They had just needed a soul and an athame, a witch's ceremonial dagger, powered by dark magic to do the deed. Items that were easy to obtain in Hell if you knew how.

Brilliant. Nadiel had truly outdone himself.

Soon, the alarm bells would ring all through the Underworld.

Then, the Ruler of Hell would have his hands full.

***

"It's not going to work," I muttered, staring at the dark cages spread out randomly in front of me. Once again, the feeling of despair and hopelessness weighed on me like slabs of stone pressing against my chest. It was just another reminder of how urgent my mission was, and how every hour I wasted could cost another angel their soul.

As a whole, the idea of glowing like a miniature sun sounded like an amazing way to neutralise the dark cages, but in theory, it would not work. As soon as my Light hit and disabled one cage, its potency would reduce and keep reducing as it countered more barriers. The Light would gradually become increasingly weaker with every cage it touched.

I looked around the vast space. What I needed was multiple sources of Light coming into the dungeons at the same time. If I could do that, the dark energy flowing through the room would be too weak to sustain.

"What's not going to work?" Marella asked next to me.

I jumped at the sound of her voice, unaware of her approach. I had instigated another meeting with the witches to finalise our deal. There were still a few important elements I hadn't worked out, but I couldn't afford any more delays. As stressful as it was becoming, I had no choice but to work with what I had and hope that the last few pieces would fall into place.

Marella's unseeing gaze swept over me. It was as if she was taking in Atlas's stained tunic, the hastily knotted hair at the nape of my neck and the slight bulge of a crystal on the upper part of my thigh. I pursed my lips and stared at her intently. I still couldn't figure out if she was truly blind or not.

"Just a plan I have to work through," I responded vaguely. I glanced behind her towards the worn wooden door in the wall. "Shall we go?"

"Yes, it will only be Hasbeth and me this time." She walked surprisingly swiftly towards the door, using her cane as a guide. Lifting the bottom of her walking aid, she did a short rap on the door.

Following, I asked, "The coven didn't want to meet again? I had assumed they would have wanted to be involved with the negotiation." I had expected to face the next few hours arguing with more than a few witches.

"Do you know how risky it was for all of us to meet you the first time?" She paused and muttered softly, pushing some loose hair behind her ears, "No, you wouldn't." Raising her voice once more, she said, "It is too risky for all of us to converge again. Hasbeth and I will be enough to negotiate with you."

The door opened and a familiar face peered out. Agatha's gaze darkened as it met mine. I thought she was going to slam the door shut in my face as soon as Marella passed through, but she kept it open. As I passed, I glanced down at her leg. There was no evidence at all of it ever being severed. I wanted to say something to the older witch, but I had a feeling that, despite healing her, Agatha would continue to hold a grudge. So, I just held her spitting gaze for a second longer in acknowledgement and then slipped inside.

It was pleasantly warm compared to the chill of the dungeons. Marella unclasped her worn brown cloak and hung it up on a peg on the wall. She turned to Agatha. "Is Hasbeth here?"

"Yes, already below," the elderly witch reluctantly said.

Marella nodded. "Excellent."

We moved towards the back of the living quarters where I could smell the faint aroma of herbs and cooking. Voices echoed through the stone walls, hushed and soft. This was not a place for laughter or warm conversations between friends. This wasn't a place of refuge or relaxation from a hard night's work. These walls were riddled with fear. Fear from the constant abuse of captors they could never escape from.

A little head full of dark curls peeked out from behind a wall. Another face framed with long brown hair popped out just below. Big eyes watched me with a mix of suspicion and curiosity. Little children with grime on their faces and hunger hollowing out their eyes. My mouth went grim. No, this wasn't a place for little children.

Agatha crouched down and pulled back the faded circular carpet that covered the hidden trap door. The hinges groaned as she pulled the door up revealing the staircase that dropped down to the room below.

We made our way downstairs into the larger room where our previous meeting had been held. Candlelight flickered around the room, illuminating Hasbeth, who busy at one of the long benches on the side. She looked like she was grinding some herbs in a small bowl.

"Where do you get the herbs from?" I wondered out aloud. From the scent, these were herbs that were found on Earth, grown from damp soil and sunlight. How had they made their way to Hell?

Hasbeth turned around. "If we get captured in the Underworld, we take precautions." Hasbeth looked at me through the bronzed mirror that hung in front of her. The head witch eyed me, disapproval evident in the slant of her dark eyebrows. "You took your time."

"I came as soon as I could," I responded, making my way toward her.

Hasbeth turned around, her long grey dress swished softly against her legs. "So, what is your answer, angel? Will you take our children with you?"

The mirror behind her caught my eyes. I opened my mouth and then closed it. The light of the candles reflected softly from the shiny surface. Looking around, I noticed several mirrors hanging from the wall.

When I initially walked down the stairs it had seemed like the room had been lit by many candles, but in reality, it was only a few with the mirrors reflecting the warm glow around the large space.

"Is something the matter?" Hasbeth frowned at me.

"Ah yes… I mean, no," I said distractedly. I forcibly pulled my eyes away from the mirror and focused on the witch in front of me. "Let's discuss our terms, but first I need clarity on a few things."

Hasbeth smoothed the front of her gown with her hands. "What do you want to know?" The sharp rap of the cane near me announced Marella's presence, as she turned to stand next to the head witch.

"My success on this mission requires me and the rest of the other angels to leave the Underworld alive." I tilted my head towards Hasbeth. "And potentially some of your children. It would be a risk to go down the known pathway toward the ferryman. A risk of being followed or delayed. I was hoping you might have access to another location."

Hasbeth frowned. "And where would that be?"

"The Elysian Fields."

She barked out a laugh. "Ah, yes, the resting place of virtuous souls. By the dark mother, why would you think we would know the location to that realm?" Her dark eyes gleamed. "What use would we have of a place we cannot access?"

No humans who dabbled with dark magic would not be allowed to pass through to the Elysian Fields. My heart sank, but I steadfastly answered. "Witches have been roaming through the Underworld, meeting with demons for centuries. I thought there would be a possibility of one of you running across the higher realm gateway."

Marella shifted her stance. The movement seemed uncomfortable. I focused on her, sensing things unsaid. "What is it?" I asked her.

She sighed. "We still cannot help you," Marella said. "A couple of us have stumbled across the gateway by accident, but none ever marked it to find it again as there was no need."

"What do you mean 'marked it?'"

Marella opened her mouth, but Hasbeth placed a hand on her arm to forestall her from answering. "We mean marking a location so we can find it again," Hasbeth interjected. "And before you ask, we do this using a spelled orb and blood."

"The same sort of spelled orb that will take me to the ferryman and back?"

The head witch nodded. "Correct."

I took a breath. "I'm going to need some additional assistance."

Hasbeth raised her brows. "Oh?" She said it with a tone that indicated refusal even before she heard what I had to say.

I carried on. "I need you to find the location of one of the angels locked in the cells."

Reaching under the tunic I wore, I unstrapped one of the quartz crystals from my thigh. There was instant tension in the room as I pulled out the crystal as if I held a spitting snake. I supposed, considering what happened before, they had a reason to be cautious. But only if they were practising dark magic. This crystal wasn't full of Light.

"If you wouldn't mind, could you place your hand on the quartz?" I asked, holding it out in front of me.

Instantly suspicious, Hasbeth responded, "Why?" I could see her body lean back, trying to create more distance between herself and the object in front of me.

I huffed out a breath, not bothering to hide my exasperation. It was not me who had broken trust with the witches. "I can show you the image of an angel. I need you to find him for me. I've implanted a memory inside the crystal and I can guide you on how to access it."

Marella leaned forward on her cane. "And where is this angel?"

"He is in one of the cells. I need the cell to be located."

I heard a scoff behind me. It appeared Agatha had stated her opinion.

"Why do you want to find him?" the blind witch inquired.

Before I could answer, Hasbeth cut in. "I want to know how you put images in crystals." There was a certain glint in the head witch's eyes as she studied the quartz in my hand. No longer was she backing away. "Where do you find these stones? I have not seen them here in Hell or the Underworld."

"You need to have an affinity and some training with crystals," I said. "Not every angel can do it in The City. And these were given as a gift."

She eyed me as if she knew exactly who had gifted them to me, but thankfully didn't voice her thoughts out loud. Hasbeth placed her hand on the rough surface of the quartz, her fingers curling around the circumference. "What do I do?"

"It would be easier if you close your eyes," I said. She did as I asked. "Now, take a big breath in and slowly out."

Her dark eyes flared open briefly. "I know how to centre myself, angel." The word 'angel' was coloured in with contempt.

I bit my lip and swallowed a flare of impatience that rose up with a biting response. "Good, then this shall go quickly." I felt Agatha creep closer to my back. "Centre yourself and let your awareness drift down your arm to the palm of your hand. Feel the cool surface of the crystal under your hand, the slight thrum of energy pulsating gently. Go deeper… yes… that's right. You are in the heart of the stone, feeling the pulse inside as if it were your own. See yourself surrounded by the clear, white energy filtering into your very being."

Meditation and visualisation were one of the most powerful tools given to the human race. The power of the subconscious and super conscious, if tapped into correctly, could alter reality. Witches were trained in their forms of meditation to harness their gifts.

With consistent practice, they could become faster in tapping into their powers to cast spells. Hasbeth didn't need much guidance to enter a deep, trance state. I could tell she was there by the way her body visibly relaxed and her features, which previously held contempt, now had melded into peaceful repose.

"In your mind, ask the crystal to show you the memory that it contains." I waited several seconds, letting her take her time with this part. "A face and form will appear."

"I see it," Hasbeth whispered in wonder. "I see him."

"His name is Rushton. Remember his face. He is who I want you to find."

Hasbeth's dark eyelashes fluttered, then opened slowly as if she had awakened from a dream. She slowly focused on my face, hand still gripping the crystal. "You will teach me how you did that. You must."

My darker self raised her head and sneered. *Look how she talks to you like you are beneath her. A mere servant. Does she not know that you can remove her head from her shoulders? I can tell she doesn't respect you. Do you know why? You haven't earned it. There is nothing about you that inspires fear.*

Fear is not the only way to gain respect, I hit back.

But it is the quickest. You don't have time to deal with these infants playing with magic. It's pathetic, really.

The last thing I wanted was an opinion from my darker self. I pushed my alter ego away but she didn't go far. I felt her hovering just on the edge of my awareness as if waiting for an opening to sneak back in. To be honest my darker self's thoughts on the matter annoyed me more than usual.

Perhaps... because they were true.

Focusing back on Hasbeth, I reversed the position of our hands so it was the head witch that held the crystal instead. "I don't have the time to see if you have the talent and then to train you," I said firmly, removing my hand and stepping back casually.

The scars on the side of her face shifted as her mouth tightened. "If you want us to find this angel you will make the time."

If I was a novice witch, I could imagine that the head witch's voice would have made me jump as if my bottom had been switched. She had that no-nonsense tone that threatened imminent punishment and a face that could have cracked stone if it smiled. But Hasbeth was far below the most intimidating person I had ever met. I wasn't used to confrontation, but I was finding myself in more and more situations where being gentle and reasonable was not working.

"My mission is time-sensitive. May I remind you that if I fail we will all fail." I let the threat hang there like a fraying rope over a fire. Marella's face blanched. She at least remembered what I said might happen if I ever became a Fallen.

"Perhaps we can consider this training as something you could do after–" Marella started to say.

"No," Hasbeth cut her off. "If you fail, that is on you. If you want extra assistance, then you will pay for it."

I was getting tired of this. Specifically this witch. "And what assistance are you exactly giving me? Two rings to the Underworld? And for that you want me to take children, *children*, with me and somehow get them safely to Earth? That task alone is barely possible." My smile was cool. "You have all failed at leaving the Underworld. That is why you are here as captives."

I shook my head and stepped further back. "Yet, somehow, I am supposed to succeed whilst orchestrating a mass escape. You do realise the Fallen will be following me." I heard the anger in my voice, sharpening my tone to thorny points. Frustration bubbled in my veins. "I do not have time to waste. I do not have time to train you when every night our window of escape gets smaller and smaller. I see I was mistaken in asking for your help. Instead of gaining from our association, I'm afraid now that it might cost me instead. I will get the rings on my own. I have been to the Fallen domain and I know where they are."

I glanced at Marella who looked mildly dismayed. "I'm sorry for wasting your time, Marella, but I'm also more sorry I wasted mine."

Turning away from the growing outrage in Hasbeth's eyes, I strode past Agatha who started to lift an arm to stop me. I shot her a hard look and she froze as if she suddenly remembered what happened the last time we were in a confrontation.

I was halfway up the stairs when I heard Marella say to Hasbeth, "I think you are making a mistake."

"And you think you know more than I do?" was the cold response.

"In this case–"

I didn't stay around to hear anymore. Pushing open the trap door, I climbed out of the hidden room beneath. Around the anger that burned within me crept bitter disappointment. A massive chunk of my plan had relied heavily on the witches' support. I would now have to enter the Fallen domain myself to steal the rings, which would only increase my chances of being caught and extend the timeline of the angel's escape. The location of Rushton's cell was also becoming more unlikely to be found.

Perhaps I had spoken too hastily. I was just so frustrated with trying to move one step forward and then slamming up against yet another delay or obstacle.

I walked towards the entrance of the witch's quarters, dodging little bodies running past and the distrustful looks from the older residents. There were young and old-looking women busy carrying wood and food back and forth from various rooms. Most had visible scars disfiguring their skin, the others I suspected hid other deformities under their clothes.

Whispers hissed around me but no one approached. I couldn't exactly blame Hasbeth for trying to squeeze every drop of advantage that she could.

These women were just surviving. They needed every tool they could get their hands on.

I sighed, my steps slowing as I approached the door. Maybe I should–

The door slammed open with a bang.

I halted to a stop, my heart beating wildly. A dishevelled-looking witch braced her hands against the doorframe, breathing heavily as if she had run a great distance. Panic etched in every feature of her face. She limped forward and raised her voice, alarm slicing through every syllable.

"They are coming! They are coming!" she screamed.

Chaos erupted. Running footsteps and things being thrown and slammed echoed from every direction. The witch who yelled barrelled past, almost knocking me over in her haste to get as far away as possible.

I didn't have to ask. I already knew who or what was about to come through the door. A door I now couldn't leave from.

The Fallen.

If they found me…. if they knew I was here...

I turned around and ran.

Chapter 25

I bolted down the passageway, back to the trapdoor. Children hid themselves in little alcoves, covering their bodies with blankets and hand made baskets filled with clothing. Women helped cover their tiny bodies in haste before they darted off themselves. As frantic as everyone was, there was a purpose to their movements. They had all done this before. Many times.

Agatha was just helping Marella climb the last stair by the time I got to the trapdoor.

"What are you doing here?" Agatha hissed in alarm, waving me away with her hand. "Get out of here! You need to leave now before they see you! If they find you here we will all be punished!

"It's too late," Marella said briskly. She took back her cane from Agatha. "They are here already." She stepped quickly to the side, bent down and pulled the trapdoor shut as quietly as she could. The slight sound was enough to make Agatha flinch and look fearfully behind us. I wondered briefly where Hasbeth was.

"Quickly, cover it up," Marella said.

I leant down at the same time as Agatha did and we both eased the frayed mat over the hidden door. Agatha quickly rushed to the side of the room and lifted a small child's table and chair and arranged it on top.

"You are going to have to hide. There is a cupboard just out of this room to the left. It has a false back. Just slide it aside and you can hide in there." Marella's instructions were hurried as she rushed past.

I turned towards her. "But what about you?"

She glanced briefly back towards me, eyes unseeing, but filled with trepidation. "The women here can't hide. They will find us eventually and it would only make things worse. Hide and don't come out until someone gets you."

I nodded then cleared my throat when I realised she couldn't see me. "I will."

They left swiftly towards the front door, though Agatha had enough time to shoot me a filthy look as she passed. I rushed out of the room and turned left as instructed. It was a small bedroom, simple furnishings with a faded blue coverlet covering a small bed, and a thin yellowish pillow thrown haphazardly on top.

An old cupboard was wedged in the back corner of the room and I ran over and pulled on a small, brass ring, opening one side of the cupboard. It creaked in protest and wobbled precariously. There were a few old dresses hanging from wooden hooks in faded, muted colours. I pushed those roughly aside and reached for the false back, carefully sliding it across.

A short, sharp scream split the air. Then, it abruptly stopped.

I froze, hands on either side of the cupboard, preparing to launch myself within. I heard a few bangs and crashes of things being thrown around and breaking and then… a low, masculine laugh. The hairs pricked on the back of my neck.

What was I doing?

This felt wrong. I couldn't hide in a cupboard while the witches were being tormented. Logic said that I would make it so much worse by leaving the hideout designated to me. What would I even do? But my conscious, my sense of right and wrong, that little voice deep within my soul, beat against the bones of my chest, telling me to *do something*.

My fingers curled against the wood and I took a few long breaths.

Creator, give me strength…

I pulled off Atlas's tunic and threw it inside the cupboard. Quickly grabbing a dress from the hook, I shoved it over my head, pulling my arms through the holes, barely noticing if it was on the right way. One sleeve was slightly torn but otherwise it looked like what everyone else was wearing.

Atlas's tunic would have been fine darting around through the dungeons in the dark, but in a line up with the other women, it would be obvious that I'd be the odd one out. The witches still managed to look presentable and clean. Atlas's clothes, which I had been wearing and abusing for some time, did not.

"Idiot, idiot, idiot, what are you doing?" I muttered to myself as I frantically looked around for a sharp object I could use. The bed had a small stand but there was only a cup of water on it. Why didn't I grab Atlas's throwing knife when I had the chance? Idiot.

There. On the floor by the base of the bed.

I knelt down and picked up a small nail. Definitely not ideal, but it would have to do.

Bracing myself, I took a breath and held the nail up. Trying not to think too closely on what I was about to do, I jabbed it into my skin and dragged it down the right side of my face. I winced. It stung fiercely. I made myself do it two more times, starting from the side of my forehead all the way down to my jaw. My flesh tore easily, and the blood welled up and over my skin. That should be deep enough.

The shouts were a bit closer. More slamming of objects against walls.

Closing my eyes, I forced myself to block out everything around me. I wove the healing strands together in my mind in an intricate weave and healed my cuts just enough to make them seem old. Then, I grabbed the cup of water from the side of the bed and scrubbed the blood away from my face.

Scars. I now had scars.

I stood up and edged towards the hallway. Carefully, I peered out. It was deserted... then a witch scurried across the corridor, holding a hand up to her face, whimpering softly. I waited until she disappeared then crept in the direction she came from, passing a few openings that led into other rooms and corridors. I paused before each one and checked to make sure there were no Fallen before moving forward again.

"What are you doing? What are you doing?" I whispered to myself again. "You have no idea what you're doing."

I heard clanging to my right and voices that raised and lowered periodically. It felt warmer in this direction and I realised that I was heading towards the area where the witches prepared and cooked their food.

The smell of baked bread and the sharper scent of something burning wafted towards me. My hands went clammy as I got closer to an arched opening towards the back of the corridor. The voices became louder.

"Eat it. Pick it off the floor and eat it. You dropped it. You shouldn't let good food go to waste." The voice was feminine and cruel. "There you go. Yes, all of it now."

As I got closer I could see benchtops lining the wall with baskets and utensils scattered around. Two long legs encased in dark brown pants dangled off the edge. Booted feet swayed back and forth like a frisky child.

I heard someone chopping wood at a frantic pace, another stirring in a pot. Soft sniffles also came from the direction of the floor. I leaned a little closer and saw that behind a wooden island bench, a woman was on her hands and knees.

"Oh, hello there. Please, come and join us."

I jerked my head up and saw the Fallen leaning to the side, watching me. She had long auburn hair that instantly reminded me of Nadia, though hers fell long and silky to her elbows and mine had been a tangle of loose curls that always seemed to find its way into my mouth. Her lips were shaped in a cupid's bow and they were twisted in a small smirk as she regarded me with glee. In her hand was a small knife which she deftly flicked around her fingers.

"You must be new. I've never seen you before. Don't be shy." Her voice had changed to sugary sweetness.

Looking into her black eyes, I knew I had little choice but to come inside the room. I walked in slowly, eyes darting to my right at the two women who were making some food on the other side of the room.

One of the witches, an older woman with grey streaks in her hair, paused in her chopping to stare at me wide eyed before resuming her work. The other witch just continued to stir furiously, eyes down and lips white from pressing them so hard together.

I walked hesitantly towards the Fallen but stopped a few feet from her. There was a fire lit in a kiln where the smell of baked bread was coming from. On the ground there was another witch with short, uneven brown hair. She scooped up what looked like burnt remains of bread and soup from the floor into her mouth, sobbing with every breath. She was young and thin, almost painfully so, and she tried hard to make herself as small as possible on the rock floor.

Booted feet hitting the ground had me turning back to the Fallen. She stood in front of me and I noticed we were about the same height. I couldn't help but wonder what her name was and how long she had been turned.

"What's your name?" she asked, a smile widening to friendly proportions. It was like watching a shark smile.

I instantly felt relief. She hadn't seen through my disguise. I said the first thing that came to my mind. "Um, Sandy."

Crack. I found myself sprawled along the floor, face stinging from the blow to the side of my face. I shook my head to clear the black spots in front of my eyes.

"It's Sandy, *Mistress*, to you." The voice was still pleasant. "And that's a terrible name. Your mother should be stabbed."

Under the sleeves of my dress, I felt my arm bands activate. The armour slid against my skin and over my chest, reacting to a combination of my fear and pain. The sobbing in front of me stopped. I looked up and the witch on the floor regarded me with large blue eyes.

Are you okay, she mouthed. I nodded.

Fingers dug into my hair and hauled me up to my feet. I instinctively reached up and gripped her wrist with one hand, trying to relieve the pressure. The Fallen shook me slightly, like I was a misbehaving dog. "You *must* be new. Don't they teach you anything in this place?" She leaned closer to my face and whispered conspiratorially, "Let me show you how this works."

"You!" She pointed at the women stirring the pot. "Are you finished with my food yet?"

The woman looked up and panicked. I noticed she had some scarred tissue trailing down her neck like rivulets. Sweat trickled down the side of her face. Her cheeks were flushed red. "Not yet, Mistress. We just have to add some of these herbs and then put it–"

The Fallen waved her hand dismissively. "Nonsense, you've taken too long already. Bring it over here."

The woman shot another panicked glance at her friend who was still chopping. The older witch quickly dumped whatever was on her board into the pot and they gave it a quick stir. She then took a ladle and filled a small bowl.

"*Now*. You are testing my patience…" The sing-song nursery voice heightened the alarm in the room. For what felt like the hundredth time, I asked myself, *what are you doing?*

The witch grabbed a spoon from the workbench and hurried over to where we were. Her hands trembled as she offered it to the Fallen angel. I was surprised the contents didn't spill onto the floor. The dark angel looked at me.

"I want you to taste it and let me know if it's any good. The last time it tasted like hound breath. They have been warned and they will be in trouble..." she said the word 'trouble' slowly and with great emphasis, "if it has not improved."

She smiled at me while still having a stranglehold on my hair. "Please, try some."

Their last attempt was obviously the remains on the floor that were being eaten. The witch brought the bowl closer to me, holding it up since I couldn't bend down. Reaching out, I filled what looked like soup in the wooden spoon and brought it carefully to my lips.

It smelt fragrant. I opened my mouth and tasted it. The broth had muted flavours with bits of what I hoped were soft vegetables. I could imagine in the coldness of the dungeons this would be a pleasure looked forward to at the end of a long night.

The Fallen didn't care if it tasted good or not. There was no answer I could give her that would leave these women alone. Like always, with those who took pleasure in someone else's pain, it was about power. Control. The witch looked at me pleadingly.

I said the only thing I could. "It's delicious."

"Really?" The Fallen's eyes widened in mock surprise. "I must try it, then." She dipped her pinky finger in the bowl and put it in her mouth. "Hmmmm…." she said consideringly, scrunching her lips together.

I didn't even have time to react. My head slammed down on the bench behind me with force. Pain blinded me like a crack of lightning and black spots danced before my eyes again. My knees buckled but she held me up with the hand in my hair and brought me close once more to her side. I felt something wet drip down the side of my face.

My darker self seethed.

"Liar!" she yelled out loud to the room. The dark angel wagged her finger in front of my nose, her inky orbs shining with malice. "Naughty, naughty liar! It tastes worse than hounds breath. *And…* you didn't say 'mistress,' which makes me very, very sad. As for you…"

The old witch screamed as she was lifted off the ground with air. I had been waiting to see what type of ability she had. Air. You could immobilise with air, lift and throw. I had even heard of Fallen angels creating multiple tornados and directing them with precision.

I wasn't aware of all the ways the elements could be used but I imagined a dark angel would know how to inflict the most pain with whatever ability they possessed.

"You have failed me one too many times, old woman. Is there even a point to you existing? Maybe I should save everyone the trouble and space, you old hag…"

"No, no, please, mistress. Please! I promise I will do better. I will make you something else." The witch was lifted higher and moved over towards the open kiln where the fire was still burning. "I WILL MAKE YOU SOMETHING ELSE!" she shrieked.

The younger witch stared in horror, clutching the pot to her chest. The other witch on the floor sobbed helplessly again. There was nothing they could do but watch.

I slowly and carefully lifted my hand behind the Fallen's back, still facing the witch that was mere inches from being burned alive. Once I had it in position, I closed my eyes and channelled.

Two bodies hit the floor.

I opened my eyes and saw the old woman in front of the kiln, grasping at her knee, whimpering in shock and pain. She rocked herself as if in a trance. I took a breath and looked down.

Auburn hair spilled at my feet. Dark eyes looked up sightlessly. There was a gaping hole in the Fallen's chest where my Light had gone through, concentrated into a laser beam. The scent of burning flesh wafted up towards me.

My darker self started laughing.

"What have you done?" the younger witch with the pot whispered. "They will kill us all."

I wiped the blood off my face with the sleeve of my dress. "Hide the body. I'll be back for it."

Stepping over the Fallen, I raced out the room. There was still at least one more of them left. I knew the only reason I had managed to do what I had done was because I had the element of surprise. It was exactly what Atlas had said. They were arrogant. They assumed they were the biggest threat in the room and in most cases they would be right. But I was a Light angel pretending to be a witch and all I needed to do was use my abilities before they used theirs.

I turned the corner and slowed down, straining to hear something to give the Fallen's location away. I crept forward, towards the main corridor that led to the door into the dungeons.

I saw Hasbeth leading a group of young women towards another room. She froze when she saw me, instantly recognising who I was. Whispering something to one of the young witches, she then waved them off. They scurried away, most of them holding hands, keeping together.

Hasbeth didn't look afraid. She powered her way towards me like a woman on a mission, as if she didn't care there were Fallen in her domain.

"You have some nerve to still be here!" She looked furious, her dark skin almost purple. "Leave now!"

"How many are there?" I asked her.

"Did you hear what I said?" Hasbeth gripped my arm as if she intended to haul me out of there herself.

I shook her off forcefully. "There is a dead Fallen in your kitchen. You need to make sure they are not discovered until I get back. I told the other witches but I don't think they have a clear head right now."

Hasbeth's mouth dropped open. "What–"

I raise my voice slightly. "Where is the other one?"

She blinked at me as if for the first time noticing the scars and blood on my face. "He is with Marella. He always comes for her. He likes that she is blind."

"*Where?*" I was stressed.

Hasbeth pointed across the corridor down an opening on the right. I spun around and headed towards it. "Wait! What are you planning–" she started to say.

"Are they any more?" I called urgently over my shoulder.

"No, but–"

I darted in the direction she pointed. This rock corridor, like all the others, had symbols painted on the wall in dark brown. They all varied and I wondered if they were symbols of protection or just signs that announced the location of things.

There were many languages and scripts that I knew, but I had not specialised in that area. These symbols were ones I could not instinctively read. Though with time I might have been able to pierce together their meaning. Being able to read the witch's language might be something that could be an advantage later.

I slowed down as the corridor branched out in two directions.

"Which way, which way, which way…" I muttered. I tried to calm my racing heart and took a breath, closing my eyes briefly.

A low masculine laugh.

There. I went right.

I passed what looked like a little school room filled with small wooden chairs and tables. The furniture looked disordered as if they were in the middle of a lesson and had to drop everything and leave.

Fabric covered the openings of a couple other rooms, but it was the room at the end that held my attention. It also had a piece of faded red cloth hanging from nails embedded high in the rock. The cloth fell to about a foot off the floor. There was a slight rip on the right side and a few other small holes where a dim light could be seen coming from within.

I inched ever so carefully closer.

"…she died before we could bring her with us. A pity." There was a slosh of water. "You are not very talkative tonight, my dove. Is there something on your mind?"

"No, my Lord," I heard Marella murmur.

"You witches get so down and depressed after a few years in Hell. What happens to that spark, that fire you all have when you first arrive?"

Marella responded, but it was too low for me to understand.

"Should you not be grateful for all that we give you? You have a home here, food, purpose... and most importantly, you get to serve the greatest of all creations." Another low masculine laugh and more water trickling. "What more could you ask for?"

At least he wasn't torturing her like I feared. The conversation, on the other hand, was typical of what I had come to expect from a Fallen. Arrogance, ego, and the intention to wound. The delivery varied from angel to angel but underneath the message was all the same. I am better than you in every imaginable way. I will take what I want and there is nothing you can do about it.

This low level of consciousness was not exclusive to Fallen angels. Oh no, it was a theme common in humans and deities alike. Empires had both risen and fallen on ego alone. The need to crush those weaker and defenceless, a timeless tale. Except in other creatures, it undulated within their life span, staying for periods, some longer or shorter than others. With Fallens, or creations that had no soul, that low level consciousness was a constant, an unending song with no deviation, only an intrinsic belief in the lyrics.

We all had the capacity to 'fall' just as we also had the capacity to get back up again.

Again, I had no plan. Somehow, I would need to get close, without him recognising who I was. Reaching up, I undid the coil of hair at the nape of my neck. My hair fell loosely down my back and over my shoulders

The Fallen's voice turned silky and smooth. "You especially should be grateful for all the attention I have bestowed on you. You are not the most beautiful witch down here or the most talented... but I, unlike the rest of my brethren, like that you can't see me or all the things I have planned for you. It makes all our sessions that much more enjoyable."

"What are you doing?" I muttered once more to myself.

Then I barrelled into the room, through the thin fabric covering the door.

"Oh! I'm sorry... I, uh... I didn't... I didn't mean..." I said, halting to an immediate stop.

I was a terrible actress – no, an atrocious one. I knew this because I remembered seeing a play once in my past life as Nadia. It was a group of six year olds pretending to be dogs creating mischief in the town. They were much better than me. My ability to lie was becoming easier the more time I spent in Hell.

My ability to do it convincingly was another matter altogether.

There were two things I had going for me. The first was the genuine shock on my face upon entering the room. To be honest, I didn't know what to expect. I knew he hadn't been physically harming Marella from the tone and cadence of her voice.

What I didn't imagine was her to be kneeling at his feet as he reclined on a chair surrounded by shards of glass.

The Fallen had that soft, male beauty found in Greek statues carved from alabaster. His honey coloured hair had a slight wave to it as it fell around his ears, a stark contrast to the sooty black armour strapped to his chest. His pants were rolled up to his knees as Marella knelt in front of him. Her shift was stripped down so she was naked to her hips, washing his feet in a basin of water.

Around her in various places across the rock floor were bits of shattered glass. It wasn't the type of mess you would see if someone had dropped a glass object and it scattered all over the ground. These small, translucent pieces were placed very deliberately in every direction across the room. It was a painful obstacle course, one with no hope of navigating for someone who was truly blind.

The second thing I had going for me was the fact I was an angel. Despite the scars on my face, I was cut from a cloth no mortal could compare with. I had hoped I would be distracting enough that my lacklustre performance would go unnoticed, but at the same time, not too distracting that the Fallen saw through my disguise and recognised me for what I was.

As soon as I spoke, I saw Marella's back stiffen. She recognised my voice instantly. The Fallen snapped his head to me and I felt every sliver of attention directed at me like he was an eagle and I, a field mouse. I turned around as if to head back towards the exit.

"Stop. Come here." It was an order.

I froze at the sound of his voice in both relief and apprehension. I turned back slowly, bowing my head and letting my hair cover most of my face.

"I said, come *here*."

Feeling the tension of what I was about to do ripple through me, I walked slowly towards them. There were shards of glass along my path and twice I stopped deliberately to lightly move them with my feet, causing a tinkling sound as they hit other pieces of glass.

Marella's head tilted at the sound. The Fallen's soft mouth flattened into a thin line. I had warned her as much as I could.

I stopped just out of arm's reach. Marella paused in her washing and the Fallen pulled his feet out of the basin and stood up. He was a head taller than me with the sleek toned build of a runner or dancer.

Dark armour covered his chest as well as over his arms and legs. A sword leaned on the back of the chair he was sitting on, the wrapped hilt peeking up over the back support. The only other weapons I could see were two short blades strapped to each thigh.

"Well, well, well... what do we have here?" His long fingers brushed the underside of my jaw and slowly tilted my face up. Dark orbs stared down at me. "Well now... what a pity. You could have been stunning. Yes, a real work of art if it wasn't for these scars." He tisked under his breath. "Somehow, you witches prefer life in the drudges of Hell instead of with us. You mutilate yourselves just to avoid our attention. It almost makes me angry."

The Fallen slid his hand down my throat, caressing the sensitive skin with his thumb. I fought not to move away. "I have not seen you before. Are you new?"

I nodded, keeping my eyes down.

"Hmm. Take off your dress."

My head snapped up. Oh, not good. Not good at all. My armour was still active and even if I did manage to retract it, my arm bands would be clearly visible. The Fallen may have not recognised me, but he would certainly recognise the similarity of my armbands and the ones Lucifer wore. The fact that I even had them on would make him instantly reassess the situation. I needed to make a move, but he was too focused on me. He would react quickly to any attack and I had to make my one shot count.

I simply needed more time. I took a hesitant step back.

He smirked, as if delighted by my reaction. "My dove, tell her what will happen if she runs."

"Just do what he says." Marella's voice was flat, devoid of emotion. "It will be worse if you resist."

The Fallen spread out his arm gallantly. "But don't let her sway you. Please, do what you feel you must. Everyone has a choice." The corners of his lips tilted up further in amusement.

The hunt. The anticipation of a chase, a fight... he was hoping for it. There was nothing more alluring than prey believing they could still get out of a trap alive.

I stepped back again, narrowly missing a shard of glass and wrapped my hands around my body as if I was protecting myself. *Think, think, think!* Abruptly, I dropped to my knees in front of him. "Please, I only wish to serve. I... do have... other skills that may please you."

"Oh?" His amusement deepened, as did his interest. "Do tell."

My hands became clammy as I spun this new lie. I continued to hide my face, hoping my nerves would translate into 'terrified young witch.' "I do have some skill in the art of healing and relaxation through muscle manipulation," I said, then winced at the tinny sound of my voice. I forced myself to keep going. "My aunt used to be a priestess of Ascelpius and I learnt much from her before I left."

Take the bait. Take the bait, I chanted in my mind.

"Interesting," he responded. He took a step closer until his feet edged into my vision.

Please, please, please, please, please...

"Maybe later."

My heart sank. Then my dress began to burn. The hem of the faded cloth started smoking and then caught on fire against my skin. I let out a short yell and jumped up, frantically patting the edge of my dress as the flames seared my flesh. The Fallen laughed as I managed to put out the flames with my hands, burning them in the process. He then stopped laughing as the cloth holding the Light filled crystal around my thigh came loose.

The crystal fell to the ground with a thud and rolled across the floor. Time slowed down. My eyes tracked its movements until it rolled to a stop. I looked back up, heart thudding in my throat. We stared at each other. It felt like minutes stretching out into forever, but it was only a few heartbeats.

We both reacted.

I lifted my hands up and blasted a bolt of concentrated Light right into his chest. At the same time a wall of fire surrounded me, cutting off my vision and heating the air dangerously fast.

"Well, well, well... look what we have here." The Fallen's voice was full of excitement. My stomach dropped. He was still alive. I must have missed or my Light failed to pierce through his armour.

"I thought you looked familiar, but the scars… the clothes, your demeanour…" He laughed again. "…very clever. Lucifer's pet, what are you doing here? And more importantly, what am I going to do with you?" The Fallen's voice came closer. "There are so many angels who would *love* to meet you."

I spun around in a circle. The flames were as tall as my head. I would have to jump through to get out. Lucifer's armour would protect my chest but I wouldn't be able to avoid getting burned. I would heal, I just hoped I would be functional.

"He won't be very happy if you harm me," I said, moving as close as I could to the wall of flame at my back.

"Yes, why is that exactly?"

I braced myself. Then I started running. Two, three steps…

"You must have one hell of a magic–"

I leapt through the wall of flame, covering my face with my arms. A flash of searing pain. Red crossed my vision, burning through my eyelids. Then I was through. I hit the floor and rolled. Shards of glass pierced through my skin. I looked up through my hair and the Fallen turned towards me.

I blasted a bolt of white, hot Light right at his head.

He was fast. So fast.

He twisted to the side and lifted up his arm. My Light hit his armour, sizzling momentarily before

448

falling away on either side like water parting against a sharp rock. I pulled all the pain and fear inside me, channelling it through my hand and hit him again. Hard. It blazed out of me, brighter and more intense.

He blocked my Light with the same arm. My Light crackled against the dark plate like white lightning.

Was that a breach in the dark metal? The Fallen winced.

Hope sparked. But before I could attack him again, pain gripped me in a red, hot vise. I gasped and my body stretched upward, my hands clawing high in the air. It felt like my blood was boiling in my veins, smoking out through my lungs. I screamed as the veins in my eyes threatened to burst. Blood trickled out of my nose and leaked from the corners of my eyes.

The Fallen spoke, his voice quiet and full of satisfaction. He was close, kneeling right in front of me, hand caressing my bare leg.

"You didn't know I could burn through your insides, did you? For all your Light magic, you are still not a match for us. You never will be."

My darker self howled at me through the swirling agony. *LET. ME. KILL. HIM. I WILL CRUSH HIM.*

His hand slid higher on my leg, travelling over my knee and towards my upper thigh. I shook as the torment increased. Whimpers escaped my lips.

"What a gift I've been given tonight," The Fallen continued to murmur. "I would very much like to be the one who trains you."

Say 'yes,' my darker self commanded. *Let me show this one his place!* If I took up her offer, I could end this. I could end him.

"I'm going to–" the Fallen started to say, then let out a short, agonised scream.

Pain scattered, rolling away from me in a rush. The relief was so intense I almost fainted. Fortunately, my vision cleared and I saw Marellla backing away from us, my shattered crystal scattered across the ground next to the dark angel. The bright Light had caused him to turn his head away. My hands came up just as the Light started to fade and he turned his head back.

For a split second, my palms covered his eyes. A spilt second was all I needed.

Light burst from my hands, intense and focused. He shuddered, twitching violently, then his body dropped heavily to the floor.

I slumped over and braced my hands on the ground next to his head. Two gaping black holes replaced his eyes. This time, the scent of charred flesh made me want to vomit.

"Is… is he dead?" Marella's hushed whisper made me look up.

I wiped the blood off my face with the sleeve of my dress. Feeling dizzy, I stayed seated on the ground. Marella's face was pale, almost ghostly. She had pulled her shift back on, covering her chest.

"You aimed well," I said hoarsely.

"I sensed… I guessed where… but I wasn't sure…" She shook and turned her face away. I could feel the emotions spilling out of her, as if she had locked her feelings deep inside of herself and now they rushed back up, too fierce to stop. Tears ran down her face.

"How long will he be gone for?" she asked through her tears, still looking away.

"I do not know." I had no idea how long fallen angels took to reform. Did they take longer if they were 'killed' by something light opposed to something dark? Would they remember how they passed?

"Marella!" Hasbeth rushed into the room, closely followed by Agatha and another witch I didn't recognise. She was older than Hasbeth with darker skin that had a natural gleam to it that it almost looked polished. Her dark hair was cut so short you could see her scalp.

"Careful of the glass," I said and slowly stood up, wobbling on my feet.

Hasbeth moved carefully through the shards until she got to Marella, putting an arm across her shoulders and holding her close. She whispered words in a comforting tone of voice. It was the softest I had ever seen her.

Agatha tsk'ed at the floor and murmured something to the other witch who quickly left the room again. "Evil," she muttered, which was a little ironic as she was a dark witch and I'm sure had done much worse during her time on Earth. Strange how perspective changes when the things you do to others are done back to you. Sometimes the law of Cause and Effect, karma as others would call it, happened quickly, and sometimes it took lifetimes.

"You have killed him. When the Fallen find out, we will all die." Hasbeth's voice sounded like a bell of doom ringing through the room. She looked down at the body at my feet with a mixture of fear and fascination.

"I will take their bodies with me. They will not find them here," I said. I could hear the fatigue setting in my voice. The pain of the Fallen's magic had drained me.

"How?" Hasbeth demanded.

"Like you said, I can take non living things with me through the mirror." My eyes glanced down. "He would now be considered non-living." I bent down and took the Fallen's hand in my own. It was still warm.

Now that I couldn't feel the heavy weight of darkness and danger emanating from him, or see the malicious intent sparking through his eyes, he just looked like any other angel in The City. I slipped off the gold ring encircling his finger.

"It appears that I don't need those rings after all," I said softly. Hasbeth frowned, watching me stand up and clasp the ring in my fist. "Perhaps you need me now more than I need you."

I started to say more, but my mind stuttered. A shiver ran through my skin.

I felt him like a heady rush of wine swimming in my veins. He was like the beginning of a storm, rolling with unleashed power and when he stepped out of the shadows into the room my breath knotted in my throat.

Lucifer. By the Creator, he was beautiful.

A dark vest wrapped loosely around his torso, giving tantalising glimpses of muscled golden skin. His pants were waist height and moulded to his frame, highlighting the strength of his thighs and the length of his legs. His midnight eyes locked onto mine and a luscious heat of awareness spread right through me. The memory of his body moving against mine was enough to set my cheeks aflame and my stomach to tighten. The heat I felt echoed in his eyes and, for one eternal moment, we stared at each other like there was no one else in the room.

Movement broke the moment.

Hasbeth, Marella, and Agatha dropped to the floor, their faces all but melding into the hard surface. Fear permeated the room. No, more than fear. Fear was what I felt when the Fallen were in the room. This was bone deep terror. Agatha was shaking so hard her knees were knocking on the floor.

The corner of Lucifer's lip lifted sardonically as he glanced at the witches. His gaze travelled over the room to the shards of the glass on the floor, the spilled basin of water, and the shattered Light crystal. Then, slowly, his eyes rested on the Fallen whose eyes I had burnt out.

I tensed slightly, wondering how he would react to me so blatantly dispatching one of his warriors. His gaze moved, taking in the cuts and scrapes on my feet, the dots of blood bleeding through my faded dress, and up to the scars curving down the side of my face and the smears of blood, which had leaked from my eyes and nose.

His eyes finally met mine once more.

Lust blazed in them like a hungry inferno and with it… pride. He tipped his head towards me like a warrior acknowledging a hit. My lips parted in surprise. I took a step towards him, wanting nothing more than to feel his energy wrap around mine. The longing was sudden and intense.

As I did, the shadows stretched out towards him and wrapped around his frame. As much as he wanted me, almost to the point of pain, he resisted. He fought the need desperately. With his eyes never leaving mine, he faded into the darkness.

I let out a sigh.

"He did not kill you," Hasbeth said in awe. "He did not kill you."

"No," I said softly, turning to face her and pulling my thoughts away from my Flame. She stood up and helped Marella unsteadily to her feet. Agatha was still on the floor, hands covering her head as if she was waiting for a bomb to explode.

"You killed one of his own and he did not destroy you." Hasbeth stared at me in disbelief. She glanced at Marella and shook her head. "It seems... I need to think..."

"I told you to trust me," Marella said. It wasn't unkind the way she said it, but it had reprimand. "This alliance is something that will benefit both of us."

Hasbeth turned to me then spotted Agatha on the floor. She said briskly, "Oh, do get up, Agatha. He is gone."

Agatha peered between her fingers like a child checking to see if the monster had truly left. When she spotted us all standing she hurried to her feet, tucking wisps of grey hair back behind her ears. At that moment the other witch who had left came back with a broom.

Agatha snatched it from her hands and grumbled, "I'll do it." She made a shooing gesture for her to leave and then started sweeping the floor slowly, avoiding looking at us.

Hasbeth cleared her throat and I could see the look of strain pass over her strong boned face. The words stuck in her throat before they came out. "Once you have taken the... Fallen away, I would like for us to talk again."

I just stared at her with blood drying on my face, letting the silence grow. Silence could be a powerful thing, filling empty spaces with unheard thoughts and doubts.

When I didn't say anything more, she shifted, uncomfortable for the first time in her interactions with me. "I will be more open to what you want," she said finally.

I continued to stare at her and let my hand fiddle with the gold ring that would gain me the access I needed to the Underworld. I let nothing show on my face, nothing except the slightest beginnings of a frown.

Hasbeth cleared her throat again, then smoothed her dress down her hips in an impatient gesture. "Fine, I will give you what you ask for. For the children." She held my gaze and inside her dark brown eyes I saw a look of pleading and fear. "Please," she added softly.

Agatha paused in her sweeping and stared at the head witch.

"I will take the Fallen with me, then I will come back to talk with you again. But Hasbeth..." my voice cooled. "If we haven't reached a satisfactory conclusion in that time, that will be the end."

I deliberately didn't clarify what I meant by 'end.' It wasn't as if I was planning to do anything to harm them, but they didn't know that. And with the body of a Fallen at my feet, it just added to the uncertainty of what I would or could do.

The dark skinned witch waited a beat and then nodded tensely in agreement.

See, I was learning. But I needed to learn faster.

I didn't have time for anything else.

Chapter 26

The Underworld trembled.

Long fissures scored the misty floor in jagged lines. The five rivers of the Underworld beat violently against the shores like angry fists, eager to crush and consume. The walls shuddered with such force that large pieces of rock crumbled like sand and collapsed into the darkness.

Hades stood by the Styx and raged. On the outside, he looked as unmoving as the cool, marble statues adorning his family's many temples, but on the inside, he seethed like a dark, brewing storm. Cerberus whined in response to his master's turbulent emotions and one of his three heads pushed up against Hades' gauntlet hand. His bident glowed with power and he fought against the magic inside him, which had responded to his wrathful anger.

Hades' voice blasted out, deep and reverberating. *"Lucifer!"*

His voice echoed through the vastness, vibrating through corridors and into crevices, making its inhabitants pause.

The God of the Underworld spun around and struck the thigh of a male Fallen who was imprisoned in the ground at his feet. Different shades of bone twisted thickly around his wrists, forearms and legs, holding him captive. If the bone started to break, more replaced it, layering over and over until it became thicker and thicker.

The Fallen screamed as the double pronged spear embedded itself into his flesh. The muscles of his leg trembled and then suddenly split like an overripe fruit.

A portion of the river rose high up over Hades's head and sharpened to a fine, icey point. Cerberus growled, long and low.

"You may have power over water, foul one," Hades voice was like soft thunder, "but the Underworld is *mine*. Use what is mine against me and I will end you here and now."

The Fallen bared his teeth and though they were in no way as impressive as Cerberus's deadly canines, the promise of vengeance in that look would have made many beings pause. But he was not just any being, he was the God of the Dead and the king of the Underworld. He held the Fallen's gaze steady and resolute, until finally the water above trembled like a branch shaken by the wind. It collapsed into itself, falling back into the river with a splash.

"You have gone too far this time, Hades," snarled a Fallen female who was also held imprisoned next to her comrade. "Lucifer will not allow these liberties you take to be without consequence."

"We will see," he replied grimly and then stabbed her in the side. She screamed in agony.

"*Lucifer!*" he bellowed once more, sliding his spear out of her body. The wound gushed blood and spilled onto the ground in a shallow pool.

"I must be missing something, because I don't believe I've given you leave to discipline my warriors."

The devil stepped out of the shadows. His voice tilted on the edge of boredom but power thrummed around him, a slow build waiting to be released. He walked towards the Fallen on the ground. With a small flex of that power, the ground that trapped them shifted and melted away like snow.

Hades' mouth twisted as the Fallen started to lift themselves up.

The God pointed his spear against the throat of the female but his glare was directed at male Fallen besides her. "I did not give you permission to move," he said. Cerberus padded over and the middle head clamped its jaws over the Fallen's skull and pressed down threateningly. The Fallen froze as blood trickled from his scalp.

Lucifer stopped a few metres away. "Is there a reason for this tantrum? I would hate to break a weapon that you so clearly cherish."

The ruler of Hell faced the ruler of the Underworld, mere strides apart. It was a distance that could be breached between one blink and the next. The air around them shivered with unleashed power and tension. Though there was only a thin tolerance on both their sides, they had never crossed the line to invite war between them. But the cold fury emanating from Hades signalled that the line was close to disappearing.

"My ferryman is missing. And since I have not sensed any other God or powerful deity in my realm, I can only conclude that it was you, or one of your *minions*, that disposed of him."

Lucifer raised a brow. "I see."

"You *see*? I see your ambition has no limits," Hades replied. With a swift motion, he stabbed his spear right through the female Fallen's neck. Her body jerked up. He twisted the point in the ground and ignored the dying gurgling that followed.

Lucifer blinked slowly, then spoke.

The sharp, acerbic syllables grated on each other, screeching in pain when they touched. They melded excruciatingly into a discordant flow that pierced through the eardrums. Cerberus flinched, letting go of the Fallen and shaking his heads as if there was something crawling between his ears. He whined softly and reared back.

Then, all of a sudden, his canine heads started to attack each other. One darted for the other's throat, the other one tore an ear. Snarls and whines filled the air as claws and fangs lashed and severed, spraying blood.

"Heed," Hades snapped out. Cerberus shuddered as if wanting desperately to obey but his form lacked the strength. With a snarl of his own, Hades passed a hand over the hounds heads and Cerberus instantly slumped, collapsing heavily to the ground. The ruler of the Underworld knelt and placed a gentle hand on one of his heads before standing up to narrow his dark eyes at Lucifer.

Hades was Cerbeus's master, the demon followed no other as loyally, but it didn't matter who held his leash. At his core, he was formed from darkness and the dark had only bent to one being and one being only.

The ground sucked the other Fallen within its depths. After a second, the Underworld surface split behind Lucifer and the Fallen emerged gasping for air, dirt falling away from his face and body. Lucifer held out his right hand and a dark sword formed from the shadows. "Go," he said to the angel behind him without looking. The Fallen scrambled up and fled back into the misty darkness.

After a couple of heartbeats, Lucifer tilted his head and sensed the space around them. He twisted the hilt of his sword slowly in his hand and pointed the tip at the dead Fallen at Hades's feet. "That wasn't part of the plan."

"Since my ferryman is gone, I believe that was just a start to paying your debts." He leaned on the spear and dug the tip further into the Fallen and into the Earth below. "Don't be concerned; they come back, don't they?"

The corner of Lucifer's mouth lifted. "We both know I didn't touch your ferryman. So this," he gestured to the dead dark angel, "was you displaying your irrational temper. Me displaying mine would be to cut off Cerbeus's heads. All of them."

Hades' tilted his head. "I have never liked you, Dark One. There are laws that govern our world, our realms, lines that shouldn't be crossed, but you always felt like you were above them. Perhaps I should call on the Gods and end this here and now. How do I know this…" he gestured with his gauntlet covered hand, "ruse, will flush out whoever did this?"

"Whoever eliminated your Ferryman will proceed to the next stage of their plan if we continue to play our intended roles. If I truly wanted your throne, ending your ferryman would not be the way I would do it. No, I would do far more than cripple you." He smiled slowly, delivering his words with purpose. "I'd make you leave the Underworld to retrieve the pieces of *her* body from the furthest reaches of existence, then, and only then, would I dismantle your power base and assume your place."

At the mere implication of his Flame being threatened had the rest of Hades' armour appear around him. They snapped in place over his body and his glare was a cold fire from the slits from his helmet. "Mention my Flame again from your filthy mouth and I will forgo this *understanding* we have and cave your head in."

Lucifer lifted his sword, the tip pointing at the God's chest, burning a deep, dark red. "I had not finished. I have no interest in the dead and where they go. I have no interest in ruling the Underworld and having to engage with the rest of your inflated family. It would simply be a waste of my time, which would be best used elsewhere. You already provide an acceptable level of order above Hell. I have no need to change things if they are already working. If I wanted to rule in your place, Hades, I simply would."

It was a struggle not to lash out at the Fallen in front of him. The instinct to protect was primal and the will to override it was eroding rapidly. But something about this whole scenario had not rung true with him. An instinctual feeling had him holding back from unleashing vengeance upon the ruler of Hell.

He was not ruled by emotion like his nephew, Ares, even though those darker emotions were ever present, churning through his form like a dark wind. As much as he hated to admit it, Lucifer was correct. This would not be the way in which the dark angel would attack. This was a wound, one he would eventually recover from.

From observation, Lucifer did not wound; he incapacitated. Asclepius was a prime example, though Hades imagined he would not be so easy as the healer to dispose of, which was why they had previously avoided conflict.

But who would gain from this discord? And why now?

"Your arrogance is astounding. You actually believe you could rule here in my place." Hades shook his head. "As I said before, you defy the natural order of things. There would be consequences even for one such as you to try and take the power over the dead that isn't yours to take. What you fail to understand is that I don't merely rule, I *serve*. Something that is far beyond your understanding," Hades paused.

"Five nights," Hades said simply. "You have five nights to find out who or what did this. In the meantime, we will continue this… charade that we are at war. But if after those five nights are up and there are no answers, it will cease to be a charade." He couldn't let his powers weaken any further than that. He would have to act as if the ruler of Hell had indeed grown in ambition and stand against him while he was still able.

Lucifer just smiled. "Excellent, I'm glad we had this conversation, Now," he said, his dark sword starting to smoke. His eyes gleamed with something sharp and feral. "Shall we begin this… charade?"

Hades pulled his spear out from the Fallen.

The Underworld shuddered once more.

***

Nadiel and Selaphiel arrived at the designated meeting point in the Underworld. Tianya stayed with the rest of the Fallen to run interference with Sirus and also to act as a fail safe in case they didn't return from the ninth level. If they weren't back within 24 hours, her orders were to find Ruin-aith and leash him with the spelled chains they used in the arena. She would have complete control over him when he was bound and force the demon to retrieve them if he decided the ninth level of Hell would be a good place to leave them.

Hopefully, if they were delayed, that would be the reason, not something more... permanent.

They knew Ruin-aith was very old and powerful, but they didn't know where he ranked in the demon hierarchy. When the Fallen arrived in Hell, he was already acting as a servant to Lucifer. Finding information about him from the demons in the upper levels had proven difficult, though there were whispers that led Nadiel to draw a vague conclusion.

One thing was clear: all the demons despised him. His role as Lucifer's lackey branded him as a traitor, even though with the bond, he had little choice.

The air was charged. There was a sense of looming danger, the sort that makes animals scatter and flee before an uncontrollable forest fire. Nadiel couldn't help feeling the edge of it, trailing around his senses just out of reach. He caught himself constantly looking over his shoulder, preparing for a fight.

He didn't like it.

Selaphiel was still smirking. She had been doing that since they had met up. The female Fallen was all but gloating with the result of her successful mission with the ferryman. She kept glancing over as the walls occasionally trembled, spitting debris in every direction. It was way too premature to celebrate. They still had a long way to go before they could act against Lucifer.

He had a plan, but it wasn't set in stone.

Once they contained Lucifer they could finally lead an existence they felt worthy of. The Fallen were craving a war befitting their stature. Yet here they were, restricted to capturing escaping demons and the occasional stray warrior angel.

It made him want to snarl.

Too long they had been kept away like ornamental weapons, only rarely coming out to show that their blades had actual purpose. The frustration was across all factions but fear held them back. They were right to be afraid, though many of them would deny ever feeling that emotion. Lucifer had demonstrated numerous times how brutal his displeasure could be. But their leader no longer reflected their own desires.

At the very beginning, Lucifer had seared his mark across all the realms in cold, calculated violence. He found the weakness of those who appointed themselves in charge and proceeded to show them otherwise by pressing on those weaknesses very, very hard. He had used the Fallen like the weapons they were and it had been a glorious time.

But once Lucifer had established his dominance, things had slowly started to change. Where once they instigated and initiated, now they just maintained. Those brave or stupid enough to question him found themselves taking a trip to the lower levels of Hell.

There were whispers that the reason Lucifer didn't launch a full scale war with The City was because he had made a deal with Archangel Michael. Another rumour was that Lucifer didn't think he could win a battle against the right hand of God, that The City had finally found a weapon to defeat the Devil.

Another deadly rumour, whispered only in the most isolated of places, was that the Ruler of Hell secretly yearned to go back to his former self and was trying to find a way to do just that.

Nadiel again, had his own theories, but the bottom line was that the Fallen were dissatisfied and Nadiel had decided to do something about it. Oh, there had been many who had tried before, but they were impatient. They didn't take their time, gathering information like little fractured pieces of glass, waiting for the time to meld it into something sharp.

Once Lucifer was safely contained there would be a fight for power. He cast another glance at Selaphiel who appeared to be humming under her breath. He had plans around that too.

"So, we are going to visit the ninth level of Hell," Selaphiel said, briefly stopping her humming. "You haven't yet told me what the eighth level of Hell is. We have all been led to believe that there have only been seven levels in total."

Nadiel couldn't help feeling slightly smug. He knew it would have irritated her beyond belief that he had known something she hadn't. He clasped his hand behind his back and tried not to show his enjoyment as he faced her.

"The seventh level of Hell, as you know, is where we hold the most dangerous and strongest demons. The ninth level of Hell is rumoured to hold the seven deadly sins. So, as you are aware, a demon from a higher level of Hell can descend into a lower of level of Hell, even though we discourage it. The barriers will let them pass because they aren't as 'dark.'" He smiled. "So what would prevent the strongest demons from the seventh level of Hell from interacting with the ninth level?"

Selaphiel frowned. "The eighth level. What exactly is *in* the eighth level of Hell?"

Nadiel's smile widened and he held up a finger. "Light. Lots of it."

Selaphiel's mouth dropped open. "But... how..."

"How is Lucifer maintaining Light in Hell?" Nadiel asked the question for her. His lips flattened. "I know how he is doing it *now*, as for before, I just have theories."

Selaphiel stared at him for a second and then threw a hand up in the air. "The Light angel," she hissed, spinning around. "Of course! She is his supply. No wonder he hovers over her like a dragon guarding a golden egg. Do the other angels know about this?"

He shook his head. "Not many have thought it through. They are too concerned with politics and fighting amongst themselves, or getting out of Hell rather than taking the time to work out how things actually work around here." He paused as the walls shook again around them. "I'd rather them not know. Most would want to weaken Hell without understanding that if we do that we would have to battle for power with the strongest of them. The demons don't like having a master any more than we do. Best to keep them in the cages they are in so we can be free to fight on one front and not two."

Selaphiel nodded. "I agree. I've fought with some of the stronger ones." Her hand twitched against her leg. "We should avoid fighting with them if we can. Not that we couldn't keep them in line." Her pride wouldn't let her believe otherwise. "I just don't see us united once Lucifer is contained. We'd have our hands full maintaining our authority against every upstart who wants their piece of power."

Nadiel was pleased she at least saw that far. "Thankfully, Ruin-aith doesn't need a gate to get us to the ninth level. He somehow has been gifted the ability from Lucifer to appear in whichever level he wishes. I believe he will be able to bypass the eighth level entirely."

As if his name had summoned him, Ruin-aith was suddenly there in their midst, his tattered cloak spreading out like tentacles. "Itsssss time." His cowl swivelled to look at them both and he raised a bone white hand, his unnaturally long fingers curled out.

Selaphiel looked at his hand in distaste and then said out loud, "This better be worth it."

"I will takess you to the place you wisssh to go. Whatss you do there isss up to you," the demon said.

"Once we are in the ninth level of Hell, we require you to remain with us until we are ready to leave," Nadiel said firmly. He needed to be clear in his instructions to the demon. If they found a loophole, they would take it.

"Yess… of course. Whysss, young masstersss? Did you think I wouldss leave you?" Did he imagine it or did the demon appear amused? "Come, we musssst make hassstte before our absssence iss noticed."

Selaphiel walked over and placed her hand over the demon's pale one. This time she managed to keep her disgust to herself. Though she couldn't resist saying, "Let's get this over with," barely under her breath.

He followed and placed his hand on top of hers.

"No," Ruin-aith said. "Itsss mussst be ssskin contact." This close to the demon Nadiel could make out the faintest outline of the his face under the hood. What he saw or sensed made the skin on the back of his neck prickle. With reluctance, he moved his hand from Selaphiel's and onto the demon's skin. His flesh was clammy and cold, like a fish.

They shifted.

Large orbs of fire hung in the air, well above their heads. It illuminated a vast chamber. If there were any walls they were further than the eye could see. It felt old and terribly ancient. A place where myths and legend bordered on reality. A place where one whispered in hushed reverent tones and bowed their head in submission.

To his right, a large cube rose out from a circular hole in the ground. The cube had arching grooves embedded in its gold coloured surface. They were layered across each other forming intricate circular patterns that were almost hypnotic. In the centre of the cubes surface was a large sapphire stone. It glowed and dimmed in faint pulses like a weakened heartbeat.

The structure made him want to back slowly away. Instead, with effort, he let go of the demon's hand and walked closer.

"So this is it," he said softly. He could feel an energy around the cube that reminded him of the barriers between the levels. The hole in which the cube hovered above appeared bottomless. He knew if he dropped something down he wouldn't hear a thing.

"One of them," Selaphiel said from behind him. He turned his head and caught her a few metres away, looking to his left. Past her he could see the shape of another cube. "It's true. I had doubted... but it's true." Her voice was touched with awe. "The seven."

The seven deadly sins. Pride, greed, wrath, envy, lust, gluttony and sloth. Demons were created from the negative thoughts and deeds of mankind. Smaller demons could manifest with an evil act from an individual or small group of people. Larger more powerful demons could manifested with a war or an event such as genocide or mass surpression or control.

The seven deadly sins were like the blood and bone of every dark deed and thought. They were the core desires that drove people to do the mildest to the most heinous of evil acts. They were as fundamental as the elements themselves.

"Thissss isss the ninth level. Ssolitary confinement for the ssstrongest of us," the demon hissed. Nadiel had kept his awareness on where the demon was as soon as they arrived, but the stirrings of anger that was unusually present in the demon's voice had him turning slightly so he could keep him in his line of sight.

"How did he do it? How did he trap them here?" Nadiel asked, reaching his hand out cautiously towards the cube. Immediately, a blue-ish white barrier appeared around the circular hole. As he suspected, it was a barrier very similar to the ones between the levels of Hell. The only variation he could immediately see was the colour. The barrier couldn't harm the Fallen, but Nadiel instinctively knew if he proceeded to touch this one he would be on his knees.

"He wasss the first sson of Light beforess he became the first sson of the Dark," the demon replied. "And he wasss armed with much knowledge."

"I want to see them all," Selaphiel said eagerly. Ruin-aith complied, leading the way. They walked around, footsteps echoing in the chamber. One by one they came across the seven cells. They were all identical except for the stone embedded in the centre of the cube.

"Which one is Wrath?" Selaphiel asked. Nadiel shot her a sharp look. Why would she want to know that?

He wouldn't be surprised if she wanted to free one of the seven just so she could see if she could fight them. Even if it killed her. Repeatedly. Selaphiel was a powerful ally but she was also a little... bent. She did things that made no sense to Nadiel. The best tactic he found to get her back in line was distraction.

Before Ruin-aith could answer, he cut in, "There is another cell there." He pointed further down where the distant edge of a cube could be seen at the edges of the firelight. "Who is in that?"

"The Massster has a few more cellss. Ssome hold beings and creaturess who are not demonss but just as powerful. Other cellsss are empty and... waiting."

Selaphiel snorted. "I'd give a tooth to find out which poor worm annoyed Lucifer to end up down here."

Nadiel gestured ahead. "I want to see an empty one."

They walked deeper into the chamber, passing another closed cell along the way before they arrived at a large, flat circular disk, hovering above a hole in the ground about the same size. The disk was the same bronze colour as the cube cages but without the intricate lines and the stone set in the middle. It looked thin, like if you slammed enough power into the centre of it you could easily shatter it. But he knew enough that looks could be deceiving.

His brain ticked. "Do you have the ability to close one?" This is what their plan had hinged on, the ability to confine Lucifer in one of these cells. Cells that were strong enough to hold one of the seven.

He hadn't given Selaphiel much more information beyond that.

"Oh no, not I. You wouldss need ssomeone with the ability to ssee the weavesss and flowss of magic. Ssomeone who could alter them. A very sspecial being."

He waited for a beat and then said, "Someone like a witch?"

Ruin-aith tilted his head. "Yasss. But not an ordinary witch. No witchessss here."

"That's not exactly true," Nadiel said softly.

"Care to fill me in?" Selaphiel asked stiffly.

He kept his eyes on the demon. "Ruin-aith here is not all that he seems. Apparently, a long time ago, he was a very naughty demon and ate some of Hades' souls. And by some, I mean a great many. That's why you are 'chained,' isn't it? They couldn't exactly risk you escaping into the Underworld every now and then for a snack. But during your feasting, you managed to consume a 'very special' soul."

"What soul?" The words came out between her teeth.

"The witch who helped Lucifer build the barriers."

There was a silence that followed after his words.

"How do you know this?" she demanded. "Who gave you this information?"

"Ezriel," Nadiel said with a confidence he didn't feel. From this moment everything was just a dangerous guess. "Lucifer brought her down to teach him the weaves to hold the demons at bay, but you killed her before he could return her back to Earth."

"I don't killss. I take." The demon's voice was sharper and the empty hood seemed not so empty for a brief second. "They becomess mine."

Nadiel's eyes lit up and he felt the first true spark of excitement. He took a step towards the demon. "Which means she is still with you, doesn't it?"

The demon didn't respond.

"I want you to release her," he ordered. "Then I want you to get her to make one of the empty cells keyed into Lucifer's energy," Nadiel said slowly.

Selaphiel placed her hands on her hips. She cleared her throat pointedly. "I see a few gaping, bottomless holes in your plan. Firstly, why would a soul who helped Lucifer set up the boundaries, now try to trap him in a cell? Secondly, the soul is not physical. How would it even do what you want it to do? Thirdly," she gave a little huff of a laugh, "and this is probably the most important one, how are you going to get Lucifer to step into a cell? He's not an idiot."

Nadiel silver brows came together. "Neither am I. The soul is going to help us because she would rather do that than return back to *him*." He pointed his finger straight at Ruin-aith who was shifting from left to right. "As for not being able to create the barriers as a spirit, you are correct. She won't, but she could most likely direct us to someone who can."

Her hands slid slowly from her hips. "Another witch," she murmured.

"Yes," Nadiel said. "And we have a few of those to choose from." He held up a finger, "And before you ask, there is one reason and one reason only he would willingly open a cell and step inside."

Selaphiel smiled slowly. "Yes... yes, you're right. He won't want to lose his precious Light angel." She clapped slowly, the ringing sound harsh against the solemn stillness that had settled around them. "You have really outdone yourself. Though, even if we bring her down here into the cage, he is going to suspect it's a trap when he opens it."

His mouth opened then closed.

"Why don't you makess ssure the trap hass already sssprung?"

They both looked at the demon. Nadiel frowned. "What do you mean, demon?"

"Change not only the cellsss to trap the Massster, Fallen. Change the barriersss to the ninth level itsssself. When he arrivess in the ninth level to get the angel he willss already be trapped."

They both looked at each other. That was... Nadiel thought reluctantly, not a bad plan at all.

"Why would we trust you," Selaphiel asked, voicing his own concerns. Her hand twitched to her side where

476

her dagger was concealed. "It would be in your best interest to betray us. To kill us while you can."

"Our bond preventsss me from harming you." His pale hands spread out. "Long have I been in ssservice to the Masster with no foreseeable end. I wissh for that end sso I may join my kind once again. Perhapsss if I am of great sservice to you, you willss let me do that once more."

"Hmmmm…" Selaphiel said, tapping her lips with an index finger. She raised an eyebrow at Nadiel. "Do we believe him?"

"We shall see," Nadiel said in a non committal tone. Frankly, he had no idea. The demon's suggestion was too good not to consider, but he needed more time to turn it over in his head. "Call the witch you consumed. The one with the knowledge of the barriers" he ordered.

For a brief second the demon's hand curved into claws. Just as quickly, they abruptly relaxed. "Yasss."

"Bring her out."

Strangely, the demon turned its back on them as if he didn't want them to see what he did. To be honest, Nadiel didn't think he wanted to. The demon's shoulders hunched over and the tattered ends of his cloak moved erratically in coils. Selaphiel tugged nervously on the end of her braid, but once she saw Nadiel watching her she immediately stopped.

Ruin-aith obviously unnerved her as much as he did Nadiel.

Suddenly, a white glow appeared around the upper part of the demon, dim at first, but then growing in both size and brightness. The demon let out a subtle hiss as if in pain, then the white light tumbled to the ground, spreading out in a flowing pool. Slowly, a figure formed as if strugglingly to remember its original shape. It was like witnessing a birth, but more disturbing.

The demon gave a shudder and then moved to the side.

On the ground was a young woman curled into a foetal position. Long, curling hair hid most of her body like a frayed blanket. The colour of her soul was wrong. Instead of the pure, white light souls emanated when first entering the Underworld, this soul's colour was dull, almost brown in places.

"What's her name?" Selaphiel asked.

"Tanaysssia," Ruin-aith hissed.

At the sound of her name, the female spirit stirred and looked up. She was lovely for a human, Nadiel thought. Petite and curvy, with strong features balanced by large almond shaped eyes. She would have been even more striking if her form had the colour of life instead of shades of bluish-grey.

She wore a long, flowing dress, which was ripped in many places. Many spirits took the appearance of what they looked like moments before they died. He wondered which demon got to her first. Or perhaps it was Lucifer himself who ended her life once her usefulness had expired.

Disorientated, she looked around, her gaze sliding past him to the darkness surrounding them. But then her large eyes locked onto Ruin-aith.

She screamed.

It was a scream of pure terror. A sound so high and full of intense emotion it sucked the breath right from you. It was like ringing a bell to a group of powerful demonic beings trapped and starved of sustenance.

Nadiel felt something shift in the air and he glanced around uneasily. No, he didn't like this. The sound continued, shrill and unending. Nadiel quickly stepped into her line of her sight, effectively blocking Ruin-aith from her vision. The scream cut off abruptly and her eyes darted widely about as if the demon had simply disappeared.

He crouched down in front of her, stealing her attention. "Shhhh… shhhh…." he said calmly. "Look at me. Look at me. There is just you and me right now." Her eyes focused on his face, as if seeking comfort from his human appearance. When she appeared to have calmed a little he smiled, hoping it came across as reassuring.

His blood was pounding as he faced the key to all his long held ambitions.

"Tanaysia. Welcome back," he said, gently. "You and I have lots to discuss."

Chapter 27

Dragging a dead body was harder than it looked.

After a short but tense stare down with the Dragarth, I hauled the Fallen through the portal to the Underworld. I grunted with effort as I pulled his legs through the mirror. The sight would have been odd, as you couldn't see the mirror from the Underworld. It just looked like half a severed body moving on the rocky floor. I had originally thought the portal mirror disappeared when you went through the other side from Lucifer's domain, but after some pondering, I figured it was just invisible.

Luckily, I was right. Otherwise, I would have been stuck in the Underworld until my soulmate decided to help me out. And since he was currently avoiding me, I didn't feel like that would be anytime soon.

The ground trembled under my feet. I dropped the Fallen's cold hands and looked up just as a spray of fine rock particles hit me in the face. Coughing, I looked around as the walls reverberated.

What was going on?

Feeling suddenly nervous, I grabbed the Fallen's hands again and pulled as quickly as I could down the wide tunnel. His head lolled back, and I tried not to look at his empty, burnt sockets where his eyes had been. I didn't know when the dark angels would wake up, but I didn't want that to be right next to the access point to Lucifer's domain. I wasn't sure if they would be able to access his realm without his permission, but I didn't want to take the chance in case they woke up and remembered exactly who had killed them. And where.

After a few harrowing turns, with the walls spitting out rocks like it was aiming for me, I dragged the male Fallen next to the female. There, that would have to do. I had left them in a shadowy corner, but I couldn't be sure a demon wouldn't find them before they recovered. I didn't want to think about what would happen if one did.

Trying to ignore the stabbing feeling of guilt, I turned and walked away. I was tired, but I had to continue my negotiations with the witches. Then I needed to fill up my quota of crystals before Lucifer declared I had broken our deal. Not that I minded. I seemed to be finding a use for the crystals anyway. He didn't exactly *specify* that after I filled the crystals, I couldn't use them myself.

I smiled, and the scars pulled along my face.

And then maybe if I had time, I'd have a hot, relaxing bath.

***

A few hours later and bereft of a bath, I entered Atlas's room.

An axe slammed into the side of the wall, millimetres away from my head. I froze, my eyes widening as I spotted Atlas on the far side of the room. His back was to an array of small to large axes, and he had his arm cocked back, ready to throw the other one in his hand.

"Atlas!" I yelled, holding my arms protectively over my chest.

"Sorry!" he yelled at the same time, just as I was about to merge backwards. "Ares' arsehole! I thought you were the bloody demon!" His eyes were wide and edged with fear. It was then I noticed he had a small gash on his forehead. His clothes which had looked tidy and clean before, were now dishevelled with a few tears slicing down the sleeves and across the middle.

"The Dragarth?" I asked, looking around cautiously, edging further into the room. "Are you hurt?"

"The demon your flamin' lover sent to train me! How did he think I was going to learn from a bloody demon? I don't even speak his bloody language! He just kept throwing things at me until I picked up the same weapon and threw it back. That's not how you train someone!" he ranted.

"Uh…" I looked back at the axe embedded in the wall. "It looks like you're learning pretty fast."

"I was aiming for your flamin' head, you nit!" he roared.

At the elevated sound of his voice, the bundle strapped to my chest started to cry.

The axe he was holding dropped with a clang. "What in Hades' flamin' river is that?" he shrieked, pressing himself against the wall as if he could also escape through it.

I stroked the bundle against my chest and bounced around a little. When the crying still continued, I used a little technique I had recently discovered. I visualised soft, white light around me, and the crying immediately trailed off.

"It's a baby," I said matter-of-factly. "A little girl, to be exact."

"What is *that*," he pointed at my chest, "doing here?" His voice dropped down to a horrified whisper.

"It's one of the witch's children. I have to take her back to Earth." I looked at him, a little confused. "Atlas, you're acting like you've never seen a child before."

At my explanation, he visibly looked relieved. His shoulders relaxed, and he slumped more comfortably against the wall, despite the many protruding weapons hanging along it. "Ohhh, the witch's get. I thought it was *your* child."

"Mine!" I said in alarm. "Why would you..." I blinked, then shook my head. "You do know how..." I stopped and closed my eyes. This was not a conversation I wanted to have. I also didn't want to engage in an exercise where I picked apart the confusing tangle of Atlas' mind. I took a deep breath and just let it go. "No, it's not my child," I said, opening my eyes.

"Yes, you said that."

I huffed out a breath. "Atlas, I said I'm going to Earth to leave the baby with the witch's coven."

He scratched his arm and gave me an assessing look under his thick eyebrows. "So you finally made the deal? What were the terms?"

I waved my hand dismissively and walked closer. "It doesn't matter. Atlas, I'm going to *Earth*, and I want you to come with me."

His face immediately went blank. "But we haven't worked out the rest of your plan. You don't have access to a portal for the warrior angels. I haven't started training you with a throwing knife. We haven't–"

"Atlas," I stood in front of him, placing a hand gently on his arm. His eyes dropped down to my fingers curled around his shirt. "None of it matters. I want to take you back home."

Hope flashed in his eyes before it flickered and died. He cleared his throat. "I can't, Sandy. If I don't finish training you, he will find me and throw me in a pit full of scorpions. That's what he said." I hadn't asked Atlas about his trauma with scorpions, but apparently, that threat was enough to make Atlas do almost anything Lucifer wanted.

I shook my head. "He won't come for you if I take you out of Hell myself. If you escaped, that would be different. But if I manage to get you out myself, it's my win. He would see it as an accomplishment," I said with certainty.

He licked his lips. "I don't know…"

"The truth is, I don't really know if I'm going to survive by the end of all this," I said gently. This thought had been playing around and around in my head for some time. "If I manage to get the warrior angels out without being killed by some Fallen or demon, that would be a miracle. And I may be able to do it," I sent a quick prayer to heaven, "but there is also a chance that I may not."

Oh, I had faith that I was meant to be here. That somehow, my meeting Lucifer in this slice of time was all for a purpose. I just didn't know what it was.

Was it to free the warrior angels? Maybe. I hoped so. But I couldn't know for sure. And just in case it wasn't, and I failed in this task, I had to look out for my friend. I also knew that I could hope for Lucifer to intervene if I was in serious trouble, but I couldn't rely on him. Not completely. Not the way he was now, despite the connection we had between us.

Shaking my head ruefully, I added, "If something happens to me, there is no guarantee you will ever leave Hell. Now is my chance before I run out of time. Atlas, you *have* to come with me. You have to let me take you home before it's too late."

The other element I had no choice but to consider was that if Lucifer decided to sever our soulmate link and submerge once more into the Darkness, losing whatever parts of his soul he had gained, he would, without a doubt, use Atlas against me.

I couldn't let that happen.

"I could help you fulfil your mission," he said quietly, as serious as I had ever seen him.

"I know," I said just as quietly. "I can do this, Atlas. I've learnt enough." I hoped. I let go of his arm and turned around, soothing the sleeping baby in my arms who had started to stir. "We have to leave now. There is something happening in the Underworld, and it could get worse the longer we wait. Also, I can't keep this baby with me here for very long before she is going to need to feed."

"How? How are you going to get me out?" he asked behind me.

I shot him a grin over my shoulder. "I'm going to have to kill you."

***

It took us staring at the portal mirror for another hour before it finally showed the Underworld. There were other places it revealed, but I couldn't be sure what type of realm it was in. Each portal mirror in the Fallen domain seemed to be locked to one location.

These ones here flickered constantly to different places. I was sure there was a way to activate the runes around the frame to fix the portal anywhere we wanted to go, which made it so frustrating. Since

I lacked the knowledge, we had to do it the hard way.

Wait and wait some more.

Considering this was a travel mode of Lucifers', the chances of any of these locations being in a higher realm were slim to non-existent. There was one that vaguely resembled Earth, but I wasn't sure enough to take the risk and waste this opportunity.

I was now familiar with the terrain of the Underworld leading from this portal mirror, so as soon as I saw the misty landscape, I said to Atlas, "Take it now."

"Sandy…" he started to protest, looking dubiously at the bottle of liquid I had given him.

I pulled open the stopper on my own dark blue vial and ever so carefully dribbled the contents into the baby's mouth. "Atlas, you can come with me, or you can stay here with him."

I didn't even have to point to the Dragarth, who was looking at Atlas like he was a three-course meal. I had to, of course, yell at the three-headed serpent again, who hissed at me in frustration as I interfered with the portal mirrors. He destroyed half the furniture in the room in response.

Atlas stuck as close to me as a second shadow, completely unnerved by the three sets of eyes that continuously stared at him. "Is it going to eat me?" he kept whispering.

"Not if you're with me." I was pretty confident the Dragarth wouldn't risk harming me to get to Atlas.

This time I told Atlas, "Though, if you stay, he'll probably eat you."

After a string of muttered half-curses about Zeus and a pig, I heard him pop the stopper and down the contents with a single gulp. "You better be right about this, Sandy. If I die down here, I'm going to come back and haunt your arse. You'll never get any sleeeeep. I'll keeeep sinnnginggg thiss son–" I heard his body hit the floor.

After a quick check to make sure the baby had stopped breathing, I crouched down to where Atlas had fallen to his side. Speed was critical. Every second mattered now. The Dragarth slithered slowly closer, his large scaled body further crushing the furniture to the floor. The forked tongues flicked in and out, and six yellow eyes narrowed in on Atlas' unmoving chest.

I narrowed my own green eyes back at the demon as I grabbed Atlas's ankles off the floor. "Don't even think about it." After a second of concentration, my body was enveloped in a subtle, warning glow of pure Light. My eyes narrowed further to make my threat clear. The Dragarth's tail thrashed around like a furious cat. With exertion, I heaved Atlas' body towards the portal. I slid him through, slowly merging backwards with him and the baby.

I smiled at the Dragarth just as we disappeared.

As soon as I went through to the Underworld, I did a quick scan for danger. There was always a risk that a demon or, worse, a Fallen was nearby. When I sensed nothing, I threw up a Light shield around us and pulled out two other glass vials with pearl-coloured liquid inside. The baby's lips had alarmingly started to turn a light blue. Trying not to panic, I dribbled the contents of the vial in her mouth, careful not to spill any.

I rubbed the column of her throat gently. "Come on, come on," I whispered encouragingly.

Kneeling down, I pulled open Atlas' mouth by tugging the bottom of his chin down. I almost spilled the liquid over his beard as the Underworld trembled once more. Using a few of Atlas's curse words under my breath, I waited for the tremors to pass, then gently poured the contents down his throat. I prayed madly that this would work. I was one hundred percent trusting the witches. They had everything to gain by helping me right now. I had to believe that.

The little baby started to cough, her eyes fluttering open to reveal honey-brown eyes. She immediately scrunched her face and started to wail.

"Shhhhh… Shhhhh…" I whispered, frantically looking around. A child's screams would be the sweetest sound in the Underworld, impossible to ignore. Looking at Atlas's unmoving chest, I was too anxious to calm her down.

"Breathe, Atlas," I said, trying to rock the baby to cease her screams. "You need to breathe."

The witches had told me to administer the second dose as soon as possible. The longer I waited, the more likely that the soul would start to leave the body and journey to whatever was their next destination. I knew I would lose precious minutes dragging Atlas's body through to the Underworld, and I didn't know what would await me on the other side.

The walls shook again, and little cracks appeared. What was going on? I tried to sense Lucifer through the link, but I didn't detect any strong emotion leaking through the cord that bound us.

It was then, of course, that the demons found us.

There were four of them. Slender and hairless, their pale pink bodies scrambled across the rock wall on either side, heading towards us. One of their elongated heads looked up, and dark gaping pits where their eyes should be directed themselves at me. A chittering sound emerged from its lips, and the others responded in kind.

"Atlas..." my voice was loud and alarmed. I placed my hand on his chest and shook him. "Wake up now!" The baby continued to cry in my arms.

They came at me all at once, leaping across the rock walls with alarming speed. I dropped my shield and lasered the one closest to me. Its claws reached out, and my concentrated beam of Light sizzled diagonally across its chest. The pieces of its body hit the ground. My shield came up again just as the other three demons slammed into it.

Sizzle.

"Atlas!" I screamed and hit his chest hard with my fist.

My shield flared at the impact and strained to hold it as they screeched and backed away. The baby wailed louder. They bunched their legs, preparing themselves to leap at me again. I quickly lowered my shield once more.

My beam of Light shot out in a molten hot line. They leapt up, but I severed one demon's legs completely off. It fell to the ground, flailing its arms in rage. One of the other demons crawled over and, with a quick movement, bit through its neck.

The demon stopped flailing.

"Get up–" slammed his chest again, "you big–" hit him again, "overly large, irritating…" My fist came down once more. "Don't you *dare* die on me, you hulking–"

The demons attacked again, this time coming at me from multiple angles. I raised my hand upwards, and the shield fell around us like a dome. They slammed into my Light, shrieking again from the pain. One opened its mouth and dragged it down right in front of the baby's head, burning its lips in the process. They scrambled backwards again, their faces bubbling over with boils.

A great, gasping breath had me looking down.

Atlas went into a fit of deep, belly coughs and opened his eyes. He glared at me and sat up awkwardly. "Well, that was about as fun as rubbing your balls against a splintered fence. Ahhhhh! What in the seven rivers is that?" he yelled, pointing at the demons. "Get rid of it, Sandy! Don't just sit there!"

A tidal wave of relief hit me, making me feel shaky. For a moment, I had thought... I took a deep breath. "They are demons, Atlas. We are in the Underworld."

Finally calming down, I dropped my shield. Both my hands came up, and white Light blasted out of me in a steady, sharp stream. The demons leapt up, but my Light had shot above them, not at them. They collapsed in pieces to the floor.

Feeling better, I put my arms around the baby strapped to my chest and shushed her gently. A softer, white Light flowed around me, calming her cries down to soft gurgling murmurs.

Once we were no longer a beacon for the demons, I turned to Atlas, who got stiffly to his feet, pulling out a sword strapped to his back. "How are you feeling?"

"Fine," he said, swinging his sword experimentally and then rolling his shoulders to loosen the joints. "Let's get out of this flamin' place." He paused, looking slightly alarmed as the Underworld shook again.

I took his word for it, hoping that his short-lived death had not caused any unseen damage. Fumbling at my waist, where I had strapped a belt and a pouch, I pulled out a translucent blue orb.

"What's that?" Atlas asked.

"This is my way back to the portal." I whispered the words of the incantation three times. I had practised this over and over again for an hour until I got the pronunciation and rhythm of the words right.

The orb turned a dark blue and pulsed once, signifying that I had been successful. I put it back in my pouch. This time I took out a dark green orb. "This one will take us to the ferryman crossing."

Saying another incantation three times, I threw the orb up in the air where it hovered, spinning slowly around. It split open, revealing a dark purple flame. Its muted glow emitted enough light that I could see it but not too much that it attracted attention. It moved forward, and we hastily followed.

Atlas paced behind me, surprisingly quiet enough that I barely heard his footsteps. It was hard to remember he was so skilled with all his loud boasting and crude language. He had proved his intelligence time and time again. I knew I never would have made it this far without him.

We didn't talk and wouldn't unless it was absolutely necessary. Voices could echo down these corridors and hit the wrong ears. The aim was to get to the ferryman as discreetly as possible. I had also warned Atlas about the spirits. Last time I was here, one had seen me, screaming at me to help them, and I found myself dragged into Hell.

They floated around us, drifting aimlessly with no apparent direction or urgency. Most of the time, they ignored our presence until we came too close to their light, then their focus sharpened and latched onto us pleadingly.

We made sure to stay as far away as we could, just in case.

I wondered if the Underworld unnerved Atlas, but every time I glanced at him, his mouth was set in a grim, hard line. I supposed after meeting Lucifer, and the Dragarth, the bar of what was terrifying was set pretty high. Everything was in perspective.

After a couple of hours, with me feeding the baby the only bottle of milk I had, the tremors of the Underworld became increasingly more violent. We had managed to skirt past a couple of demons and, when pressed, eliminate a few more. When we couldn't determine a way around them, Atlas acted like a brilliant distraction. His roaring and cursing – and sometimes thumping his chest like an ape – stole all the attention, and then I quickly finished them off from behind. The tactic had been working well. I started to believe that we could do this without much trouble, that I could get Atlas and this tiny baby girl home.

Then we arrived at the river and saw the boat.

It was lying on its side on the banks of the river Styx like a shipwreck washed up on the shore. My eyes glanced up and down the river's edge frantically. There was no sign of the ferryman.

"Where is he?" I hissed.

Atlas shook his head wordlessly.

Looking around cautiously, I edged closer to the shore. Maybe there would be footsteps. Maybe he just went for a walk? I knew that was ridiculous as soon as I thought about it, but part of me refused to believe our way out was closed just when we were so close.

As I approached the sandy banks, I saw splatters of blood. Some were dark red, almost brown, and some were also black. Both looked relatively recent. Had there been an attack on the ferryman? Perhaps that was why the Underworld was trembling. I could see no obvious footprints or disturbances near the boat itself, but the water could have washed away any tracks. I also had no real knowledge of tracking, so even if there was some sign or indication of what happened here, I wouldn't be able to tell.

Defeated. I felt defeated.

What was I supposed to do now? How was I supposed to get Atlas and the baby to Earth? I couldn't go back. I didn't have another set of potions to take them through the portal mirrors. I clenched my fists in frustration.

I turned back to tell Atlas we needed to come up with another plan, but the words turned to ashes in my mouth. A long curving blade was held at his throat, and behind him, a Fallen. Atlas's face was pale. He held himself still, but I saw his left hand moving incrementally towards the knife in his belt.

I shook my head slightly. His hand stopped. There was no way he would be able to attack a Fallen successfully. Even if he did manage to grab his blade without being noticed, it wouldn't matter. If he caused a sliver of trouble, the Fallen would kill him.

She was shorter than most angels, coming almost an inch below the top of Atlas' head. Her skin was the kind of brown that reminded me of a doe's pelt with hints of gold shifting through at certain angles. Her dark hair hit the tops of her shoulders, blending in with the armour that covered her chest.

She wore armour. My heart sank into the pits of my stomach.

I tried not to panic. It was so much different when it was just my life on the line. But when it was Atlas'...

"Come closer," she said, her voice echoing around us.

I tentatively moved towards her, wondering how I could get close enough to take her out without hurting Atlas.

"Stop," she commanded.

My feet jerked to a halt. I desperately wanted to use my Light, but I couldn't see a way I could hit her.

"The child. Put it down on the ground."

I glanced at the drowsy baby's face, eyes half closed as the warmth from my body comforted her. I knew as soon as I put her down on the cold, rocky ground, she would start screaming again and draw every demon in the area towards us. I glanced back up into the Fallen's dark, empty eyes and knew putting this baby down was a death sentence.

My stomach twisted as I looked at Atlas and the knife against his throat.

"You're taking too long," she said.

Drops of blood started to slide out from beneath the blade. Atlas kept his eyes on me but didn't move. I knew he was afraid like I knew he was trusting me to get him out of this, even knowing what I was up against.

Pulse hammering, I slowly knelt down and started to unstrap the baby from my chest. Atlas's life was in imminent danger. The baby... hopefully, had a little more time. *Please let her have more time*, I prayed fervently as I undid the knot across my shoulder.

The thought of leaving her here, vulnerable to the horrors lurking in the dark, made me want to scream. My hands trembled as I gently put her down, surrounded by the dark grey cloth that had held her to me.

She stirred, shifting uncomfortably, eyes flickering open.

"Leave her," the Fallen ordered.

I stood just as the baby started to whimper. As I took a step away, I tried hard not to flinch as she began to cry helplessly. The high, keening sound echoed around us, and I felt the clock ticking inside my head as her life slowly counted down.

Use me, my darker self whispered. I stiffened.

The Fallen gestured with her head towards the left. My eyes followed towards the opening of another tunnel, almost hidden around a bend. I moved slowly away from the crying baby, feet dragging with every step. My opportunity to get close to her crumbled away, leaving me scrambling desperately for a solution.

As I walked towards the tunnel, I turned my body slowly so I could see Atlas and the Fallen angel. I couldn't use my Light to burn. The Fallen was wearing armour and to disable her, I would have to hurt him. I had the ability to heal Atlas from grievous wounds, but I couldn't bring him back to life once his soul departed his body. The only option I had was to blast her with pure Light. Hopefully, that would break her contact with Atlas and allow me the space to eliminate her.

It was a massive risk. Almost too much. She could kill him before I had a chance to take her out.

Use me, my darker self tempted once more. The Creator, give me strength.

The baby wailed behind me, and the darkness stirred around us with eager, reaching hands. I was running out of time. If I wanted to save them both, I had to act now.

In every lifetime, there comes a time when you don't know what the right thing to do is. But doing nothing ends up being the worst choice to make.

I channelled heat into my palm, fervently hoping for the best but no way near prepared for the worst. I started to lift my fingers and froze.

Yellow eyes glimmered in the dark.

The demon launched just as the Fallen started to turn around. It went straight for her face. She immediately let go of Atlas and stepped swiftly to the side, slicing downwards with her knife.

"RUN!" I screamed at Atlas.

He didn't hesitate. Finally freed from the knife at his throat, Atlas bolted away from the Fallen and headed straight my way. But the dark angel was quick. Rock shot out from the ground in a jagged pillar in front of him. He slammed against it with bruising force and fell to the ground.

He didn't move.

Fear fueled the fire in my veins. My Light shot out in a bright torrent and slammed into the Fallen. She flew backwards through the air, sizzling with Light, but not before she threw something with her right hand. The object glinted high in the dark like a falling star and then hit my stomach, deflecting off the armour I had activated earlier.

The figure of the Fallen slowly got to her feet. I had hurt her, but nowhere near enough.

Atlas stirred on the ground, and the dark angel glanced over.

"You have now cost him his life," she said with a grim smile. The rocks around Atlas trembled.

Use me, my darker self hissed. *Or do you want him to die?*

My eyes widened. The need to protect my friend was overwhelming. With tears in my eyes, the words almost escaped my lips, but the sound died in my throat as the most bizarre thing happened.

Several more demons jumped out of the shadows.

They all looked the same. Grey skin, patched with silvery scales, and four muscular arms, which ended with one gleaming black talon. Their heads were wide, hosting a wide mouth bearing rows and rows of sharp, elongated teeth. For a second, I thought they would attack me or Atlas, who was an easy target on the ground.

Instead… they went for the Fallen. All of them. She went down amongst a pile of long grey limbs.

I ran towards Atlas and heard a low groan as I knelt down next to him. He had a large gash in the centre of his forehead that was bleeding profusely. I had no time to heal him now.

"We have to get up now!" With effort, I grabbed his arm and hauled him up, wrapping an arm around his waist to support his weight.

I turned towards the baby, who was still yelling her tiny lungs out. Then my body locked up as if each and every muscle was encased in ice, halting me in my tracks.

A lizard demon held the baby girl in its arms.

It stood upright, almost as tall as me, with a long tail that was tipped in small thin spikes. Carefully held in its arms was the baby who struggled pitifully. All it had to do was to curl its claw-tipped fingers, and the baby would die.

My heartbeat became louder than the thoughts racing through my mind, drowning them out completely.

Then the demon stretched out its arms. "Take the childs," it said in a low, raspy voice.

I stared at it in shock.

"We must make haste before the Fallen defeats us."

Us? What was going on? Was this demon helping us? That was... impossible. I struggled to compute what was happening.

"Put the baby down," I said, Light sparking along my fingertips. "And back away."

Surprisingly, the demon immediately did as I asked, carefully placing the child on the ground. It moved backwards, still facing me. "We don't have much time," it said once again, this time with more urgency.

I quickly made sure Atlas could stand on his own. He swayed only slightly, then steadied, wiping the blood running down the back of his face. He pulled out yet another sword strapped to his back and glared at the demon. Tougher than he looked.

I walked over and scooped the baby up in my arms, watching the demon cautiously.

"You must follow me," the lizard demon said, turning and gesturing with an arm. "I will lead you out of here."

A quick glance over my shoulder showed me that the dark angel was on her feet and still fighting. Dark metal flashed, and the number of demons had reduced dramatically.

"Why?" I demanded.

"Because we hate the Fallen," it hissed. "We are tired of being slaughtered for your training or their entertainment."

I blinked at the implications of that. Another set of choices. This one harder, riskier, and stupidly insane.

"Where would you take us?"

Atlas sucked in a breath and looked at me, hearing the consideration in my voice. "Sandy–" he started to say.

The demon opened its mouth with a scary smile. "Why, the Elysian Fields. I was sent to take you there."

Chapter 28

"Did I get my head knocked in and I'm hallucinating or did you get your head knocked in and that's why you're acting like a crazy person?" Atlas growled at me, his eyes trained on the back of the reptilian demon's head.

We quickly followed the demon through the misty terrain of the Underworld with no certainty of where we were headed. Even though the demon was with us, we still avoided the deeper pockets of black that bloomed in corners and crevices. Even the monsters had their own monsters roaming about.

"I know this is a bit unorthodox, but–"

"Un-a what?" Atlas cut me off, confused.

"Ah, it's a bit unusual," I corrected. "But we didn't have many options. This seemed like the best one," I muttered at the end.

"I'm sorry," he whispered harshly. "How in Hades' sizable balls was *this* the best option!"

We had been trekking for almost an hour, and I thankfully managed to calm the baby down for most of that time. She had finally fallen asleep against my chest and I pondered, not for the first time, the desperate circumstances the witches were in to send one of their babies with me.

Me, a magnet for all things dark.

"I couldn't take you back and we couldn't stay where we were. And I don't have any idea of how to get you out of here."

"But a demon, Sandy. A *demon*. You know they don't have souls, right? You were aware of that because... *he could be taking us to Hell!*" he hissed furiously.

"I thought about that," I whispered back. "The last time I was taken into Hell, Lucifer was not happy." I still remembered fragments of the conversation between my Flame and the female snake demon who had orchestrated my torture. Back then, he had destroyed the demons who were with me and insinuated what would happen if he found me back in Hell.

I stumbled and almost tripped as a thought struck me. "Perhaps the demon is taking me back to Lucifer? They might think I've tried to escape."

Atlas let out a string of curses. Then he stopped. "Maybe he is helping you?" His voice was hopeful. "Do you think he is helping you?"

My eyes widened. This was an angle I hadn't considered. Then, I abruptly shook my head. "No, it isn't his style. It's too obvious." My Flame was more likely to just point in the right direction, and would be happy for me to stumble and almost impale myself to get there. Leading me by the hand to the place I needed to go didn't feel like him.

"I am taking you to the Elysian Fields," the demon said again, without turning back, obviously overhearing our whole conversation.

"See?" I said, and lifted one shoulder, as if the demon's response mattered.

He glared at me.

I sighed. "I am concerned, but I know we still have options. A demon I could probably protect you from, and have. More than one in fact. A Fallen... we were lucky, Atlas."

That ended the conversation for a while.

The Fallen in the witches domain had been unaware of who I was and what I could do. I had the element of surprise. Here, the dark angel had attacked deliberately and seemed to at least have an idea of my capabilities.

What I told Atlas was true. We had been lucky. If the demons hadn't intervened, I probably would have lost both Atlas and the baby.

Was I worried that the demon was lying to us? Absolutely. What did it have to gain? Unless I was wrong, the demon had inferred that it knew we were trying to free the angels trapped in the dungeons and simply didn't want the Fallen to create more of themselves. Maybe it was as simple as that. Or perhaps we were heading towards Lucifer... or a Hell Gate.

I could help the thoughts and possibilities racing through my head. As outwardly calm as I appeared, I was anything but on the inside.

I could probably sense a Hell Gate before we got too close. The overwhelming negativity would prickle along my skin like burning needles. But perhaps there might be a horde of demons waiting just as I sensed the Gate. Or perhaps the Gate was something we fell into, like an endless dark hole ending into a pit of fire. Or perhaps there would be—

"Just up here," the lizard demon said, walking up a slope that twisted around the corner. We had taken so many corridors and turns, some I didn't even realise were there. If we had to return to the river, we would be completely, utterly lost.

My skin turned clammy and I strained to sense movement around us in the dark. I was waiting for an ambush. I was waiting for an attack. Would I be able to protect us all this time?

Light flared against my fingers as we walked upward and turned cautiously around the corner.

It was a small chamber, about twice the size of Atlas's room in Lucifer's domain. Dominating the space was a small body of water, crystal blue in colour with white flowers blooming delicately on the surface. A thin sheen of mist rolled softly over the top before disappearing like a cloud of smoke against the dark rocks. Just behind that was two white columns, cracked, parts crumbled away like insects had been slowly gnawing at it over the centuries.

Between these pillars stood a gateway.

A shimmering pearlescent sheen of liquid stretched between the columns. It rippled and moved as if trying to escape its confines. My mouth gaped open. If a horde of demons filed in behind us banging together a knife and fork, I probably wouldn't have even noticed.

There was no doubt about it. This was the gateway to the Elysian Fields. Now that I was in front of it, I should have noticed we were approaching the elusive portal much earlier. I was so prepared to feel the dense, violent energy of a Hell Gate that I had been numb to feel the opposite.

It was like standing in front of a window by the sea, after being buried alive for a year.

"It's real," Atlas whispered in awe.

"Yes." It was the only answer I could manage.

The hunt for this gateway was notorious. In The City of Light, I had heard the warrior angels were trying to find the access point from the Elysian Fields into the Underworld. They had been strategizing for a long, long time on how to get the angels out of Hell. But each attempt to find or source information on its location had ended in failure. This portal was a closely kept secret amongst the Gods, even from The City, who would only use it for the highest of intentions.

And we found it.

The demon moved back against the wall as if its very presence hurt it. "Here. Now go."

I shot the demon a disbeliving look. I had expected some sort of treachery, but I never thought the demon would do exactly what it said it would.

I took Atlas's hand in my own and guided him around the pool, my eyes trained on the demon, just in case. As we got closer to the portal, the feeling of lightness intensified. I took a deep breath, and tears of relief welled up in my eyes. I didn't let them fall. We weren't completely safe yet.

"Go through," I said to Atlas. "I'll follow right behind you."

He hesitated, then squeezed my hand. "Don't make me wait long, or I'll come back out and get you," he said sternly.

I just nodded.

He let go of my hand. After a second, I felt him leave.

I stared at the demon and it stared right back at me.

"Why?" I asked.

The demon flashed its serrated teeth. "Go, angel. Perhaps we shall see you again." Its tongue flicked out as if he wished it was longer and he could taste me. "Soon, I hope." He moved, and left down the pathway we had come.

Running a comforting hand down the baby's back, I turned towards the gateway and merged through.

***

Sunlight.

That was the first thing I felt. Warm, golden rays gently caressed the exposed parts of my skin. I tipped my head up, seeking its warmth like a babe at its mothers breast. My eyes caught on the bluest of skies, a vivid wash of colour that seemed almost surreal.

My head dipped down. Oh. Beautiful.

Rolling, emerald green grass spread out in front of me, intersected only by a shimmering curve of water that glistened like a mermaid tail in the light. Trees rose up from the ground, some like giants providing pockets of shade. Other trees had branches that dipped low, offering their fruit to anyone passing by.

There were spirits here, weaving through the grass and walking along the shore of the river. But unlike the Underworld, they weren't pale imitations of their former selves. Here in Elysium, they glowed with vitality and awareness.

The air sang with harmony and peace and my body sagged, knees hitting the ground. A colossal weight, which felt like it was welded across my shoulders, slowly started to slough off me in chunks. The heaviness peeled away, as if the sun burned through each and every layer.

I felt my skin prickle with the need to unfurl my wings, and I ached to spread them out and absorb the energy like a healing salve. I thought it had started to drizzle, but at the first taste of salt against my lips, I realised I was crying.

A soft moan made me look sideways.

Atlas lay stretched out on the grass, arms and legs splayed as wide as they would go. His head was tipped back in bliss and a half smile graced his lips.

"I think I shall stay here, Sandy," he said, eyelashes fluttering. "First, I think I'm going to have a long nap. Then I'm going to find something to drink. After that, I'm sure there is a busty woman I can convince to have a tumble."

The creases on his forehead had smoothed out and I was reluctant to break his contentment. As much as I wanted to linger, we could not stay.

"We can't stay, Atlas. We don't belong here."

"I'm a hero, a mighty warrior. Of course I belong," he said matter of factly with his eyes still closed.

"I'm not disputing your accomplishments. I'm disputing the fact that you are not dead."

One brown eye opened. "Minor detail. I deserve a break from that cursed place."

"Perhaps a break on Earth?" I suggested. "We need to get this baby back to the witches." The baby was peacefully asleep. I wondered how much longer it would be before she demanded another feed. I didn't have another bottle on me.

"You want me to leave *this*," he said, gesturing to the splendour around us. "To go with you to a dark witches' den. Sorry, Sandy, you're on your own. I'm going to take a nap now."

I sighed. "Atlas, if we don't leave soon, a Guardian will come to remove us. They don't take kindly to those lingering where they don't belong."

He muttered something incoherent.

I changed tactics. "All right then. I was excited to see your camp grounds when I took you back home. I've never seen an army before. One worth seeing," I clarified, looking at him from beneath my lashes. "I guess I have to look elsewhere before I return to the Underworld. Who knows if I will get the opportunity again." I let out a reluctant sigh. "Perhaps the Kolaiths..." I ventured.

Both eyes snapped open. "You wouldn't!"

I shrugged.

He sat upright and glared at me. One finger pointed menacingly in my direction, which was a feat in the Elysian Fields. "The Kolaith's have rudimentary skills in the battlefield. In fact, I'd be surprised if they didn't piss their pants like little boys, once they see our army storming towards them. They're barely weaned off their mother's tits, coming up with battle strategies my niece who is only five summers old could outwit! Impressive army…" he sneered. "You would be seeing the worst Greece had to offer."

I stared at him. "So are you coming with me?"

He sat up. "Yes, I'm coming."

I turned my head around to look at the portal where we had entered from. All I saw was a tree and rolling green hills. Confused, I reached my hand out to touch the bark. Just as it made contact, the bark rippled and my fingers slowly slid right through.

The portal was hidden well. Though, I needed a way to remember where it was when I returned back to the Elysian Fields. I obviously couldn't access the Underworld through the Ferryman, since his sudden disappearance. So I had no choice but to come back here.

After a moment of consideration, I pulled out a crystal from my pouch. From the location of the river in Elysium, I could determine the general area of where the portal was located. I knelt down and, after a minute of scraping with one of my knives, I embedded the crystal into the ground. Dusting my hands on my dress, I stood up. Hopefully, I'd be able to see it, if not sense the energy when I was near. For now, it was the best I could do.

I turned around and reached down for Atlas's hand, who was on the verge of collapsing back down onto the grass. I pulled him up, then reached up to touch the gash on his head. The bleeding had stopped but the swelling made him look like he had an emerging horn coming out of the centre of his forehead.

"Let me just take care of this," I said. This time, channelling the healing light came so much easier for me. I didn't have to pierce through a circling noose of dark energy to access my other gifts.

"There," I said, once the swelling had gone back down and all evidence of his time in the Underworld had disappeared. "We can't have you going back to the army looking battered and bruised." I smiled at him. "You need to come back looking stronger than ever."

I was grateful for that hint of a smile that touched his lips and reached his eyes. I had done it. I had got him out.

Freed from the density of the negative realms, I closed my eyes and shifted us out.

***

Selaphiel pushed the door open to the witches domain with a burgeoning sense of anticipation. A few witches scurried along the hallways just up ahead. As soon as they noticed her black eyes trained on them, they let out a short, sharp squeal and scattered like cockroaches in different directions.

Pathetic, really.

The human population was like an infestation of ants. No matter how many times you stepped on them, more seemed to appear from under rocks and cracks in the ground. They were so breakable, weak, and constantly terrified of *something*.

Tonight, that something was her.

She smiled and spotted a shivering witch hiding in a shadowy corner beneath a chair. Selaphiel jerked her head forward like a viper. "Boo!"

The witch screamed, covering her face with her arms and hands,

"Stop playing," Nadiel reprimanded from behind. "In and out, remember?"

She rolled her eyes and turned around.

Tanaysia, the spirit of the witch who had helped Lucifer create the barriers, moved slowly in front of Nadiel, as if every movement hurt. She supposed being swallowed by a demon for centuries would probably have a damaging impact on your soul. Though, despite her sickly soul colour, she seemed to be functioning remarkably well.

Nadiel scanned the area as if his gaze could burn through the walls. "If every witch is not in front of me within the next 30 seconds, I will find you and throw you into the arena. I promise you, you will not like that." His voice echoed threateningly down the long hallways. Then he slowly started to count.

There was silence for a few of those seconds and Selpahiel started to warm up to the idea of a hunt. Then, unfortunately, the sound of rapid footsteps started to get closer and closer. Witches streamed out of corners and and passages, some flustered, some panicked, and some completely terrified. Even the witch under the chair managed to crawl out and kneel on the ground in front of them as if she was about to be sacrificed.

Selaphiel sighed and rolled her eyes again.

When the count ended, it appeared that there were around thirty witches gathered before them. Selaphiel was honestly surprised there were so many. Though, she was never one to visit the witches domain herself. Her brand of entertainment was usually found elsewhere.

A tall, dark skinned woman came forward, pushing her way through the crowd. She had a strong energy, and held herself well despite the fear she could all but smell steaming off her. The scars that ran up the side of her face were deep, leaving even grooves like ripples in the sand. A flash of several different demons scrolled through her mind as she tried to determine which one could have left its mark.

"How may we serve you?" she asked. By coming forward the witch signalled herself out as the leader. Her eyes were appropriately lowered, her voice submissive but the set of her shoulders spoke a long, barbed line of defiance.

Interesting. Maybe there was still some play to be had.

"Is this all of you?" Nadiel asked.

"Mostly. Some of us are out doing our chores." Her eyes kept straying to the spirit hovering in front of them. Some of the witches had yet to notice her. Selaphiel figured their attention was locked on the biggest threats in the room and everything else had yet to fall into their line of vision.

"Go," Nadiel said to Tanaysia. "Find one."

The witches tensed as the spirit glided forward. They parted in alarm as she moved through them, her eyes locking on each and every witch. Some of the children cried. Another witch moaned and fainted on the floor. After a few moments, Selaphiel wrinkled her nose as the distinct smell of urine permeated the air.

Disgusting, the lot of them. But unfortunately they needed these humans. They needed one witch to show potential. They needed one witch to have the ability to alter the barriers. If not, their plan and everything they had been working for would incinerate into ashes. But they had come too far for that to occur. Selaphiel would *not* let that happen. If she had to scour the Earth, turning covens inside out, burning through villages just to find the right witch, she would.

Tanaysia moved back towards them. She faced Nadiel and then shook her head slightly.

Anger gripped her, the need to let it out intensifying with every breath. She lifted her eyes to Nadiel and let the violence just shimmer there. She felt satisfied to see him look slightly alarmed, because he knew, in the next few minutes, someone was going to die.

She stood up, a slow uncurling of her body like a shadow growing taller with the passing of the sun. With one soft, light step she was next to the closest witch, the reek of her stench infiltrating her nose. A glint of metal flashed and the witch slipped to the floor, holding her stomach as her insides tried to spill out. It took almost another two kills before the screaming began.

They started to flee, like a herd of antelope spotting a lioness amongst the grass. But she had already pounced, and she knew the kill she wanted the most. She moved gracefully through the bodies, her blade flashing in and out, feeling the spray of blood on her skin cool her temper like a summer shower.

The dark skin witch was helping a couple of children up from the floor, urging them to move quickly. Her brown eyes caught her own and in them Selaphiel knew she saw her own death staring at her, only moments away. Her jaw trembled but she steadied it, with a flash of her own defiance in her eyes.

Selaphiel smiled. Oh yes, she would enjoy this. For her strength, Selaphiel would gift this witch her time. She would make this kill slow.

The door slammed open.

Selaphiel broke eye contact to glance at the distraction. Two witches stood in the doorway. One was elderly, with steel, grey hair and a face that resembled a prune. The other was a much younger blonde, with a cane in her hand. Her gaze roamed around the room as if frantically trying to latch onto something to steady it.

Selaphiel immediately dismissed them and turned back, her body craving the last death it needed.

"Her," Tanaysia said. "It's her."

Selaphiel whipped back around. Tanaysia's finger was pointing straight at the blind witch. The grey haired woman next to her gripped her arm in alarm.

The spirit's head bowed as if defeated. Her voice came out in a pained whisper. "She is the one you need."

Nadiel moved towards the witch until he stood right in front of her. "What is your name?"

The blind witch swallowed, then said, "Marella."

"Hello, Marella," he said almost kindly. Selaphiel saw the excitement sparking behind his eyes. "You need to come with us."

Chapter 29

We arrived just as the sun began to set. The sky was a wash of burnt oranges and Fuschia pinks as the sun gave a dazzling farewell before the encroaching night.

My feet touched the grass, and I smiled reassuringly into Atlas' pale, terrified face. I had discovered he wasn't exactly comfortable with heights. Not that he would have known this before we took off, as I was the first angel that he had ever flown with.

With effort, I unclasped his hands from around my waist. His stranglehold loosened, and he hissed at me, "Get this screaming brat off me!"

The baby had started crying just before we landed. I loosened the knot I had tied around his chest and carefully manoeuvred the child, who was cradled against his back, into my arms.

I rocked her gently and rubbed her back, but she would not settle. "I think she is hungry," I said.

"Then let's dump her and go!"

I ignored him and cast my eyes to where the witch's orb had hovered. We were at the edge of a sleepy little village, half surrounded by a lush, wild forest. The smell of baked bread and cooked meat soaked into the air with delicious abandon, washing over the other earthy smells from the domesticated animals. Soft chatter from nearby windows was pleasant to my ears. They were happy, harmonious sounds of family and close community.

But the orb that stopped near a dark wooden doorway at the edge of the forest served as a reminder that this pleasant little village was not all as it seemed. A coven of witches had taken up residence here, and they were certainly up to no good.

I cast my gaze down at the innocent bundle crying in my arms and then back towards the house in front of us. It seemed wrong to leave this child here, to grow up amongst women who would no doubt teach her to follow the dark paths without a second glance backward. But I knew my interference in her destiny would end here. She had chosen this life, and she would continue to make choices as she grew up into a young lady. It would ultimately be up to her as to where her path would take her.

At least I had gotten her out of Hell.

I squared my shoulders and walked up to the door, feeling Atlas' brooding energy hovering close to my back. As I reached the doorway, the orb above us disappeared, having fulfilled the end of the spell. I lifted my hand to knock, and the door opened.

A man stood on the threshold.

Thick, bushy eyebrows drew together, a startling contrast to his shiny bald head. The rest of him was large, a mix of muscles and a slight overlay of softness that came with eating for your taste buds. His cream shirt was casually opened at the neck, and his dark pants were slightly smudged with something dark around the knees.

"What do you want?" the man asked rudely. "We don't have any handouts 'ere."

"That's not how you speak to a lady," Atlas snarled behind me.

My eyes wanted to roll around to stare at him in shock, but I resisted the urge.

"She don't look like a lady," the man answered back, but his tone was less aggressive as he eyed Atlas' looming form over my shoulder. Indeed, I did not with my stained and torn dress. I looked exactly like the beggar he thought I was. "That baby is causing a din. What do you want then, Miss?"

"I was told this baby belongs here."

"Here?" he scoffed. "There is no baby mother—"

"Henry," a soft, feminine voice said behind him. "Please introduce me to our guests."

Henry moved his shoulder backwards, and a petite, dark-haired woman stood close by, warmly lit by the light of the lamps within the house. She barely came up to his elbow, her features plain with the skin around her cheeks blemished with the scarring of pimples. Her dark hair coiled neatly at the nape of her neck, making a thin silver necklace adorned with a red garnet even more pronounced against the neckline of her dress.

She looked harmless... except she was not.

Now that I was out of the unrelenting negativity of Hell, I felt the darkness of her energy as clearly as if it reached out and brushed against my skin. She glanced at the crying baby in my arms I was unsuccessfully trying to soothe, then discreetly up at the spot where the orb had vanished.

"I do not know who they are, Mistress. They just turned up with a baby, claiming it's one of ours."

She placed a delicate hand on his arm as she ran her eyes over Atlas and then myself. She stopped at my face, and a slight tick in her cheek told me she wasn't exactly pleased with what she saw. "I'll take it from here, Henry."

He let out a slight grumble, but he obeyed her without question. Turning, he lumbered around the corner, his shadow briefly darkening the space before flowing after him.

"Would you like to come inside?" she offered sweetly, opening the door wider. "It is no place for a baby out here in the cold."

Atlas scoffed.

I held her gaze. "No, thank you. I'm just here to give you this child. It's one of yours." I reluctantly held out my arms.

She reached out, and her hand brushed my own as she took the baby from my arms. I felt a brush of energy as we touched, and I quickly pulled my hands back.

"Angel," she murmured softly. "How unusual. Eloise!" she called out, her head turning to the right. "Come here, please." She didn't hold the baby comfortably, close to the body and tucked in. She held the baby like someone holding a muddy animal, reluctantly and unwilling to ruin their clothes.

There was a light patter of footsteps, and then I caught a glimpse of the arms of a young girl wearing dark grey with a pattern of small white flowers. "Yes, Mistress?" came a soft voice.

"Please take this child to Martha. Tell her it needs to be fed… and bathed."

"Of course." The arms reached up, and the elder witch gratefully passed the baby on. My heart gave a small twinge as the little girl disappeared out of sight.

Her attention returned back to us, and I could see her thinking, nails tapping against the wooden doorframe. "Who gave you this child?"

"Hasbeth."

The nails stopped abruptly. "You're from the *Underworld?*" she hissed in shock.

"No," I said dryly. "I came from Hell."

Her eyes widened.

"My bargain with the coven has been completed." I wasn't quite sure if I needed to say that, but I felt like I had to end this encounter in some way.

"Wait!" She took a step forward, and I felt Atlas tense behind me. "How many of us are down there?"

I hesitated, then said, "I saw about twenty or thirty of you. There… could be more in other places."

Her eyes narrowed. "How did you get the baby out?"

"With great difficulty." My tone let her know that was all I was willing to say on the subject.

She took another purposeful step towards me.

"That's far enough, witch," Atlas said menacingly.

She eyed him up and down and then laughed softly. "I could crush you with a few choice words."

"Not with my blade rammed down your throat," he replied calmly.

I could feel her intent to cast before the sound left her lips. I held up my hand and let my power crackle around my fingers. "My bargain has finished," I said firmly. "I will not divulge anything else. I am no friend to your kind, and I am quite capable of holding my own against your coven. Any delays to our departure will not be met kindly."

She seemed unperturbed. Her light brown eyes all but glowed. "You are most interesting. An angel traversing into Hell and leaving with a witch's baby. I didn't know your *kind* made bargains with the other side. If you feel so inclined to do so again... my door will be open."

"It won't happen again."

She smiled. "Never say never. I will remember your face."

I stared at her for a couple of seconds, then said, "We're done here." I turned and placed my hand on Atlas' arm, urging him to follow.

"We have kin down there. You could save more of them." Her voice was soft with a tinge of sadness. I didn't believe it for a second.

"Then perhaps don't send your kin to the Underworld," I replied brusquely.

We walked past the first row of trees in the forest. I could feel her eyes stamping themselves onto my back, and I resisted the urge to scratch at the spot between my shoulder blades. Instead, I snapped my wings open and pulled Atlas around in front of me.

"Let's get you back home," I said.

He looked at my wings with trepidation. "Maybe I could live here."

My mouth lifted. "You don't mean that."

"Bloody flying angels. Like damn bloody birds. Bloody unnatural..."

He continued muttering and cursing as I wrapped my arms around his waist and took off.

***

"Mistress!"

Chantelle, the Grand Mistress of her coven, closed the door with frustration. She should have taken that angel and her companion and ripped every drop of information she could from that winged body. If she had time to prepare and plan, she could have done it, but without preparation, she wasn't certain she could have subdued the angel. She had been to Hell and managed to come out. Impossible. That alone might have been worth the risk to take her.

But Chantelle had hesitated. Someone who had survived that would be dangerous... even though she didn't look it.

Or perhaps it was the man behind her who was the formidable one. Though, she hadn't sensed anything unusual about him except for an utter willingness to protect the angel. She would have liked to get her hands on him as well. If either of them had left a strand of hair or a drop of blood, she would have been able to bind their energy to hers and eventually track them down. But they had refused her invitation inside, so she had lost the opportunity.

Some of the witches were *alive*. The revelation took her breath away. Imagine the knowledge those women would have had from their time in Hell.

Her frustration soared once more. "Blast it all!" she shouted and stamped her foot.

"Mistress!" The call came again from Martha.

Growling under her breath, she picked up the front of her dress and hurried to where the source of the voice came from. The sound led her to the fireplace, where Martha knelt by the floor in front of a medium-sized wooden tub they usually used for washing dishes. She was holding the baby swaddled in a white cloth. Thankfully, the child was not crying anymore.

"What is it?" she asked sharply.

"It's the child, Mistress. You have to see this. I don't know what it is?"

Her curiosity piqued, and she glided over to where the other witch knelt. Was the child a hybrid? Perhaps a melding of demon and witch. A flicker of delightful possibility pushed back her earlier frustration. She looked down at the baby.

Her eyes widened.

The little girl was a couple of months old, all soft rosy skin, if not a little underfed. There were no visible horns or any other markings that would deem her to be anything but human. But that didn't stop Chantelle from throwing her head back and laughing in sheer delight.

Oh, bless the Dark Mother. Bless all the witches in Hell. May their souls be forever in the Dark Mother's embrace. She wondered if the angel knew what a gift she had given them.

The baby's skin had been written on with dark brown paint. Names, carefully drawn with an ancient, cursive script. They covered her chest and stomach. They ran down her arms and curled around the back of her legs. Every part of her that had been covered by clothes was filled with the script. Names that would have taken decades to possess. Perhaps even more.

Demon names.

Once you embraced the Dark Mother, you never left her side, no matter how far or long you travelled.

"Thank you, my sisters." Chantelle smiled. "Thank you very much."

***

The Goddess Isis reclined on the ornate cream chaise littered with deep blue cushions. She twisted the jewelled goblet in her hand and took a sip, careful not to drop any liquid on her golden sheath dress, which clung to her body. She barely noticed the rich flavours swirling through her mouth as her thoughts spun in a multitude of directions.

She was so distracted that it took her a moment to notice when Archangel Michael entered the room.

He wore all white, a long robe with a wide blue sash belted intricately at the waist. His face was pleasing to behold. Michael had a type of beauty that both comforted and attracted, like looking at a stunning piece of art that reminded you of the richness and joys of life. Though that type of warmth had its own danger, the danger of trust given without thought or consequence.

Long, gold hair fell unadorned about his shoulders, unlike her own dark locks, which were entwined with gold thread. Angels from The City tended to dress simply, unconcerned with differentiating themselves from their followers. It was something Isis admired, even though she wouldn't adhere to the practice herself. Gold helped conduct her energy, and her jewels amplified it.

Her lip twitched. And she supposed it looked good.

"Michael," she said and respectfully stood up to greet him.

His violet-blue eyes took in the room she had created in Kryptos. It was simple elegance. A couple of comfortable, luxurious chairs, excluding her chaise, were set around a rectangular table that was filled with fruit and refreshments. The floor was sandstone, peppered with pots of lush greenery that carried a fresh, earthy scent. A stone water fountain trickled nearby, adding to the peaceful ambience.

A stark contrast from the last time she had been in Kryptos.

"Isis," Michael returned the informality warmly. She gestured to one of the seats, and he sat down. "I apologise for the delay. I came as soon as I was able," he continued.

She turned around to seat herself once more on the chaise. "No matter. I was perfectly content to be alone with my thoughts for a while. I find I rarely get the chance these days."

"What was so urgent?" he asked gently. "I don't usually leave The City of Light, but your message was insistent."

Archangel Michael and herself weren't exactly friends, but they did respect each other's positions. And sometimes in the realm of the Gods, that was enough to declare yourself at least allies.

She took another healthy sip of her drink. "I met with Lucifer." It was hard to even sound out his name. Once she did, the notes of it seemed to have a life of their own, as if they summoned a small amount of the owner's energy making the room feel colder.

Michael's attention sharpened.

"He asked for a key to move through time. I gave it to him."

The Archangel processed the information and its implications. "I see."

"You're not going to ask me why?"

Michael looked at her directly. "I suspect it was because you felt you had little choice."

She looked briefly away. "I owed him. He did me a favour a very long time ago. He also threatened my

Flame… and I believed him. That's all it took for me to leave something so very dangerous in his hands."

His voice was soft. "You have no need to explain yourself to me."

Her amber eyes met his. "But I do. He wants to use it to hurt you. He *will* hurt you. He will go after *your* Flame."

Michael stilled, concern flashing across his face. Then he placed his elbow on the arm of the chair and rested his lips against his fist. His eyes went distant as if he imagined himself somewhere else. After several seconds he abruptly shook his head, eyes suddenly clearing. "He hasn't made up his mind. It hasn't happened yet."

That was the paradox with time. If Lucifer intended to go back in time and alter it, they would both remember that he had done exactly that. Or at least Michael would if the alteration directly affected him.

"It doesn't mean it won't happen," she warned. "I thought you should know."

He inclined his head. "I thank you for informing me."

She studied him. He did not look affected by her news. If their situations had been reversed, she would be acting very differently. She might not be so kind. "You are not concerned? He hates you," she said curiously.

"I am aware." She caught the touch of sorrow in his words, though his face betrayed nothing. "And he would have the right to those feelings. I will not begrudge him that. Worried?" His eyes glowed slightly, and his lips lifted in a rueful smile. "I have faith. Everything has always been as it must."

"Your faith does you credit, even though I do not understand it." She tilted her head at him. "Or perhaps… your faith lies in another. One with a heavy burden to bear. I wonder if it is wise to put so much on one soul."

Archangel Michael stood up. "She is stronger than she seems. She just needs to be aware of it."

Isis rose with him, the heavy gold necklaces around her neck clinking together softly. "I hope for your sake that she is. For I saw his intentions, and I would not wish that upon you."

"You and I both know everything comes and goes in cycles. A balance will come. It must." There was pure belief in his eyes, a conviction rooted in the soul.

Isis took a breath. "She is surrounded by darkness. Is that truly a balance? What if she, too, becomes lost?"

Michael didn't say anything, but his pause gave him away. At least, it gave him away to someone like her.

The Goddess let out the breath she was holding, her eyes widening at the unseen she caught with her vision. "There is another. You have another."

"Farewell, Isis," Michael said and turned to go, his form starting to shimmer.

"I hope that person is powerful enough," she called out behind him. "For all our sakes."

Chapter 30

It was almost midnight when we finally found the Tarigan army. According to Atlas, they seemed significantly smaller in size since the last time he had seen them. I wasn't sure how much time had passed on Earth since Atlas had been taken. It could be weeks or days.

From the information I had gleaned from the way Hell worked, time moved much faster there compared to Earth. Either way, I didn't let Atlas know about the time discrepancies. His death grip on me during our journey was borderline torture, and his cussing had barely ceased.

"There, Sandy!" Atlas yelled in my ear, causing me to flinch. "There are our banners!"

I looked across to where he pointed. Red and white flags rippled gently in the breeze from various places around and within the army. I couldn't make out the design this far up, but it looked like some kind of animal in red at the centre of a white background. I could see the smoke from fires like thin, twisting columns rising to the night sky and the cloth cover of tents pitched densely towards the middle. Small specks of people moved about like ants around the circumference, hopefully still unaware of our presence.

There was a little cloud cover, but not enough that if someone looked in our direction, they wouldn't notice something unusual.

"Where should we land?" I asked, my wings keeping us hovering in the air.

"Over there," he said, pointing to a little cluster of trees a little way off from the camp. "We'd have to walk a bit, but it's better than being bloody shot in the arse by my army before I can announce myself."

A sudden thought popped in my head, and I smiled. "How about I make a celestial entrance? It can't hurt your reputation to be returned to your people by angelic means?"

He paused, then said, "They could still shoot us. Some of them aren't that bright."

I activated my armour, welcoming the feel of cool metal sliding over my skin. "If it looks like there is going to be trouble, I'll fly us out quickly and cover you. Where would be the best place to land?"

"In the middle of the command centre. Where all the big tents are."

I flew us straight over the army, the anticipation of mischief making me smile. Once I reached the tents, I held us steady and started to glow.

Light burst from my skin in bright rippling waves, illuminating every strand of my hair, which billowed up in whisps from the breeze. My wings shone like twin moons, large and glistening, and I sent a calming wave of energy radiating outwards as we started our descent. If I could sing, I would have, but I hadn't trained in Archangel Gabriel's temple, so I decided not to try in case I ruined the effect I was creating. It wasn't long before I heard shouts of alarm and the scrambling of frantic movement. Bright flares of torchlight lit up all around us.

"If they shoot me, I'm going to kill them," Atlas muttered.

My lips twitched. They may very well shoot at us, but I was confident that with their steadfast belief in the Gods, they might hesitate in attacking, just in case we were one of the Gods they worshipped. There was nothing worse than offending a God before going into battle. Gods could be vindictive creatures and easily wronged. Lives could be lost in the hundreds just for giving the slightest offence.

Men surrounded us with drawn weapons just as our feet touched the ground. Hushed whispers and pointed fingers greeted us. Fear and awe, they warred with each other, charging the air and battling for dominance. I let go of Atlas and turned to face them, dimming my Light until my features shone through. Fear lessened, and awe intensified. Disbelief flashed across weathered faces, and tears shone on grimy cheeks. Some men dropped to their knees in absolution.

Beauty helped, no matter what it was dressed in. Or... smelt like.

Then someone spoke, their voice piercing through the murmurs. "Huntagon? Atlas Huntagon?"

Atlas squinted in my Light, trying to see the source of the voice. "Braxtus?"

A man stepped away from the crowd, copper hair and armed. His mouth was slack with shock, brown eyes disbelieving. "We thought you were dead! Is it really you? Are you a spirit come to fight with us in battle?"

"No, you fool! Do I look like I'm dead to you?" Atlas scowled and took a step forward, hands arrogantly on his hips. "My abilities were needed elsewhere." He gestured to me.

There was a rumble of talk through the crowd as they digested the information. Someone ran away, shouting, "Atlas Huntagon has come back! The Commander has come back!"

"You work for the Gods now?" another man asked through the crowd.

"I did," Atlas lied. "But now I'm back to take care of you sorry lot. I hear you have been suffering without me. Damn near got yourself killed," he continued to lie.

There was a wave of agreement. "You have really come to lead us again?" Braxtus asked with relief, "and with the Goddess' blessing?"

Apparently, I was a Goddess. I wondered which one they thought I was.

Someone muttered, "Jacrum ain't going to be happy."

"What's that?" Atlas said, cocking his head. "Jacrum, you said? Why wouldn't my old friend be happy that I'm back?"

"Of course I am happy," a loud, clear voice parted the crowd. People shuffled around, and a dark-haired man made his way through. He was dressed almost identically to the way Atlas had been when I had first met him. A red and white striped cloth was tied over dark brown pants and a cream coloured tunic. On top was a brown leather breastplate that looked a little worn but well cared for.

"Ah, so you're the unlucky bastard who took over being Commander while I was gone," Atlas said. He flashed a friendly smile. "I'm glad the army was left in capable hands while I was gone. How was the battle with the Kolaiths? Did we destroy them once and for all?"

Jacrum cleared his throat as an awkward silence descended. "No. No, they are not all dead." He scoffed as if Atlas had made a joke and looked around at the men. "As if it would be possible to kill all of them."

Uh oh. I saw Atlas' body tense at his friend's words. His voice was a low, menacing growl. "What do you mean?"

"I can't fill you in on a week's worth of battle strategies in a couple of minutes. It doesn't matter now anyway; we are fighting the Anthreans now."

Atlas rocked back on his heels and stared. "Are we?" he asked slowly, deliberately.

Understanding his tone, Jacrum carefully responded, "You are not Commander anymore, Atlas. I am."

And there it was. The age-old reason for why people went to war, killed their neighbours, strangers, and family. Power. Those who didn't have it yearned for it. Those who had tasted it fought with their dying breath to retain its sweetness. It was a poisoned well for a dying man. The more you consumed, the more you lusted, and the more it killed you.

It was a rare soul who let power willingly slide out from their fingers. Unfortunately, as much as I loved Atlas, he wasn't one of them.

Fear and love were the only two motivations in life. They were the baseline for any decisions and every choice. The rare souls who could let power go wielded it from a place of love rather than a place of fear.

I wanted to intervene. I wanted to pretend to be the Goddess these men thought of me as and declare Atlas as the Commander of the Tarigan army once again. But I sensed that it would be more harmful than helpful. Atlas would want to be Commander on his own merit, not because I told everyone he had to. In addition, as an angel, I was not supposed to interfere in the decision-making of men. Though that didn't stop me from feeling ridiculous just standing there.

I must have made some small movement, for Jacrum turned his attention on me and swiftly knelt down on one knee. "Forgive me, Goddess. I did not mean to ignore you. Thank you for bringing Atlas Huntagon back to us. His presence has been missed." A few more men in the army dropped to their knees and bowed low.

"Which Goddess is she?" someone murmured.

"Aphrodite!" one declared.

"Why would Aphrodite take Atlas?" a hushed whisper asked, confused.

Another low voice. "Artemis. Does Artemis have wings?

"That's Hermes."

"Does that look like Hermes to you?"

"It's Nike, you fool!"

I opened my mouth. "I–"

Atlas spread his hands wide and turned to face the men gathered around him. "Before I left with the an... ah... Goddess, we were preparing to battle the Kolaiths." He stared the crowd down with his piercing brown eyes. "We hate the Kolaiths," he sneered. "They are cowards! They are liars. Enemies pretending to be friends. They owe us a debt." He slammed his hand into his fist to punctuate his words. "Why... haven't... they... paid?"

I had no idea about the history between Atlas and the Kolaiths, but every time he mentioned them, it was filled with rabid disgust and disdain.

"We followed your plan," Jacrum announced confidently, nodding at his men. "We still took too many losses. Even then, we kept following your plan until it was too–"

"Then the plan should have changed!" Atlas roared angrily, pacing around like a caged tiger. He seethed and stilled, taking a breath. "The plan should have changed," he said, still loud but less deafening. "You don't stick to a plan, you bloody... you don't stick to a plan if it's not working! You change! You adapt!" He glared at Jacrum. "How many losses did we take?"

"Too many," Jacrum said fiercely. He pointed a finger at Atlas' chest. "Do not blame this on me. It was *you* who left us without a leader right before battle! What do you think that does to an army without its Commander? What do you think that does to its morale? Try winning a war like that! If you become our leader again, how do we know you won't leave?" There was an answering murmur in the crowd. "You have a higher calling, don't you?" His voice was borderline sarcastic. "You could disappear on us any moment. We need someone here who will actually be *in* battle!"

Maybe I should look offended. I tried frowning delicately. But even though I was supposedly a

Goddess, I was practically ignored besides the occasional fretful glances. I tried glowing a little more.

Atlas glared at Jacrum. "I am not needed anymore. If I was, I would still be there!" I winced as he pointed his finger downwards. Luckily no one mentioned the telltale gesture. "We are debating this like bloody women! Let the Gods decide who should lead!" He pulled out his sword. "We will do this the old-fashioned way. If I am meant to lead us to glory, I will beat you in single combat. If I have fallen out of favour, I will die. That is the way of warriors, not blabbering women!"

My frown became more realistic.

Jacrum shifted on his feet, glancing quickly around at his men. "I think we should have this conversation in private, in my tent. Let us go and–"

"What?" Atlas said in a loud, sharp growl, leaning forward. "Why are you hesitating? You're not *afraid*, are you?"

The army surrounding us let out a simultaneous, "Ohhhh…" as they recognised the insult. Their eyes darted swiftly between Jacrum and their former Commander like the fight had already started.

Jacrum stiffened. "No. I'm not afraid. Do not insult me, Atlas." He was afraid. I could feel the tension of his fear, even though he fought not to show it. I could tell he wanted to say more but felt he could not. Fighting Atlas was not an option he wished to entertain, but it appeared that he had no choice if he wanted to keep the respect of the army. "Fine. We shall fight at sunrise and let the Gods decide," he finally said grimly.

I felt a little relieved. Atlas was weary. We had flown for most of the night and had been up for many hours trekking through the Underworld on high alert. He needed sleep and food. He needed to recover before he would be able to fight at his best.

"No, we shall fight now," Atlas said.

I shot him a look.

"There is no need to delay," my friend continued. "Unless you need your beauty sleep?" The men around him chuckled.

The new Commander's glare was cold. "I thought *you* might. You look a little worn, Atlas. I wouldn't want you to feel that I won unfairly."

Atlas smiled. "I wouldn't feel anything, Jacrum. If you won, I'd be dead! The fight will be held in honour of the Gods! We can't get more fair than that! We shall do it right here. Move back, move back." He gestured with his sword at the crowd. "Make a wide circle. Braxtus," he pointed at the copper-haired man at the front, "alert the rest of the generals who haven't moved their arse here and bring me my sword, spear, and shield," he commanded.

Atlas turned towards me and took a few steps to my side, and lowered his voice. "Are you staying?"

My eyes widened. "How can I leave you now? Why didn't you wait until morning? I know you are tired." I put a hand lightly on his arm and frowned in concern. "Are you sure this is a good idea?"

Atlas's lips were grim. He turned his head to make sure no one was close enough to overhear and moved his head closer. More people had gathered, but they had formed a large circle around us. Jacrum had disappeared, presumably to prepare for the fight. Or he could have run away, but I doubted it. "I couldn't wait until morning, Sandy. I'd be dead by then. Jacrum would make sure I was quietly killed and claim it was the will of the Gods or some cowshit."

My face must have shown my surprise because he chuckled darkly. "It's what I would have done if I was him." His bushy eyebrows drew together. "Don't interfere with this fight, Sandy. I mean it. No matter which way it bloody goes or by Ares' balls, I will curse you to have the face of a donkey's arse and to fart like one, too."

I'd heard this threat before. Well, the first part of it. The latter part was new.

"I could heal you," I offered quietly. "Give you some energy so you can fight."

Atlas scowled at me. "No. I don't need healing." He tapped his finger to his head. "Here. Here is where the fight is won or lost. All else doesn't matter." He gave me a pointed look. "Remember that."

My teeth worried my lower lip. "I would have thought that just by bringing you back you would go back to being Commander. I thought they would see this as a sign." Surely descending through the sky surrounded by Light was a sign from a higher power. What else could I have done?

He grinned at me. "They do, but you didn't say anything, so Jacrum made it seem open-ended. A God or Goddess would have ordered me reinstated. Jacrum took advantage of that. Tricky bastard." I opened my mouth, but he waved my unspoken words away. "I'm glad you didn't. It needs to be this way. If you did, I would always have to watch my back with my old friend." He frowned in thought. "It would be easier to kill him."

Humans. They were brilliant and backward at the same time.

"Someone bring the Goddess a bloody chair!" Atlas yelled to the side at a few of the men. Several of them instantly scurried away at his tone.

"Commander," a young soldier said from the side, holding out a shield and a spear. As Atlas' brown eyes focused on him, he belatedly corrected, "I mean, Atlas, sir. Sir." His face flushed red.

"It's alright, lad, just give me my damn weapons." Atlas walked over and grabbed the large metal shield by its leather strap, lifting it so it covered his forearm and almost up to his shoulder. He slid his short sword back into its sheath and grabbed the spear the soldier held out reverently.

"I'd wish you the luck of the Gods, sir," the boy said with awe in his eyes. "But clearly, you already have it," he said with a quick, besotted look in my direction.

Atlas just nodded, then started moving lightly on his feet. He jogged slowly for a few minutes, then stretched his limbs. During this process, another soldier brought me a small wooden chair to sit on. He tried to hastily dust it with his tunic but ended up just smearing the dirt around. I smiled at him and nodded, which made him even more flustered that he tripped over backwards and landed sprawled at my feet. His comrades laughed, and he all but ran away, apologising profusely.

I sat down gingerly. To my relief, the chair didn't give way under me. I was thrown back to the time I sat beside Lucifer and watched another battle in front of me between a Fallen and a demon.

The battle then made me grip the arms of my chair hard enough to dent the wood. But this time, my anxiety was significantly higher. Atlas was my friend. Even though his death would mean he would be reborn once again at some point in time, I still did not want to watch him die.

A cold wind blew across me as I watched Atlas twirl his spear in smooth, circular strokes. The breeze became denser, and a warning tickle travelled its way up my spine. Suddenly alert, I turned my head slowly to the left. My breath caught in my throat.

A man stood next to me.

Dark gold armour moulded across a powerfully built chest and shoulders, and a rich crimson cape fell across his back in regal folds. A multi-layered leather skirt rested on muscular thighs, leaving a gap of dark bronze skin on display before being covered again by metal greaves, which went all the way down to his ankles. Dark leather boots covered his feet, clean and new as if never worn before.

My eyes travelled up to his face, which was looking ahead. Bold, handsome, and savage. His hair was cropped close to his head, a dark brown that was just a shade lighter than black. At my perusal, the face turned, and gold eyes flecked with red speared straight into me.

I instantly knew who I was looking at.

Ares. The God of War.

I turned back to look at Atlas and the rest of the soldiers, but they didn't seem to notice an actual God in their midst.

"They are not aware of my presence." Ares' voice was low and smooth, more refined than I expected it to be.

It was strange. I had been around Lucifer, demons, and Fallen for some time now, and yet, this God, this particular one, made me nervous. It wasn't that he was a God; it was that quiet, contained violence that bled through his energy field. This God could go from nothing and then extreme rage in the time it took to blink. That made me nervous.

Lucifer burned cold. This one burned hot.

"Are you here to watch the fight?" I asked softly. I spotted Jacrum moving through the crowd, armed in a similar fashion to Atlas.

"I've had my eye on Atlas Huntington for a long time now. When he disappeared, I was most disappointed. Would you be responsible for that?" Ares' voice was deceptively mild. It would be a truly blind fool who would overlook the threat beneath that hovered lightly over my pulse point.

Jacrum stepped into the circle, a determined expression settling over his face. Atlas stopped moving around and stood facing him, relaxed, calm, and centred as I had ever seen him. It was my friend who was going into battle, yet it was I who currently felt in more danger than he was.

I took a breath and kept my eyes on the fight just about to start. "No, I didn't take him. I just brought him back."

"Where was he?"

"Hell."

"And who exactly took him?"

I sighed. "Lucifer."

If my skin could burn from his gaze, it would have.

Jacrum darted forward, shifting from left to right as he ran towards Atlas. He jabbed his spear straight at Atlas's neck. Atlas leaned swiftly away and then blocked a follow-up blow of Jacrums shield against his own.

"I would have made the first move," the God murmured.

"He is just getting his rhythm," I replied, worried for my friend. Jacrum was fresh, Atlas was not.

Jacrum jabbed with his spear, and Atlas blocked by slamming his shield down. Jacrum swung his shield around almost in a decapitating move, but Atlas gracefully ducked under and up. Then Atlas followed up with a series of intricate spear thrusts in rapid succession. Jacrum managed to deflect, but it looked difficult. The former Commander started to move back instantly on the defence.

Atlas pressed forward, swiftly darting to the side and then leaping up and thrusting down hard with his spear making a loud clang as metal hit metal. Jacrum stumbled back, then reimagined his footing.

"There we go," I said softly.

"Hmmm," the God responded, then said offhandedly, "Why did Lucifer take Atlas Huntington to Hell?"

I decided to tell the truth. "He wanted to train me in the art of strategic thinking and thought Atlas would be useful for that purpose."

"You?" I heard the slight amusement, and it irked me. "You are not a warrior."

"So I've been told," I responded dryly.

The crowd started shouting encouragement and curses. Money exchanged hands, a flash of copper coin appearing and disappearing quickly. With the battle of Commander and former Commander in front of them, I was again virtually forgotten, left in my invisible conversation with one of the most violent Greek Gods in existence.

Atlas struck again with his spear, but this time Jacrum trapped the spear against his side with his own, holding it in place. Immediately, Atlas swung the edge of his shield out and sheared the tip of Jacrum's spear with a resounding *crack*. The tip fell uselessly to the ground.

"Well played," the God said approvingly.

Jacum quickly backed away and pulled out his sword. Moving slowly around, Atlas let his spear drop and pulled out his own sword from his sheath. Then they came back at each other, the dust powdering the air as their feet moved swiftly, the heavy clang of meta was accompanied by grunts of exertion.

If Atlas was good with his spear, he was much better with his sword. Jacrum was pushed further back, the strain showing on his face. I relaxed a little, feeling a little more confident in my friend's success. He was tired, I had seen it before in his eyes, but in this fight, you wouldn't have been able to tell.

They were good, but they did not hold a candle to the Fallen. In comparison, their movements were slow and clumsy, lacking the innate grace and lightning-quick reflexes of those imbued with power. But it didn't matter how skilled or unskilled they were, it was still a fight where someone would lose their life.

"Why does the Dark One want to train you?"

I glanced sideways at Ares, whose eyes were still locked on the fight. "He thinks I have potential."

"You do not have the element that makes a great warrior," the God responded flatly.

"And that would be…" I trailed off.

"Hardness. Ruthlessness. But I'm more concerned about his interest in you. Are you someone I should be watching?" he asked softly. "Do you somehow wear a mask I am unable to see beneath?" He turned his head, and the red flecks in his gold eyes smouldered. "Are you a lioness that I mistook for a deer?"

I fought not to swallow and said clearly. "I am what you see. No more, no less."

A gasp had my attention pulled back to the fight. First blood had been drawn. I could see the splatters of wetness staining the sand. With only the moon and the golden glow of the torches all around, the blood looked dark, like demons' blood. Jacrum was limping, and I noticed his shield was cracked. His panic had accelerated as his eyes darted around the crowd as if looking for a way out.

"He knows he has lost," I said quietly.

"He lost a while ago. He was never the better fighter, but at least he didn't run from the fight," Ares said almost approvingly. "He will die a warrior and not a coward. Why did you bring him back from Hell?"

My response was automatic. "Because he is my friend."

There was a bit of silence as we both watched Atlas wear down the former Commander slowly but surely. "Friend or lover?"

I raised my eyebrows at the unexpected question. "Friend. A male and a female can be friends without being lovers."

"It would usually be love that would drive someone to save another from Hell."

I glanced at him sharply. That comment hit a little too close to home. Was he aware of my history, or was that just a casual comment thrown my way to test my reaction? "Or loyalty," I responded. He inclined his head. "I find it interesting that the God of War should talk of love."

His lip curved just the barest of fractions. "Love is just another type of war."

I belatedly realised that Ares' Flame was Aphrodite, the Goddess of Love. It was hard for me initially to wrap my head around the pairing but as I thought about it more it made sense. We were all drawn to our opposites to balance us out, to challenge and push us towards becoming our best selves. That is if we allowed them to. From my understanding, Ares and

Aphrodite seemed to have a turbulent relationship, a constant push and pull throughout the ages.

Though, it probably still fared better than mine.

"If you want to look at the calibre of a man, look at his history. Analyse how he has fought and won his battles and how he has acted in between. You start to see his character, his strengths, and his weaknesses. Much can be learned from history if you delve far enough."

I watched my friend fight and nodded in agreement. "Atlas is a good man, loyal, intelligent, if not boastful," I let a small smile creep across my face, "and courageous. He has been through much, and he still hasn't been broken by his experiences. If another human had been to Hell... they would not be as he is now. I see why you have had an eye on him."

"Yes," the God acknowledged, "but I was not talking about Atlas."

I jerked my head around again, but Ares was looking back at the fight. My mind raced and came to one conclusion. "You don't want to go there," I said quietly.

"I will do as I please."

"You don't know what he is capable of."

"I have seen plenty."

"You have seen when he has been uninspired. Poke at what you think his weaknesses are and you will see him when he is inspired. I promise you, you do not want that." My fingers clenched around the material of my dress.

The God of War was not phased. "He is crossing lines, and by doing so he is encouraging me to cross a few of my own."

There was another gasp, and I saw Atlas' spear embedded into Jacrum's shoulder. In the few seconds that I had looked at Ares, he had somehow managed to retrieve it from the ground and deliver a debilitating blow. The blood drained from Jacrum's face, and he slowly stumbled to his knees. I didn't like watching this, so I lowered my eyes.

My instinct was to heal and fix, but I could do neither. I didn't know what I would have done if it was Atlas kneeling on the ground. Would I have been able to do nothing? I wasn't sure.

"What line do you think he has crossed?" I asked instead.

"He is interfering with my Uncle's domain. That is enough. Though Hades has not yet asked for assistance, I will give it if he does." The violent energy around him swirled as if stirred by an eager hand. I did not know what Ares was speaking of, but I wondered if it had anything to do with the disturbance in the Underworld when I had left.

Ares was legendary in battle. Very few could match his prowess. What would happen if he joined Hades in the Underworld? What would happen if more Gods did? Was Lucifer becoming a threat they couldn't now ignore?

"Goddess, can you bless my sword?" a voice suddenly interrupted.

I turned to my other side, and a large man knelt next to my chair, his blade out and resting on the inside of his arm.

"Pardon?" I asked, confused as to what I should do.

"Goddess, could you please bless my blade? May your strength guide my sword in the next battle. I shall spill the blood of hundreds in your name."

I looked at him in alarm. "I... I ... I don't... I mean..." I stuttered.

"Just put your hand on his sword," Ares commanded.

I reached out and brushed my fingertips over the cool metal.

The soldier immediately bowed his head and thanked me profusely, slowly backing away from my chair.

There was a collective shout from the crowd. "Atlas! Atlas! Atlas!" And then collective gasps. I glanced up just as Jacrum's body slumped to the ground, a sword embedded in his chest.

Violence. Death. It was everywhere. I had the sudden urge to get away. "Why are you here?" I asked Ares. "Why are you telling me all this?"

"I want you to pass on the message when you return to Hell."

Some of the tension I had been holding escaped.

"You thought I would detain you," the God murmured, as the scent of fresh blood washed over us both. "It was an option, but I will not act yet until asked." He waited for a beat. "Though, that might happen sooner than you think."

The threat became heavier. I stood up, and Atlas turned towards me, a grim smile on his face, nodding solemnly. Now that the fight was over his weariness was evident, settling like a heavy cloud around his shoulders, dropping them down. Men surrounded him, cutting him off from my vision, slapping him on the back, and cheering the return of their Commander.

Jacrum's body was left forgotten on the floor.

"What would you do if someone came after your Flame?" I asked the God beside me. "How far would you go? What and who would you destroy? You talk about lines crossed, I talk about obliterating them. They took me away from him once before, and you got a creature you wished was never born. Do not do it again because he will not care about whose blood is spilled, innocents, Gods, angels, friends, family, even children. Please," I said, looking at the God of War who would never know my Flame like I did. It didn't matter if he was dark now. If someone deliberately took me away from him now, if it wasn't my choice, Lucifer would annihilate them and everyone around them.

I was afraid. Afraid for everyone else.

"He is not rational," I continued. "You have codes, honour, lines you won't cross. He doesn't. Not when it comes to me. Not the way he is now. If you care about your people, the ones that follow you and trust you to keep them safe, don't set him off. He will violate everything you hold sacred under the sun. You know his weakness. He also knows yours. He knows everyone's," I finished in a whisper.

Ares' face was granite and calculating. If he heeded what I said he didn't show it. "I'll be around," the God of War said. "Convey my regards."

Then he was gone, leaving the breeze to whip my hair around my face.

"Sandy!" Atlas said, grabbing my arm. "What are you bloody staring at? I was calling you, but you were too busy mumbling to yourself." He leaned closer and whispered in my ear. "The soldiers think you are the strangest Goddess they have ever seen. By Ares's balls, could you have at least tried to look normal?"

I opened my mouth and then closed it again. I could have told him about Ares, but the weight of the conversation I just had and the fight to the death, left me feeling drained. The urge to leave became stronger.

"I'm glad you won," I said earnestly.

"Of course, I bloody won!" he scowled, wiping sweat off his brow with his forearm. "You didn't think–"

"Commander," a soldier interrupted. "Apologies Goddess, but there is a message from–"

"Yes, yes in a minute!" Atlas roared at the younger man. "Get me something to eat will you?"

The man scurried off.

"I better leave," I said with a slight smile. "It looks like you will be busy for a while."

Atlas looked momentarily deflated. "You aren't going to stay for a bit?"

"I can't," I answered back softly. "I have to return. I have to finish what I started."

He looked uncomfortable, sifting his weight from side to side. "Well... don't get your fool brain killed. And ask the demon king for help! You need to work out how to open those cages and get a portal to the Underworld. Have a plan, but know all plans are flexible. Don't let the Defeated Ones–"

"Atlas," I said reassuringly, stepping closer. "I'll be okay." Impulsively, I leaned over and hugged him tightly. The smell of sweat and man washed over me, but strangely it was a scent I knew I would miss over the next couple of days.

Atlas had made Hell bearable. He had given me strength and hope, and I would miss him terribly. It was almost overwhelming to think I would be on my own to face the darkness. It had been easier to face what was coming when I had a friend.

After a moment of startled stillness, he hugged me back even tighter.

I immediately heard whispers around us.

"...he is in love with a Goddess."

"Maybe she took him away to have strong sons."

"Like Hercules!"

"Hercules!"

"She's pregnant?"

"She must be."

"I bet Zeus got mad, and that's why she had to bring him back before he killed the Commander."

"You're all worse than a bunch of loose-lipped whores in a pleasure house!" Atlas roared again, pulling away. "Get back to your posts!" He turned back to me, brown eyes serious and intense. "You need help, Sandy, come find me." He jammed his finger into my shoulder. "I mean it."

It meant a lot that he would say that after all we had been through. But I couldn't involve him anymore. The more time I spent with him, the more I would put him in danger. I just nodded and took a step away, throat tight and eyes prickling. "Bye, Atlas, and thank you for everything."

I turned away quickly and spread my wings out. There was a collective gasp around us. The white feathers of my wings shone brightly, imbued with my Light. With a beat of my wings, I launched myself into the air, feeling the cool breeze stream across my face. The stars glittered all around me, lighting my way through the misty veil of clouds.

I wanted to fly over the ocean and breathe the fresh air of the forests. My soul yearned to feel the beating heart of mother nature until the soft blush of dawn spread across the sky.

But I dared not linger. The temptation to stay would be too strong, and there was still one last place I had to go before I left Earth.

The place where it all started.

Chapter 31

I flew. My soul guided my wings straight into the past, to a place where a tiny village used to nestle amongst the rolling green hills. Where a cool lake glimmered amongst lush trees and singing birds, and an apple tree grew, bountiful with its crimson red fruit filled with tart sweetness.

Nearby would be a little cottage, old but sturdy, worn but clean. A path would wind through the hills towards its wooden doorway, where pots of rosemary and mint grew on either side.

As I got closer and closer with every beat of my wings, my mind coloured in more memories. Me running as a child, laughing as my father yelled to put my shoes on. Me lying on the grass, entwining my hair with flowers and daydreaming as I looked up into the clouds. Me finding my father on the ground, struggling to breathe, hysterical as to what to do.

Happy memories, painful memories... they all entwined in my head, filling in the gaps around the comet of love that had blazed through my life, irrevocably changing the fate of the Earth and those above and below.

The ghost of my former self had been with me for a while, pulling and pushing me to reconnect and remember. And I had. Nadia was with me now; her feelings, her thoughts, and her dreams had integrated with my own.

But now it was time to let her spirit go.

I was her, but I was more than her now. The Nadia who had loved Lucifer would not be able to navigate the turbulent relationship we had now. I could no longer view him through the lens of her experience, as beautiful as that was. I had to see him as he was now; the monster and the angel.

I had evolved and become his match. I was his Flame, in my highest form, and I would need every scrap of experience that had made me who I am to counter the darkness that encompassed him.

I flew lower, skimming through the clouds, feeling the white mist pass through the fine feathers of my wings. I broke through the clouds just as the sun emerged from the horizon, washing the land in bronze and burnt orange.

The landscapes around me became familiar, though what I saw on them wasn't. The tiny village had become a massive town. Building filled streets upon streets, spreading out like cracks on dry land. Lamp lights illuminated the darkness as if they were trying to replicate the light of day. Dogs barked, and people trudged through with carts and baskets, preparing for the day ahead.

Life had inevitably grown and spread, building upon the past until I couldn't even see an echo of what once was.

As I flew onwards, a part of me didn't want to see the place I had lived and loved so utterly changed. But my intuition pulled me forward; I sensed there was something I needed to see.

I didn't know what I expected, but it wasn't an enormous field of wildflowers.

My breath caught in my throat, and my feet came down. My wings pushed me back until I hovered in the air. The gently rolling hills where my feet had run constantly from my cottage to the apple tree were covered in a sea of blue, white, yellow, and pink flowers. The flowers were bright and perfect as if each one was captured in the fullest bloom of its life. The scent washed over me with its gentle perfume, and I closed my eyes and took a great deep breath.

Nadia had loved flowers. I remember picking a handful every morning during spring and summer to decorate the window sill with my mother's blue vase. Lucifer had brought me flowers from all over the world, amazing and delighting me with their unique shapes and vibrant colours. But it was still the wildflowers I loved best, the ones that grew near my home.

I looked across to a familiar hill. The apple tree was gone, but I knew where that was.

Flying down, I landed right in the middle of the field. Pulling my wings back in, my hands automatically reached out to caress the blooms, feeling their silky petals brush against my fingertips. Dawn's rays touched my skin, and I tipped my face to the rising sun as I walked through the field of flowers towards where my cottage had once been.

Tears pricked my eyes. It wasn't because it was just incredibly beautiful; the tears were because I could feel the weavings of the spell in the air.

Magic. Magic had created this. Old magic that had lived on this land for a long, long time.

I didn't have to wonder who had created these flowers and had preserved them here. There was only one being in creation who had loved me with an intensity that had changed the balance of Heaven and Earth. There was only one angel who had dove straight into Hell to wait lifetime after lifetime on the possibility that I might one night end up there.

Lucifer. This was his tribute. A declaration that honoured the love and loss of his Flame.

"Oh, Creator," I whispered. "If only he was Light, what a future we would have had together."

The field of flowers ended, and a familiar curving pathway began, leading right up to a little sandstone house. In some ways, it was a relief not to see my old cottage, where the memories of my death were still fresh, like a bruise blossoming under the skin.

The house was much bigger than mine had been, with an arch outside the front door that had creeping vines curled prettily around its frame. Two windows spotted faded blue curtains that were partially drawn, and the chimney was smoking steadily, indicating that the owners were awake and had already started their day.

I was curious as to who lived here after all this time and what they thought about the magic of the land they were on. But now was not the time to indulge in my curiosity and answer potentially awkward questions. Perhaps the mystery would be solved at a later time.

Shaking my head and smiling, I stretched out my wings once more and flew up towards the bright patch of green grass where my apple tree once stood. My feet touched the ground, and I sat down, pulling my knees up and resting my chin on my hands. You could see so much from up here. I could see, in its entirety, the little piece of Earth I had once called home.

I let myself take it all in and reflect on how far I had come in such a short time. The change in me was as if I had lived a few lifetimes of my own in Hell. I was certainly not the angel I had used to be when I left The City of Light. I didn't think I could ever go back to her and just live my existence in the shining halls of light.

I lay back on the grass and stretched my arms wide. It felt so good to bask in the sunlight. Almost too good. Strangely, I had acclimated to the crushing weight of negativity that had slowly gotten heavier and heavier, and I had forgotten what it was like to be free from it all.

Free… that was the word.

Free from the responsibilities that weighed so heavily on my heart, where every action I took could be the tipping point that caused my end or someone else's. Free from questioning myself over and over again. Free from the death that surrounded me and free from the pain.

But being free meant also being away from *him*.

And that was something my heart wouldn't let me do. Whether he knew it or not, Lucifer needed me. I refused to believe he was meant to stay, lost in the darkness, doomed forever to live with the shadows as a vessel of pain and destruction.

I curled my fingers into the grass around me.

I was going to save him.

I didn't know how or what that meant for the rest of the world, but I was determined to be the light that showed him another way like he had been for me all that time ago. He hadn't fallen again into the darkness, so there was still time… not much time, but enough to hope.

And I could go as deep as I must on just a teardrop of it.

I had much to do. I pushed myself up and stood with a sense of determination, wrapping the strength of my faith around me like the most impenetrable of armours. I couldn't linger any longer. I still had to find a way to free the warrior angels from their suffering before they turned dark. I still had to find a way to get them out of Hell. In my head, a plan was taking shape, but there were still a few pieces that were missing.

I wasn't trained to be a warrior, but slowly, in my own way, I was becoming one, despite what the God of War believed. I had the biggest challenge ahead of me and everything to lose. I had to be smarter, stronger, and more resilient than I had ever been before. I had to be one step ahead of the Fallen, the witches, the demons, and even my Flame.

It seemed an impossible task in impossible circumstances. But greater things had been achieved by people less able than I.

I had to face the music. No… I had to fall into it.

"Goodbye, Nadia," I whispered, taking one last look at the field of flowers below.

I stretched my wings out and prepared to descend back into Hell.

Bonus Chapter - Lucifer's POV

Lucifer's footsteps barely made a sound as he walked across the dusty pink marble floor of Asclepion. The sanctuary was famed for its beautiful architecture and advanced healing practices. He had been keeping an eye on the temple for months, waiting for Asclepius to make a visit and bask in the adoration of his followers. Once a year he graced his favourite place of worship with his presence, magnanimously healing a few of the sick himself.

People from all over Greece chose to move to Epidaurus, where the sanctuary stood, desperately hoping that Asclepius would heal their loved ones. Only a handful were given the honour, the rest had to rely on the renowned temple practices to fix their ills.

Little did Asclepius know that this year would be his last.

Healers and servants moved past him. Some blatantly staring, others bowing profusely, incorrectly assuming he was another God. A few of the more intuitive ones scurried out of his way, sensing the deep darkness burning through his blood, seeking to create as much distance as possible.

Anticipation had his dark eyes gleaming as he neared the ornate double doors to the Tholos, a large circular room that was used for offerings and sacrifices to the God of Healing. He could sense Asclepius' presence inside, hear his smooth, confident voice amongst those of his followers.

The double doors opened with a touch of his will. No one turned around as he walked towards the back of the crowd gathered before the dias. Asclepius stood before his people dressed in a white robe, edged with a thick, elaborate gold border. The fine cloth was pinned to his left shoulder, with a gold brooch in the shape of a starburst. In his right hand he held a golden rod with a large snake coiled around it, the head curving up towards the top.

The God laughed, his light brown beard swaying gently with each shake of his shoulders. "If you had healed the lady, I would have been suspicious of your bloodline, young Gallaine. She was almost at the ferryman's river by the time you brought her to me."

Lucifer stared at him from the back, remembering the last time he had seen the God and his part he had played in the death of his Flame. His rage smouldered, burning like red embers in his eyes. Oh yes, he would enjoy this.

A few people at the back glanced casually over their shoulder at him, as if sensing a prickling of danger, like a scorpion crawling along your spine. The red glow emanating from his eyes rooted them to the ground.

"Now let's talk about the sound therapy chamber you have developed. Was the design I gave you followed precisely? If one measurement was off the whole room would lose its effectiveness," Asclepius continued.

More people from the back started to turn towards him as the crowd sensed the growing tension blooming amongst them. It was like a wave surging in the dark waters of the ocean, slowly rippling outwards. Heads continued to turn until finally, the God noticed the disturbance amongst his followers. Irritated at the attention being diverted away from himself, Asclepius tilted his head up, his eyes searching the crowd.

They found his. Dark glowing eyes clashed with bright golden brown ones.

Asclepius' gaze narrowed as if trying to place him. He supposed he did look different from the last time the God had seen him. He had clothed himself in black. His new ability to blend into the shadows made it a necessity. His hair was left loose untamed, his blue eyes a forgotten memory. Gone was any softness, any weakness he had inherited from The City of Light. The deep recesses of Hell had birthed a new warrior, hardened with loss and rage, sharpened with vengeance and polished with the highest gleam of power.

There were debts to be paid, and he had come to collect.

Asclepius' eyes widened. "What are you?" he boomed. "Who are you to defile this holy place?"

Lucifer smiled. There still wasn't any recognition in Asclepius' eyes but he knew the God could clearly see his energy field, his aura. Most humans held an array of different colours around them, symbolising their health, their character and their past, present and future selves. Gods generally had a golden aura, angels a deep violet, but his... his was just black. All black.

He let his wings out, and the great length fanned out from his body in a dark sweeping wave. Gasps echoed around him, and cries of alarm. There was even the sound of drawn steel. They had never seen someone like him before. He was the first of his kind. An enigma. An unknown. An abomination that shouldn't exist.

So they had no idea what they had unwittingly let into their doors.

People edged around him and ran out the Tholos. He let them. He was only here for one person only.

"I haven't begun to defile it yet." His energy lashed out and wrapped Asclepius in dark bands.

The God cried out in pain and struggled within his confines. Men ran at him from all directions, shouting and brandishing weapons. With his eyes still locked on Asclepius, he lifted two fingers. The screams rose, shrill and terrified. Then there was the scent of burning flesh. Metal clanged to the floor. He stepped through the drifting ash.

"Wait!" Ascelpius said, struggling. Panic edged his voice as he realised he couldn't shift his form away. "I... I do remember you. You look different from before."

Sadly, the Greek God of healing didn't have any defensive or offensive abilities that worked from a distance. He could affect the body by touch, but he wouldn't be afforded that opportunity. More people entered the room. More people died screaming. Smoke wafted between them, staining the air with death. He continued to move forward, walking up the stairs with smooth, easy strides.

"Yes, yes I remember! From The City!" His eyes darted wildly around the room. He muttered something under his breath. "You need to be healed? I can cure you from whatever ails you. You are clearly sick and in need of help. I can do more for you than any being alive. My powers can defy even death. If you just tell me how you ..."

Lucifer grabbed him by the throat. In the corner of his eyes, he caught a glimmer of gold. "Too late," he whispered insidiously.

"No!" Ascelpius yelled as they shifted out of the Earth realm and away from the help he had been desperately waiting for.

Lucifer merged them into the ninth level of hell. The lightness of the Earth realm shuddered away, and the weight of darkness pressed all around him. To him, it felt like a warm thickness, ripe with potential. But to the God, whose distress was evident in the clammy texture of his skin, it must have been suffocating.

Lucifer stepped back from Ascelpius and unravelled his dark coils from his body. The God would not be able to leave now, no matter how hard he willed it.

"Where are we? I demand you take me back!" The bravado rang false, masking his growing fear. "Are you so arrogant that you don't understand the force of Olympius that will descend upon you? My father is Apollo! You dared to lay hands on me. For your transgression you will be punished. The City will be punished. If you return me at once I can see what I can do to buy you some leniency, as I can see you are clearly infected my some sort of deadly parasite, but even that will not be enough for the deaths at my temple! You killed my people!" The God forcibly softened his voice placatingly. "Return me now, angel, and we can see how we can repair this."

He used air and Ascelpius slowly raised up from the ground. The Greek God hissed in alarm. Lucifer held out his palms and several thin black spikes appeared in his hands. "Unfortunately for you, I'm not an angel anymore."

One of the spikes shot out and embedded itself in the God's stomach. Ascelpius screamed in outrage.

"For a healer, your pain tolerance is pitiful. I've killed humans with more fortitude than you." Another spike shot out into his thigh.

"What do you want?" Ascelpius screamed, twisting from the pain. "What are you?"

"I want you to remember," Lucifer crooned softly. Another spike flew into chest, another into his shoulder. They were tipped in poison, designed to inflict excruciating pain. The God could heal himself in time, working slowly through the darkness, but Lucifer didn't plan on gifting him that time. "I want you to remember the last time we met. As for what I am, by the end of it you'll have many names for me."

"I can't remember every encounter I've ever had! I'm a God. I've met millions of people over my lifetime!"

Luicfer summoned the fire. It circled underneath Ascelpius like a coiled snake, growing steadily brighter and larger with every second. The bottom of the God's sandals started to melt.

"Wait! Stop! There was a girl!" the God said desperately, face tight with pain as his blood stained across his clothes. "You brought a girl to one of my temples for healing, but she was too sick!"

Lucifer's eyes gleamed. "She was infected by demon blood."

The flames curled higher. "Yes!" he yelled, sweat dripping down his face. He kicked his legs up, trying to avoid the hungry glow beneath. "I couldn't heal that. You must understand, such evil is beyond any healers skill."

Lucifer walked around the twisting God. "Ah, but you told me otherwise. Do you remember what you said?"

When he said nothing, Lucifer reached out with his will. His arm snapped up at an unnatural angle. The sound was loud and shattering in the quiet. Ascelpius screamed.

"Stop! Yes!" his voice pleaded. "I said I could help with the demon who infected her!" He let out another shout as his arm clicked painfully back into place. It seemed Ascelpius' legendary healing abilities weren't just a rumour. Even amongst the darkness in the lowest levels of Hell, the God could still use his abilities.

It would be interesting to see how long he could keep it up.

"You lied," he said conversationally, as blisters began to swell on Ascelpius' legs. He continued to kick them high in the air, giving himself only seconds of relief at a time.

"I saw an opportunity to help millions! Can you begrudge me that? The witches had access to certain elemental magics that were the key to saving more lives. No one could save her. NO ONE. But the blood you took helped me saved others."

His words ignited a wave of fury. Lucifer's will lashed out once more and Ascelpius' leg snapped at the knee. The God's eyes bugged out.

"Do not make it sound as if you were acting out of the hightest good for all," his voice roughened to crushed glass. "Everything you've done is to stroke your ego, your pride. You heal because it makes you look good and you thrive off the adoration and praise. If you received no accolades for your work you wouldn't lift a finger to help a soul. Gods," his lips twisted. "Your egos are larger than mountains. Just know it was your *ego* that allowed me to capture you today. It was because of your ego, that you did not think to have protection. Basking in your own glory, you forgot how weak you truly are, especially when faced with someone like me."

His other leg snapped and Lucifer felt the dark satisfaction at the shrill scream that echoed through the lower level. The air stirred, the indescribable hunger from those he had caged before reacted to the pain.

"There was a cure," he continued. "But I wasted too much time with you to find it sooner. And that... that makes me angry."

The God's robe caught on fire.

"Please!" Ascelpius shrieked in desperation, writhing like the flames beneath him. He looked like a broken puppet tangled in his master's strings. Fire burned across his thighs, inching its long fingers towards his chest. His golden skin turned dark. "Please! I can bring her back. I CAN BRING HER BACK!"

Lucifer dampened the flames momentarily. They sizzled down to a pleasant glow. "Oh?" he asked deceptively.

Ascelpius' clothes had burnt away. He panted in pain and slowly his blackened skin began to return to its normal golden hue. The short reprieve allowed him to snap another leg back in place. The tension in his body eased a fraction.

"I didn't lie when I said Hades can return a soul. I can ask him to locate her in the Underworld and with my powers I can give her life! I can return her to you!"

His boots stopped circling around the God and he stared into wide golden brown eyes. "That would be an idea if her soul turned up in the Underworld, or in any known lower realm in existence. I can only conclude that she is still in the lost realms, roaming in an endless barren wasteland full of dangers." His eyes glowed red. "For that, you will pay. You amongst many others who have wasted my time. Time I could have spent saving her."

Ascelpius panicked. "Please! I know you are an angel. Your kind does not do this! You do not DO THIS."

His voice was velvet and his wings shimmered in the low light. "Do I *look* like my kind? This is what happens when you have nothing left to lose." His hands wove together in complicated formations. Geometric symbols appeared in flashes of dark light. "I will hear your screams to the end of days. You will be locked here, alone, with only the sound of your despair. You will beg for mercy and you will receive none. You will live out an eternity of torment, the price for your part in her death."

"No, no, no, nonononononono!" Ascelpius struggled within his air bonds. "You cannot do this! The Gods will come for you! You will start a war! They will tear you apart!"

The Devil smiled. "Let them come. I will be waiting."

He held the spell in front of him and said the word of power. It cut through the air and hit the God with physical force, stealing the breath from his lungs.

Ascelpius looked down at his chest and then back up at Lucifer. "What have you done?" he whispered in horror.

"What you deserve."

Flesh parted like a seam down the middle of his body. The God's golden skin turned inside out, revealing the pink, glossy insides of his body. Lungs, spleen, kidneys and heart all rolled across the surface, pulsating and moving with life. Slowly, the shape of Ascelpius' body turned into one large, flesh ball. The screams became muffled, but still continuous.

Lucifer tilted his head. It was the first time he had used that spell, but he rather liked its effect. Dramatic, but it got the point across.

He floated the pulsating, screaming mass across to one of the empty cells. Setting it down in the centre of a circular metal disk, he activated the cage until the metal snapped up in various pieces, forming a cube. The curving lines on the surface glowed blue as it absorbed the energies of the God, containing his power within.

The debt Ascelpius owed him would never truly be paid. Not for him. But his torment eased some of the burning rage inside him.

It would be enough, for now.

Please Help!

If you enjoyed reading this book, please help me continue my dream of being an author by writing a review on Amazon and/or Goodreads. To an author, reviews are pure GOLD as they help others decide whether they should purchase your book and if they will find the same joy in it as you did.

And if you REALLY loved this book, please consider sharing it on social media and to all your friends who love a mythical dark fantasy romance read.

Thank you for reading, and love to you all!

Vx

Author

Verusha Robbins lives in Sydney, Australia with her husband, Aaron and their sparkly ray of sunshine daughter, Ally. She has a cat called Odin who loves to sleep anywhere she is stationary, which isn't very long.

Verusha has written since she was seven years old and has always been drawn to fantasy and romance books. She has travelled all over the world but her most favourite places besides home are Egypt and Ireland. An introvert at heart, she loves nothing more than being warm and curled up with a good book with her family nearby.

You can follow Verusha's journey here:

Facebook: https://www.facebook.com/VerushaRobbinsAuthor/

Instagram: https://www.instagram.com/verusharobbins_author/

TikTok: https://www.tiktok.com/@verusha_robbins_author

Other books by Verusha Robbins

Much of Verusha's success in life can be attributed to her intense interest in Personal Development. She has compiled several books in this genre jointly with her dad, Virend Singh.

Verusha realises that when you put the effort into developing yourself, the rewards are amazing - you become happier, healthier, focused and more effective; your relationships improve; overall, you attract better outcomes in life.

If personal development is important to you, please check out Verusha's other publications at www. inkNivory.com